THE
LIBERTY
INTRIGUE

ALSO BY TOM GRACE

THE

LIBERTY

INTRIGUE

A NOVEL

TOM GRACE

DG
DUNLAP GODDARD

PUBLISHED IN THE UNITED STATES OF AMERICA.
MANUFACTURED IN THE UNITED STATES OF AMERICA.

ISBN-13: 978-0-965-60401-7 (trade paperback: acid free)
ISBN-13: 978-0-965-60402-4 (ebook)
LCCN: 2011945364
A CIP catalogue record for this book is available from the publisher.

The Liberty Intrigue is a work of fiction. Names, characters, places, dialog, and incidents are products of the author's imagination or are used fictitiously. Any resemblance to actual events, locales, or persons, living or dead, is entirely coincidental.

Jacket Design by Jeremy Bronson
Author Photograph by Angela Carson

QUANTITY PURCHASES
Companies, professional groups, clubs, and other organizations may qualify for special terms when ordering quantities of this title. For information, email Special Sales Department at info@dunlap-goddard.com.

For Kathy, always

Liberty, when it begins to take root, is a plant of rapid growth.
—GEORGE WASHINGTON

Government is not reason; it is not eloquent; it is force.
Like fire, it is a dangerous servant and a fearful master.
—GEORGE WASHINGTON

PART ONE

★★★★★★★★★★★★★★★

I

"TODAY WILL BE A GOOD DAY."

Kwame Gyasi Cudjoe, the Most Exalted Excellency and Supreme Leader of the Democratic Republic of Safo, made this pronouncement from an ergonomic recliner upholstered in the leather cut from the hide of an endangered African elephant that he had personally hunted and killed. Cudjoe's flying throne was bolted to the floor in the salon of the presidential helicopter. A standard Russian-made Mi-26P helicopter could carry sixty-three passengers, but the amenities added for the comfort and protection of the African leader cut that number in half.

Cudjoe's powerful frame was clad in khaki fatigues and his combat boots gleamed like polished black onyx. No cartoon general, the strongman wore a single star on his battle dress uniform that he earned during a storied military career, one that ended with the coup d'état that won him control of the entire nation. He wore dark sunglasses, despite the shades being drawn over the porthole windows, and slowly swirled a glass of English whiskey in his left hand.

The Safolese dictator traveled light today, his only guest on the flight from the capital being a swarthy Iraqi named Latif.

"I think you will be quite satisfied with the demonstration, Excellency," Latif said, his eyes on the metal briefcase beside Cudjoe's throne.

"That is what I am paying you for," Cudjoe replied. "Satisfaction."

Officially, Latif was an engineering consultant to the Safolese government employed for his expertise in mining and mineral extraction. One of Cudjoe's first official acts after seizing control of the country was to nationalize the mines. After all, maintaining a steady flow of gold and diamonds from the earth was essential to replenishing the nation's coffers.

Few aside from Cudjoe knew that the engineer's identity was a fabrication to conceal a fugitive. Prior to the US-led invasion of Iraq, Latif had engineered chemical weapons for Saddam Hussein. For his efforts, he was made the five of diamonds in the US Military's "Most Wanted Iraqi" playing cards. In homage to Latif's infamous past, Cudjoe's briefcase contained the Iraqi's fee in uncut diamonds.

At twenty-two, Tanu Baafi was the youngest member of the eight-man security detail aboard the helicopter. The reedy lieutenant's decade-long climb through the ranks began when he was conscripted as a boy during the civil war that followed Cudjoe's coup. One of the few boy soldiers to reach manhood, he had made a profession out of the only skill he possessed.

It was the height of the dry season and the tall grasses of the vast northern savanna stood sun-bleached and brittle as straw. The flight ended at a large rectangular clearing of scorched earth. Baafi studied the scene outside the porthole window as the helicopter slowed to a hover. Several khaki-colored military trucks lined one side of the clearing, showing at least forty soldiers. Two large, open-sided tents formed a command post with an array of communications and weather gear. A windsock fluttered limply, indicating a mild wind blowing out of the Sahara.

A lone transport stood at the far southern end of the clearing—a Bofors FH77 Archer. It was an articulated, six-wheeled truck consisting of a four-man armored crew cabin in front and a 155mm, self-loading Howitzer turret in the rear. The barrel of the field cannon stood at a high elevation, aimed at an unseen target several miles distant.

The helicopter landed in the center of a large letter H painted on the ground on the opposite side of the clearing from the Archer. Baafi and half the security detail deplaned first, followed by Cudjoe and Latif, and the remainder of the men.

The general in charge of the field test and several members of his staff snapped to attention as their commander-in-chief approached. Cudjoe parted his security detail and saluted the officers, then turned his attention to the general.

"Report," Cudjoe commanded.

"Sir, the weather conditions are ideal for the test. The forecast for the next few hours is warm and dry with clear skies and light winds out of the north. There is no sign of the Harmattan."

Cudjoe nodded, thankful to avoid an encounter with the dry, dusty sandstorms that raged out of the Sahara this time of year. "And the munitions?"

"The gunnery crew reports that the weapon is fully operational and ready for the test. Three 155mm rounds have been loaded with fuses set for an air burst fifty meters above the target."

"Does that meet your specifications?" Cudjoe asked Latif.

"Yes, Excellency, it does."

Cudjoe returned his attention to the general. "And the target?"

"We've established a wide perimeter around the target area and the troops have been equipped with protective gear for the test."

"Good," Cudjoe said. "You may proceed."

The Safolese leader and his guest were shown to seats beneath an open tent with a clear view of the Archer and an array of large LED screens displaying terrain and weather data. After the flight, Cudjoe preferred to stand, locking his gaze on the long slender cannon pointed skyward.

The Archer shuddered as the Howitzer roared and the first shell flew into the air. The turret adjusted slightly for the second round, then the third. In a mere thirteen seconds, three volleys arced across the savanna.

THE WOMAN DID NOT HEAR THE ARCHER'S THUNDER AS SHE SAT weaving a basket, but noticed that the many birds that populated the massive acacia tree had suddenly grown silent. She then heard a faint whistling growing louder like an angry kettle on the fire.

There was an explosion overhead, followed by a puff of smoke that appeared above the treetop. The birds scattered as tiny metal fragments rattled through the branches. After two more explosions marked the sky, the three smoky clouds formed a triangle over the small village. Some of the woman's neighbors looked up from their chores while others ran for shelter.

As she watched the wisps of smoke, the woman detected the aroma of bitter almonds. Several birds fell from the sky and landed nearby, their bodies wracked by death spasms. The woman pressed the fabric of her *boubou* tight against her mouth and nose, praying for the nightmarish scene to end. Her breathing came in panicked bursts and her heart raced inside her chest. Dizzy and nauseated, the woman collapsed against the trunk of the tree.

CUDJOE WATCHED THE AIRBURSTS OVER THE VILLAGE ON THE monitors. Remote cameras fitted with telephoto lenses captured the scene, including the deaths of many birds as they attempted to flee the upper limbs of a large acacia tree.

"Baafi," Cudjoe called out.

Baafi approached and snapped to attention. "Yes, sir."

"You are a good observer. You will be my eyes," Cudjoe said. "The general is sending a squad of men to inspect the village. Go with them and report back to me."

"Yes, sir."

Baafi collected a radio headset and joined the rest of the survey team as they boarded a truck for the test site. Kijiji was only a few kilometers downwind from the Archer, so the heavy truck closed the distance on the rutted path quickly.

One kilometer north of the village, the truck stopped so the occupants could don chemical suits. Baafi felt his body temperature rising inside the suit as he secured the seals around his wrists and cinched a web belt with a holstered pistol around his waist. He took a few slow, deep breaths to suppress a growing sensation of claustrophobia.

The truck stopped just north of the village and the survey team covered the remaining distance on foot. The village was a typical collection of cylindrical buildings with conical thatched roofs joined by low walls to form a compound. In a noticeable break from tradition, no one came out to meet them.

Baafi heard nothing but the rustling of the multilayered chemical suit and his own breathing. The wind barely fluttered the leaves of a large acacia tree. All else was still and silent.

He followed the team into a large building that served as the entry into the compound. Inside, they found an elderly man, likely the village chief, lying on the ground. His eyes were rolled back such that only white was visible. Foamy spittle ran from his mouth.

More bodies lay inside the compound—adults and children and the livestock either dead or dying. The poison unleashed by the Iraqi engineer spared no one, not even the flies that feast on the newly dead. Baafi had seen death before and had on orders killed many, but the murder of this village felt evil.

The temperature inside Baafi's suit was climbing. With sweat beading across his forehead and soaking his uniform, he steadied himself against a doorway to counteract his growing light-headedness. As his vision cleared, he noticed the traditional mural painted around the opening. Though common to this region of Africa, intricate geometries on this doorway seemed impossibly familiar. His eyes swept back and forth across the design and he knew that he'd seen *this* pattern before.

One of the few memories Baafi retained from his abbreviated childhood was of his mother decorating the doorways of his village. He was perhaps five and his mother had taken a break from painting to get a drink of water. Imitating her, he stuck his hand in a bowl of ocher paint and made a full handprint on the wall. His mother reprimanded him, but incorporated the mark he'd made into her design. The hidden handprint was their secret and only they could see it. Near the bottom of the right jamb, Baafi found his mark.

Baafi fled the courtyard, fearing that his suit had failed and that whatever had killed these people was beginning to affect him. He bent over, hands on his knees, gasping and overheated. Gradually, his heart rate returned to normal and he realized he wasn't dying. He then heard footsteps approaching from the village.

"You okay, man?" the squad medic asked, looking through Baafi's face shield.

"Yes, just getting hot."

"I'll be glad to get out of this suit, too, but not until we're clear of the area and hosed down. Understand?"

Baafi nodded. The medic patted him on the shoulder and returned to his work collecting blood samples from the victims. Baafi had seen enough of the village and would remain outside its walls. He spotted the acacia tree and felt that eerie sense of déjà vu again.

As a boy, he and his friends had climbed in a tree like this one. To see such a great living thing amid so much death seemed comforting. He found himself drawn toward it. Baafi was only a short distance away when he spotted the woman seated at the base of the tree. A partially woven basket having tumbled from her lap, she lay back against the trunk with both hands holding the cloth of her dress against her mouth and nose.

Baafi squatted in front of the woman and saw that she was not breathing. Gently, he lowered her hands into her lap and pulled the printed cloth of her *boubou* away from her face. Though the years and grief over the loss of a son had left their mark, he instantly recognized his mother's face. And the lies of his mother's death and the razing of his village by Dutannuru rebels were laid bare.

2

VICTORY OR DEATH

The letters flowed from the fat tip of a black marker, the indelible ink bleeding into the camouflage fabric stretched taut over the combat helmet. Ross Egan peered over the shoulder of the young man who carefully rendered the block letters onto the brow of the helmet on his lap. So intent was the soldier on his task that he failed to notice his audience.

" 'These are the times that try men's souls'," Egan quoted.

Upon hearing the unique sound of English spoken with a flat mid-American accent, the soldier bolted to his feet and in a fluid motion donned his helmet and snapped a crisp salute.

"At ease, sergeant," Egan said reassuringly. "I'm a civilian."

"Orders, sir. You are *bwana*—master of the power plant."

"I'm just the guy who keeps the lights on, but if it will make you feel better," Egan stiffened his stance to offer his best approximation of a salute. "Now, at ease."

The soldier set his feet shoulder width apart but remained ramrod straight.

"May I see your helmet?" Egan asked.

"Yes, sir."

With both hands, the soldier removed his helmet and placed it in Egan's hands. The engineer read the brave words in the waning daylight and pondered their meaning.

" 'Remember the Alamo', sir."

"Hmm?" Egan responded absently.

"William Barret Travis. These were his words."

"They were indeed. And like you, Travis borrowed them from another soldier locked in a desperate struggle for liberty." Egan handed the helmet back. "Why are these words now yours?"

"I fought in the last war, the one that split my country."

Egan studied the soldier's face. "How old are you?"

"Twenty-three."

"You would have been just a boy—" Egan quickly reconciled the two facts, "—a boy soldier."

"I was from a small village in what is now the demilitarized zone. Early in the war, Cudjoe's men raided it in retribution for our support of the rebels. All the women of the village, my mother and my sisters, were raped and murdered. My father, the village elders and other men were forced to watch before they too were executed. I was taken with the other boys and made to—"

Egan held up his hand to halt the soldier's painful narrative. "I know what they made you boys do. There is a special place in Hell reserved for the Glorious Leader."

The soldier nodded. "I am a husband. My wife has just given me a son. I gladly risk my life to protect theirs."

"I understand."

Egan extended his hand to the soldier, who accepted it with a strong, firm grip. Though more than twenty years his senior, Egan knew both the man's pain and his motivation.

"Victory or death," the soldier offered.

"For us all."

Egan left the soldier to his duties and resumed his walk around the grounds of the power plant. He knew every square foot of the place, having rebuilt much of it from the ground up. The facility had been badly damaged in the civil war, stripped of all but the heaviest pieces of equipment and abandoned by Cudjoe's retreating forces. The same was true of all the territory ceded by Safo—lands that emerged as the Republic of Dutannuru.

During the 1960s, the Safolese government dammed the Umoja River and built the 300-megawatt power plant. The plant stood near the tip of a peninsula formed by a sharp bend in the river. Unfortunately, from the Dutannuru point of view, the plant was on the wrong side of the river.

The agreement that ended the civil war divided the two nations down the center of the Umoja River. The power plant, which was the primary source of electrical power for Dutannuru, stood squarely on Safo's side of the river. Over Cudjoe's strenuous objections, the diplomats straightened the border at the river bend and severed ten square kilometers of the jungle peninsula in Dutannuru's favor. As the Safolese army withdrew from the ceded peninsula, they left nothing behind but wreckage.

A pair of fences ringed the power plant, a ten-foot high electrified inner fence to deter human intrusion surrounded by a five-foot high livestock version to ward off jungle fauna. Due to a recent spate of incidents along the Dutannuru-Safo border, the army's corps of engineers had augmented the power plant's defenses with fortified gun emplacements. Combat troops were now in place and ready should open hostilities commence.

The dull thump of rotor blades grew louder until a military helicopter appeared over the power plant.

"Sir," the soldier he'd just spoken to called out as he ran toward Egan.

"Yes?"

"Orders, sir. I'm to take you to the helipad. You have a visitor."

"All right."

Egan kept pace with the soldier as they briskly strode across the open yard. An officer dressed in fatigues emerged from the helicopter, followed by a pair of khaki-clad civilians. Both toted shoulder bags, the woman of the pair protectively cradling a digital camera. The trio hunched down beneath the whirling blades and trotted out toward them.

As they closed the distance, the officer returned the salute offered by Egan's escort and dismissed the soldier before turning to the engineer. Egan's gaze darted from the officer to the civilians. From beneath the brim of the woman's jungle hat, he noted the hint of a distantly familiar smile.

"Niki?" Egan shouted over the din as his mind put a name to the lovely face.

Clear of the rotors, Niki Adashi stood and nodded, her face beaming. Slender and nearly as tall as Egan, she threw her free arm around his neck in a friendly embrace.

"You remember me!" Niki said happily.

"It hasn't been that long," Egan replied.

"Please come with me," the officer said, interrupting the reunion.

Egan nodded and the trio quickly moved away from the helipad.

"It is an honor to meet you, sir," the officer said once they were inside the command post. "I am Major Opoku. I apologize for my abrupt arrival."

"Not necessary, major," Egan replied, "but why are you ferrying out visitors with God knows what about to happen?"

"Orders, sir. These people represent the international media."

From the tone of Opoku's voice, Egan knew the man was less than thrilled with the idea of shepherding reporters into a likely battle zone.

"I'm Edward Turcott, freelance journalist with the *Times*," the man said as he thrust his hand toward Egan. "I gather from your meeting outside that you are already acquainted with Ms. Adashi."

"I am," Egan replied.

"Excuse me, Major," Turcott interjected, "I know you gentlemen have business, but the daylight is waning and we'd like to have a look around before dark."

Niki stood quietly by Turcott, holding a long lens camera in the crook of her arm the way a big game hunter would have cradled a Holland & Holland .375 Royal Deluxe.

"And I thought you came halfway around the world just to visit an old friend," Egan said to Niki.

"Sadly, no," Niki said. "I am here in the event that Cudjoe attacks. President Mensah wishes the world to know."

"I can think of no one better than you to capture Dutannuru's plight," Egan said. "I assume your selection for this assignment wasn't purely by chance?"

"Like you, I place my trust in higher powers," Niki replied with a knowing smile.

"As I said, I'd like to have a look around," Turcott reiterated perturbed. "President Mensah assured me that Ms. Adashi and I would have full access to this facility."

"Your access is not quite as full as you think," Egan replied. "Talk to whomever you like, but you cannot enter or photograph the interior of the powerhouse."

"Why not?" Turcott asked.

"National security," Opoku interjected tersely. "If you take any unauthorized photographs or enter restricted areas, you will be imprisoned."

"You're joking," Turcott snorted haughtily.

"I am not," Opoku replied stonily. "Go now."

Turcott retreated from the trailer quickly, thankful to be out of Opoku's sight. Niki shared a quick glance with Egan and an unspoken promise to talk when they had an opportunity.

"I can't believe Mensah has you running a press tour," Egan said once the door closed behind Niki.

"He kills two birds with one stone. You are the primary reason I am here. The Embassy of the United States has issued an evacuation notice to all of its citizens in Dutannuru. President Mensah has ordered that you be brought to the capital and evacuated with your fellow countrymen."

"He knows better than that."

"The President warned me that you might be difficult." Opoku turned to the duty officer. "Do you have the secure line I requested?"

"Yes, sir. You can take the call in my office."

Opoku led Egan into a small room at the end of the trailer. A light on the multiline phone blinked expectantly. Opoku picked up the phone and identified himself, then waited. After a moment, the major's posture stiffened as if a superior officer had entered the room.

"Yes, Mr. President. He is with me."

Opoku listened for a brief moment before offering the handset to Egan.

"Mr. President," Egan said warmly.

"Ross, your government has chartered a plane that will depart the capital in one hour. I think you should go."

"Is that why you sent Niki?"

"No, but I will not complain if her presence results in your achieving a longer life. I do not wish you to suffer the fate of Archimedes. You are too valuable, my friend."

Egan recalled the murder of the brilliant Greek mathematician during the chaos that followed the fall of Syracuse to the Romans during the Second Punic War.

"This is as much my fight as yours," Egan countered.

"And the first thing Cudjoe will attack is *your* power plant."

"We always knew that would be the case—plus it just irks the Illustrious Leader that we can keep the lights on and he can't. All the more reason for me to stay. And if Cudjoe does take this plant, he'll find it just as he left it."

"I hope it does not come to that."

"You and me both, but if there's no other choice..."

"Very well. Give Major Opoku this phrase: *Mtoto shupavu sana.*"

Egan smiled and repeated the phrase. Opoku nodded and left the command post without him.

"Maggie used to call me that," Egan said.

"She was right, and you remain a *stubborn child.*"

Egan heard the rustle of papers over the phone.

"I have received some new intelligence," Mensah continued. "Satellite images from just a few hours ago show Cudjoe has moved additional forces into the border region near the power plant. There are staging areas for armored troop carriers and attack helicopters. My generals believe the attack will come soon."

"The US government is providing you information?" Egan asked, incredulous.

"We acquired the images from a private firm."

Egan detected the bitter undertone in Mensah's reply. When the prospect of a second war over Dutannuru had emerged, many of the world's leading political figures made speeches urging dialog and brokered negotiations. Shuttle diplomacy by the globetrotting American Secretary of State resulted in little more than a well-staged photo opportunity for the saber-rattling dictator. A UN resolution denouncing Safo's increasingly hostile stance toward its smaller neighbor was killed by nations that were quietly trading arms for access to the vast natural resources of the repressive people's state.

"There was a time when the United States stood shoulder to shoulder with nations like Dutannuru in defense of liberty."

"A pragmatic approach is the current political fashion," Mensah offered. "And the pragmatists believe Dutannuru's days are numbered."

"Pragmatist is just a polite way of saying pessimist. I believe in the people of Dutannuru."

"I, too, believe in my people. And in you. May God be with you in the coming storm."

"May He be with us all, Mr. President."

Egan left the command post and resumed his tour of the grounds around the power plant. The automatic lights that normally flickered on at sunset remained off—the facility and its defenders cloaked themselves in the jungle darkness. Above him, a clear, moonless sky sparkled with the tiny lights of distant stars.

The younger soldiers were restless, eager for snippets of news, rumors and speculation about the looming conflict. Veterans of the last war knew from experience that the future would take care of itself and that a soldier must concern himself with the present. Those who were off-duty ate or slept, knowing both those activities become elusive in battle. Others ritually inspected and cleaned their weapons and equipment to ensure all was in peak working condition.

The jungle takes on a different character at night, and the presence of so many men had disrupted the natural rhythm of the nocturnal creatures. Darkness and silence enhanced the palpable sense of anticipation.

Egan's iPhone vibrated silently in his belt holder. He checked the screen and read the text message: LOOK UP.

He holstered the phone and scanned the sky. The message was an application that he'd written to text him whenever the International Space Station was passing overhead. He remembered a cool, July night in his childhood when his parents woke him and sat with him in front of a grainy black-and-white television to watch Neil Armstrong and Buzz Aldrin walk on the moon. He had retained a passion for space exploration to this day.

Egan heard the metallic click of a camera shutter.

"Wishing on a star?" Niki asked, her face subtly up-lit by the faint glow of the camera's LCD screen.

"Not quite," Egan replied, his gaze still fixed upward.

Then he saw it. The bright object streaked out of the northwest, moving diagonally across the sky.

"Look there," Egan said, pointing skyward.

"A meteor?" Niki asked.

"A space station," Egan replied.

"With war so close, it is hard to imagine that people can accomplish something so extraordinary. It is very fast."

"Has to be," Egan offered, "or it would quickly come crashing to Earth."

"Might not be such a bad thing," Turcott opined as he uploaded a story from his iPad. "I think the manned space program is a colossal waste of time and money."

"So says the man whose livelihood depends on technologies born from man's hopeful desire 'to slip the surly bonds of earth' and 'touch the face of God'."

"*Touché*," Turcott conceded, "and very poetic."

"My wife was a great reader of poetry. I guess some of it rubbed off on me. *High Flight* is one of my favorites."

Niki laughed fondly. "She described her attempts to expose you to literature as *cultural diffusion*. I think of her often. She was a good woman."

Egan nodded. "Our time together was too brief, but I'm thankful for it."

They watched the ISS hurtle across the night sky until it disappeared behind the distant jungle canopy. The pointed tip of a crescent moon emerged over the eastern horizon.

"And may that be the only thing we see lighting up the sky tonight," Egan said. "Though it'll mean you wasted a trip out here."

"Wars are like cabs in Manhattan," Turcott said. "There's always another one just around the corner."

"I took some interesting pictures and met an old friend," Niki offered. "However it turns out this trip will not be fruitless for me."

"Do you shoot landscapes?" Egan asked.

"If I like the scenery," Niki replied.

"Come with me."

Egan led Niki and Turcott toward the power plant. The complex of buildings seemed eerily quiet in the darkness. They skirted the main buildings and approached a guarded gate. After a quick check of his credentials, Egan escorted the reporters onto the upper deck of the dam. The lake formed by the dam spread lengthwise to the east. To the west, a steep cliff-face of concrete fell to the river valley below. He stopped at a point near the center of the dam.

"Oh my," Niki gasped.

From this vantage, the thin sickle moon hung low in the sky over the far end of the lake, reflecting perfectly in the placid water. Niki unfolded a tripod and quickly calculated the settings required to capture the image.

"That is what really should have brought you here," Egan said. "Not another war waged by a murderous parasite."

"Not a fan of Kwame Cudjoe?" Turcott asked.

"Hardly," Egan replied. "The thug seized power in a coup that threw his country into civil war and led to the deaths of tens of thousands. He took three-quarters of the land along with the major oil fields, mines and industry, leaving Dutannuru with next to nothing. A decade later, Cudjoe has nationalized everything, his people are starving, tens of thousands more are dead, and his nation is a total basket case. And right next door, the spit of land he left in ruins is fast becoming the economic lion of Africa. This isn't a war—it's a heist. And the cop who used to patrol this beat is nowhere to be found."

"If war comes again, do you think it will go badly for Dutannuru?" Niki asked.

"Wars rarely go well when an enemy is massing on your border."

"If you're an American, why are you still here?" Turcott asked. "That helicopter we arrived in was sent to whisk you away from this place before hostilities commence."

"My wife came here with the Peace Corps when all of this was Safo. The government then was ineffective and riddled with corruption, but foreign aid was welcome and she fell in love with the people."

As he spoke, Egan watched Niki patiently work her camera. Sensing him, she paused.

"I was still a girl when I met his wife," she explained to Turcott. "Maggie became part of our community, like family. I miss her to this day."

Egan nodded. "Bettering the lives of the people here was my wife's calling. After we married, I returned with her and this is where we made our home. That's why I refuse to leave."

Niki finished shooting the moonlit landscape and detached her camera from the tripod. Ripples on the far end of the lake disturbed the reflection, wakes radiating from the black silhouettes moving in a straight line toward the dam. She saw that Egan had noticed the incoming boats as well.

"Are those boats Safolese?" Turcott asked.

"Don't know," Egan answered, "but it's probably not a good idea to wait here to find out."

Niki quickly stowed her tripod and they all headed back the way they came. The moon illuminated the plant buildings and cast long, dark shadows.

"What are you hiding in there?" Turcott asked casually.

"Nothing," Egan replied with a hint of evasion.

"Then why all the security? I've been inside power plants before, if that's your worry. I did a piece on the Three Rivers Gorge project in China a while back."

"That's cutting edge hydro. What's in there isn't nearly as impressive."

Turcott eyed him suspiciously. "When you say it like that, you just make me more curious."

"We all need a little mystery in our lives."

As they neared the end of the dam, a figure climbed onto the walkway and strode toward them. It was Major Opoku.

"Ah, I have found you," Opoku said, relieved.

"I thought you returned to the capital," Egan said.

"I volunteered for duty here. I am now on the general's staff."

"I'm sure he's glad to have you."

"If war comes to Dutannuru here, then this is where I must be."

"Spoken like a patriot, Major," Egan said warmly. "And speaking of war, we spotted some boats on the east end of the lake heading this way."

"Safolese patrol boats. We are monitoring them as well as troop movements along the border. The helicopter that brought us here," Opoku said to the reporters, "has been redeployed. We have confirmed reports that Cudjoe ordered a test of chemical munitions on a small village in northern Safo earlier today. Many were killed."

"Shouldn't these two be evacuated?" Egan asked.

"Like you, they volunteered to be here and the helicopter was required elsewhere. Cudjoe may use chemical shells against us. We have protective suits, helmets and body armor for you all."

"Cheery thought," Turcott offered.

"Thank you," Egan added, grateful for the consideration.

"I also bring a request from the general. He asks if you would address his men."

"Why me?" Egan asked, taken aback, "I'm just a civilian, and a foreigner to boot."

"You were part of the First Council," Opoku countered. "Your role in creating Dutannuru is well known. Words you wrote are taught to our children. The general heard you speak at the First Council. He believes you are a wise and honest man. With war so close, he asks that you speak to his soldiers. In your words, he believes they will find truth and courage."

"I would be honored," Egan said.

"Then all of you, please follow me to the command post."

Opoku's arm seemed in constant motion, saluting the junior officers and enlisted men they encountered while crossing the compound. Niki and Turcott both noted that the men accorded Egan with equal respect.

"The general asks that you speak at nineteen-hundred hours," Opoku said as they reached the command post. "He apologizes for making his request on such short notice."

"Unnecessary. I just need a little time to collect my thoughts."

"Of course," Opoku said. "Use the duty office. You will speak from there."

"May we join you?" Niki asked.

"Sure," Egan answered.

Opoku left Egan with Niki and Turcott in the duty office. He provided them with cold sodas and promised to return when it was closer to the time of his address to the troops.

"So just what are you," Turcott asked Egan as he settled onto a small couch beside Niki, "one of Dutannuru's Founding Fathers?"

"More like a founding friend of the family," Egan replied as he sat down behind the desk. "I advised President Mensah when the council drafted the country's constitution."

"He's too modest," Niki protested. "The name of Ross Egan is honored in Dutannuru."

"How well do you know Mensah?" Turcott asked.

"He was godfather to my son."

"I see."

Niki reviewed the images stored in her camera's memory. Most were of young soldiers preparing to shoulder the burden of war.

How many would pay the price of this war in maimed bodies and lost lives? she wondered. *What would be the cost?*

Niki reached her photographs of the moonrise over the lake. Turcott glanced at the beautiful images.

"You were right," Turcott admitted. "We should've come here for the scenery."

"That and the people," Egan offered.

"Are they really all that different?"

"No, but that's the point. Where it really matters, the people of Dutannuru are the same as those back in the States or anywhere else in the world. They all want to live peaceful and productive lives."

"Then why is Dutannuru going to war?" Turcott asked.

"Dutannuru is not *going* to war," Egan answered. "War is *coming* to Dutannuru."

"But can't they negotiate with Cudjoe?" Turcott pressed further. "End this thing before it starts?"

"Can you negotiate with a burglar as he's kicking in your door?" Egan countered.

" 'All war represents a failure of diplomacy'," Turcott replied.

"Bet you learned that Tony Benn chestnut in some political theory class," Egan said with a chuckle. "Was your prof a tweedy Marxist?"

"Progressive feminist, actually."

"Same difference."

"Diplomacy is a tactic of war," Turcott offered. " 'Supreme excellence consists of breaking an enemy's resistance without fighting.' "

"Sun Tzu—I see you're up on the classics," Egan said. "Hitler skillfully employed both diplomacy and blitzkrieg in the pursuit of his ambitions. This is true throughout history."

"So tell me, what is war?" Turcott asked sharply.

"Are you familiar with the Ten Commandments?" Egan asked.

"Of course, but how do they relate to war?"

"They provide context. Oh, and for reference, I'm using the variation where only the first three commandments are religious and the rest are civil."

Turcott nodded that he understood and Egan continued.

"Offensive wars are based on breaking the Tenth, Seventh and Fifth Commandments, in that order. It starts when the leadership of one nation covets the wealth or property of another, breaking the Tenth. Acting on this desire with the use or threat of force is theft, breaking the Seventh. The aggressor breaks the Fifth when it uses lethal force to take what it desires. Cudjoe's actions follow this pattern. Now, there can be pretext and antagonism between rival nations, but when you distill an offensive war down to its essence, you always find a thief trying to steal something."

"Wasn't the US invasion of Iraq an offensive war?" Turcott asked.

"No, it was an offensive action taken in the context of a larger war, like D-Day. A better analogy might be the use of atomic bombs on Japan—both were hotly debated actions taken with the sole intent of protecting American lives. The United States didn't start the Second World War, but it did launch a number of offensive actions to end it and restore the peace. Along the same lines, Israel has launched what some have called unprovoked attacks on its neighbors in order to prevent those neighbors from acquiring nuclear weapons. These were in fact offensive actions in an ongoing defensive war that has existed since Israel's founding. That is the right of the aggrieved nation." Egan set his elbows on the desk and leaned forward. "Should Safo attack, Dutannuru must drive them back and accept nothing less than unconditional surrender."

"Do you see why the general asked him to speak?" Niki asked Turcott. "Now, will you please give the man a moment to prepare his thoughts."

Turcott conceded the point and returned to his article. Egan gave Niki a grateful wink, then turned pensive. As she uploaded her images to the press pool back in the nation's capital, she found her eyes drawn to Egan's face. He was lost in thought, oblivious to her observation. The years, she decided, had been kind to him.

Turcott, too, wondered what kind of man he'd stumbled upon in a place he didn't know existed just a few days ago.

3

"IN THIS LAND, GOD CREATED THE ANCESTORS OF ALL MANKIND."

Egan's clear tenor voice resonated from the two-way radios carried by the soldiers defending the power plant. He wore a wireless headset and spoke from behind the desk. Adashi and Turcott sat silently on the couch. Opoku stood in the doorway.

"And in that act of creation, he endowed us all with certain rights that no one can take from us. Greater minds than mine summarized the most sacred of these rights as life, liberty, and the pursuit of happiness.

"A decade ago, the people of this land paid a terrible price to reclaim their patrimony. As was their right, they threw off the burden of a failed and corrupt government that had bankrupted the nation. As was their right, they rejected the tyrant who murdered his way to power and made war on those who resisted him.

"Those brave and hopeful rebels, who sacrificed all for the promise of providing a better world for themselves and their descendants, knew that terrible civil war could only end for them in victory or in death. There could be no surrender. They would accept no chains. The people of this land chose to live free or die.

"And many did die to restore the freedoms now enjoyed by the people of Dutannuru. We owe a debt of honor to those patriots, a blessed obligation to defend that which they redeemed with their blood.

"The memory of that civil war remains fresh among those who survived it, all but the first generation born in liberty bear the scars of that conflict. That war left one people divided into two nations.

Those who toiled in the warm light of liberty took what was left them and prospered. Their kin, blessed with far greater natural resources, struggle to survive as the fruits of their labor are squandered for the glorification of a madman. The only difference between the people of these two nations is on which side of the Umoja River they stand.

"This unnatural division is the work left undone, a task we had hoped to complete in peace but are now forced to undertake in war. The army massing on our border is not the enemy—they are *our family*, and they are tormented by a great devil. What comes is a war of two nations, but one people. Dutannuru does not seek this war, but will fight it if we must. We will fight for all that we hold dear, and not just to protect our freedom, but to win back theirs. The only way this war can end is with *one* nation.

"For all Dutannuru—*Victory or Death!*"

"LISTEN TO THEM," OPOKU SAID PROUDLY.

The defenders of the Umoja power plant responded to Egan's address with a roar of approval. Like the troops at Trenton and the Alamo, the defenders' courage found voice in chanting the famous motto—*Victory or Death*.

"Quite a speech," Turcott said flatly as he made some notes.

"It was a beautiful speech," Niki countered as she snapped another photo of Egan seated behind the desk.

Egan waved her off and removed the headset. "I just told them the truth."

"That is why I asked you to address my men," a voice boomed from outside the room.

Opoku stepped aside and cleared the way for General Darko. A squat man with the build of a water buffalo, he crossed the room beaming and extended a beefy hand to Egan.

"You touched their hearts," Darko said. "Your words are stronger than any fear of the unknown. I thank you."

Egan stood and shook the general's hand. "I'm glad to help."

"We expect the attack will come soon," Darko said, turning serious. "I am going to visit with my men. Will you come with me?"

"Of course."

"May we join you?" Niki asked, camera in hand.

The general nodded and led the way out with Opoku and the others in tow.

4

THE NEXT HOURS PASSED QUICKLY AS EGAN AND DARKO SPOKE with small groups of men positioned around the power plant. The soldiers, who would likely take the brunt of the expected attack, seemed both nervous and resolute, knowing their fight was in the service of a greater good.

"You've attracted quite a following," Turcott said to Egan as they walked toward the next group of soldiers.

"Must be my fifteen minutes of fame."

Between stops, Opoku remained at General Darko's side, quietly relaying orders from an incoming report to his commanding officer.

"That is very interesting," Darko said, turning to face Egan. "The government is broadcasting your speech nationally."

"You're kidding," Egan replied.

"I am not. President Mensah liked what you said very much and he wished all of Dutannuru to hear your words."

After Opoku's two-way squawked, he switched the radio to send-receive mode. He wore an earpiece and throat mike under his helmet, so what little they heard of the conversation was one-sided jargon.

"What is it, Opoku?" Darko asked on completion of the report.

"Sir," Opoku replied, "activity along the border has increased significantly within the last twenty minutes."

"Have they crossed?" Darko asked.

"No, and the reports we're getting are confusing. There doesn't appear to be any coordination..." Opoku paused as another report came in. "Sir, a Safolese helicopter is hovering at the border requesting permission to approach and land here for the purpose of parley."

"This is very odd," Darko mused. "Do we have a visual on this helicopter?"

"Yes, sir. It is unescorted and running with full lights on."

"Is it carrying any weapons or external tanks?"

Opoku relayed the question and waited a moment for a reply.

"Our forward observer reports the helicopter is a large military transport," Opoku said. "No weapons are visible."

"Is there any further information on the chemical weapon they tested? How it was delivered?"

"No, sir."

Darko considered all that he'd heard for a moment.

"If they wish to talk, I will let them talk. Permission granted. Tell the Safolese that we will provide an armed escort to accompany them from the border to this facility. They are to fly in formation with our escort, and they are to keep their communications open and maintain contact. Inform them that their escort is under orders to fire on them should they deviate from their instructions. All troops are to remain on full alert."

"Yes, sir."

Opoku moved off to begin issuing orders to the groups affected by the inbound helicopter.

"Might this be a ruse?" Niki asked Egan.

"Darko's not buying it," Egan replied. "Cudjoe pulled a fake parley once during the last war and killed a lot of people."

Egan, Niki, and Turcott followed the general back to the command post to await the arrival of the Safolese representative. Opoku kept pace with the general, feeding the commanding officer a steady stream of updates.

The Safolese helicopter and its escort of two Dutannuru attack helicopters followed a course that routed them downwind of the power plant on their approach. The huge Mil Mi-26P dwarfed its escorts, causing Egan to wonder if the helipad could accommodate the aircraft's forty-meter length. It hovered over the pad as floodlights washed it in search of weapons. Satisfied that the helicopter posed no visible threat, Darko granted permission for it to land.

The helicopter descended slowly, the pilot aware of the weapons trained on the aircraft should he make any suspicious moves. He landed it lightly and powered down the twin Lotarev turboshaft engines. The escort helicopters remained aloft, hovering in position to act if necessary. Slowly, the long rotors wound to a stop. As the dust settled, the emblem near the nose of the aircraft became clearly visible.

"Is that Cudjoe's helicopter?" Darko asked.

"Intel confirms that the markings match those of the helicopter assigned to transporting the Safolese head of state," Opoku reported.

"This makes no sense at all," Egan said absently.

"How so?" Niki asked, still snapping photos of the idle aircraft.

"There is no reason to believe Cudjoe is inside that helicopter, and I can't imagine his handpicked flight crew would decide to defect on the eve of war."

"Maybe Cudjoe *is* in there and he just wants to talk," Turcott said.

"God, I hope not," Egan shot back. "That windbag gives marathon speeches at the drop of a hat. It's possible he's sent an emissary to offer us a chance to surrender the power plant now and walk away without a bloodbath. But I just can't believe he thinks that Dutannuru would simply roll over."

The helicopter's forward door opened and the pilot descended the steps. He was in a flight suit with his helmet tucked under one arm and the other clearly visible. The holster for his sidearm was empty. He took a few steps away from the door and stopped, squinting in the bright light at the command post.

Darko motioned for Opoku and a pair of armed soldiers to accompany him and the four strode toward the pilot. On seeing the rank insignia on Darko's uniform, the pilot snapped to attention and saluted.

"At ease," Darko replied as he returned the salute. "Why are you here, Captain?"

Egan could not hear the exchange but found it odd when the general and Opoku both turned in his direction. A moment later, one of the soldiers jogged over.

"Sir," the soldier said, "the general requests your presence."

Egan nodded and followed the soldier onto the helipad. Without asking permission, Niki impetuously joined him.

"You sure you want to do this?" Egan asked in a half-whisper.

"What's the worst that could happen?"

Egan arched an eyebrow at her but offered no reply as they neared the men standing on the helipad.

"This is the man who made the speech?" the pilot asked, surprised to see a Caucasian face.

"Yes," Darko replied firmly.

"Very well," the pilot cocked his head toward the helicopter and nodded.

A moment later, the rear door of the helicopter opened and three men in military uniforms slowly filed out. Like the pilot, they were unarmed and held their hands up at shoulder level as they spaced themselves alongside the helicopter. The braids on their uniforms indicated the men were part of an elite unit.

Niki gasped, but continued taking pictures when a forth man emerged from the helicopter into the light. He was tall and thin and dressed like the others except that his uniform was disheveled and bloodstained. He walked purposefully toward them, arms hanging loosely from his sides, but unlike the others he was armed. In his right hand, he carried a machete, its blade blackened with dried blood. A small plastic cooler hung from his left.

The soldiers accompanying Darko trained their rifles on the man, who halted a safe distance from the group. He looked directly at Egan.

"Are you the man who made the speech, the man who said that we are one people?"

"I am," Egan replied.

The man's jaw tightened and he seemed on the verge of tears.

"I—" the man said, struggling to keep his voice even, "heard you."

The man set the cooler on the ground and dropped onto one knee. With his head deeply bowed, he held out the machete in his open palms. Unsure what to do, Egan turned to Darko, who nodded that he should accept the offering. Egan approached the man cautiously, hoping the soldiers still had their weapons ready in case the man suddenly attacked.

As Egan reached for the machete, he noted the man's hands were trembling. They steadied when Egan removed the blade, as if relieved of a terrible burden.

"For the people of Safo," the man said, "I surrender to our Dutannuru kinsmen."

Egan studied the bloody weapon and the kneeling man awaiting a response.

"On what terms and on whose authority do you speak?" Darko interjected.

"General," Egan replied, "I believe he speaks as the leader of Safo."

Darko's eyes widened, incredulous that the young officer had somehow seized power.

"Are you the leader of Safo?" Egan asked softly.

The man nodded, his head still bowed.

"Please stand and tell us what has happened," Egan asked.

The man rose up, tears glistening on his face. He stood at ease with his arms behind his back, his gaze fixed on Egan.

"My name is Tanu Baafi," he began. "I was a member of the security detail protecting President Kwame Cudjoe. I led a coup against him and he is dead. I killed Cudjoe. I am now leader of Safo."

"Why did you kill Cudjoe?" Egan asked.

"Today, he tested a terrible weapon."

"We know. He used it on a village in the north."

Baafi nodded. "I went to that village. It killed everyone. He planned to use this weapon here, against you. Many would have died. The only way to stop Cudjoe was to kill him."

"We are grateful," Egan said, speaking in even, measured tones.

"Do you control the army?" Darko asked.

"I killed Cudjoe before he was to meet with his generals. I went in his place. Most of the generals accepted me as their commander. Those that did not were relieved of duty and imprisoned. The army has been ordered to withdraw from the border and return to base."

"Can you prove any of what you say?" Darko asked warily.

Baafi picked up the cooler and, cradling it in the crook of his left arm, opened the top.

"Our generals asked me the same question," Baafi replied. "This satisfied them."

Baafi tilted the open cooler slightly to reveal its contents. Inside was a pair of human heads.

"One is Cudjoe. The other, a man named Latif. Latif made the weapon for Cudjoe. Their bodies are inside the helicopter."

Egan had met Cudjoe once, before the civil war, and had seen the tyrant's distinctive face in the news many times during his brutal reign. One of the heads in the box had certainly belonged to Cudjoe. He stepped forward and closed the cooler lid, then offered his hand to Baafi.

"For your Dutannuru kinsmen, I accept your offer of surrender."

5

EGAN STOOD INSIDE THE CAVERNOUS POWERHOUSE, STARING through a gaping hole in the floor at the twisted remains of a seven hundred ton generator. Turbine Number 4 was twelve meters in diameter at its widest and, upright, equaled a three story building in height. The turbine lay unnaturally on its side, ejected from its concrete and steel housing at the base of the Makola Dam.

"Can you fix it?" a woman's voice called out.

Egan looked down the length of the powerhouse and found his questioner at the near side of Turbine Number 2 walking through the wreckage toward him with a small retinue in tow. Maya Randell's petite frame was clad in tailored safari wear accented with an Emaa Da patterned kente cloth scarf. Her black hair was drawn back in a single tight braid emphasizing the almond shape of her face.

"S'cuse me?" Egan shouted back.

"You heard me. Can you fix it?"

"I can fix anything dats broke, ma'am," Egan thundered back, exaggerating the Yooper dialect of Michigan's Upper Peninsula, "but dat dere is definitely gonna cost ya more dan fifty bucks."

Maya laughed, recalling her first encounter with Egan. She and her husband Burton were both fresh out of graduate school and honeymooning across America when their VW camper hit a deer in Michigan's Upper Peninsula. Egan was a teenager at the time, working in his uncle's auto shop when the damaged vehicle was towed in. The accident occurred during the height of the summer tourist season and the hotels were full, so Egan's parents took in the stranded newlyweds for a week while their camper was being repaired.

The gangly redhead had impressed the Randells with his home-made computer and various electrical projects that rivaled thesis work by their fellow graduates from MIT. They recognized Egan's potential and made a point to keep tabs on the promising young man.

Maya's bodyguards and personal assistant stopped several meters back and she closed the remaining distance alone. Egan stood a foot taller than Maya, so he bent slightly to meet her embrace and kissed her gently on the cheek. The young bride who became a tech boom billionaire embraced Egan as warmly as his family had greeted her so many years ago.

"Then it's a good thing I have a bit more money now than I did then."

"You and Burton made more in interest in the last ten seconds than that old camper cost new," Egan said as he released her.

"And that ratty old thing is still in our garage. Boys and their toys."

"Sentimental value," Egan said sympathetically. "So what brings you here?"

"Checking on my investment, of course," Maya replied. "But seriously, can you fix *that*?"

"I'm afraid Turbine Number Four is down for the count. One and Two are up and running now. Three and Five are damaged, but repairable. The dam wasn't damaged at all and the powerhouse can be put back in order in a few months."

"What happened?"

"I visited here a couple times back before the civil war and Number Four had problems from day one," Egan explained. "Last summer, it was down for some scheduled maintenance and a number of cracks and cavities in the turbine blades were repaired with welds. Routine stuff, but they didn't rebalance the turbine wheel afterward. The few workers who survived the accident said it was vibrating like crazy and then—*Bang!* The rotor came flying out of its seat and did all this. We'd heard rumors, but had no idea how bad the accident was. It knocked the plant offline completely for several weeks and cut the Safo's total power supply by about a third. Most of the power made here goes to an aluminum plant, so that loss of power cut directly into

Cudjoe's flow of hard currency."

"Cudjoe was going to make war on Dutannuru for energy?" Maya asked.

"He had a lot of reasons to go to war, but I think this accident pushed up his timetable. Mensah has made repairing this plant a national priority, now that this land is back to being one nation."

"I know," Maya said with a knowing smile. "He told me where I could find you."

"I leapt at the chance to get out of the capital. I can't go anywhere in public."

"That's what you get for being all white and freckly," Maya chided. "At least you finally have some gray to mute that red hair. Now I, on the other hand, am the perfect shade of mocha for this part of the world."

"You're about as African as I am Irish, and neither of us can walk the streets of the capital without getting mobbed."

"Ross, you are a national hero, or I should say, *international* hero."

Maya pulled a copy of the *Wall Street Journal* out of her shoulder bag and spread it out on a worktable. Above the fold was the now-iconic photograph of Egan accepting the Safolese surrender.

"This image is everywhere, and Niki is in very high demand."

"Good for her," Egan said.

"Good for *you*, and that's why I'm here. You've done some brilliant work in Dutannuru, and not just with electricity. This republic is the one bright spot on the African continent and your influence on its government is undeniable."

"Oh, I can deny it. Helping Mensah create an honest government here was Maggie's dream. She dedicated her life to these people."

"And you honored her sacrifice by helping make that dream a reality. Dutannuru was in as bad a shape as this place when it broke free, and now it enjoys one of the highest GDPs per capita in the world. The people here have jobs. Hell, they have food! All of the children are in school. And where else in Africa can you find a growing middle class? Every health statistic shows marked improvement. Dutannuru even has an immigration problem because folks in the neighboring countries know a good thing when they see it. And speaking of neighbors, when was the last time one sovereign nation asked to peacefully unite with another?"

"Mensah has provided wise leadership for his people."

"And a wise leader seeks good counsel," Maya said, "You've provided that to President Mensah. He told me that you've been invaluable to him in the unification and reconciliation process."

"*E Pluribus Unum*. There's a lot to be done," Egan admitted, "and he'll be missed when he steps down at the end of the year."

"There's talk in the legislature of you succeeding Mensah as president."

"That would be something," Egan said with a laugh. "Thankfully, the constitution of Dutannuru bars foreigners from elective office."

"No such prohibition against you exists in the United States."

Egan and Maya studied each other carefully for a moment. She then gave him a slight nod that she was serious.

"That's insane. I'm about as qualified as..."

"As *any* native born citizen of the United States who is over the age of thirty-five," Maya interjected. "Those are, of course, the bare minimum requirements for holding the highest office in the land. I prefer a resume of substantial accomplishments as well, but the last election taught us that it isn't a necessity. Article Two also contains a residency requirement, but my lawyers have reviewed the clause and have assured me it's not an obstacle."

"But I've never run for anything," Egan said.

"Neither did Washington or Eisenhower. They both won fame on the battlefield, but yours came through peace. Everything you've done for Dutannuru has prepared you to lead." Maya stabbed a slender finger at the newspaper photograph. "This defining act has thrust you onto the world stage and it forces us to rethink our plans. Our dream of bringing power to the people must grow beyond electricity or we waste an incredible opportunity to save our country before it's too late. The world needs the United States, and the United States needs you."

"This is the last thing I would ever have wanted."

"I know," Maya replied sympathetically, "but you have had greatness thrust upon you. And it looks good on you."

Egan crossed his arms and stared down at the shattered turbine as he considered Maya's proposition. The engineers he'd trained could restore this power plant without him, while the country he'd helped found would soon elect new leadership. It was a time of change in Dutannuru, a perfect moment to step away and start something new.

"It's been a while since I last visited my folks," Egan said. "This is something I should talk over with them."

"Absolutely." Maya moved next to Egan and slipped her arm around his waist. With her free hand, she patted his forearm supportively. "But fair warning, I've already spoken with your father."

"And what did he say?"

"It's his idea. I just happen to agree with him."

"He is most definitely *not* a fan of the President," Egan said with a chuckle. "When do you need my answer?"

"You have a little time to think it over," Maya replied, "but soon. The election is less than two years off and we'll need every bit of that time to make a credible run."

"Fair enough," Egan said as he picked up the newspaper. "The President will be hard to beat—lousy leader or not, he is a savvy campaigner."

"And he's got all the unions, most of the press, and some major big-money backers solidly in his corner," Maya added. "It'll be tough, but he is definitely beatable."

Egan caught a hint of a conspiratorial smile on Maya's face, and her eyes sparkled with a glint of mischief.

"Why do I get the feeling you and that devious husband of yours already have an intriguing campaign strategy in mind?"

"The way to beat our President is to give him everything that he *thinks* he needs to win."

PART TWO

★★★★★★★★★★★★★★★★

Eleven Months Later

6

NIKI ADASHI STROLLED CONFIDENTLY ACROSS THE LOBBY OF THE Willard Hotel, the heels of her leather boots tapping lightly on the marble floor. She wore a stylish, full-length camel hair coat with a colorful scarf loosely wrapped over her head and a woven bag dangling from her arm. She was pulling on a pair of leather gloves when she spotted Egan seated by a window.

"Right on time," Egan said with a smile as he rose to greet her.

Niki offered a cheek and he gave her a friendly peck.

"This is not an event I wish to be fashionably late for," she replied. "And I must say you are looking very handsome this evening."

Egan, dressed in black tie formal, nodded a thank you and slipped on a navy overcoat.

"Do you have the invitation?" Niki asked.

Egan patted his left breast pocket and felt the stiff embossed cardstock. "Right here."

They exited through the revolving door and out under the glass canopy protecting the hotel's Pennsylvania Avenue entrance. It was just past sunset and the temperature hovered in the high twenties under a clear evening sky. Egan offered his arm and the pair moved briskly up the street. Niki easily kept pace with his long-legged strides. On the opposite side of the avenue, a handful of ice skaters glided under the lights in Pershing Park.

Continuing past the Treasury Building, they cleared the first security checkpoint before proceeding up East Executive Avenue. A fresh layer of unblemished snow blanketed the immaculate grounds of the South Lawn, as if ordered expressly for the evening's festivities.

The pillar of effervescent water rising out of the fountain glowed with an internal light.

Egan studied the elegant façade of the White House as they walked and found the scene worthy of a rendering by Currier and Ives. The home of the American President was designed to make an impression, and it did so to great effect. Egan felt a swell of patriotic pride that he was, tonight, an invited guest in a place that was once home to Thomas Jefferson and Abraham Lincoln.

A small fountain in line with the sidewalk marked the east entry to the White House grounds. There, Egan and Niki were cleared by both Secret Service and a representative of the White House Social Office before passing through the wrought iron gate.

"Welcome to the White House," the Secret Service agent said as he returned their credentials.

"Thank you," Egan replied.

They followed another couple along a broad walk to the illuminated colonnade that defined the entry to the East Wing. The covered porch was decorated for the holidays and glowed with the warmth of the festive season.

Through the doors, a uniformed Secret Service officer made a final cursory check of their credentials and then pointed them through a metal detector.

"I think we're finally in," Egan offered as he cleared the magnetometer without a beep. He had been briefed on the security procedures and brought only a photo ID and the key card to his hotel room.

At the coat check, Niki removed her scarf to reveal her black mane coiffed in an up-do with a halo of ringlet curls. Egan helped her with her coat and received his first glimpse of the red beaded gown that wrapped Niki's lithe form. Delicate spirals of gold hung from her ears like tinsel and around her neck she wore a braided gold torc. Niki completed her transformation by trading her boots for a pair of Manolo Blahniks. In heels, she stood eye to eye with Egan.

"May I escort you to the Residence, ma'am?" a chiseled Marine in full dress uniform asked.

"You may," Niki replied, accepting the young man's offered arm.

The Marine led them down the East Colonnade. The windows were adorned with large magnolia wreaths dressed in red and famed with green boxwood garlands, beyond which lay the Kennedy Garden under a blanket of snow. The colonnade ended at the Visitor's Foyer, where an arch of decorated garland accented a large bronze bust of Lincoln. A pair of large paneled wood doors beneath an ornate elliptical transom stood open, providing access to the central hall that ran the length of the Residence's Ground Floor.

The polished marble on the walls glistened and a series of intersecting vaults ran the length of the broad corridor. Barely a third the way down the hall, the Marine guided them up a long marble staircase, at the top of which Egan caught a glimpse of the East Room to his right.

They turned left into the Entrance Hall, and then up the Grand Stair to the second floor, arriving at the Yellow Oval Room.

"This is where the President and the First Lady will host the reception," the Marine said as they reached the door. "I hope you enjoy the evening."

"Thank you," both Egan and Niki replied.

As the Marine withdrew, he gave Egan an approving smile, then performed a perfect about-face and headed back toward the stair.

"I have to thank you again for asking me to accompany you," Niki said as they entered the Yellow Oval, her voice barely above a whisper.

"You deserve a better seat to this particular event than in the press pool. And based on the looks you're getting, I should be the one thanking you."

A White House photographer documented their arrival at the reception. Inside, dozens of couples milled about. Some faces Egan recognized, but most were unknown to him. A beautifully decorated twelve-foot tree stood on the opposite side of the oval, flanked by two windows decorated with wreathes.

"What are you thinking about?" Niki asked.

"Maggie was always better at social events than me. She would have really enjoyed this. My being here is a fitting tribute to her life's work."

"May I offer you a drink?" a server asked.

Niki requested a white wine, Egan a cranberry juice over ice.

As the server withdrew, the President and the First Lady appeared in the doorway. She was draped in golden silk brocade, the delicate fabric shimmering in the light. The President, known for his cool demeanor, wore his tailored tuxedo as comfortably as James Bond.

"Good evening," the President said warmly—all conversation in the room stopped. "My wife and I are thrilled that you could join us tonight to honor President and Missus Mensah of Dutannuru. Our guests will arrive soon, and we will join you shortly. In the meantime, enjoy."

The First Couple nodded to a few friends, then turned and swept away.

"Did you see that dress?" Niki asked softly. "I might as well be wearing a paper bag."

"It's rude to outshine a bride at her wedding," Egan chided, "and equally rude to do so to our hostess on such an important occasion. But as elegant and attractive a woman as the First Lady is, she can only dream of wearing a dress the way you do."

Niki blushed and dropped her gaze with a bemused smile.

"I could never—"

"Niki," Egan said, cutting her off. "The only polite response to a compliment is *thank you.*"

"Thank you."

"You're welcome."

After their drinks arrived, a couple broke away from a group of guests near the tree and moved toward them. The man looked to be in his early forties, thin and wiry with a hatchet face of sharp, angular planes. The woman on his arm was an attractive brunette, well into her second trimester.

"Ross Egan?" the man asked.

Egan nodded and offered his hand. "And you're Daniel Page. A pleasure to meet you."

Page accepted Egan's hand in a firm, boney grip. "The pleasure is mine. It's an honor to meet a recipient of the Nobel Peace Prize."

"Once the President and the guest of honor arrive, the place will be thick with them."

"Indeed," Page chuckled. "And this is my wife, Elena."

"Delighted to meet you," Elena said with genuine warmth. "What you did in Dutannuru was quite simply amazing."

"Thank you," Egan replied, shooting a quick glance at Niki. "And I assume you saw the photograph of that famous night."

"Why yes."

"My guest is the photographer," Egan said proudly. "May I introduce Niki Adashi."

"You were there?" Elena asked, amazed.

"Yes," Niki replied.

"Oh my," Elena gasped, her free hand shot to her abdomen.

"Another kick?" Page asked.

Elena nodded. "This child is a gymnast, I swear. Would you mind sitting on the couch with me for a moment? I have about a million questions to ask you, but I simply *must* get off my feet."

"Of course," Niki replied.

Arm-in-arm, the two women moved to one of the finely uphol-stered sofas.

"I won't let my wife monopolize your guest," Page promised.

"Judging by the other ladies gathering around them, I think she might be the perfect icebreaker."

"I have to admit, I'm surprised you know who I am. Are you into politics?"

"Not really, but I have a friend who is, and she made up a set of flash cards so I'd know who's who. If I remember your card correctly, you managed the President's last campaign and even wrote a book about it. So, I guess we have that in common."

"You ran a presidential campaign?" Page joked.

"God no. I co-wrote a book with President Mensah. It's coming out after the first of the year."

"Then you'll be hitting the promotional trail about the time we start campaigning in earnest." Page sipped his drink, his flinty eyes still locked on Egan.

"Our schedule looks brutal, but it's only for a few months. Then I can slip back into obscurity. I can't imagine the gauntlet you and your boss have to run through until November."

"We should have the nomination sewn up before my next child is born," Page said confidently. "Then we'll get a bit of a breather before the convention and fall campaign."

"You don't think Governor Lynn will give you a run for your money?"

"I thought you weren't into politics."

"I'm not," Egan replied, "other than to educate myself on who the candidates on my ballot are and their views on key issues. I take voting seriously."

Page tapped his glass to Egan's. "Here's to an educated voting public."

Both men took a sip to complete the toast.

"Regarding the Governor of the great state of Pennsylvania, I think an intra-party challenge to a sitting president is a suicide mission."

"She must think the President is vulnerable if she's willing to take a shot."

"That, and she'll be four years older next time around, and running against a field of young up-and-comers. In the governor's mind, it's now or never. I admire her nerve, but her campaign is quixotic."

Egan chuckled.

"What's so funny?" Page asked.

"As a guy who knows a little about windmills, I find the thought of tilting at them amusing," Egan explained. "My father owns a wind farm in Michigan."

"I see. And as I recall, your field of expertise is electrical power?"

"Yes."

"Given that and your notoriety over that business in Dutannuru, I'd wager that you would be a more formidable opponent than Governor Lynn."

"Then it's a good thing I'm not running."

"Good for the President. Another thing that would be good for the President is your endorsement."

Egan shook his head in disbelief. "You're joking."

"I'm a campaign manager. I never joke about contributions and endorsements. You're a hot commodity, so your endorsement translates into votes."

"But I don't belong to any party," Egan said.

"All the better," Page countered. "Independents will decide this election."

"Fame is a poor substitute for making an educated decision. The President has a record to run on and the voting public should decide to retain him based on that and not the endorsement of an actress or a rock star. I won't shill for any politician, but I will give every candidate, including the President, my fair consideration and make my decision privately."

Page studied Egan carefully for a moment, and then nodded.

"I respect that, but I had to ask. You don't seem at all pleased with the notoriety that comes with winning a Nobel Prize."

"If I'd won a Nobel for having discovered something that benefited mankind, that would be one thing. The path to peace was shown to us two thousand years ago, and it remains the road less traveled. All Mensah and I did was transplant a shoot from the American tree of Liberty in Africa."

"No small feat."

"Perhaps, but the prize really belongs to the people of Dutannuru for seizing peace out of war. The real demonstration of that comes in a couple weeks."

"Oh?" Page asked.

"I've heard it said that the only job better than president is ex-president. Mensah is popular enough that if he wanted the job for another term, the legislature would have offered an amendment to the people and changed the constitution on presidential term limits. Like George Washington, he sees the importance of holding power for only so long. The beauty of our system is that we peacefully create ex-presidents."

"Not too soon, I hope," Page said wryly. "Otherwise, I'm out of a job. Speaking of jobs, we do have one that might be of interest you. Would you consider being our next ambassador to Dutannuru?"

"Is Quimby stepping down?"

"No, but there's another post opening up unexpectedly and we're thinking of shifting her there. You'd be a perfect fit for Dutannuru and I see no problem getting you through the confirmation process."

"I'm committed through the first half of next year, but my publisher would shoot me if I didn't consider your offer seriously. It's the kind of publicity I think she'd kill for."

"It wouldn't hurt us either. We're looking at making the shift in late spring, but I would appreciate it if you would keep this between us for now. I'll let the President know that you are open to the idea."

"Fair enough."

The President and the First Lady returned to the Yellow Oval with the guests of honor and their entourage. Page excused himself and joined his wife, and Niki returned to Egan.

Instead of a formal receiving line, the two presidential couples made a slow circuit of the room with the hosts making the introductions. Egan and Niki held their place, waiting their turn.

"Is this not exciting? We are going to meet the President," Niki said in a low voice.

"We've already met Mensah." Egan replied.

"Not him, the President of the United States," Niki said with the pride of a recently naturalized citizen.

As the two presidential couples moved toward them, Egan caught the President sharing a quick glance with his campaign manager. Page gave an almost imperceptible nod of his head.

"These two, I believe I should introduce to you," Mensah announced to the President and the First Lady. "It is with great pleasure that I present Ms. Niki Adashi, a daughter of Dutannuru and a fine photographer who has recently won the Pulitzer Prize for her work in my country."

"Ms. Adashi, my wife and I are delighted that you could be with us tonight," the President said warmly.

"Thank you, Mr. President," Niki replied breathlessly. "Madam, everything is just beautiful, and your dress is simply stunning."

"The White House Staff is amazing," the First Lady agreed. "As for my dress, I honestly think Marcia Amagansett could make a sack of potatoes in a dress look divine."

"Dear, you are no sack of potatoes," the President chided affectionately.

"And this," Mensah continued, "is a very good friend to me, and to all the people of Dutannuru—Ross Egan."

"Your reputation precedes you," the President said as he extended his hand. "I am truly honored to have you here with us tonight."

A White House photographer captured the meeting between three recent winners of the Nobel Peace Prize.

"Thank you for inviting me here to honor my friend. This is a unique privilege." Egan then turned to the First Lady. "The graciousness of a house is a reflection of the people who make it their home. Thank you for your hospitality."

"You're welcome," the First Lady said with a soft smile. "I hope you both enjoy the evening."

THE RECEPTION IN THE YELLOW OVAL CONTINUED FOR ANOTHer forty-five minutes, then the guests were ushered down the stairs into the Entrance Hall where the majority of those invited to the state dinner waited. Egan and Niki crossed the marble floor, a checkerboard of light and dark polished stone and found a spot along the colonnade.

After a few moments, the President, his wife and the guests of honor descended the Grand Staircase. The United States Marine Band played four *Ruffles and Flourishes* followed by *Hail to the Chief* and the national anthems of Dutannuru and the United States.

After all the guests had filed through a formal receiving line, the two presidential couples walked down the Cross Hall to the State Dining Room that was exquisitely decorated for the holiday season. Both presidents spoke briefly as the guests enjoyed a five-course meal that would have earned any restaurant that equaled it a James Beard Foundation Award.

"I wish I had not worn so tight a dress," Niki moaned as the dessert plates were cleared away and the guests moved on to the opulent

East Room for the evening's entertainment.

"The great thing about tuxedos is they have these fasteners on the waist that allow you to loosen them a bit."

"You men are very fortunate indeed."

"I thank God and my father for my Y-chromosome each and every day."

As they stepped into the East Room, Egan was immediately struck by the size of the space. It was larger than any place he had called home. Fresh garlands with blue hydrangea and eucalyptus accented the four fireplaces in the room, which had magnificently decorated fir trees standing at each end.

Seating for all the guests was arranged in a semi-circle around an area that contained an array of traditional and electronic instruments. Once the guests were seated, the President moved to center stage.

"The musicians who will entertain us tonight," the President began, "have been the joyful stewards of the modern soundtrack of the Christmas season for many years. I am very pleased to present *Mannheim Steamroller*."

"I enjoy this group very much," Niki said as the musicians appeared from the adjacent Green Room and took the stage. "Maggie played them for me during her first Christmas in my village."

Mannheim Steamroller performed an hour-long set of seasonal music in their uniquely elegant style, culminating in their stirring rendition of *Stille Nacht*.

The musicians took their bows to an audience that included some of the nation's most powerful people, all on their feet applauding the outstanding performance. And as they clapped, several members of the audience felt their cell phones vibrating in their pockets. Others rushed to quell their contribution to a cacophony of disparate ring tones.

"What's happening?" the President tersely asked his campaign manager, alarmed that a situation might be emerging somewhere.

"I don't know," Page replied as he fumbled with his phone.

Egan watched as Niki fished a thin handset out of her clutch purse. Having left his phone at the hotel, he was one of the few people in the room not trying to quell a buzzing or chiming gadget.

"That's very strange," Niki said, puzzled, as she read the luminous screen.

"You got an odd text, too?" a Texan in a tuxedo asked, his brow furrowed as he read the message on his iPhone.

Niki nodded. "I have never received a text message without a sender's name or a number."

The Texan glanced over Niki's shoulder. "I got the same damn thing."

"What's it say?" Egan asked.

Niki turned her phone toward him. It read:

WHO IS I?

7

TWO ARCTIC CAT SNOWMOBILES CRUISED ACROSS THE FROZEN lake—a gray-white slab of solid ice ten times the size of Manhattan. An early freeze roared out of Canada in a series of blasts that sealed the vast lake completely by Thanksgiving weekend. Six weeks of polar temperatures had thickened the ice to eighteen inches at mid-lake and the winter fishing season was in full swing.

Mike Unden rode beside his father Jacob toward a cluster of shanties out on the lake. The structures ranged from simple wooden sheds to elaborate constructions outfitted with all the amenities. A mix of pickup trucks, SUVs and snowmobiles were parked chaotically on the ice as several fishermen set up beside one of the larger shanties for bowl game tailgate party.

Mike eased back on the throttle, slowing his sled to a crawl as they neared his father's unusual shanty. Inspired by a visit to Disney's Epcot, the old farmer had built a small geodesic dome with an elongated airlock entry that he called his igloo. The entire structure could be easily broken down by two people with a ladder and a ratchet wrench and fit in back of a trailer pulled by Jacob's F-150.

Once assembled, the igloo was anchored to the ice to keep it from blowing away in the gusts that roared across the lake. A small satellite dish mounted atop the dome hinted at the simple comforts hidden inside.

Both men parked their sleds and dismounted, the elder a tad slower than his son.

"How you doing, Pa?" Mike asked.

"Little stiff, but a bad day of fishing beats a great day of work."

"So I've heard. Let me help you with the cooler."

Mike unwound the bungee cords holding a large rectangular cooler to the back of his father's Bearcat Z1 XT. The utility sled was a steady draft horse compared with the thoroughbred that was Mike's CFR 1000, but both men shared a passion for their winter mounts.

As Mike hefted the cooler, his father unlocked the igloo's outer door and they stepped into the dome. The bright morning sun shone through triangular windows, warming and illuminating the interior. The shanty floor, like the rest of the dome, was made from insulated panels that sealed the structure tight.

"How's the hole?" Mike asked as he set the cooler beside a bench that served as the igloo's kitchen counter.

Jacob opened a hinged door in the floor to reveal the lake below. Several inches of new ice covered the top of a hole in the center of the exposed frozen lake.

"Needs a reaming."

"On it."

Mike grabbed a six-inch offset auger and quickly reopened the hole in the ice. As his father unloaded bait from the cooler, Mike dragged a small generator and propane tank out of the igloo. Just to the left of the entry, he plugged the generator into an electrical box and connected the propane tank to a quick disconnect gas line. He pulled the starter cord, bringing the four-stroke engine rumbling to life. Satisfied, he returned inside.

"You got power for the TV and the heater's ready to go."

Mike slipped off a glove, picked up the remote and flipped through the channels. It was too early for the pregame shows, so he stopped on a documentary about the Vietnam War.

"You wanna watch this?"

Jacob glanced at the screen and shook his head. "Saw enough when I was there. See if you can find me a western."

Skimming through the satellite guide, Mike settled on *The Treasure of the Sierra Madre*.

" 'Badges? We don't need no stinking badges!' " Mike quoted in a poor imitation of the infamous bandito.

"Don't quit your day job," Jacob opined as he looked over his fishing lures.

Mike turned on the small propane heater and set the temperature. It wasn't enough to turn the igloo into a sauna, but it would keep his father comfortable. That was the trick with his father's condition. Jacob Unden was a tough old bird—just not as tough as he once was.

"Better get going if you want to get your ride in before the game."

"Yeah, yeah." Mike tugged his gloves back on. "Call me if you need anything."

"Like you can hear me over your sled."

"Love you, Pa," Mike said as he headed out the door.

Jacob paused and waited for the sound of his son's snowmobile. He heard the muffled thunder of the engine, the shift in pitch and volume as the sled quickly raced away.

"I love you, too, son."

Jacob settled on a lure, tied his line and baited the hook. The igloo had all the comforts of home, including a battered La-Z-Boy chair whose cushions fit Jacob's body like a glove. Mounted to the floor beside the chair stood a rod holder. He dropped his line into the hole and set his rod.

Too early to justify a beer, he poured a cup of black coffee from a Thermos and surveyed his tiny refuge. He enjoyed many fond memories of this place, including, he smiled, the conception of his son one January morning when the fish just weren't biting.

He walked over to the heater and warmed himself. Outside, a wispy trail of smoke rose out of the exhaust vent. Jacob set his coffee cup down on the counter and pulled a small screwdriver out of his tackle box. He gently loosened the screw on the crimp collar that held the heater's flexible exhaust pipe in place by a half turn and slid the end of the pipe back. Immediately, he felt the hot exhaust leaking through the gap. Jacob put the screwdriver away, picked up his coffee cup and settled into his chair.

★

AROUND NOON, MIKE UNDEN DROVE HIS SLED UP TO THE IGLOO and parked. He'd enjoyed a great ride both on the trails and racing across open stretches of the lake. It was cold, but the wind was light under a perfectly blue Dakota sky. He slipped off his helmet and opened the outer door.

"Hope you got that chili simmering, Pa, cause I'm hungry."

Mike did not smell the tangy aroma of his father's four-alarm chili as he entered the igloo. In fact, he smelled nothing at all. His father sat slumped in his chair, head back, lifeless. Shards of a broken coffee cup lay on the plywood floor.

Almost immediately, Mike felt he was having trouble breathing. His head spinning, he lunged back through the doors outside and drew in as much fresh air as his lungs could hold. After his mind cleared, he disconnected the propane tank to kill the heater. Then he dialed 911.

8

COPPERHEAD, MONTANA

HOMER HOPPS RECLINED IN A LEATHER CLUB CHAIR IN THE MAIN hall of the ski lodge, warming himself by a roaring fire. At six-eight, his long, jean-clad legs stretched across the floor, ending in a pair of worn cowboy boots. With a vintage National guitar laying across his lap, he seemed lost in thought as he strummed a haunting melody.

The lodge, with its stone floors and soaring timber vaults, had been designed to accommodate hundreds of skiers and snow boarders, though only a handful enjoyed its partially completed runs. Envisioned as a year-round resort destination, Copperhead fell victim to the faltering economy. And when promised financial assistance from the state failed to materialize, the dreams from which it was born evaporated in a spiral of default and foreclosure.

Like the Torrences in Stephen King's *The Shining*, Homer and his wife Suzy served as caretakers of the ill-fated resort. And both were thankful that no paranormal evil had taken root. Instead, the couple in their mid-fifties with children grown and gone had to deal with spiders, miners, and rogues.

"It's almost six," Suzy announced.

Homer looked up and smiled as his wife approached, firelight glinting off his round spectacles. His melody transitioned into George Harrison's love song *Something*.

Suzy bowed down and kissed Homer's balding pate. A shoulder-length fringe tied back in a ponytail was all that remained of his once lustrous head of hair.

"Dinner's ready, and you've got a long night ahead," she said.

"Call me a lot of things, my love, but never late for a meal."

Homer strummed a final flourish as he pulled himself vertical, then set the steel body guitar back in its lined case. He unclipped a two-way radio from his belt and pressed the talk button.

"Double-H to Captain America. You read me cap'n? Over."

UP THE MOUNTAIN FROM THE LODGE, A SMALL GROUP OF SNOW boarders reveled under the lights in the confines of their private halfpipe. Aside from the adjacent intermediate slope, it was Copperhead's only functional downhill run.

A boarder clad in arctic white cammo raced up the right side of the halfpipe, cleared the edge and sailed into the air. In a fluid motion, the airborne body twisted into a 520-degree rotation and bent into a back flip. Feeling the tug of gravity, the boarder spun upright and floated down the near-vertical side of the run.

"Way to rock that Kassaroll, Captain America!" shouted another boarder from atop the halfpipe.

Heart racing with adrenaline, Deb McColl responded with a howl and pumped her fists after successfully landing the trick. Her reverie was short-lived as a jolt of static crackled inside her star-spangled helmet and Homer Hopps's voice filled her ears. She shot for the end of the pipe and slid to a stop.

"Talk to me, Double-H," McColl responded.

"Soup's on and it's almost time to go to work. Round up your posse and head back to the ranch."

"Loud and clear, Double-H. See you in ten."

McColl signaled the rest of the boarders that this was their last run, then turned and headed down to the lodge.

9

ROSS EGAN SAT BENEATH A POOLSIDE PERGOLA STARING OUT AT the Atlantic Ocean. Though a cool night by Florida standards and cold compared to Dutannuru, he sat comfortably in a pair of khakis and a golf shirt with a pull-over windbreaker. In one hand, he swirled a fine California Syrah in broad-bowled wine glass while the other held an exquisite Ramon Allones Gigante Double Corona. Modest waves crashed ashore in a predictable, soothing rhythm.

"...and if he stays healthy, the Packers could make it to the Super Bowl," Leon Egan opined. "Isn't that right, son?"

"Uh, yeah," Ross replied, drawn out of his thoughts to answer his father.

"That's a stirring vote of confidence," conservative talk radio host Garr Denby shot back as he flicked a long ash off the end of his cigar. He then turned to their host. "What do you think?"

"The Pack has played well all year," Burton Randell conceded, "but they had a relatively easy schedule. Carolina dropped a couple more games, but when they lost, it was either in the final seconds of regulation or in OT, and against a quality opponent. Any of those games could have gone their way. The Panthers are the most danger- ous wild card team I've seen in years."

Following an evening of good food and college bowl games, the gentlemanly quartet had retreated to the pergola to enjoy the waning hours of the year with good wine and cigars. To the west stood the Florida retreat of Maya Randell and her husband. The Raffles Hotel in Singapore, where the Randells enjoyed their twenty-fifth anniver- sary, served as the architectural inspiration for the colonial-style villa.

Egan was there with his parents, Leon and Rhetta, who wintered in a condominium just up the coast near Vero Beach. The Randell's twin daughters were in Palm Beach with their husbands celebrating the arrival of the New Year, their young children left in the capable hands of their doting grandparents.

Ross's cell phone buzzed like an angry hornet. He glanced at the screen and smiled before he answered.

"Yes, Mr. President."

Mensah's hearty laugh poured through the receiver. "You only have about seven more hours to say that. Then I will just be another old man in Dutannuru. I just called to wish you a most happy New Year, my friend."

"And to you, as well. I was just thinking about you. How are things in the capital?"

"The New Year arrived five hours ago, and the celebration shows no sign of abating. I think it will just flow into today's inaugural celebration."

"The people of Dutannuru have much to celebrate, not the least of which is your years of good stewardship. Today is the first time they've greeted a new year without the threat of war."

"Yes, this is a happy day," Mensah said. "But also a busy one for me."

"I appreciate your call and I look forward to spending time with you after your return to private life."

"That will be good. I must go now, but I will see you soon."

"Can't wait," Ross replied.

"If only it was *our* president," Denby remarked sarcastically as Ross pocketed his phone. "I'd be out celebrating in the streets if I thought his last hours in office were ticking away."

"You've got another year before that happens," Burton said, "and only if most of the voters feel as you do."

"Gallup and Rasmussen seem to think so, and my Arbitron numbers have never been higher," Denby offered. "The mood of conservatives across the country is absolutely electric. The only problem is there's no Reagan to galvanize it." Denby turned to Egan. "Or somebody like your pal Mensah."

"I can guess how you feel about the President and Governor Lynn," Ross said, "but what about the six Republicans?"

"Vegas is having an easier time picking the Super Bowl winner than figuring the GOP nominee," Denby replied. "There are two governors, an old senator, a quirky congresswoman, a four-star general, and a media billionaire. Any of 'em would be better than what we got now, but no one is a clear favorite. I read your book, and *you* would stand as good a chance as any of them, and better than most after what you did in Africa."

Maya stepped out onto the terrace and glided toward the four men.

"The management of Raffles Palm Beach is sorry to inform you gentlemen that it is closing time at the Winston Churchill Bar," she announced. "So if you are quite through discussing the state of the British Empire, it's time to stub out those nasty cigars and come inside. The ball drops in five minutes."

In response, the quartet each took a final draw on their cigars and lofted four perfect rings of smoke into the air.

" 'A woman is only a woman,' " Burton offered, " 'but a cigar is a smoke.' "

"You can quote Kipling all you like," Maya shot back at her husband, "but you better not have smoky lips if you expect to get some sugar at midnight."

Burton looked at his wife and the remnant of the Corona in his fingertips, and stubbed the cigar out.

HOMER HOPPS STOOD IN FRONT OF A LARGE, FLAT SCREEN TELEvision watching a band he could not name play live from an outdoor stage near New York's Times Square. He tried to keep an open mind with regard to music but some trends in popular culture simply eluded him. He was the only person in the windowless meeting room watching the celebration. Deb McColl and the rest of her rogue programmers sat glued to laptops and workstations, young men and women fueled on energy drinks and salty junk food.

"*Go* or *No Go* time, people," Hopps announced. "Con Ed?"

"Go," a twenty-two year old Cal Tech grad replied.

"EMS?"

"Go," another rogue answered.

"Network feeds?"

"Go."

"Package?"

McColl looked up from her screen at Hopps. "Go."

A devilish smile curled the ends of Hopps's mouth. "All systems are *Go*. On my mark, we are T-minus two minutes. And...mark."

"WHERE ARE THE KIDS?" LEON ASKED AS HE SAT ON THE COUCH beside his wife.

"Camped out in the play room. They held on as long as they could," Rhetta explained, "but the last one nodded off about forty minutes ago."

They gathered in the den, an immense flat screen displaying the scene in Times Square. Despite the cold, a record crowd filled Broadway and the intersecting streets in the great annual tradition.

"Ross, would you do the honors?" Maya asked as she handed out noisemakers.

"My pleasure."

Ross gently twisted the cork from a bottle of Roederer Estate Brut and felt it release with a soft pop. He then filled six champagne flutes with the effervescent liquid and distributed them.

"The ball's dropping!" Rhetta said excitedly. "I love this part."

"...5...4...3...2...1..." they counted down with the crowd in New York City.

At the stroke of midnight, Times Square went dark. The celebratory shout died in its first syllable as the mood shifted from joy to confusion.

"What the hell," the host of the program exclaimed before the network cut his microphone feed.

Television cameras powered by stand-alone generators continued to broadcast the eerie scene of a packed Times Square plunged into darkness. Celebrants wearing illuminated necklaces and deely bobbers appeared like tiny fireflies flickering in the shadow.

Calls from police officers to remain calm could be heard over the murmuring crowd.

"I hope this isn't..." Rhetta said, her voice quavering.

"Power's gone out, dear," Leon reassured his wife. "That's all."

The first seconds of the New Year passed like an eternity. There was no panic, no sudden rush to flee the darkness, just a stillness of anticipation. The people in Times Square were waiting for a sign. And then it came.

It started with the jumbotron screens that covered the Times building, then spread from screen to screen. A cryptic message:

WHO IS I?

"My God," Denby roared. "It's a college prank. Probably one of those egghead schools, like Stanford or MIT. No offense."

"None taken," Maya replied.

Burton set his champagne flute down on the bar and checked an incoming message on his cell phone.

"But what does it mean?" Rhetta asked.

"It means those brainy engineers flunked freshman English," Denby answered sardonically.

The conservative talk show host's sharp humor was a clear sign of his relief that a tragic event was not unfolding. Instead, the Times Square blackout would provide a rich vein of humor for his next broadcast.

The surreal scene continued for another thirty seconds before the messages disappeared. Then the lights of Times Square blared back on to full intensity and the LED illuminated ball completed its descent. Fireworks erupted from the rooftop and the celebration, somewhat subdued, resumed.

"Whoever's responsible for that stunt ought to be strung up," Leon grumbled. "The memory of 9/11 is still too fresh for the folks in New York. Like when those idiots flew Air Force One low over the city just to take a picture of it."

"They blew what could have been a perfect PR moment," Denby

agreed. "Most of the people in New York City voted for the President, and his ham-handed staff goes and scares them half to death. If they'd gone public, they would have had thousands of people out cheering as the plane flew over."

"Regardless of whoever is responsible for this little shenanigan," Maya announced, "this is still the start of a new year. You all have my best wishes for one filled with love, family and happiness."

"Hear, hear," Denby seconded.

"Bravo," Maya whispered into her husband's ear. "Please extend my congratulations and continued good wishes for the New Year to our team."

"Already done," Burton replied proudly. "And I'm sure they're not waiting another two hours to pop the corks in Montana."

Champagne glasses clinked and a round of kisses and embraces were exchanged. Maya saved Ross for last and approached him with a mix of expectation and concern.

"Happy New Year," Ross said as he embraced her.

Maya kissed him on the cheek and then whispered in his ear.

"Last year was a good one for you, and God knows you deserved it. May this year bring with it all that we hope."

"Amen to that," Ross replied softly.

Maya gave Ross a tight squeeze before slipping from his embrace and turning toward the others.

"I must beg your indulgence for a moment. Now that it is officially the New Year, Ross and I must attend to a small business matter. We will return to you shortly. For those who feel the need for something sweet, I whipped up a decadent chocolate mousse that's in the refrigerator."

"Decadent is the operative word here," Burton agreed as he pulled a tray of chilled glass vessels containing a dark frothy substance topped with a raspberry. "Maya makes it from her grandmother's recipe and a whole mess of dark chocolate went into this."

"I'll bet it pairs nicely with the brut," Denby speculated.

"You'd win that bet," Maya replied. "Now save us some. We'll be right back."

✯

MAYA LED ROSS TO A SMALL ROOM ON THE NORTH END OF THE villa. Three sides of the room featured large arch windows that, in daylight, overlooked a colorful garden. It had bamboo plank flooring and a ceiling paneled in painted beadboard. The plaster walls and wood trim were finished in off white and pastel hues. What could have easily been a sunroom retreat was instead the home office from which Maya and her husband managed their business empire.

Ross sat on a white wicker sofa as Maya retrieved a thick leather folio from a locked desk drawer. She sat beside him and carefully laid out a set of bound contracts on the glass-topped coffee table. Beside the contracts, she set a pair of fountain pens made from wood taken from the original US Navy frigate *USS Constitution*.

"So, this is it," Ross said.

Maya nodded. "The birth of Terrafuma Energy. All your years of research, your life's work, have led to this moment. A moment that will change the world."

He leaned forward and studied the cover of the contract. It bore the logo of a company that would exist as soon as he and Maya added their signatures to these documents. While the paperwork before them was thick with legal boilerplate, the essence of the agreement was simple. For his part, Ross would invest Terrafuma with his intellectual property—a permanent license on the revolutionary technologies that he created. Maya would provide the considerable financial resources required to establish this new private company. They were equal shareholders in this venture, a dream they both nurtured over the long years of research and development.

"There are only two things I can think of that I was more excited to sign," Ross said. "My wedding license, and my first driver's license."

"Only one was worth more," Maya opined.

Ross removed the cap from one of the pens and flipped to the tabbed signature page. Slowly, he guided the pen through the loops and curves of his name. Maya then added her signature to consummate the deal.

They completed the remaining copies quickly and Maya returned all but Ross's copy to her locked drawer.

"So, now it's official," Maya declared as she returned to the sofa. "You are the first billionaire of the new year. On behalf of those of us who have created something worthy of earning three significant commas of net worth, I welcome you to the club."

Ross shook his head and smiled. "Thank you."

"Now before we can celebrate, we must attend to Terrafuma's first client."

Maya tapped a few keystrokes into a handheld remote to activate a secure teleconferencing program. A moment later, a flat screen wall monitor glowed with a view into a room half a world away. Looking back at them was an Asian man with a round face and graying black hair. It was Chen Yung-Chin, leader of the Standing Committee of the National People's Congress—a position of power second only to the Chinese presidency.

"Good day, Chairman Chen," Maya said with a polite nod of her head.

"And to you, Ms. Randell," Chen replied.

"It is my great pleasure to at last introduce to you my associate, Ross Egan."

"I am delighted to finally make your acquaintance," Chen said. "We share a similar background in electrical engineering. Speaking as one engineer to another, your work is most revolutionary."

"Thank you," Ross replied.

"I trust that your review team was satisfied with our demonstration at the Dongjaio Power Plant?" Maya asked.

"Indeed. Their only disappointment was in not seeing how your innovation was accomplished."

"Will respect for our intellectual property be an issue?" Egan asked.

"It will not," Chen vowed. "Separate installations will be provided as defined in the contract. All activity within those installations will be the sole responsibility of Terrafuma Energy."

"And the payment terms we proposed?" Maya asked.

"Most unusual," Chen replied, his eyes narrowing, "but what you offer is also most unusual. China's investment in US Treasuries has lost considerable value due to actions taken by your President and his most significant supporter. Paying Terrafuma in Treasuries is agreeable assuming that you can meet the timeline."

"Our project team is ready to scale up the work at Dongjaio as soon as the contracts are signed," Maya said. "From there, they will move on to your other power generation facilities."

"Then I suggest you make arrangements for that work to commence as soon as possible. I will sign the contracts upon the conclusion of this call," Chen promised. "The first transfer will be made into Terrafuma's account at the open of business tomorrow."

"And the other matter we discussed?" Maya asked.

"Ah, the *favor*," Chen said, smiling conspiratorially. "Consider our warming interest in joining the President's New York Climate Exchange an act of gratitude from the People's Republic of China."

"We look forward to the fruits of those discussions," Maya said with a polite nod of her head.

"Until we speak again." Chen returned the nod, and then terminated the call.

Ross turned to Maya. "That went well."

"And the President will be thrilled with the prospect of China joining his climate exchange. A diplomatic and environmental coup—it's the kind of accomplishment that may help him win the election."

"It'll certainly do something to his chances in the fall," Ross agreed.

"Yes, but first we must help him through the primaries. Four years ago, Governor Lynn lost her party's nomination by the slimmest of margins, and there are many who now regret their decision to back the President. She presents a formidable challenge for the nomination."

"And serious contenders draw the big money."

"They do indeed," Maya said. "And as my dissatisfaction with the President is known in certain circles, the governor and I have an area of common interest."

"When do you meet?" Ross asked.

"In a few days. And instead of a campaign contribution, I'll make Governor Lynn and her husband an offer she can't refuse."

IO

THE ROSE BOWL STADIUM ECHOED WITH THE ROAR OF more than eighty-seven thousand football fans. John Sarcobosco strained to hear the count amid the din, his body tense in a deep three-point stance, coiled like a spring awaiting release.

"Blue 48, Blue 48—Mustang, Mustang!" Cincinnati quarterback Al Kresta called out from the shotgun. "Hut!"

The center to Sarcobosco's left snapped the ball back and the offensive lineman lunged forward. He was immediately met by his counterpart on Florida's defensive line, a two-time All American slotted to go in the upper rounds of this next NFL draft. The parabolic microphones on the sidelines easily caught the crash of helmets and shoulder pads, transmitting the bone-jarring sound to millions of television sets around the country.

The Cincinnati line held off the Gator blitz. From inside the pocket, Kresta drilled a pass onto the numbers of his favorite receiver of the day. Tomeo hauled his catch in with both arms and sped for a seam through the Florida secondary. In the short field—on third and goal from the eight—the Gator cornerback and safety weren't giving Tomeo much room, closing on him in an instant.

As the two defenders slammed into Tomeo, the receiver felt arms tightening around his chest and waist. Like hitting a brick wall, Tomeo's forward motion stopped abruptly, the defenders' momentum plowing him down onto the field. The safety tried to wedge his hand into the cradle of Tomeo's forearms, attempting to dislodge the football and cause a fumble.

Both hands on the ball! Tomeo imagined his coach shouting—the running back's mantra drilled into him over years of practice.

Tomeo would not fumble—not today and not now. The impact of his shoulders hitting the ground jarred him. What air remained in his lungs shot out in a blast, but he held on to the football.

The whistle blew. The play was over. From beneath a pile of bodies, Tomeo lifted his head and saw the grass around his face was green. The white line he had tried to cross was barely an arm's length away.

The two Gators pulled themselves up. Sarcobosco eclipsed the sun and held out a friendly hand.

"Took a hell of a shot there, bro," Sarcobosco said. "Ready for another go?"

With one hand still on the ball and the other wrapped around Sarcobosco's meaty forearm, Tomeo pulled himself upright.

"Job ain't done, Little John. Job ain't done."

Tomeo handed the ball to the linesman, who spotted it inside the one-yard line.

Fifteen seconds remained to play in the first major college bowl game of the New Year. The score: Florida 24—Cincinnati 20. Cincinnati had to score a touchdown to win; a field goal wasn't enough. They had one last shot, fourth down with barely a yard of field between them and a victory. All they had to do was find a way past the stifling defense of the undefeated Gators. The Gator nation chafed that they wouldn't be playing a week later in the BSC game, though no one could argue that the schedules played by the top two teams were any easier.

As his teammates moved into the huddle, Kresta scanned his team's sideline. The offensive coach and several assistants were all gesturing frantically, a coded language of hand signals indicating the final play of the game. All but one of the signalers was a decoy, and quarter-by-quarter his team changed who sent in the plays. The noise generated by the largely hostile crowd doubled in intensity.

Thirteen seconds.

"Rip, Tight, 36-under, T-Bird, Charger," Kresta sounded clearly to his brothers in arms, looking at each squarely as he spoke. The car names were his team's playbook code. "On two! On two! Nobody jumps offsides! Go!"

The offensive line formed off the center, each of the large, muscular men crouching down into a deep low stance. Cincinnati set eight men up front, with Kresta immediately behind the center and a pair of running backs lined up in back of him.

The Gator side of the line of scrimmage was just as formidable, a wall of men intent on defending a thin strip of land with every last ounce of their strength. The game would end in a display of blood and guts, smash mouth football.

Ten seconds.

"Hut!" Kresta shouted.

The Gators' left side defensive end surged forward, the only one of the sixteen men on the line to flinch. The linesmen blew their whistles and tossed penalty flags.

The clock stopped with nine seconds to play and both teams stood up.

"Offsides. Number eighty-two on the defense." The head referee announced to the stadium and television audience. "Half the distance to the goal. Repeat fourth down."

The one-hundred-yard long field had been reduced to little more than the length of the football. The penalized defensive end's head hung low, knowing he'd just made his teammates job that much harder. A signal from the sideline traded the player out.

Both sides parted as the linesman reset the ball and the referee whistled for play to resume. No huddle. Both sides quickly moved into position. Kresta scanned the defense and noted a slightly different look with the replacement player.

"Corvette!" Kresta shouted, telling his teammates to run a mirror image of the previous play. "Corvette!"

Sarcobosco planted his tree trunk thighs and crouched low, his back as level as a cornerstone.

"You're going home with nothing," the All American defensive tackle growled.

Though slightly larger than he, Sarcobosco noted that the tackle's hind side was set low. He lowered his head and locked his eyes on the goal line.

"Hut!" Kresta shouted.

"I'm gonna stuff you like a turkey," the tackle boasted.

"Hut!"

Sarcobosco surged forward, driving his shoulder down and under his opponent's pads and into the man's chest. The battle to move the line between the two sides became a simple mater of leverage. Sarcobosco had the upper hand, driving forward and up, pressing the tackle back on his heels. As the tackle stumbled over the foot of a teammate, Sarcobosco took full advantage of the misstep.

Sarcobosco's head was still down, shoulder planted squarely in the tackle's numbers, when he saw the goal line below. He'd driven the line forward.

Kresta fed the ball to Jakes, the halfback, who slipped along Sarcobosco's right hip and surged toward the goal line. A pair of linebackers rushed in to fill the gap and swarm the ball carrier.

As the whistle blew, a pile of bodies lay atop the goal line. Sarcobosco pulled himself up to his full six-four and looked down at the tackle he'd pancaked. The man was flat on his back like a stranded turtle.

"First round draft choice, my ass," Sarcobosco said with a derisive snort.

The line judge who signaled the play dead ran up with one fist in the air, signaling no score. The Gator fans roared their approval. The head linesman made no ruling on the play.

"What do you got?" the head referee asked his two linesmen.

"The ball carrier didn't break the plane," the line judge replied.

"I didn't have a clear view," the head linesman offered.

"Alright then."

The head referee picked up the ball and set it on the three-inch line, then signaled a first down for Florida.

"What?" Sarcobosco roared. "I crossed the goal line with Jakes in my back pocket!"

"This is bullshit!" Jakes agreed, stripping off his helmet. "We're being jobbed!"

"Still going home with nothing," the Gator tackle taunted as he headed toward his sideline.

"And you'll be lucky to go in the seventh round with those grass stains on your ass," Sarcobosco countered.

"I scored, man. I know it," Jakes groused.

"Damn straight."

Two seconds.

As the Florida offense and Cincinnati defense ran onto the field for what would be the final play of the game to seal the Gator victory, the head referee felt the pager on his belt vibrate. The signal from the replay official in the press box was not unexpected. He switched on his microphone and stepped in front of the camera.

"Official time out. The previous play is under review."

The head referee then jogged over to the sideline and picked up the phone connecting him to the replay official.

"What do you see?"

"First angle...can't tell," the voice on the phone replied.

The jumbotrons at both ends of the stadium replayed the dramatic goal line stand.

"Next angle...again, it could go either way. I need the overhead shot down the line. Okay, there's the snap and ...oh shit."

"What?" the head referee asked.

"The feed cut out. My screen's black."

The crowd in the stadium gasped as the jumbotrons and electronic displays around the stadium all went blank.

"We lose power?"

"We still got lights in the press box, and the network is still broadcasting," the replay official replied. "Just nothing on...what the hell?"

One by one, a series of white letters appeared on the stadium's screens. They spelled out the message:

WHO IS I?

II

"IF I MAY SPEAK CANDIDLY, MR. PRESIDENT," THE DIRECTOR OF Central Intelligence said, "we have no idea how these intrusions were executed. This isn't just a single event, but a series of well-orchestrated, complex operations. We have to consider the very real possibility that the Chinese or the Russians are behind this."

The President nodded pensively, but said nothing. He was seated in an exact replica of the Appalachian oak rocking chair favored by JFK. The DCI and the Director of the FBI sat on the adjacent couch. Levi Knopper, the White House Chief of Staff, sat in a chair opposite the directors.

"Is there *any* direct evidence implicating anyone?" Knopper asked.

"No," the FBI Director replied. "And no one has claimed credit for these three cyber attacks."

"So what do we know?" the President asked pointedly.

"The first attack, during the recent State Dinner, was a simple, mass cell phone text to guests attending that event. The message was routed through several carriers simultaneously, with the message apparently originating outside of the United States."

"Apparently?" Knopper interjected.

"The CIA and NSA ran down the international trail to a blind end," the DCI replied. "The text messages could just have easily originated within the US, meaning the trail we followed was a ruse."

"We are still trying to determine how these messages entered the system, and how the sender acquired the cell phone numbers for your guests that evening. Even the White House didn't have numbers for all of the attendees who received the message. It's possible that three or more of the local cell towers were used to track guests entering the White House grounds and to strip their phone numbers."

"What about Times Square?" the President asked.

"Completely different type of attack," the FBI Director replied. "This wasn't a blanket disruption of the city's power grid, but a surgical disruption of power to specific buildings and signage. The police, fire stations and hospitals closest to Times Square were unaffected by the attack. They tied into dozens of electrical and communications systems remotely and they covered their tracks very well. All of the servers identified as access points were rebooted at 12:01 and their memories wiped clean. A similar approach was used at the Rose Bowl, though that incursion was limited to the stadium's jumbotron displays. The one thing these attacks have in common is a total lack of physical evidence."

"Since the text incident at the White House went largely unreported," the DCI added, "the more public attacks are being viewed largely as a publicity stunt."

"A publicity stunt?" Knopper snapped. "For what, terrorists?"

"A movie," the FBI Director replied. "At least that's the buzz running all over the Internet. The domain name who-is-i.com is taken, along with several variations. No luck so far in tracking down the registered owners. No one at any of the major studios has heard of a movie with this tag line for a marketing campaign. A few offered that if this was done to promote a movie, it's brilliant."

"Brilliant until it lands the people responsible for it in jail," Knopper countered.

"Given that no one has been hurt, no property has been damaged, and each attack has been benign in nature," the FBI Director offered, "I doubt anyone would receive a prison sentence for this."

"The courts will make that decision," the President said. "What I'm concerned about is if the intent is not benign."

"We are operating on that assumption until proven otherwise, Mr. President," the DCI offered. "And regardless of the intent, we need to know how this was accomplished in order to prevent it from happening again."

"Gentlemen, I do not want this happening again. I plan to attend the BCS Championship game and the only thing I want to see on the jumbotrons is a football game."

"Our technicians are at the stadium now isolating the electronic screens from the outside world," the FBI Director offered. "And we're establishing a false front so anyone attempting to access the screens will think they've gotten through, so we can track them. That said, I don't think they'll hit the BCS Championship Game."

"Why?" the President asked.

"The previous intrusions were unique and out of the blue. The other three major bowl games played this week went unaffected and the people behind these attacks have to know we will be all over the championship game as well as the NFL playoff games through to the Super Bowl. They have little to gain."

"Very well," the President said. "Keep me apprised of your progress."

"That will be all for today, gentlemen," Knopper announced as he stood up, signaling an end to the meeting.

The two directors thanked the President and exited through the northwest door into the corridor. Knopper closed the door and checked the latest messages on his Blackberry.

"What do you think?" the President asked.

"I think they'd both better get their respective acts together to figure out what the hell is going on. Hmmm."

"What?"

"Governor Lynn's husband is back in the hospital with chest pains," Knopper replied.

"Shame it's not Lady Macbeth's heart," the President grumbled. "If he dies, she'll be center stage for coverage of the funeral, and on the eve of the opening primaries no less. How the hell do I run against a grieving widow?"

"You're getting ahead of yourself. The report says chest pains, and the former senator is alert and undergoing some tests. It all sounds routine, but take the high road and call the governor to express your concern."

The President shrugged his shoulders but knew his chief of staff was correct. "What else is on the schedule?"

"You have China's ambassador this afternoon—apparently there's been some positive movement on their participation in the climate exchange."

"It would be great if we got them on board."

"Also, Peter Sturla is in town on business. Daniel Page asked if we could squeeze in a meeting."

Sturla was the President's single most important financial backer. The multibillionaire international financier traversed the global economy like a great white shark and had most of the western world's leaders on speed dial. Through his investment funds, Sturla shifted positions on dollars, euros, and yen like chips on a poker table. And after fifty largely successful years in the game, even his slightest moves caused tremors in the world currency markets.

"I think we can *always* find time for Peter Sturla," the President said.

"They're up next, Mr. President."

Knopper departed the Oval Office, and returned a moment later with the two visitors. The President stood in the center of the Oval, atop the Great Seal of the United States.

"Peter, it's good to see you. I wasn't aware you were in town."

As the President shook Sturla's right hand, he placed his left on the financier's shoulder, making the gesture warmer and more personal. The President stood a full head taller than his guest and was nearly thirty years his junior.

"Mr. President, it was not my intent to impose upon you, but Daniel thought you might have time for a friendly visit."

"Daniel thought correctly," the President said with a nod to Page. "Please, have a seat."

The President indicated a pair of chairs for Sturla and himself, leaving the couch for Page and Knopper.

"You look well," the President offered.

"As well as a man of my age can expect. I have no complaints. I must commend you on your efforts regarding oil exploration off the coast of South America. I think it will do much good for our Latin American neighbors."

What Sturla did not say was that the company doing much of that exploration stood to reap huge profits, and that he was that company's largest individual shareholder.

"Though I think it's important for the US to curb its appetite for foreign oil, the oil we do buy should come from as close to home as possible. It will help in repairing our long neglected relations south of the border."

"That is good," Sturla said. "Daniel briefed me on some of the initiatives you propose for your second term."

"We've accomplished a lot, but there is still work to be done. The past two years were especially difficult with Congress being so evenly split, but I think we can push the balance back in our favor. The people are tired of Washington gridlock."

"As in your last campaign, you have my wholehearted support."

"I know I can count on you, Peter."

Sturla's support went far beyond the maximum contribution an individual can make to a candidate during an election cycle. Through political action committees, 527 groups, and his financing of ultra left-wing organizations, Sturla wielded subtle but considerable influence over American politics.

"My help extends beyond your re-election to the campaigns of like-minded, progressive candidates seeking congressional seats and gubernatorial offices. Your presidency remains our best opportunity to intelligently remake this country. Rest assured that defeating those who oppose our shared vision is my highest priority."

"We can't let our opponents continue spreading their lies," the President sighed. "The American people are incredibly naïve about how the world really works. If it wasn't for us, the Republicans would eat them alive."

"Very true, Mr. President," Sturla said. "I understand that you are meeting with the Chinese ambassador this afternoon."

"I am," the President replied, knowing that the financier's connections in governments around the world ran deep.

"Then I hope your discussion with the ambassador will prove fruitful."

12

MICHAEL UNDEN SLIPPED THE BAG OF SHELL CASINGS FROM THE 21-gun salute into his coat pocket and then accepted the offered hand of his neighbor.

"Mr. Hansen, it means a lot that you'd come up from Florida for my dad's funeral," Unden said.

"Your pa and I go back a long way, and he and your ma were there when my Dottie got sick. It's only right."

"Still, it was good of you to come. See you back at the house after all this is over?"

"You betcha."

Hansen ambled away, stopping briefly at the space in the mausoleum wall where the ashes of Jacob Unden had been placed beside those of his wife. He placed a hand on the cold slab of marble, his fingers gliding over the carved names.

"It was a fine service," Pat McGivney offered as he approached Unden. "Nice to see your father buried with full military honors. He deserved it."

Unden's grip on the folded flag in his arms tightened.

"Dad didn't talk much about that, least not until recently. He saw a lot more than any kid should."

"It was a trip to hell that I'd rather not repeat either," McGivney agreed, "but your dad did good. You don't just shake the Medal of Honor out of a Cracker Jack box."

Unden smiled. "I was just glad to get out of my combat tours in one piece."

"Had it been, maybe a lot of the jihad nonsense we've had to deal with ever since could've been avoided. But that's neither here nor there. Both you and your pa were good Marines. Semper fi."

"Semper fi," Unden echoed softly.

"Mike, we need to get together to discuss your dad's estate."

"Anything wrong?"

"Just some things I'm looking into," McGivney replied. "Tax code stuff. I should have a clear read on it in a couple days."

13

NEW ORLEANS, LOUISIANA
JANUARY 9

THE CROWD CHEERED AS THE PRESIDENT AND HEAD REFEREE jogged out from the sideline onto the Superdome field. He wore dark gray pants, a white button-down shirt open at the collar and a windbreaker with the presidential seal over his left breast. At midfield, they met the captains of the two undefeated teams squaring off in the BSC National Championship game.

"Captains," the head referee announced, "allow me to introduce the President of the United States—"

Though a few stray boos could be heard, the audience at the final college game of the season was largely respectful of the nation's commander-in-chief. The referee paused until the crowd noise ebbed before continuing.

"—who will toss the coin this evening. The University of Michigan is in blue and Stanford University is in white. Here is the coin."

The referee held out his hand and the cameraman zoomed in on the large silver coin resting in the open palm. The pristine coin looked like it had just been struck.

"On this side we have the Block S representing Stanford University. Should this side land up, Stanford will have won the toss." The referee turned the coin over. "On this side we have the Block M representing the University of Michigan. Should this side land up, Michigan will have won the toss. Mr. President."

The referee handed the coin to the President, who grasped it between his thumb and forefinger to test its heft. He was attempting to judge how strongly to toss it, knowing a poorly executed effort would guarantee ridicule on the late night talk shows. What the President wanted was a nice clean arc with the coin spinning all the way until it landed on the BCS emblem painted at midfield.

Glancing up at the jumbotron, the President saw a close-up of the coin in his hand as he prepared to make the toss. He gave it the old one...two...and on three flipped the coin. He followed the perfect upward arc of the coin, but lost it in the lights.

And then the entire stadium went black.

The crowd murmured nervously in the darkness, emergency lights providing only a faint illumination. Secret Service agents with flash-lights and weapons drawn raced onto the field to secure the President while other elements of his protective detail donned night-vision goggles and swept the stadium for potential threats.

"Give me a *W!*" a small group of football fans shouted when the first letter appeared.

"Give me an *H!*" with the second.

As if it were a cheer for their favorite team, the fans spelled out what had become a familiar question:

WHO IS I?

14

"DAMN IT!" THE PRESIDENT RAILED. "YOU ASSURED ME THAT they wouldn't attack the BCS game."

"Mr. President," the FBI Director's voice sounded calm and clear over the speakerphone, despite the early hour of the call. "I said it was highly unlikely that those responsible for these incidents would hack another bowl game."

The President paced inside the confines of his office aboard Air Force One, fuming over the latest appearance of the mysterious message: WHO IS I?

"Don't play semantics with me," the President snapped back. "*You* didn't just look like an idiot in front of millions of people. The first primaries are a week away and I'm standing in the middle of a football field when the lights go out? The right-wing media is going to have a field day with this—I'll bet the attack ads are already in the can. The stadium was supposed to be *off-line*. You said there would be countermeasures in place to stop it. What the hell happened?"

"The plan, as per our briefing yesterday, was in place. We are still sifting through the data to determine exactly how this intrusion occurred."

"Did you learn anything that will help catch these bastards?"

"Watching this incident unfold in real time has provided a lot of data—intel that was lost in the previous attacks that could be the key to identifying those responsible. This time they cut the power from the city grid and we're tracing back those access points. The hack into the jumbotrons is a little trickier, but we believe it was backfed from the network satellite. As in the previous events, this intrusion displays a remarkably high degree of sophistication and adaptability."

"It sounds like you admire these criminals," the President remarked sharply.

"One can admire ingenuity while deploring the aim. And frankly, sir, we have no idea what the aim of these attacks is. So far, no one has been injured and no property has been damaged," the FBI Director explained. "In fact, it appears the perpetrators of these attacks are taking great pains to ensure that no emergency or life-safety services are affected. If these incidents are just a prank, I'm all for a slap on the wrist and putting these folks to work in our cyber-warfare units."

"And if it's not?"

"That's why we're investigating these incidents as if our nation is under attack, sir. Until we know for certain, we err to the side of caution."

"I appreciate that, but these people have invaded my house and have made me look like a fool on national television. If you wish to retain your position in my second term, you will catch them, and catch them soon."

"I understand, Mr. President," the FBI Director replied.

The President tapped the button on top of the speakerphone and ended the call.

"Don't you think you were a little hard on the guy?" Daniel Page asked.

"Hard? I thought I showed remarkable restraint. What I really want is some heads on spikes."

The President pulled a couple diet sodas from a small refrigerator, handed one to Page, and opened the other as he sat down in the leather executive chair behind his desk.

"Yeah, the late night guys and Denby are going to have a lot of fun with this," Page admitted, "but if you can keep a sense of humor about it, the whole thing will blow over in a couple days. I'll have the writers work up some material for your upcoming appearances. My advice is to just laugh it off."

"Easy for you to say when you're safely hidden behind the scenes," the President groused.

"If I don't get you across the finish line in November, I'll be just as unemployed as you but without the perks that go with being a former president. Trust me on this."

The President took a swig of his soft drink and nodded. Page was the best in the business, having moved him from a state legislature to the White House in record time.

"Mr. President," a woman's voice sounded over the intercom on his desk.

"Yes, Arleen?"

"The White House has an incoming call from Governor Lynn. Do you want them to patch it through?"

The President turned to Page, who nodded that he should take the call. At last report, the Governor's husband was resting comfortably and undergoing a series of tests on his heart.

"I would be delighted to talk with the Governor," the President lied.

"I'll put it through on line one."

A moment later, the button for line one of the desktop phone flickered to life. The President picked up the handset and answered.

"Governor Lynn, how is your husband?" the President asked with well-feigned sincerity.

"Thank you for asking, Mr. President. Bobby's well, though it was quite a scare. The doctors have ruled out another heart attack, but he's undergoing a battery of tests to determine what happened."

"After my father's struggles with heart disease, I understand something of what you're going through. Please know that you and your husband are in my thoughts and prayers."

Page rolled his eyes to the ceiling but remained silent. After all, protocol must be observed.

"Mr. President, I'll cut to the chase. This latest incident with my husband's heart has forced us to seriously re-evaluate my decision to challenge you for our party's nomination. I have scheduled a press conference for tomorrow morning where I will formally announce my withdrawal from the race and encourage my supporters to back your re-election campaign to the fullest."

Taken aback, the President found himself momentarily speechless.

"Well, Governor," he finally said, "I can't say that your decision is unwelcome, just something of a surprise."

"For us both," Lynn admitted with a tinge of regret. "And I'm sure this concession call is not nearly as satisfying as it would be after thumping a rival at the polls, but in this matter, my family has to come first. My decision to challenge you was based on policy differences we have and I hope that we can work toward a resolution that will benefit both the country and our party."

"My door is always open to you, Governor," the President offered. "And I look forward to your input."

"I appreciate that, Mr. President," Lynn replied. "It's late and I won't keep you any longer. Have a safe flight back to Washington."

"And again, my best wishes for your husband's speedy recovery."

"Thank you, Mr. President."

The President cradled the handset with a pensive look in his eyes.

"So, what was the old bat's decision?" Page asked derisively.

"She's out of the race," the President replied.

"What? She quit just a week before Iowa? She wasn't that far behind in the polls. I had her pegged to hang on 'till Super Tuesday."

The President was familiar with the pool among his campaign staffers as to when Lynn would concede defeat. To his best recollection, no one picked a date prior to mid-January.

"Thank God for Philly cheesesteaks," the President said with a smile. "Bobby Lynn's latest round of chest pains has caused the Governor to reassess her run against me. Our primary season is over before it began."

"You really should send flowers," Page offered. "She just saved the campaign a ton of money that we can bank for the general election."

"Or not," the President said with a devious smile.

"What do you have in mind?" Page asked.

"We don't have to bank it all. In fact, I don't mind if we blow our entire primary budget on the primaries."

"But you're running unopposed."

The President's smile widened. "On the *Republican* primaries."

15

"...AND YOU'RE LIVE IN FIVE...FOUR...THREE..."

The producer continued the countdown with his left hand. A pair of digital clocks on the studio wall tracked both the actual time and the seconds remaining to the start of the program. Around the country, local radio stations wrapped up their top-of-the-hour news briefs. Millions of listeners heard a crackle of lightning followed by a rumbling thunderclap.

"This is C-P-R," the basso profundo announcer said mellifluously, "Conservative Private Radio."

Garr Denby bobbed his head to the opening chords of David Bowie's *Through These Architect's Eyes*, feeling the groove of the theme song to his nationally syndicated show as he readied himself to go on the air.

"From the heart of the republic for which *he* stands," the program announcer said, "Garr Denby is on the air."

"Greetings friends," Denby began. "It is *I*, your courageous captain of conservatism, your ribald raconteur of the republic, here to once again discuss, dissect and otherwise delve into the body politic. And do we have a lot of ground to cover today.

"First off, last night's BCS game. Phenomenal game, and that double overtime finish ensures it will rank among the legendary college championship games. But for me, your humble correspondent, the high point of the game occurred before opening kickoff—and I'll tell you why in two words: *Coin toss*.

"Yes, the BCS coin toss, which turned out to be ironically symbolic of this failed presidency. Our intrepid leader, once again, inserted himself into a popular venue with maximum exposure and minimum risk of a screw up. The game itself was decided in the time-honored way, with the better performing team earning victory. But the coin toss was symbolic of this administration butting into a private exchange for the purpose of deciding winners and losers.

"To be fair, this analogy is a bit of a stretch in that both teams represented prestigious institutions of higher learning that receive substantial amounts of government largesse in the forms of grants, subsidies and federal student loans. So, from the President's point of view, he couldn't lose, as most of higher academe is firmly latched onto the government teat. The same could not be said of the NFL, where the teams are privately held businesses. If the President tosses the coin at the Super Bowl and one of the team owners, I shan't name names, isn't a supporter of the regime, I can imagine the President using a two-headed coin.

"Now, I don't know who is behind these WHO IS I? attacks, but the incident yesterday was a piece of poetic genius. Cutting the power just as the President tosses the coin perfectly captures the essence of his decision making process—arbitrary and often *in the dark*. I, for one, look forward to permanently turning out the lights on the President and his socioeconomic reign of terror next November. The sooner this cabal of Marxist retreads is tossed on the ash heap of history with their failed ideology, the better it will be for us all.

"Moving on to the even bigger story of the day, the President's road to re-election just got a little easier with the unexpected withdrawal of his lone challenger for the Democratic nomination. Pennsylvania Governor Isabelle Lynn announced this morning that she was ending her campaign for the presidency. She cited concerns over her husband's health in light of his most recent hospitalization just a few days ago.

"The former Senate leader's ongoing heart woes are well known, and perhaps the strain of yet another campaign was more than he could handle. His doctors report that Bobby Lynn did not suffer another heart attack, and he remains under observation to determine the cause of this episode. I cannot fault the Governor's decision—family trumps all and I wish the Lynns the best as they deal with this matter.

"I, for one, was looking forward to what surely would have been a bloody, bare-knuckled fight for the Democratic nomination. The President's popularity has waned so far in the three years since he ascended to office that members of his own party see him as vulnerable to a challenge. It was 1980 all over again, with a president so ill suited for the job that many in his own party thought he ought to be replaced.

"Doubtless, a great sigh of relief emanated from the Oval Office and the President's re-election headquarters as his campaign dodged a bullet. He barely beat Lynn in the last go-around and her challenge posed a serious threat to the President, as she stood a very good chance of pulling off the upset. The President recognized the danger of Lynn's challenge and was headed into the primaries loaded for bear with a war chest that, by most estimates, dwarfed what he had four years ago.

"I am certain the White House statement regarding Governor Lynn's decision will be filled with praise, acknowledging her valuable contributions to the Democratic Party and our nation's political discourse. What will be missing from this statement will be an expression of gratitude for saving the President's re-election campaign hundreds of millions of dollars—money it can now use against whoever survives the Republican primary campaign. I say *survive* because there is no clear GOP frontrunner.

"And unlike 1980, when the Republicans had a charismatic candidate who could clearly and optimistically articulate the principles of conservatism as the antidote to the nation's progressive malaise, we have a large field of decent folks that will likely cannibalize each other on the road to the nomination. Governor Lynn's withdrawal from the race is a huge gift to the President. It allows him to conserve his considerable resources for the fall, when he will take on a battered candidate with a serious financial disadvantage.

"Of course, idle minds are the devil's workshop and I suspect that the mainstream media lapdogs and the political dirty tricksters toiling to re-elect our dear leader shan't be idle long. Their attention will be singularly focused on bringing forth the weakest, most moderate, milquetoast candidate in the GOP field. And you can bet the President's get-out-the-vote campaign and community organizers will be out in force in those states with open primaries. Back in a moment."

16

"...*BACK IN A MOMENT.*"

Mike Unden pulled into an angled parking spot on the street but remained in his pickup truck until the end of Garr Denby's opening segment. He'd been a fairly regular listener of the thought-provoking and often humorous talk radio program since his first tour with the Marines. Beyond sports and family, a fair percentage of the email correspondence he shared with his father while stationed in Iraq covered topics explored by Denby.

An icy wind blew down 4th Street as he exited the truck, his boots crunching on the thin, dry layer of packed snow. Unden stepped up onto the sidewalk and made his way to a two-story brick office building that, according to the carved cornerstone, had stood on that spot since 1912. A brass sign by the door read:

MCGIVNEY & MCGIVNEY
LAW AND ACCOUNTING

He stomped the snow off his boots as he moved through the vestibule into the reception area. After a bell chimed to announce his arrival, Pat McGivney poked his head out of the kitchenette.

"Mike," McGivney said warmly. "Just getting a cup of coffee. You want one?"

"Yeah, sure. Black."

"Just head on into the conference room," McGivney pointed to an open door. "I'll get your coffee and grab the files from my office."

Unden nodded and went to the conference room. He slipped his wool cap and lined work gloves into the pockets of his heavy Carhartt jacket, then hung the coat over the back of a chair and sat down. The room was tasteful but understated, furnished with an oval wooden table and comfortable chairs.

"Here ya go," McGivney said as he set two ceramic mugs on the conference table, both emblazoned with a silhouette of ducks in flight. "The darker one's yours."

McGivney placed a thick file and a legal pad on the table opposite Unden, then closed the door and took a seat.

"How're ya holding up?" McGivney asked.

"Pretty good," Unden replied. "House is quiet now that it's just me and the dog. Work keeps me busy."

"Running a farm like yours is tough duty, even this time of year," McGivney agreed. "Always something to do. That's what I wanted to talk to you about. Aside from a few charitable bequests, your dad left the bulk of his estate to you. He had a couple small insurance policies and his IRA. The rest of his estate is tied up in the farm."

"So what do we need to do?" Unden asked.

"A couple years ago, this would have been a simple matter of transferring ownership of the farm LLC from your pa to you. Same with the deeds, vehicle titles and bank accounts. Then the death tax came back."

A decade earlier, the previous president called on Congress to enact a series of tax cuts to restore economic confidence in the wake of a mild recession and a terrorist attack on the United States. Congress complied, but in order to win bipartisan support it did so only on a temporary basis, with the Republican legislators thinking the tax cuts would be made permanent at a later date. The later date never came, and the current president and his allies in Congress allowed some of the cuts to expire in the middle of a debilitating recession. This inaction triggered the double-dip recession that snuffed out any faint signs of recovery.

Among the taxes that were reinstated was the estate tax, a levy on the transfer of wealth from someone to his or her heirs. Popular among progressives, the tax effectively prevents those who create wealth from passing it on to their children and grandchildren when they die—a final punishment for having done well.

"How bad is it?" Unden asked.

"Bad. The tax is little over half the value of your dad's estate."

"Half?"

"I know, and seeing as most of the assets of the farm are in land and equipment, there's little cash on hand to cover the tax. Then there's the issue of timing."

"Timing?"

McGivney nodded. "Your pa died on New Year's Eve—which is *last* year. That means the death tax is due *this* year, on April 15. We can file for an extension, but it just pushes the day of reckoning off until the fall."

"Even if we have a great season, I can't grow nearly enough wheat to cover half of what our farm is worth."

"The death tax was touted as a way to get fat cats to pay their fair share, and to break up huge family fortunes," McGivney explained. "Dirty little secret is that loopholes in the tax code protect those fortunes while this tax punishes small but successful businesses when the owner dies. Back when this tax was previously in effect, I had your pa buy an insurance policy to cover the tax. It wasn't cheap, but it protected the farm for your mother and you. Then the tax was phased out and, after a bad season, your dad let his policy lapse. He was already sick when it became clear that Washington was going to let this tax come back, so insurance on him couldn't be bought at any price."

"So how does the damn government expect me to pay this tax? What am I going to do?" Unden asked.

"There's frankly only one thing you can do: sell the farm."

17

"I'D LIKE TO WELCOME OUR FIRST GUEST THIS EVENING," ELLIS Springfield announced to the television studio audience and to millions of viewers later that night when the program aired. "I am truly honored to have him here with us tonight, and his story is just incredible—Nobel Peace Prize winner Ross Egan."

Springfield stood and motioned to his left. The camera panned around to catch the opening of the stage curtain as the band launched into some jazzy intro music. Egan stepped onto the brightly lit stage and flashed an uneasy smile at the audience, much of which was offering him a standing ovation. He waved and then strode over to Springfield's desk where the host shook his hand warmly. Both men sat and waited for the applause to die down.

"Ross," Springfield began, "a year ago almost to the day, you were in the African jungle, on the border between two nations on the brink of war. You're an American, and I'm thinking if it was me, I'd have been on the first plane out of there. You stayed—and given the way things turned out, thank God you did—but I have to ask: Why?"

"To honor my wife's memory," Egan replied.

"How does sitting on a ticking bomb honor your late wife?"

"Maggie dedicated herself to bettering the lives of the people of what is now Dutannuru. She gave her life to that cause."

"What do you think Maggie would say about all that's happened?" Springfield asked.

Egan glanced down for a moment, and then looked back at Springfield with a smile. "She'd tell me not to get too big a head over my Nobel, but she would be happy that the people of Dutannuru now enjoy the fullness of liberty. As she hoped, life in Dutannuru is significantly better."

"I read your book over the weekend, which I must say was riveting." Springfield held up a copy of *The Dutannuru Miracle* as the number two camera zoomed in on the cover.

"Thank you. President Mensah and I were lucky to work with a talented writer and great editor. They helped us tell the story well."

"So, describe *The Dutannuru Miracle*."

"To be honest, what happened in Dutannuru wasn't a miracle. The men and women who framed Dutannuru's constitution simply built on the genius of our nation's founding fathers, and the results they got were what they expected. It may sound corny, but it's hard to go wrong when the people are guaranteed their rights to life, liberty and the pursuit of happiness."

"But what about the assassination of Cudjoe?" Springfield asked. "That caught the world by surprise. Doesn't that qualify as a miracle?"

"Not if you think about it as the natural reaction of an individual given the choice between liberty and tyranny. The United States exists because thousands of men and women acted just as Tanu Baafi did," Egan explained. "They chose liberty and staked their lives and fortunes to win it for themselves, their children, and all of us."

"So, you were a guest at the White House recently. How was that?"

"Incredible. The President and First Lady are very gracious hosts and visiting the White House during the Christmas Season is—" Egan paused, searching for the right words. "The pictures I've seen of that night don't do it justice. Honoring President Mensah with a full state dinner was symbolically meaningful to Dutannuru and really classy on the President's part."

"Over the past few weeks, this WHO IS I? thing has popped up several times, but I understand the first time was actually *at* that state dinner."

"Several people, including my guest, got that odd message on their cell phones," Egan replied.

"Did you?"

"Later. I didn't bring my phone to the White House, so I got it back at the hotel."

"There are rumors in Washington that you might become the next ambassador to Dutannuru."

Egan chuckled. "That's all they are."

"You haven't been asked?"

"I don't think that kind of offer would come until after the election."

"What about politics? Do you see a future for yourself there?" Springfield asked.

"I can honestly say I have no interest in seeking *any* political office."

"Will you return to Dutannuru?"

"At some point, but I have no immediate plans," Egan replied. "President Mensah and I will be lecturing at college campuses in support of our book over the next few months, starting with my wife's alma mater—Hillsdale College. That's about as far out as I'm planning for the moment."

18

LYDIA HILL ENTERED THE CLIFFORD Y. STEPHENS AUDITORIUM with a group of her fellow College Democrats. Clearing security, they quickly found a block of seats and settled in. Half of the 2,700 seats were already taken and the crowd streaming down the aisles would soon fill the room to capacity.

Six identical wood podiums bearing the crest of Iowa State University stood on the stage, arranged in a shallow arc so the candidates could see each other as well as the moderator and the audience. Stagehands rechecked connections and put the finishing touches on the scene. Around the auditorium, strategically located cameras were manned and ready to capture the debate for viewers nationwide.

An announcer asked that everyone inside the auditorium switch off their cell phones to avoid interference with the broadcast. Hill complied.

★

COPPERHEAD, MONTANA

HOMER HOPPS PERCHED ON A HIGH BACK BAR STOOL WITH A guitar across his knee and watched the off-air feed from Iowa. The stage stood empty awaiting the candidates and, off to the side, he espied the moderator chatting with officials from the host university. Deb McColl and her band of rogues had tapped into the 24-hour cable news channel at their New York studio, just ahead of the satellite uplink. In the corner of the large flat screen display, a digital clock counted down the time to broadcast.

"Deb," he called out. "Do we have a lucky winner for our Golden Ticket?"

"We do," McColl replied. "GPS on her phone places her inside the auditorium."

"Excellent. Buttrey, are you and your spiders ready?"

Ken Buttrey swiveled around from his station to face Hopps. "The site is locked, loaded, and ready for prime time."

"And what say you miners?" Hopps called out.

"The databases are waxed and stacked," Harry Dailey reported, "and the parsing engines are stoked hot enough to flash fry an elephant."

Hopps smiled and strummed a few chords with a Spanish flair. "Ladies and gentlemen: *¡Viva La Revolución!*"

WITH THE AUDIENCE SEATED AND THE DOORS TO THE AUDITO-rium closed, the house lights dimmed and the stage became an island of light inside the cavernous space.

Kathleen Kilar thanked the president of Iowa State University for his hospitality and took her place behind a desk built atop the orchestra pit. The host of a long-running news interview program, Kilar took her seat, adjusted her blazer and did a final test of her lapel mike and earpiece.

As the network's dramatic theme music for the current election cycle blared from the auditorium speakers, she heard the voices of the anchors in New York turning over the broadcast to the local team. In the pit below her, a stage director used hand signals to count down the remaining seconds to air.

"Good evening, I'm Kathleen Kilar and welcome to tonight's debate between the candidates vying to represent the Republican Party in this fall's presidential election. The first tests of the electoral waters come next week with the New Hampshire primaries and here, in the Iowa Caucuses."

Lydia Hill watched the projection screens that flanked the stage as Kilar explained the debate format. Hill felt a vibration in her coat pocket and the blare of Jimi Hendrix's wailing rendition of the Star Spangled Banner.

"I know I turned it off," she said embarrassed, feeling the judging eyes around her as she fumbled for her phone.

She thumbed the mute switch and checked to see what had set it off. A simple text message filled the otherwise blank screen:

who-is-i.com is live in 7...6...5...

The numbers quickly counted down to zero.

A ripple of applause caused Hill to look up from her phone. The six Republican candidates strode on stage in single file, each smiling and waving to the audience as they moved toward their podiums. The order in which they appeared was determined by luck of the draw.

"You got the debate on your phone?" a man behind her asked incredulously.

Hill glanced down and saw the scene before her streaming live on the tiny screen. A text crawl running along the bottom of the image announced:

who-is-i.com Is NOW live.

"From left to right," Kilar continued, "we have businessman and publisher Duncan Widmer, retired US Marine General Quenton Hook, the former Secretary of State and current Florida Governor Lila Oates, Idaho Senator Cal Neuske, former Colorado Governor Rick Walterhouse, and Texas Congresswoman Jacqueline Vogel."

Kilar paused for applause as the candidates smiled and waved to voters both in Iowa and around the country.

"The first question is for everyone," Kilar said, "starting with Congresswoman Vogel. Congresswoman, what is the single greatest challenge facing the United States today?"

Vogel composed herself for a second, and then looked out at the audience. "The single greatest challenge facing the nation today is the same challenge that faced the Founders of our great country—the erosion of our individual liberties to an expansive and increasingly tyrannical government."

Known for her terse rhetoric, Vogel felt no need to elaborate. Hill glanced down at her phone and saw, word for word, Vogel's response as if taken from the dialogue of a play. Beneath Vogel's answer was a simple commentary.

OPINION.

Walterhouse offered a different answer: correcting the damage caused by the recent nationalization of healthcare. Almost as quickly as he spoke, his words appeared on Hill's phone.

OPINION.

Neuske, Oates and Hook respectively offered the economy, taxes and terrorism, and all received the same commentary from WHO-IS-I. Then Widmer took a sip of water and addressed the question.

"As you can see from the responses elicited so far from this question, our nation faces a number of difficult challenges, and this has been true throughout our proud history. But of the many problems sitting in the in-basket of whoever occupies 1600 Pennsylvania Avenue next January, in my mind the most daunting is the nation's debt."

OPINION.

"Never before has our debt been so high, not just in terms of inflation adjusted dollars, but in terms of GDP."

US DEBT LEVEL IS CURRENTLY AT AN ALL-TIME HIGH IN INFLATION ADJUSTED DOLLARS. US DEBT AS PER-CENTAGE OF GDP WAS HIGHER IN EARLY 1940S.

Hill tapped on the link that appeared beneath the commentary and the screen filled with a colorful graph tracking US debt over time against both metrics.

"If left unchecked, CBO projections put the national debt equaling the GPD in ten years."

CLARIFICATION—CONGRESSIONAL BUDGET OFFICE RECENT UP-DATE PROJECTS GDP/NATIONAL DEBT PARITY IN 9.2 YEARS. OTHER ESTIMATES INDICATE NATIONAL DEBT WILL SURPASS GPD WITHIN THREE YEARS. INCLUDING UNFUNDED PORTIONS OF ENTI-TLEMENT PROGRAMS, US DEBT IS 840% OF CURRENT GDP.

"Our national debt is a nuclear bomb on a quick countdown to detonation, and the results of that explosion will be an economic Armageddon that'll make the Great Depression look like a mild market correction."

HYPERBOLIC RHETORIC. SUBJECTIVE COMPARISON.

"Check this out," Hill whispered.

She held her phone so that her companions could watch the running analysis on each candidate's remarks.

"How are they doing that?" the young man beside Hill asked as he turned on his phone.

With a flurry of thumbed keystrokes, the computer science major accessed the WHO-IS-I site and connected to the same live feed.

"Since you brought up the national debt, Mr. Widmer," Kilar said, "I'll start with you on the related issue of the deficit. The federal budget deficit for the current fiscal year is the largest in the nation's history..."

CONFIRMED.

"... and this has been true for each of the previous three years..."

CONFIRMED.

"...How would you tackle this problem?"

"Kathleen, every person who works for a living understands that running a deficit simply means you're spending more money than you make," Widmer replied. "Common sense says that to solve the deficit you either have to make more or spend less..."

STATEMENT IS LOGICALLY CONSISTENT WITH AC-COUNTING FORMULA: REVENUE LESS EXPENSES EQUALS A SURPLUS OR DEFICIT.

"...but common sense is a scarce commodity in Washington these days..."

OPINION. NO ACCURATE MEANS OF MEASURING SCARCITY OR SURPLUS OF COMMON SENSE.

"...The President has chosen a two-prong approach of increasing spending..."

IMPRECISE. FEDERAL SPENDING DETERMINED BY THE HOUSE OF REPRESENTATIVES.

"...to stimulate the economy during down times..."

KEYNESIAN ECONOMIC THEORY.

"...and simultaneously increasing taxes to raise government revenue..."

INDIVIDUAL TAX RATES AND FORMS OF COMPENSA-
TION INCLUDED IN GROSS INCOME INCREASED DUR-
ING THE FIRST TWO YEARS OF THE CURRENT
ADMINISTRATION.

"…Ironically, the increase in taxes, on those who actually pay taxes, has resulted in *lower* revenue to the treasury, making the deficit
bigger, not smaller…"

REVENUE COLLECTED BY US TREASURY IS DOWN
41.3% FOLLOWING INCREASE IN TAX RATES FOR
HIGH INCOME EARNERS.

"…To attack the deficit, I would cut taxes across the board for all
taxpayers and slash government spending. It worked on the 1920
depression…"

CONFIRMED. REDUCTION IN US TAX RATES AND FED-
ERAL GOVERNMENT SPENDING IN 1920 REDUCED
SCOPE AND SEVERITY OF ECONOMIC DEPRESSION.
ECONOMIC BOOM FOLLOWING 1920 DEPRESSION
LASTED TO 1929.

"…and it will work again today."

REASONABLE PREDICTION BASED ON HISTORICALLY
ANALOGOUS ECONOMIC DATA.

"This is *so* cool," Hill said. "It's fact checking everything they're
saying *as they say it*. Keep your screen up—I've got to spread the word."

"SHE'S TEXTING," McCOLL ANNOUNCED.

"That's it, young lady," Hopps urged. "Reach out and touch
someone."

One of the large wall monitors displayed the shape of Iowa rendered in dark blue with a single red dot in Ames. Another red dot
appeared, quickly followed by several more. Most were clustered
around the college town, but others began to scatter throughout the
state.

"Pan back to show the whole country," Hopps ordered.

Iowa shrank as the rest of the continental United States came into view. Red dots appeared on the map at a geometric rate. Digital counters at the bottom of the screen tracked emails and text messages forwarding information about WHO-IS-I and the number of unique users accessing the site. After only ten minutes, both numbers eclipsed one hundred thousand and were growing so quickly that the lowest digits were a blur.

"How're we handling the traffic?" Hopps asked.

"Like we got ten lanes of freeway," McColl replied. "WHO-IS-I has officially gone viral."

19

GARR DENBY LEANED BACK IN AN UPHOLSTERED BLACK LEATHER
executive chair and surveyed his private studio. He was dressed in
khaki shorts and a golf shirt, his arms crossed, smiling with an unlit
Padron Family Reserve cigar nestled in the corner of his mouth.

In a career that dated back to his high school days, he had broadcast from booths inside mobile trailers, skyscrapers, and everything in
between. Some, Denby swore, were no larger than a restroom stall.
Not so in the Taj Ma Garr.

He had worked closely with the architect and engineers, leverag-
ing his decades of experience in radio to create a studio tuned to his
performance style. From the shape of the room down to the place-
ment of the monitors and controls, no detail was left to chance. He
strongly believed that people performed better in a comfortable,
functional workplace and he wanted the best for himself and his staff.
It simply had to be right, because this studio complex was the nerve
center of his one-man radio empire.

Denby spent much of the weekend preparing for today's show.
The thick stack of laser printed pages offered solid assurance that his
three hours of broadcast brilliance would expire long before he ran
out of material. Rarely did he find himself at a loss for words.

As the theme music flowed over the studio speakers, Denby
leaned forward toward the microphone. He rested his elbows on the
desktop and pulled the cigar from his mouth. He slowly rolled the
cigar between his fingers and thumb, measuring the bulk of the tightly
wound Manduro Toro.

"My friends and loyal listeners," Denby began as the music faded,

"I am in a fine mood today, my normal optimism elevated to a heady level of exuberance. And while the debate last Friday played a role in enhancing my naturally positive outlook, it was not the cause but rather the vehicle.

"Now don't get me wrong in thinking that I was disappointed in the performances of the six GOP contenders. After all, it wasn't a real debate but a series of overlong sound bites as the candidates ran through snippets of their stump speeches as they tried to stay on message. I am not enamored with the form and substance of political debates, as they rarely permit direct argument between the candidates. These staged events are little more than casting calls with actors reading for the part of the president.

"In that regard, all six of the President's challengers proved they were more than his equal, but sadly, that ain't saying much. None of those seeking the nation's highest elected office tripped on the way to their podiums or mispronounced the capital of Uzbekistan—which, by the way, is Tashkent. I'll take geography for three hundred, Alex.

"As I said, my joy lies not so much in what I heard during last Friday's debate, but in what I saw. And *not* on my television. What I saw were the new green shoots of the First Amendment sprouting in the soil of the twenty-first century.

"Those of you who listen to this program with any regularity have heard me opine on the incestuous state of the mainstream media's alliance with the political left. Much of what passes for print and television journalism is barely disguised cheerleading for the progressive—read socialist—movement.

"The Founding Fathers of this great land saw a skeptical free press as a powerful check on the abuse of power by those in power. Over the past century that detached skepticism has morphed into slavish sycophancy for the left and open hostility for the right. Opinion, which in a more civilized era had no place outside the editorial pages, is routinely found in the simplest of news stories. Cars crash, but SUVs *kill* people. Five percent unemployment is a recession for a Republican president, but ten percent is the new normal and a sure sign of recovery for our dear leader. Sometimes this leftward bias is subtle, but often it's as subtle as a brick.

"And under the current administration, the great slobbering love affair with all things left has devolved to such blindly obedient idiocy that I finally declared independent, objective media in this country is officially dead.

"So what, you may ask, did I see during the debate that arrested my cynicism? What glimmer of hope did I find that has me ready to light up and waft billowing clouds of aromatic cigar smoke around my studio? The answer is three little words: WHO IS I.

"Shortly after the debate started, I received a call from a friend who urged me to visit this website. Now, all I know about WHO IS I are the pranks they pulled at Times Square and the bowl games. I especially liked when they left the President in the dark. So I figure they've pulled another one somewhere, but it's not at the debate.

"I hemmed and hawed, but she was insistent to the point that she wouldn't hang up until I saw what was happening on this website. So to humor her, I split my big screen like I do when I'm watching a couple football games and I took a look. It came right up and literally, my God, I was on my feet. I couldn't believe what the geniuses behind this site had accomplished. I caught it just as Winder made a remark about Neuske's voting record on taxes and the site brought up a full listing of every vote Neuske has made that raised or lowered a tax. And not just the votes, but it rated the votes on their economic impact. What I found interesting is that the site separated the tax bills in which Neuske was in the voting majority versus those when he was in the minority. And where you stand when you lose is as important as when you win. The follow up of the debate posted on the site allows you to drill deeply into the data without encountering a single iota of opinion. In the immortal words of Jack Webb's Sergeant Joe Friday: *Nothing but the facts ma'am.*"

Denby put the cigar to his lips, held a flame to the end until it glowed red, then loudly exhaled a cloud of smoke toward the ceiling.

"That, my friends, was the sound of freedom expressed in my own personal way. Under the First Amendment, Congress can make no law abridging the freedom of speech or the press. Control of the media was a power that the people of this country vested in themselves, not in government. In the hands of the people, control over the media is exercised in the marketplace. The people either buy your newspapers and magazines or they don't. They watch your news programs or they don't. They listen to me on the radio, and they *do*," Denby lofted another cloud of smoke with a laugh, "or you're a zero-share like every left-wing hack who thinks they can compete with me in the realm of ideas.

"So Congress passed no law co-opting the mainstream media, rather it was a gradual shift in the journalism schools and editorial boards that transformed a free and independent press into one that is for all practical purposes the communications wing of one political party. Thankfully, the people still retain some power over the media and they vote every day with their wallets. The red ink bleeding from most of the nation's newspapers isn't just because of the Internet or the recession—or in their words, the sluggish recovery—but because the people are not buying what these propagandists are selling. If I wanted to read party talking points, I'd get them from the party.

"I'm a little long with this opening monologue, but this is important. The folks behind this upstart website caught our attention with their outlandish and technically brilliant pranks, but have now captured our interest in providing a source of unbiased information. I hope their site can handle the traffic, because it's going to be huge over the run of this campaign. And I don't envy any politician who plays fast and loose with the facts—I get the feeling WHO IS I will call them on it immediately.

"And before we pause for a brief profit break, I must say for the first time ever, I am really looking forward to the next occasion when our President publicly opens his mouth."

Denby hit the mute button as the show went to commercial, then leaned back and sent a series of smoke rings toward the ceiling.

20

"OF THE MANY DUTIES THAT COME WITH BEING THE PRESIDENT of Hillsdale College, one in which I take immense pleasure is introducing our guest lecturers. The list of those distinguished individuals that have illuminated this stage with their wisdom is both long and storied, and I am honored and humbled to welcome this evening's speakers."

Joan Saccary looked out at the packed auditorium as she spoke. She noted cameras located near the foot of the stage, there to broadcast the event to a wider audience of cable and satellite viewers. She stood at a podium to the right of center stage, where three comfortable chairs were staged around a low circular coffee table.

Ross Egan listened to Saccary's introductory remarks from the shadows just off stage. *We've come full circle, Maggie,* he thought.

"Are you nervous, my friend?" Mensah asked, his voice just above a whisper.

"Yeah," Egan replied honestly. "Talking to an auditorium full of people is your gift, not mine."

"The trick is to pretend this is just a conversation between the two of us. And if you speak the truth, from your heart, then you have nothing to fear."

"I knew a lady," Saccary told the audience, "who twice in her life had lost her country. She lost it the first time as a very young woman when, in Czarist Russia, the Bolshevik Revolution occurred and she barely escaped with her life. She came to Cuba, started from scratch, once again built up a very successful competence, and was doing very well. And this time, as an elderly woman, again, she lost her country when Castro took over.

"Now, losing one's country once would be enough for most of us, I suppose. Losing it twice would be enough for the toughest person in the house—but not for this indomitable lady. She came to the United States where again she started from scratch and again built up a very successful competence.

"And now, as a very elderly person, I heard her tell this story on more than one occasion and invariably someone in the audience, when she was finished, would say, 'You poor, unlucky woman. How you have suffered. What an ordeal you have been through.' And her answer is always the same: 'Me, unlucky? Ah, no. I am one of the luckiest women who ever lived. Twice I have lost my country. Twice I have had a country to which I can go. When you Americans lose your country, where will you go?' I heard her ask the question more than once. I never heard a convincing answer."

"Our speakers tonight stood at the brink of war in defense of the young nation that they help build from the ashes. For their accomplishments in the cause of liberty and peace, they were jointly awarded the Nobel Peace Prize. Ladies and gentlemen, I give you the former President of Dutannuru, Xavier Mensah, and Ross Egan."

Mensah and Egan walked on stage to a thundering wave of applause. They shook hands with Saccary at center stage, and then Mensah moved to the podium while Egan and Saccary seated themselves on stage.

"Thank you," Mensah said, beaming at the audience. "Thank you for such an enthusiastic welcome. On behalf of my good friend, Ross Egan, and myself, we are delighted to be here with you tonight.

"*The Dutannuru Miracle*—a good title for a book, no? Hopeful, as miracles are good, especially for those who benefit from them. Enigmatic, as miracles are both mysterious and unexpected. And if you are a religious person, as I am, miracles inspire a sense of awe because they are the handiwork of God.

"But is what happened one year ago truly the result of divine intervention or something more in the realm of our understanding? I would posit that the incident that turned war into peace was not a miracle. Rather, it was the aftershock of a miracle that occurred over two centuries ago—in this country.

"Throughout history, political power rested on the ability to seize it. The right to rule was secured by force of arms and legitimized as the will of God or the gods. The Pharaohs of Egypt and the Caesars of Rome were actually deified in their lifetimes, such that offenses against their authority were both treason and heresy.

"Europe's Christian monarchs could not claim godhood without offending the religious sensibilities of their subjects with such blasphemy. Instead, they legitimized their claim on temporal authority as a divine right bestowed upon them and their descendants by God.

"If I recall my instruction in classical literature correctly, the reigns of Uther Pendragon and his son, Arthur, were the result of a supernatural figure bestowing upon Uther the legendary sword Excalibur. I cannot imagine what form of government would result if the mere possession of a piece of metalwork granted the owner absolute political authority, but I believe it would not be a good one.

"Edward Bulwer-Lytton wrote a famous line in his play *Richelieu*: 'the pen is mightier than the sword.' As a statesman, I must concur. And I would rather possess Thomas Jefferson's pen than any tyrant's sword, including Excalibur.

"The true miracle occurred *here*, when the Founders of this nation recognized that the natural flow of power is not from God to king to subject, but from God directly to each and every person, and from those individuals to governance of their choosing. What seems obvious to you and I today was a radical, treasonous thought in the eighteenth century. This nation fought two wars over the principle of individual liberty—the first to create the United States, and the second to purge the injustice of slavery.

"The hope of the American Revolution was countered with the monstrous terror of the French Revolution. Then Nietzsche declared God dead and Marx authored a manifesto promoting revolution against the existing social order in favor of state ownership of all property, allegedly for the benefit of the workers. This ideology pays lip service to popular government, including single-party elections. Mao Zedong was brutally honest in his observation that all political power comes from the barrel of a gun. This is true of tyrannies, but not republican democracies.

"The Americas are the new world. Africa is the oldest of the old world, home to the most distant ancestors of every person on the planet. We have in our long history experienced tribalism, imperialism, colonialism, fascism, Islamism, communism, socialism—just about every flavor of *ism* you can imagine. Republican democracy is a rare sight in African politics.

"Following our civil war, the fledgling nation of Dutannuru lay in ruins. It would have been a simple matter for those of us in the ruling council to declare martial law and assume to ourselves dictatorial powers. What we did, instead, was most unexpected. We took a seed from the great tree of American liberty and planted it in the fertile soil of Dutannuru. Our miracle, if we must call it that, is a direct descendant of *your* miracle."

Mensah paused as the audience rose to its feet and applauded.

"Thank you so much, you are very kind. Now, I wish to cede the floor to my good friend, Ross Egan."

Another round of applause erupted in the auditorium as the two men exchanged places.

"They are ready for you," Mensah said as he shook Egan's hand in passing.

"Thanks," Egan replied, thinking it was like having Sinatra open for Tiny Tim. He waited until the applause waned.

"Freedom is the ability to choose. That famous photo at the power plant was the culmination of a choice made by an incredibly brave young man—a choice between liberty and tyranny.

"Tanu Baafi was just a boy when he was rounded up and conscripted into the Safolese army to fight in the civil war. And despite years of indoctrination to blindly obey the orders of his superiors, when the truth was revealed and Baafi found himself with the opportunity to choose, he chose liberty.

"The Founders of this nation pledged their lives, fortunes and sacred honor to secure liberty for themselves and their descendants. Baafi had no fortune to lose, but he risked both his honor and his life in an act that most of us would consider suicidal—he struck down a brutal tyrant.

"When I asked Baafi why he killed Cudjoe, he replied: *Se wokum owo a, na woatwa ne tiri preko.* It means: when you kill a snake, cut off its head to ensure that it's dead. Cudjoe was greatly feared, and for good reason. Taking the head off of that snake proved to all that it wouldn't ever come slithering back.

"The essence of freedom is choice. Years ago, I remember watching a movie about a saxophone player with a Russian circus who defects in New York City. There's a scene where he's in an American supermarket for the first time and the aisles upon aisles of shelves, fully stocked with the dizzying array of products, overwhelms him.

"I've spent the better part of my adult life living outside of the United States, and this, too, was a choice. My wife and I were both born in the great state of Michigan, but the dreams of youth can take you to the farthest corners of the world. I'm still a US citizen, and I'm proud to say that I've voted in every election since I turned eighteen," Egan chuckled. "And all by absentee ballot.

"I worked in Safo before the coup and the civil war, and in Dutannuru thereafter, and that experience has made me appreciate our freedom to choose our leaders. Honestly, I have to shake my head in wonder that so many people in this country take that freedom for granted. Tanu Baafi proved just how important the choice of one person can be, and while I hope that none of you ever has to make *that* choice, I encourage you to elect those who will defend all of your rights. Thank you."

Egan nodded to the applauding audience, then joined Mensah and Saccary at the seating area. Stagehands swiftly removed the podium to provide the entire audience a clear view for the question and answer session.

"To get this portion of the program started," Saccary announced, quieting the buzz of conversation in the audience, "I would like to ask the first question. And as a good lawyer, I already know the answer, but I thought you might find it as interesting as I. Gentlemen, how is it that you decided to launch the international tour supporting your book, *The Dutannuru Miracle*, at Hillsdale College?"

Mensah turned to Egan. "If I may?"

Egan nodded his assent.

"If I am to answer this question properly, I must start by directing your attention to the beautiful woman seated in the front row. Please stand, dear."

A statuesque woman clad in a tailored suit accented with a patterned scarf and distinctly African jewelry rose and wagged a finger at her husband, before turning around to face the audience.

"This is my wife, Esi. In addition to bringing much joy to my life for many years, for which I am thankful each day, Esi is also a woman of great accomplishment. Before she was the First Lady of Dutannuru, my wife was an economist. She consulted with many private and public institutions and was published widely. She also taught economics for a few years, here at Hillsdale College."

The audience applauded Esi Mensah, recognizing her as one of their own. Esi bowed her head and then returned to her seat.

"President Mensah is being modest," Saccary offered. "I am certain that our economics faculty and many of the students in our higher level courses recognize her name. Doctor Esi Mensah is a distinguished scholar and an expert on both the theories and practical application of Austrian economics. Her work is most clearly evident in the astonishing economic recovery made by Dutannuru in the past decade and serves as an impressive, on-going case study."

"That is where I pick up the story," Egan said. "My wife Maggie was an economics major at Hillsdale when Esi was teaching here. Naturally, their paths crossed, and beyond the student-professor relationship, they became close friends. It was through Esi that Maggie, a girl from Michigan's Upper Peninsula, fell in love with a small but wonderful place in West Africa. Maggie did a stint with the Peace Corps in Safo, and I followed her there after we were married. The rest is laid out in the book, but the point is that our part in the Dutannuru miracle can be traced back to a classroom on this campus, where my wife first met her dear friend and mentor. We chose to launch our book tour at Hillsdale College because this is, for us, where the story began."

21

THE BALD EAGLE GLIDED EFFORTLESSLY ACROSS THE SKY, THE undersides of its outstretched wings aglow with the first rays of morning sun. The light wind bore the majestic bird on a straight line over the cornfield toward the Blackwater National Wildlife Refuge.

"That's something you don't see every day," Frank Crusca said admiringly. "It's a good sign."

"Assuming you don't shoot it," the Vice President replied. "Then my protective detail would be obliged to turn you over to Fish and Wildlife for prosecution."

The two men were alone in the blind—a lidless wooden box measuring twelve feet long by four wide and four deep. The box was set a few feet into the ground and the exposed sides were camouflaged with dry corn stalks.

The acres around the blind were littered with the stubble of last fall's harvest. Interspersed in the ruin were patches of snow and a large flock of decoys staged to lure Canadian geese. The Vice President's Secret Service detail reclined in insulated ground blinds, scanning the area for threats instead of migratory waterfowl.

"If old Ben Franklin had his way, the turkey would be our national symbol instead of that bird," the Vice President continued, "the wild kind, not what you get at the supermarket."

"I prefer the kind of wild turkey that comes in a bottle. Speaking of which..."

Crusca retrieved one of the two identical, stainless steel Thermos bottles from under the bench and filled his mug with a steaming brown liquid. The Vice President held out his mug and Crusca topped it off. Both men had brought a supply of coffee to the early morning hunt, but only the Vice President had fortified his with a healthy dose of Irish whiskey.

"A wee nip to cure what ails you," the Vice President offered before taking a cautious sip. "*This* the Micks got right."

As he nursed his coffee, Crusca scanned the sky and scratched the head of the Labrador retriever seated by his leg. His weapon this morning was a 12 gauge Benelli Super Black Eagle II loaded with number-2 steel shot. The Vice President opted for his trusted Remington 870 Wingmaster.

"Perfect morning, even if it is a bit on the cold side," Crusca said. "Thanks for inviting me to join you."

"Given all that you and the union have done for me and the President, it's my pleasure."

The Vice President tapped his mug against Crusca's in a light toast, and then took another sip.

"You and your boss have done a lot for us, and we plan to back you hard all the way to November."

"I appreciate that," the Vice President said warmly. "And so does the President. We've made solid gains for working people in our first term, but there's a lot more left to do."

"Preaching to the choir," Crusca said. "But there is something the union would like you to handle for us."

"We all but gave you two auto companies," the veep chided.

"I'm serious. Eisler is going to introduce a bill in the Senate that negatively affects our pension fund. A similar bill will be introduced in the House. We expect the Senate vote to split on party lines, and there's a good chance Ward'll break ranks and vote yes."

The Vice President nodded. Ward was one-term senator from a normally conservative district, and a no vote on stronger regulation of union-managed pension funds would end his chance for re-election.

"Breaking ties in the Senate is one of my many important duties. And I'll do what I can to keep the troops in line when it comes time to vote. After all, that's what friends are for, right?"

Crusca nodded.

The Vice President reached under the bench and picked up the union leader's heavy Thermos bottle. He unscrewed the top and poured off little more than a cup of coffee onto the ground, quickly emptying the flask. With a half-turn, the shallow insert twisted out to reveal a hidden chamber containing a six-inch stack of one-ounce gold coins. At current prices, the coins were worth over one hundred thousand dollars.

"Yesiree," the veep said as he reassembled the flask, "that's what friends are for."

A goose call dangled from a lanyard around Crusca's neck. He set his mug down on the bench and, with both hands, pressed the reed to his lips and blew into the instrument. Instead of a melodic tune, the union leader modulated his breaths to produce an incredibly realistic imitation of a goose. He paused for a moment and then repeated the call.

The dog was up on all fours, head cocked, listening. In the distance, both men heard the reply. Crusca called again, and the veep scanned the horizon, trying to pinpoint the direction of the response.

"Just below the top of the west tree line," the veep said.

"I see 'em."

A ragged line of eight geese flew along the property line that the farm shared with the nature preserve. Crusca played out another series of calls and the flight turned, circling in on the faux gaggle in the surrounding field. Both men shouldered their weapons and waited for the birds to come into range.

"Next pass," the veep said, aiming his shotgun at the large goose near the rear of the flight. "You take the front of the line. I'll shoot at the back."

"Got it," Crusca replied, selecting his target.

A gust of wind altered the flight path of the incoming geese. The birds quickly lost altitude and the Vice President bolted up to clearly track his target over the corn stalks surrounding the blind.

The dog spun at the sudden movement and its thick tail slapped the side of the Thermos filled with Irish coffee. The flask spun, then toppled forward onto the plywood floor. The loose cap flew off, ejected by a rush of steaming liquid. Both hit the dog's hindquarters. The eighty-pound Lab bolted forward with a yelp and rammed headfirst into the Vice President's groin.

The jolt of pain that accompanied the canine punch below the belt momentarily blinded the Vice President. Every muscle in his body seemed to contract. As he folded over, knees buckling, the Remington discharged.

A dense cloud of steel shot tore into the left side of Crusca's rib cage—the area exposed as he trained his weapon on the geese. The pellets shredded tissue and shattered bone, the blast destroying the man's lungs and heart. Falling limply with the blow, he was dead before he hit the ground.

"Oh my God!" the Vice President yelled. "Help! I need help, *now!*"

22

"...MADE GREAT STRIDES THESE PAST THREE YEARS AND THE SPIRIT and determination of this great nation remains strong." The President paused for dramatic effect, imagining the applause echoing in the House chamber. "Thank you. God bless you, and God bless the United States of America."

"Time," David Wagner, the White House Director of Communications called out.

"Fifty-two minutes and four seconds," an aide with a digital stopwatch replied.

"Factor in the applause and we're still under an hour. That'll keep the networks happy. They can squeeze in a few commercials before the opposition rebuttal."

"Who's handling that?" the President asked.

"Winfield," Wagner replied.

Emory Winfield, a three-term Republican senator from Ohio, was the Senate minority leader. His party's gains in the midterm elections had erased the Democrats' super-majority and divided the upper house fifty-fifty. The even split evaporated before the new Congress could be sworn in due to the sudden death of a Republican senator from Arkansas during the Christmas break that year. The Democratic governor appointed himself to fill the vacancy.

"What do you think, Mr. President?" Wagner asked.

"Those last changes are good. I think we got it."

"Then we'll lock it down and get it set for tonight. Thank you, Mr. President."

"Thank you," the President replied warmly.

"Mr. President," an aide said. "You have a ten-thirty with Daniel Page."

The President nodded, collected his notes from the podium and crossed the corridor between the Roosevelt Room and the Oval Office. He sat in the oak rocker and gazed out at the wintry landscape of the White House grounds. The capital was gripped in a cold snap that sent the temperature plunging to a record low.

At precisely ten-thirty, the President's secretary knocked at the concealed door between their offices and escorted in the President's campaign manager.

"Good morning, Mr. President," Page said.

The President rose and met Page in the center of the Oval, where the two shook hands.

"Let's talk in my study," the President said.

He led Page through the ornate door on the room's west side, down a short corridor and into his private study. The President sat in a leather club chair and propped his feet on an ottoman. As Page took a seat on the couch, the President switched on the array of flat screen televisions to the 24-hour news channels and muted the sound.

"How are we doing?" the President asked, his eyes skimming the news crawls at the bottom of the screens.

"On-line contributions are down."

"Down?"

"We expected it after Lynn dropped out. You're running unopposed, so a lot of your voters won't get interested in the campaign until the fall—which is fine because we don't want these folks getting message fatigue. Don't worry about it. Your core is intact, we're just operating in a behind-the-scenes mode. The goal for now is just to have you at your job, looking presidential."

"And the war chest?"

"Still on track to have the largest presidential campaign fund ever. The unions are one hundred percent behind you, as are all of your big backers. Sturla is rock solid, just like last time. I wouldn't worry about the bank."

"Did you learn anything from Iowa and New Hampshire?"

Page shook his head. "We reviewed all the exit polling and didn't find any surprises. Neuske is strong among seniors, but he's splitting the vets with Hook. Oates is doing well with Republican women in all age groups. Small business owners are split between Widmer and Walterhouse. Vogel is running strong with the more libertarian conservatives. It's a mixed bag of nuts. Neuske took Iowa but came in fifth in New Hampshire. Walterhouse squeaked a win in New Hampshire, but barely took third in Iowa."

"Just like our side, four years ago—too many candidates."

"There's not much to separate one from the pack. In the first two contests, the spread between first and last was just a hair bigger than the statistical margin of error. In terms of delegates, Walterhouse is the front runner, but a stiff wind could change the order."

"How's their fundraising?"

"Can't match ours," Page replied. "Each candidate has a small core of financial backers, but the big money is sitting on the sidelines until a serious contender emerges. We were essentially in the same position four years ago, until we broke out on Super Tuesday."

"What if no one breaks out?" the President mused.

"Nobody wins the nomination on Super Tuesday, but it usually thins the pack."

"I think it's in our best interest if the pack remains thick for as long as possible."

"I agree," Page said with a smug grin. "And we're working on a strategy in the open primary states. We had a strong primary team in place across the country, and I'm putting them to use."

"Good. How are we coming with the opposition research?"

"All of them have something we can spin if and when the need arises. Oates is pretty clean, but with her it's just a matter of guilt by association with the previous administration."

"That always plays well with my core voters, but I'm not so sure I want to face her in the fall."

"You don't think you can beat her?"

"It's not that. I just don't want the Republicans to be the first major party to nominate a woman for president—and a black one no less. We're the ones who are supposed to break down the race and gender barriers. I'd like to see her sprint to the finish but come up short."

"I can gin something up that will do a little short-term damage and play in the end like a GOP sexist dirty trick."

"Just so long as it doesn't tie back to us."

Page arched a quizzical eyebrow at the President. "Who is going to look? For the media to turn on you the story would have to involve you in bed with either a dead woman or a live boy."

"What the hell," the President growled as he fumbled for the remote control.

Page turned his head and saw a picture of the Vice President on all of the news channels. The President brought up the sound on one of the broadcasts.

"...involved in an apparent hunting accident early this morning. Reports from the scene indicate that the Vice President was not injured in the incident. Another individual, as yet unidentified, was pronounced dead at the scene. Officials are waiting until the family has been notified before releasing the name. Back to you..."

The President muted the audio and shook his head in disbelief.

"The man is a political disaster," the President said.

"Depends on who he shot," Page replied. "A bullet between Garr Denby's beady little eyes would probably bump your approval rating up ten points. Of course, you'd probably net fifteen if he'd offed himself."

"I couldn't be so lucky."

The President and his running mate started the previous presidential campaign as rivals for the nomination. The wide field of Democratic candidates that year thinned considerably after Super Tuesday; the former Maryland governor's ambitions were among those derailed. While failing to connect with the voters on a national scale, the Vice President was a loyal party man with strong union ties, an honest working class background, and the good fortune to have been born and raised on the southern side of the Mason-Dixon line. His resume and contacts complimented those of the victorious nominee and helped propel the ticket to victory in November. But since that time, the gaffe-prone politician had proven to be far less useful.

"This is the last thing I need right now. Instead of staying on message, my people have to waste time on damage control."

The President's secretary appeared at the door to the study.

"Let me guess," the President said before the woman could utter a syllable. "Chief of Staff. Press Secretary. Secret Service."

"And the Vice President. He's en route back to Washington."

"I'll meet with the first three in the Oval in five minutes. Patch my running mate through to me here."

"Yes, Mr. President."

As the secretary disappeared down the corridor, the President turned back to Page.

"You want to know what the worst part about this is?"

"Aside from the Vice President accidentally killing someone?" Page asked rhetorically.

"Yes, though it's a close second. Tonight I will give one of the most important speeches of my presidency. Sitting behind me, leering over my shoulders will be the Speaker of the House and that—that *jackass*."

23

"THE VEEP IS MOVING," MCCOLL ANNOUNCED.

"I was beginning to wonder if the police were going to arrest him," Hopps replied.

"C'mon, Double-H. You *know* that shooting was an accident."

Hopps strummed a couple chords on his guitar. "Now how could I possibly know that, darlin'?"

"That man is so freaking incompetent that if he had planned on offing Crusca, he would have missed," McColl explained. "Then Crusca would have taken him out with his bare hands."

"Of that, I have no doubt. Any guess on where they're taking him?"

"Looks like his personal residence. Nice thing about a Secret Service detail is all their electronics make them easy to track."

"And the veep still has the package?"

"Based on the security cameras in the police station, Crusca's Thermos has not left his person. Signal is strong. I still can't believe Taylor and Buttrey hot-wired a gold coin."

"Gold's a great conductor," Hopps offered. "It makes a fine antenna, and the coin was more than big enough to accommodate a bit of microelectronics. The real trick was making sure the dealer had our coin in the stack he sold Crusca."

The wall of screens in front of McColl displayed images from traffic and security cameras along the motorcade's route and a map with their current location. McColl's band of rogues had little difficulty hacking the surveillance feeds. While some relished the idea of hacking the Secret Service communications, Hopps decided it was an unnecessary risk. Their electronic footprint was large enough to track without resorting to eavesdropping.

A short time later, the motorcade reached the Vice President's personal residence near Baltimore.

" 'Home again, home again, jiggity-jig'," Hopps said as the rogues tapped into feeds from the cameras installed on and around the property by the Secret Service.

Once inside the gates, the SUV carrying the Vice President headed for the main house while the rest of the retinue peeled away toward the carriage quarters. An agent opened the front door just as the Vice President emerged from the vehicle. The Vice President gave his protective detail a sheepish wave and headed for the front door.

"Aside from the Secret Service, the house is empty," McColl reported. "His wife is in D.C. getting her hair done for tonight. We know he's called her since the shooting."

"To tell her not to worry," Hopps mused. "Being pragmatic, he probably told her to continue with her schedule for the day, but to clear tomorrow to deal with the Crusca situation."

"The story's breaking," a rogue from Ole Miss reported.

Starting with the cable news channels, sketchy reports emerged of a shooting involving the Vice President. The blogosphere quickly caught up with postings on the incident.

"*Que sera, sera*," Hopps said. "Where's our hapless veep?"

McColl brought up a three-dimensional computer model of the Vice President's home acquired from the electronic archives of the architect who built the house for the previous owner.

"Internal motion sensors have him heading down into the basement," McColl answered. "Confirmed by GPS on the tracker."

A tracking dot floated ghost-like through the virtual model. The dot moved through a large entertainment room and stopped at a door.

"Bringing the basement security camera up," a rogue announced.

A black-and-white image appeared on one of the monitors, showing the Vice President punching an access code into a keypad beside a heavy wooden door. The left pocket of his coat bulged and the fabric on that side was taut, as if weighted. The door, which had a rounded top and bowed out slightly, looked ancient and weathered. At eye level, the door featured a small, circular metal door.

"What kind of door is that?" McColl asked.

"Having spent some time in wineries, " Hopps said, "I believe that door was cut from the top of a fermentation barrel. The little port hole you see is where the vintner would lower a dipper into the barrel to see how the wine was aging."

"Makes sense," McColl said. "That's the door to the wine cellar. Somehow, I never pictured the guy as a wine snob."

"Perhaps a rare bottle of *LaFitte* isn't the only thing he has stashed away in there."

"Got the access code to that door," a rogue said. "The keypad and the room's environmental controls are wired into the alarm system."

The Vice President eased the cypress door open and disappeared inside. The heavy construction surrounding the wine cellar caused the tracking dot to flicker. He reappeared on the camera feed a few moments later, Crusca's Thermos in hand. After securing the wooden door, the Vice President playfully flipped the Thermos in the air and caught it.

"Now we know where the honorable Vice President keeps his bribes."

24

"MR. SPEAKER," THE HOUSE DEPUTY SERGEANT AT ARMS ANnounced from the door to the House Chamber, "the President of the United States."

Representatives and senators, Supreme Court justices and cabinet members, and the many guests who filled the balcony—all rose to applaud the nation's chief executive. Some applauded in enthusiastic support of the President and his policies, others more out of respect for the office than its current occupant.

The President moved slowly down the aisle followed by the congressional escort committee. He shook hands and warmly greeted his friends and supporters. For some, he signed copies of the speech he would soon deliver.

The applause continued as the President ascended the rostrum. He found two manila envelopes on the House Clerk's desk. He handed one to the Speaker of the House and the other to the Vice President. The two men locked eyes for the brief moment of the exchange, the Vice President noticing that none of the fury that the President expressed during a private meeting that afternoon had waned. Though the President had not demanded his resignation, if offered it would have been quickly accepted.

Turning from the leaders of the House and Senate, the President faced the audience of elected officials, dignitaries, and millions of Americans on the other side of the cameras.

"Mr. Speaker, Mr. Vice President, members of the Supreme Court and diplomatic corps, distinguished guests, and my fellow citizens," the President began. "The Constitution of the United States requires that the president 'shall from time to time give to Congress information of the State of the Union and recommend to their consideration such measures as he shall judge necessary and expedient.' "

The text of the President's speech slowly scrolled up the face of the twin teleprompters, staged to his right and left, just outside the frame of the primary camera televising the speech.

"My predecessors have done so in times of peace and in times of war, in times of prosperity and in times of depression, in times of blissful tranquillity and in times of grave uncertainty. The success our nation has enjoyed since its founding was not preordained. In each age, the people of this great nation have been tested, and to each challenge, the people rose up *united* in their resolve."

Applause filled the chamber and the President smiled. In honoring the past, he offered all those assembled something on which they could agree. Still, he noticed members of his own party were more enthusiastic than those of the opposition.

"When I assumed the office of President three years ago, our nation was at war and our economy was tumbling into the worst economic downturn since the Great Depression. Millions of Americans were out of work, and millions had lost their homes in foreclosure. Unbridled greed on Wall Street brought ruin to Main Street. That is the challenge that the American people elected me to solve."

The applause here was decidedly lopsided. The most enthusiastic were those up for election in the fall who needed party funding for their campaigns. Scanning the audience, the President noticed a flicker on his left teleprompter. The text of his speech disappeared and was suddenly replaced with the following message:

HYPERBOLIC ORATORY.

SEVERITY COMPARISON OF CURRENT ECONOMIC CONDITIONS WITH RESPECT TO EQUIVALENT TIME-FRAME OF THE GREAT DEPRESSION DEPENDS UPON INDICES OF MEASUREMENT.

COMMENT REGARDING UNEMPLOYMENT AND HOME
FORECLOSURES NON-SPECIFIC. UNEMPLOYMENT
RATE OF 1% EQUALS 1.65 MILLION PEOPLE OUT OF
WORK. IN THE YEAR PRIOR TO PRESIDENT'S INAU-
GURATION, LESS THAN ONE MILLION HOMES REPOS-
SESSED BY MORTGAGE LENDERS.

CAUSALITY ERROR. FOR-PROFIT ACTIVITY OF PUB-
LICLY TRADED ENTITIES IS NOT PRIMARY CAUSE OF
RECENT ECONOMIC BOOM-BUST CYCLE, MERELY EF-
FECT. FINANCIAL SECTOR REGULATION COUPLED
WITH EXPANSION OF MONEY SUPPLY CAUSED SPE-
CIFIC FINANCIAL SECTOR ACTIVITY RESULTING IN
ECONOMIC BOOM AND SUBSEQUENT BUST.

The President's eyes remained locked on the scrolling critique.
His mouth hung slightly open in astonishment. It was like receiving
back a grade school essay and finding the teacher had bled over the
document with a red marker. The President felt his cheeks involun-
tarily flush before his attention snapped back to the silent chamber.

25

THE PRESIDENT FLED THE CAPITOL AS QUICKLY AS DECORUM would allow. He had accepted the polite compliments of his partisan fellows and avoided the condescending looks of the opposition. An unusually gifted orator, the President was thrown badly off tonight and some in the House Chamber doubtless took pleasure in his discomfort.

Throughout the hour that the President spoke, the right teleprompter had dutifully reproduced his speech while the left one dissected his words almost as quickly as he enunciated them. After his initial shock, he had avoided looking directly at the offending device, but he knew from the occasional glimpse that it was still mocking him.

The Secret Service quickly guided him down secured corridors to the waiting motorcade. The President ducked into the first limousine and was quickly joined by his wife.

"What happened up there?" the First Lady asked sharply, as soon as the doors closed and they were alone.

The President ignored the question, suppressing what he was certain would be a profanity-laden response. Instead, he speed-dialed his chief of staff, Levi Knopper.

"Good evening, Mr. President," Knopper answered. "And yes, WHO IS I did parse your SOTU address. It went live just as you entered the chamber."

"I know. The bastards *hacked* my fucking teleprompter."

"What?"

"My teleprompter! I had my speech running on one screen while the other was chopping it up like a sushi chef."

"I figured the scroll was acting up. It definitely rattled you."

"You think?" the President snapped back.

"Net traffic went through the roof during your address, yet the site never crashed." Knopper reported. "NSA has never seen anything like what these guys are doing, and they've still had no luck tracing the source."

"This latest attack is a major security breach. Whoever is behind these incidents has breached telecommunications and power systems, satellites, and now the US government. This *cannot* be a group of teenage geeks in their parents' basement. There must be some serious money behind this effort, and with this stunt they crossed the line. I want a conference call with directors of the FBI, CIA, NSA and the Attorney General as soon as I'm back in the White House."

"The AG?"

"Federal laws must have been broken in the commission of these attacks. I want these criminals prosecuted to the fullest extent of the law. Set up the call."

"Yes, sir," Knopper replied, before the President rang off.

The President pocketed his cell phone and turned on the limousine's satellite television to watch the opposition response. Senator Emory Winfield appeared on the small LCD screen, speaking from Senate chamber.

"...honor to address the nation and offer a thoughtful response to the President's State of the Union address. It is your good fortune that my response will be brief in the extreme," Winfield said wryly. "In reaction to the disastrous first two years of this administration, in which the President's party also enjoyed strong majorities in both houses of Congress, the people acted to restore the balance of power between the executive and legislative branches of government.

"The President outlined his goals for the remainder of his first term, a list of populist and progressive giveaways that smack of election year pandering. The reality is that the President can offer the moon, but has little chance of moving any legislation through Congress. The President's promises are empty.

"The President complains that the conservative opposition offers no ideas or programs and is simply the party of 'No.' While there is no truth to the President's first charge, the second we wear as a badge of honor. The only thing that the President's conservative opposition lacks is the votes to overcome his veto.

"From now until the next Congress is sworn in, and hopefully a new president, nothing will get passed and, sadly, nothing will get repealed. And anyone who tells you otherwise is *not* telling you the truth.

"In closing, for those interested in a thorough and dispassionate analysis of the President's address, I heartily recommend that you visit the website listed at the bottom the screen. As the Good Book says: *know the truth and the truth will set you free.* Thank you, and good night."

Across the bottom of the screen appeared the address:

WWW.WHO-IS-I.COM.

26

"FROM SEA TO SHINING SEA, IT IS *I*, YOUR BRILLIANT BEACON OF truth in these turbulent times," Garr Denby said over the waning chords of his opening theme song. "The pooh-bah of political punditry, the courageous crusader of conservatism, and the rakish rogue of the republic for which we stand.

"I thank you all for joining me in what is the largest radio audience in the world each and every busy broadcast day. Today I have a treasure trove of material to dive into and only three hours in which to do it.

"On a low note, our bumbling Vice President was apparently responsible for the death of a man in a hunting accident. I say *apparently* because the White House spin machine wound up to full speed to obfuscate this incident. The honest truth would serve the administration far better than their typical C.Y.A. effort, but that's what we've come to expect from this bunch.

"The known facts are fairly straightforward. The Vice President was hunting Canadian geese with a long-time supporter, auto union boss Frank Crusca. The two men were accompanied by the Vice President's protective detail. They were hunting from a blind in the middle of a cornfield, on a private farm, when Crusca suffered a fatal gunshot wound to the chest and was pronounced dead at the scene. The police investigating the incident have released no specifics on the shooting.

"The conspiracy theorists are all working themselves up into a lather over this, but if *and only if* a court of law decides otherwise, I'm chalking this up as nothing more than a tragic accident. The Vice

President appeared visibly distracted during the State of the Union address last night, so much so that I think he was the only person in the room who didn't notice his boss's erratic performance.

"I take no pleasure from this tragic incident and will not make light of it. My prayers go out to the Crusca family and to the Vice President.

"Next topic, the President's State of the Union address. For years, we have been told of the President's golden gift of elocution, that he was the greatest orator since Cicero. All I need to say about last night is that the delivery matched the content.

"What I have learned from my sources in Washington is that the wizards behind WHO IS I not only treated the American people to the same real-time fact checking that they delivered during the Republican debates in Iowa, they were kind enough to let the President see it as well.

"One of the President's beloved teleprompters apparently went rogue on him and switched out his speech with the straight feed from WHO IS I. If you were wondering why the President seemed to favor the left side of our television screens last night, the teleprompter on the other side was refuting nearly everything he said, as he said it.

"For those of you who want to see a side-by-side comparison of what the President said and an unbiased, objective analysis of the speech coupled with the in-depth research supporting the facts, I whole-heartedly encourage you to visit WHO IS I. We've posted the link on our website, and I believe this is the first time in the history of this program that we've mentioned a website without crashing it.

"I've said it before many times—if you want to know who the left fears, just look at who they're demonizing. Not a crumb of complaint out of them after the Iowa debate, in fact the mainstream media's opinion of WHO IS I at that point was largely favorable. But these same news outlets and the left's kook bloggers are in full blown apoplexy over the WHO IS I veracity dissection of the President's State of the Union address. Not one of them has disputed the facts, because they can't. Instead, they are ripping into the anonymity of the people running the site. They are trying to deflect our attention away from the facts by stirring up a controversy about personality.

"When it comes to facts, personality is irrelevant. As long as the message is true, the personality and even the identity of the messenger is beside the point. Truth is truth.

"Of course, this is the kind of thing that gets you into trouble with the relativists. These modern thinkers like to tell us that there are many truths, and each truth is equally valid and there are no absolute truths. This *nuanced* and *enlightened* approach is absolute, unadulterated hogwash!

"The declaration that there are no absolute truths is itself a contradiction, the kind of flawed logic a first year philosophy student should be able to sniff out in a second. That's assuming, of course, that these first-years aren't at some elitist university filled with egghead intellectual professors who've never worked a day in the real world because it's beneath them and their utopian socialist ideals.

"If there are no absolute truths, then the statement that there are no absolute truths must be false, otherwise it would be an absolute truth that, per their premise, cannot exist. Truth is truth, and the facts are the facts. The refreshing thing about WHO IS I is that the folks behind it are providing the unvarnished truth. If a politician makes what appears to be a statement of fact, it measures that statement against the truth and lets the chips fall where they may.

"The conspiracy theorists on the left attempting to assassinate the character of the people behind this incredible expression of the right to free speech have totally missed the point. The clearest analogy I can think of is in the UK in the 1960s. The state controlled all broadcast media through the BBC and British rock music, which was *everywhere* in the US, could hardly be heard in its own homeland. The entrepreneurial, free market answer to this iron fisted, socialist government restriction was to broadcast rock music from ships just outside England's territorial waters. WHO IS I is the political equivalent of pirate radio in 1960s England.

"For those of you new to the program, I am not now, nor have I ever been, a member of any political party. I am a conservative, and it is my conservative philosophy that forms the foundational bedrock of my political viewpoint. Conservatism is based on the premise that each person is a unique individual and that each, by virtue of his or her existence, possesses certain innate rights.

"Parties may adopt political philosophies, but the primary purpose of a political party is the acquisition of power for use in forwarding its agenda. I am not interested in acquiring political power, but I have an acute interest in the motivations and intentions of those who seek to govern.

"Now, I'm running a bit long in this segment, so we have to take a break and do more to stimulate the economy over the next few minutes than our feckless president has done in the past three years. Back before you know it."

The bumper music poured from the studio speakers as stations airing the program cut away for commercials. Denby glanced at the digital clock that counted down the seconds remaining in the break, then pulled together his notes for the next segment.

"The guest is holding on line one," Denby's producer announced from the control room.

"Thanks," Denby replied.

Beside Denby's notes lay an advanced reading copy of *The Dutannuru Miracle*. Post-It notes sprouted between the pages, thickening the unbound side. Denby pressed line one and took the call off-air.

"Ross, how the hell are you?"

"Beat, but I can't complain. The book tour is going very well."

"I'll say. Your book is dominating the bestseller lists, but we'll get into that shortly. Don't want to waste any good material, and there's nothing worse than dead air."

"I'm of Irish descent," Egan replied. "Once I get talking, the difficulty is shutting me up."

"Then you and I are twin sons of different mothers," Denby said with a laugh. "Hang on—we're coming back from commercial."

Egan heard a click on the line as his call was linked to the on-air feed. Denby announced his return to his listeners over the sounds of Booker T and the MGs classic *Green Onions*.

"...unlike most radio talk shows, I rarely have guests on this program. And for good reason—the content of this show is rooted in things that I want to talk about. That said, there are occasions when I invite a guest to join me, and that's because I think both you, the listening audience, and I will benefit from the exchange. Today is one of those rare occasions.

"On the line with me today is Ross Egan, a brilliant engineer from Michigan's Upper Peninsula who ran power plants in Africa and earned the Nobel Peace Prize for having actually *done* something that stopped what promised to be a horrifically bloody war. Ross, welcome to the program."

"Thanks, Garr," Egan replied. "I'm a longtime listener, first-time guest."

Denby laughed. "How'd you listen to me in Dutannuru?"

"Podcasts. My dad bought me a subscription to your website years ago and he renews it as my annual Christmas present."

"So I'm the gift that keeps on giving," Denby joked. "Ross, I want to start by thanking you for two things. First, you won the Nobel Peace Prize—so I have to thank you for restoring some sanity to a selection process that in recent years has defied logic."

"I was as surprised as anyone when they announced that President Mensah and I had won," Egan admitted.

"It was shocking. I mean, you two weren't running a terrorist organization. You weren't promoting an extreme environmental agenda based on some really bad science and outright lies. And you didn't win solely on the *hope* that you might actually do something for peace sometime in the future. What you did actually resulted in, dare I say it—*peace*."

"Those are the exceptions rather than the norm. I'm humbled to be part of a group that includes Mother Teresa and the Dalai Lama. Why else do you want to thank me?"

"For your book, *The Dutannuru Miracle*. Being an influential member of the media, I received an advanced copy months before it was published and I wore the book out. For those of you watching on the webcam, I'm going to show you what's left of this book."

Denby held up the soft cover copy of Egan's book and the cover slipped off.

"I devoured this book like nothing I've read since the *Federalist Papers*. I wore out a Hi-Liter and burned through two pads of Post-It notes tagging important statements and ideas. I could go on and on about the nuggets of pure truth I found in these pages, but what you and President Mensah did in Dutannuru proved something that I have always believed."

"And what's that?" Egan asked.

"There is nothing special about the United States that made it the greatest nation on Earth. And what I mean by that is, there is nothing unique about our geography or natural resources that allowed this nation to prosper like no other in the history of human civilization. A version of American exceptionalism is reproducible anywhere, and the success Dutannuru has enjoyed since its birth just affirms my belief that the human spirit, unfettered by tyranny, will flourish."

"Dutannuru more than proves the point, Garr," Egan agreed. "When the United States emerged as a new nation, it was rich in natural resources, had ample open land, vast oceans to protect it from attack, and the populated areas of the thirteen states were relatively undamaged by the Revolutionary War. Conditions were ideal for the sort of experiment in republican democracy proposed by the Founders. Dutannuru, by comparison, had more in common with Germany or Japan following the Second World War. Infrastructure in the cities was largely destroyed. Thousands of people were homeless, and we had a flood of refugees from Safo before the border closed. The economy was non-existent and much of the equipment in the power plants and factories was either looted or wrecked. Dutannuru's military was a rag-tag group of citizen-soldiers with little in the way of equipment or munitions. Couple that with the fact that this tiny new nation shared a long border with a dangerous enemy and the prospects for Dutannuru's immediate survival were far worse than those of the newly formed United States. On its first day as a nation, Dutannuru ranked well below Haiti in GDP, and even Zimbabwe's pathetic economy was enviable in comparison."

Denby interjected, "There's a line you use in the book: 'Dutannuru was a Stone Age nation that came into existence at the start of the new millennium in a technologically advanced world.'"

"The only thing Dutannuru had going for it was the fact that our country was so devastated that even Safo thought the effort to conquer it was more trouble than it was worth," Egan asserted.

"But that changed last January," Denby offered.

"Yes. Dutannuru's progress since it sprang from the rubble had been, as the title of our book implies, miraculous. It was the classic tale of the grasshopper and the ants writ large, with Cudjoe in the role of the grasshopper."

"And the people of Dutannuru were the ants."

"Right. The people of Dutannuru under President Mensah's leadership established a nation governed by the rule of law and served by a government with constitutionally limited powers. Entrepreneurship flourished in this environment, driving up demand for foreign goods and services to support the growing domestic economy. Unlike many of our neighbors, contracts mean something in Dutannuru. Payment of one's obligations is matter of honor."

"So while the people of Dutannuru are making lemonade out of the lemons left to them after the civil war, Cudjoe and his band of thugs are running Safo like a criminal enterprise for their personal benefit," observed Denby.

"Despot is too kind a description for Kwame Cudjoe," Egan said bitterly. "He brought utter ruin on Safo, bankrupting a nation blessed with incredible geography and abundant natural resources. His government didn't spend a dime on infrastructure, and the loss of a critical hydroelectric plant meant they couldn't even keep the lights on."

"So with the chill of an economic winter in the air," Denby said, "Cudjoe the grasshopper looked across the river and saw the ants of Dutannuru rich with the abundant fruits of their labor. Like a good socialist, he decided a little wealth redistribution was in order."

"As Thatcher said, 'The problem with socialism is that you eventually run out of other people's money'," replied Egan. "And from ancient times right up to the Iraqi invasion of Kuwait, the pages of history are filled with stories of tyrants waging war to replenish an empty treasury. It's nothing more than armed robbery on a national scale."

"You touched on this point a moment ago," Denby continued, "but you don't consider what happened that night at the Umoja Power Plant a miracle. It seems to me like the stuff of a great Hollywood movie."

"I can't wait to see who they cast as me," Egan laughed. "Honestly, no one in Dutannuru considers the events of that night miraculous, any more than people here consider the peaceful end of the Cuban Missile Crisis a miracle. I'll admit it was certainly a relief and the answer to many fervent prayers, but Cudjoe's death was simply the end of a national nightmare. The real miracle is liberty."

27

DANIEL PAGE STOOD IN THE CENTER OF A WINDOWLESS ROOM ON the upper floor of a ten-story office tower. The new glass and steel building was one of many dotting the Rosslyn-Ballston business corridor. Its sole tenant was the Committee to Re-elect the President.

Page intently studied a cluster of nine LCD screens that formed a single large display. Feeds from the major 24-hour cable news networks appeared in windows located in the upper corners of the wall screen, floating above a graphic map of the continental United States. Hawaii and a detached, out-of-scale Alaska floated off the California coast.

A column set over the Atlantic listed the six GOP candidates and their current delegate count. Fourteen states glowed brightly in contrast to the remaining thirty-six—states in which votes were being cast today to select the Republican nominee for president in this election cycle's Super Tuesday. Seven of the states were shown in dark blue as their primary contests were over, with the remaining primary battlegrounds rendered in light gray. For presidential hopefuls, Super Tuesday separates the wheat from the chaff.

Four of the seven previous primary contests were closed, meaning that only registered party members could participate in selecting the party nominee. The remaining states held open primaries that permitted any registered voter to vote on either the Republican or Democrat side of the ballot.

The gauntlet of today's primary contests would demonstrate a candidate's ability to wage a viable national campaign. By emerging from the pack on Super Tuesday, a candidate stands to win not just a trove of delegates needed to claim the nomination, but the gravitas needed to attract the money vital for fueling a campaign through to November. For losers, the morning after Super Tuesday combines the bitter taste of failed ambition with the sobering reality of an empty campaign war chest.

Page tracked the four closed primary states voting today, but the eight open states and their 375 delegates held his deeper interest. In the last campaign, he used the momentum of a strong Super Tuesday performance to eliminate nearly half of the field of Democratic presidential candidates and propel his man into the White House. This time around, his aim was to prevent any of the Republican candidates from developing that kind of momentum.

The day opened with Florida Governor Lila Oates emerging as the clear frontrunner after she took all ninety-four of her home state's delegates in a winner-take-all victory at the end of January. Solid polling in the four closed primary states provided Page with a reasonable idea of how those delegates would be divided, especially delegate-rich California and New York. Offsetting the favorites in these states was the goal of the stealth primary campaign he was waging.

"Just wait for me out here," the President told his security detail as he entered the room.

The leader of the stern looking quartet nodded and quietly ordered his team into position at the two entries to the room. The Secret Service had the entire building in full lockdown mode for the President's brief visit to his campaign headquarters.

"Mr. President," Page said warmly. "Welcome to the war room."

"I was in the neighborhood and thought I'd drop by. I've only got a moment, so lay it out for me."

"If the previous primaries are any indication, we expect strong voter turnout across the board. That plays into our crossover strategy. Absentee voting is at an all-time high in Georgia, New Jersey, Alabama and Tennessee," Page said with a smirk, "particularly in urban areas that went for you in the last election."

"And our community organizers?"

"The grassroots support for various Republican campaigns is surprisingly robust. I've seen reports of vanpools and shuttle busses taking voters to the polls. These folks are proving very helpful in ensuring the voters have no problems with these sometimes complicated ballots."

"Exit polls?" the President asked.

"By the numbers, Oates started the day as the frontrunner, but only because she won Florida. Anything less than a win in her home state and she would have packed it in last week."

"Just don't let her build up too much momentum. I don't want her in a position to win the nomination."

Page nodded. He also knew the President didn't want to face an opponent with Oates's intelligence, quick wit, and compelling history. The lady's accomplishments refuted the liberal social script, causing most on the left to view her as the GOP's most dangerous threat to their political power. Page would do all he could to prevent the President from facing off against Oates in the fall, when she would very likely fillet his boss during the debates.

"The reverends are slamming her as a sell-out to her race and an ingrate to those who paved her way," Page reported. "She won't be in the driver's seat come June."

"Good," the President replied.

"And if things play out the way I think," Page continued, "all six of your potential opponents will still think they have a real shot at the nomination come morning."

28

"MY FRIENDS, LET'S GET RIGHT TO IT," DENBY BEGAN, SKIPPING his usual show-opening patter. "The dust from the Super Tuesday primaries has settled and we are no closer to knowing who will face the President in the general election than we were twenty-four hours ago. I say *no closer* not because yesterday's vote should have decided the matter, rendering the votes moot in the remaining states along with D.C. and various territories. I say *no closer* because we still have exactly the same number of candidates as we had yesterday, and not one is so far back as to count them out.

"At this stage in the game, with this wide a field of candidates, you would expect to see a couple floundering with delegate counts in single or double digits. These would have issued statements about reviewing their options, meaning they were checking how much cash they had on hand and deciding whether or not to cut bait.

"For the purposes of full disclosure, I have met all of the candidates seeking the GOP nomination at one time or another over the years, and my relations with them ranges from friendly to simply polite. I am not a member of the Republican Party, so I was unable to cast a vote for any of them in my home state of Florida last week because this state holds closed primaries. For the record, I think it's a good idea that party members alone select the party nominee.

"Governor Oates, who I do know well as she is the Governor of Florida, was running sixth until her victory in our winner-take-all primary made her the first candidate to win over one hundred delegates. She and Colorado Governor Walterhouse are the current frontrunners, both surging over two hundred yesterday, but the rest of the pack is clustered in the low 100s with only sixteen delegates separating number three from number six. A decent showing by any of these four in the Kansas, Louisiana and Washington primaries on Saturday could do for them what Florida did for Oates.

"I personally like all six of the candidates running. They all have some decent ideas on how to get the country back on track. Most have worked in the private sector and understand there is a world outside the Washington Beltway. Two have positive records as elected state executives—valuable leadership experience our current president never added to his thin resume of achievements. I won't endorse anyone until the party has chosen its standard bearer. What I will advise is that you follow the Denby Doctrine: Wherever possible, vote for the most conservative candidate."

"Polling is not so much a science as an art form. I always find it interesting when a pollster asks me a question, usually political in nature, and I disagree with the premise. That said, polling for Super Tuesday really took it on the chin, especially in states with open primaries. In the states with closed primaries, the pollsters got it pretty much on the money. But the states with open primaries saw their turnout numbers *way* up. Drilling into the data, my crack team of political analysts found that voter turnout in predominantly Democrat districts was *unexpectedly* high. In these same districts, we found trends favoring candidates who were polling poorly elsewhere.

"Now, there are two ways to read this trend of traditionally Democrat districts voting heavily in a Republican primary. One is that even the hardcore, genetically bred, union rank-and-file, true believers are dissatisfied with the President and his anti-America agenda. The other is that a concerted effort by hardcore, genetically bred, union rank-and-file, true believers is underway to damage the effort to select the most viable opponent to square off against our dear leader. I wonder which it could be."

"I'll end this segment with a news item from my impressive heap. There is a story out of Charleston about a woman who has uncovered a case of identity theft possibly involving the assisted care facility where her father resides. It is not unusual for facilities of this kind to assist their residents in acquiring absentee ballots for upcoming elections—patriotism being a distinguishing characteristic of many of our seasoned citizens. The only election her father missed was when he was busy shooting at Nazis in World War II. Her dad was my kind of guy—a decorated, cigar-smoking veteran and a conservative to boot. The daughter appreciated the nursing home's effort to assist their patriotic residents until last week, when her father voted in the South Carolina Republican primary. The story notes that the father suffered a severe stroke last November that left him in a coma.

"There is no way of knowing for whom this veteran's vote was cast in the primary, and he might have even agreed with the pick. We will keep tabs on this story as the investigation develops, but I find it interesting. What political party do we know that has managed to locate missing ballots in a tight Senate election to affect the outcome, so many ballots that certain precincts had over one hundred percent voter turnout? For a party that has enjoyed the broad political support of dead voters, a little help from those in a coma shouldn't be hard to conjure."

29

EGAN NODDED TO THE AUDIENCE THAT WAS APPLAUDING HIS half of the presentation. After a few months on tour, he had finally grown comfortable on stage and developed a natural rapport with the audiences. The standing-room-only crowd that packed the Lady Bird Johnson Auditorium was on its feet, which still caused him some embarrassment, but he would accept applause over stony silence every time.

As Egan returned to his seat on the stage, the university president stood and motioned for the enthusiastic audience to return to their seats.

"Gentlemen," the university president began as the last ripples of applause died out. "On behalf of the University of Texas, I thank you for sharing your incredible experiences with us. What you both accomplished in Dutannuru shows what common sense and hard work can do for a community and a nation."

The audience concurred with another round of applause.

"We now move into the question and answer part of the evening, after which our two guests will be signing copies of *The Dutannuru Miracle*. Now I direct your attention to the two staff members with microphones standing in the aisles. If you have a question for our distinguished guests, just raise your hand and they will come to you. Otherwise, I have plenty of questions, but this being Texas I know y'all won't be shy."

Several hands shot up and the young man roaming the right side aisle approached a coed near the front of the auditorium. Standing at her seat, she received the microphone.

"My name is Olivia Iglesias," the young woman announced is a sultry drawl. "And I read your book this past weekend and could *not* put if down. And y'all here who haven't read it, I highly recommend you do. I'm pre-law/poli-sci, and most of the required reading is theory. In Dutannuru, y'all put your theory to the test and proved it works. It's the best case study I've ever read, and the most riveting."

"Thank you, Olivia," Mensah said. "You are very kind."

"I hate to correct you after such a nice compliment," Egan offered, "but the course President Mensah took in rebuilding Dutannuru was not based on an untested hypothesis. The principles behind Dutannuru's political and economic climate were proven conclusively by the Founders of the United States, and again by Reagan in the 1980s."

"What Ross and I did in Dutannuru was not new," Mensah added, "but it works *every* time it is tried. Dutannuru was in dire straits and we needed what you Americans call a 'sure thing.' Ah, we digress. What is your question, my dear?"

"The government of the United States has, for much of the past century, drifted away from its founding principles. The results of that progressive slide to the left are apparent. Under the current administration, that slow but steady drift has turned into a swift current. Across most of the country it feels like we're rushing downriver toward a steep waterfall in a leaky barrel. I look forward to casting my first vote in the presidential election this November, and I really want to vote for someone who understands what made this country great and who will strive to restore what we've all lost to this progressive erosion."

"I share that desire, Olivia," Egan said.

"My question is directed at you, Mr. Egan. Will you *please* run for President of the United States?"

Egan looked dumbstruck by the question as the audience applauded in thunderous agreement. Mensah rose from his chair and walked to the edge of the stage beaming proudly.

"What a marvelous suggestion!" Mensah gleefully bellowed over the applause. Pumping his fist in the air, the former president led a chant that shook the auditorium walls: *Egan! Egan! Egan!*

30

BARBARA JONES TAPPED THE NUMBER TWO BUTTON ON HER CAR radio, switching to the local news/talk station from an old country station that had slipped into one of its lengthy commercial breaks with a pharmaceutical ad for improved male performance.

"And in Austin last night," the newscaster read, "a book tour stop by a pair of Nobel Peace Prize winners turned into an impromptu campaign rally, clips of which have gone viral on the Internet. During the Q and A session that followed the lecture, engineer Ross Egan was implored by an audience member to seek the nation's highest office. A reporter on the scene spoke with the young woman who posed the question."

"What Mensah and Egan did with literally nothing in Dutannuru truly was miraculous," Olivia Iglesias explained. "Texas has weathered this recession better than most states, and our pain is tiny compared to where Dutannuru was when Mensah came to power. If you look at what he and Egan did in those first years and compare that to what our President has done in the same amount of time, you'll see real quick who knows how to get the job done and who doesn't."

Jones pulled into a parking space in front of the elementary school and followed the signs to her precinct voting place. The line was longer than she recalled from previous elections at this time of day, but it moved quickly and she was soon in the booth with her ballot. She scanned the names of the six Republicans on the ballot and moved her pen to the oval beside Lila Oates's name. The tip hovered over the ballot for a moment as Jones considered her vote. Earlier that week, she had finished listening to the audiobook version of *The Dutannuru Miracle* and was deeply moved by the story of the war-torn nation's resurrection.

As much as Jones admired Oates, she still longed for a candidate whose accomplishments and optimism inspired her. She had cast her first vote for JFK, but the rest had gone to the candidate she found least objectionable. At her age, she wanted and expected more out of those seeking high political office, and too often was left disappointed.

Not this time, she thought.

Barbara Jones guided the tip of her pen down to the bottom of the list of candidates and filled in the oval beside a blank line. Then she wrote in neat block letters the name of the candidate she deemed most qualified to serve as president: Ross Egan.

31

THE PRESIDENT RECLINED IN AN UPHOLSTERED LEATHER CHAIR, his feet up on an ottoman scanning the cable news channels as the pundits dissected the returns from several of the previous day's closed primaries. A briefing book lay across his lap, its pages covered with Post-It notes and scrawlings in its margins. The President's personal secretary rapped at the frame of the open door and peered into the room.

"Mr. Page is here for your two o'clock."

"Show him in," the President replied as he stood and handed her the briefing book.

A moment later, while the President was pulling a bottle of water from a minifrige, his secretary returned with Page in tow.

"Mr. President," Page said warmly as he entered the room.

"Can I get you something to drink?" the President asked.

"Depends. Got anything stronger?" Page wore a sly smile.

The President motioned for Page to close the door as he traded the water bottle for a couple of cold beers. Like college boys, they twisted off the bottle tops and flipped them into the corner wastebasket.

"Good for two," Page said.

"Downtown."

They tapped the bottles in a toast and the President motioned for Page to take a seat on the sofa.

"In a word," Page began, "the Republicans are screwed. There's just under six hundred delegates left to be divvied up and even with a clean sweep of the table, not one of them can crack a thousand, much less reach what they need to clinch the nomination."

"Oates and Neuske looking to broker a deal?"

"Hell yes, but the rest are looking to play kingmaker. To pull off the nomination, someone has to promise the moon to at least three of his or her rivals. I think this will run into June before a deal is cut. And if one of the frontrunners stumbles, the rest of the pack is right on their heels."

"How's the media treating it?" the President asked.

"Our analysts are making the rounds, opining that the confusion is symptomatic of Republican dysfunction. Most are taking our spin on it. Best part, this chaos on the Republican side has made you look more presidential as you go about your duties above the fray. And since we're not running any ads, there's no voter fatigue."

"The best campaign investment I ever made."

"Perhaps," Page said, "but how would you like to go one better?"

The President studied his campaign manager curiously.

"How so?"

Page pulled an iPad from his briefcase, tapped the glass screen a few times and held it up for the President to see. The grainy clip apparently shot from a cell phone camera showed a capacity crowd in an auditorium chanting a name over and over.

"What am I watching?" the President asked.

"A book tour event. The figure standing on stage leading the crowd is Xavier Mensah. The audio is a bit rough, but the audience is chanting for Ross Egan to run for president."

"It's a stunt," the President said dismissively.

"From what I hear, it was totally spontaneous. A college student who had read their book practically begged Egan to do here what he and Mensah did in Dutannuru."

"But it won't work here anymore. We're past that."

"Maybe, but I think we can still use this expression of yearning on the right to our advantage. Polling of you against a nameless Republican has you behind by double digits. That'll tighten up once your opponent has a name and we can go after him. You won your first term with fifty-three percent of the vote, and that was at the *height* of your personal popularity. If the election were held today, you would be lucky to hit the high forties."

"You got a lot of faith in me."

"You don't pay me to lie to you—you pay me to win. A two-man race is won by taking a majority of the voters, but you can take a three-man race with a plurality."

"Egan didn't strike me as political," the President opined. "You think you can get him to come out as an independent this late in the game?"

"He's *not* political," Page concurred. "He's a patriot. Egan has tremendous name recognition right now, thanks in no small part to the Nobel Prize and *Time* naming him and Mensah their *Men of the Year. The Dutannuru Miracle* is still a top five bestseller and their lecture tour is drawing sellout crowds at college campuses across the country. You may have lost some of the independents who voted for you last time, but the center-right voters are not wild about any of the choices they're being offered."

"You sure that's not just us?"

"I can't take all the credit for the lack of a GOP nominee. Everybody in the race has some political baggage, but Egan is a fresh face. An idealist. An *outsider*. Your core voters are solidly behind you, but the rest are up for grabs. If Egan runs, I bet he'd take a majority of the grassroots conservatives and split the right with the GOP nominee. Instead of losing by ten percent in a two-horse race, you could win by fifteen in a three-horse race. And this is with no change in the number of votes we expect to cast for you."

"Interesting," the President said. "The trick, of course, is convincing him to run."

"The trick is convincing the kind of people who can bankroll an independent presidential campaign that Egan has a shot at winning. Those are the folks who'll get him in the game."

32

"WE ARE BACK FOR THE THIRD AND FINAL HOUR OF OUR DAILY excursion into boisterous and brilliant broadcasting with me, your humble host, the gregarious Garr Denby. Now, I don't often have guests on this program as the only opinions that truly matter here are my own, but from time to time I violate this self-imposed programming rule when it suits my purposes. Such is the power of the host.

"My guest today once again is Ross Egan, one of the architects of the Dutannuru Miracle and co-author of a book by the same name, Nobel Peace Prize winner and recipient of more accolades over the past year that you can shake a stick at. Welcome, Ross."

"Glad to be here," Egan said warmly. "And thanks for having me as a guest for a second time this year. That must be some kind of record."

"Indeed, and one that you can add to your growing list of honors."

"Not bad for a Yooper, eh."

"Not bad at all. And for you folks on the east and Left coasts, a Yooper is someone who lives in the U.P., which is shorthand for Michigan's Upper Peninsula. I know this because I have seen *Escanaba In Da Moonlight*."

"You saw it, but I lived it," Egan said with a laugh.

"Now, Ross, the reason I asked you here today is to discuss speculation swirling around the blogosphere and among columnists in the mainstream media that you intend to make a run for the presidency as an independent."

"While I am an independent, I have no intention of running for president."

"A handful of websites cropped up recently that are actively promoting your candidacy—"

"They're not mine," Egan interjected. "This book tour I'm on is hectic enough. I can't imagine what I'd have to endure to run for president."

"As a conservative, think of a media colonoscopy without the benefit of anesthesia."

"I've never run for anything and have no desire to be president. What I am very much looking forward to is returning to a quiet life in northern Michigan this summer."

"The surprising thing about these sites is that their traffic is very heavy, indicating a great deal of interest in you as a candidate. Some are even collecting names for petitions, both to encourage you to run and to use as a basis for placing your name on the ballot in every state."

"Again, I have nothing to do with these sites and I am not running for president. Honestly, though, I can't complain too loudly. Our book sales are up and we're back at number one."

"A second rumor has the GOP putting feelers out to you as a possible running mate for whoever wins the nomination."

"I hadn't heard that one," Egan laughed. "How can I be on their ticket if I'm not even a member of the party? And if recent history is any indication, the party elite don't particularly like folksy candidates who hail from the heartland."

"The wrong pedigree to join the Washington ruling class," Denby offered.

"An engineering degree from Michigan Tech isn't exactly a diploma from the Kennedy School of Government."

"Yeah, *your* education proves that you can actually do something productive, something that's of real benefit to people," Denby said.

"I think this whole thing got started when an enthusiastic young lady down in Texas asked me to run for president," Egan explained.

"I believe that's sound bite number three," Denby said to the broadcast engineer.

"*My question is directed at you, Mr. Egan,*" a woman's voice said, her voice slightly muddy due to the poor quality of the recording. "*Will you please run for President of the United States?"*

"That's the one," Egan agreed.

"It has been watched over one *million* times. Also, your name has appeared in several recent polls."

"Oh, God," Egan groaned. "How bad is it?"

"You actually fared quite well. A Quinnipiac University poll shows your name recognition among voters is very high, especially among young voters."

"Probably all those tour stops on college campuses."

"Might be. Along with high recognition, these folks have a strong positive opinion of you."

"I'll try not to let it go to my head."

"This is where the fun begins," Denby continued. "These hypothetical match-ups are like playing fantasy football—entertaining but utterly meaningless. All the polls show the President trailing in head-to-head match-ups against all six of the GOP candidates, and trailing further against a generic conservative. That tells me that the American electorate learned their lesson and won't repeat the same mistake twice."

"All the more reason for me not to run. The voters have plenty of choices already."

"Ross, your name has surfaced in the latest polls, and you are running very strong among conservatives and independents. Your numbers are actually better than any of the GOP candidates among those voters, but the real surprise comes among traditional Democratic voting blocs. While black Americans are still solidly behind the President, they have a very positive view of you. In a head-to-head race against the President, your draw in this group is in the mid-twenties, which is better than Governor Oates's, who is regularly savaged by the civil rights crowd as a sellout."

"Garr, this is a classic case of the grass being greener on the other side. The President was the new guy four years ago, and now he's suffering from a case of familiarity breeding contempt."

"Oh, I had contempt for the President long before he got elected, and what many of his voters are suffering from is an acute case of buyers' remorse."

"Exactly right. The voters are looking at what they got and wondering if they can do better this time around. I'm a fresh face with no political baggage, and I'm linked to something that everyone across the political spectrum agrees was a good thing. Who in their right mind can argue that a war between Safo and Dutannuru would have been better than peace?"

"The arms dealers selling weapons to Cudjoe," Denby replied, "but they don't vote. And no one can say the people of Dutannuru are worse off now than they were a decade ago."

"Or even a year ago in the former Safolese parts of the country. If the US economy were humming along, we wouldn't be having this discussion. Instead, the country is stuck in a stubborn recession with no apparent end in sight and that makes people consider alternatives. I'm nothing more than a political daydream. And I'll bet none of the candidates, including the President, are wasting a moment's thought on me."

"I am heartened to hear that you have no plans to mount a third-party run for president. Based on your strengths and ideological tilt, you'd siphon off more votes from the right than the left and almost assure us of four more years of utter failure."

"I think there's enough contrast between the two parties to offer the voters a decent choice in November. For me to run, as you correctly point out, would be redundant," Egan said. "Whoever wins this fall must win a majority in order to govern effectively in our current economic and political climate."

"Well said," Denby replied. "Since you are not running for president, what's next for you?"

"Mensah and I take the book tour abroad to Europe, Africa, India, Australia, New Zeeland and Japan. After a little vacation to visit with some friends in Shanghai, I return to Michigan in May to deliver the commencement address at my alma mater, Michigan Tech. Then I'll go back to work."

"In Dutannuru?"

"Naw. I've been away from home for a long time and left Dutannuru in better shape than when my wife and I arrived. I've honored her dream, and now it's time for me to find a new challenge."

"There you have it. Ross Egan is not running for President of the United States as an independent. We will be back after the break."

33

"Just initial here, here, and here," Pat McGivney said, indicating several clauses in the legal document. "And sign and date here."

Mike Unden did as instructed, numbly agreeing to portions of the contract with each stroke of the pen. With his signature, he conveyed title to the acreage of his family's farm save for a small split of land immediately surrounding the house and outbuildings.

As McGivney reviewed the closing documents, Unden stood up and walked slowly around the living room. His eyes stopped at the shadow boxes on the wall that contained the medals and campaign ribbons won by several generations of Unden men. In the center of his father's box was the Medal of Honor. His gaze shifted from the field of stars on the medal's ribbon to the triangular box that contained the flag that had draped Jacob Unden's coffin.

"Is this what you fought for?" Unden asked.

"Huh?" McGivney asked, looking up from the papers.

"Is this what my grandpa, my pa and I all risked our lives for? How is it right for the government to take away my livelihood? Hell, some of my ancestors were on this land for centuries before the white man ever set eyes on it. They ain't just taking my way of life, they're robbing me of my heritage and, maybe someday, my legacy."

"You won't get an argument from me," McGivney replied. "Some folks in Washington think that nobody who manages to eke out a good living has the right to pass more than a few pennies on to their children. They say this death tax is only for the rich, but it's killed a lot of family businesses and family farms around here. Frankly, the tiny amount of revenue they get from this tax can't possibly justify the damage it causes to families and communities."

"Sure as hell killed my future."

McGivney nodded but had little to offer as consolation. He tucked several copies of the contract in his briefcase, then folded the last copy into an envelope and handed it to Unden.

"Once you deposit that cashier's check in your account, swing by the office and we'll finalize your tax return. Then you can get on with your life."

"Yeah," Unden said with a snort. "Get on with my life."

34

"GRATZI, THAT WILL BE ALL," THE ARCHBISHOP ANNOUNCED TO bring an end to the public portion of the papal audience.

As the flicker of flashbulbs ceased, the small group of reporters covering the meeting between the Holy Father and the two most recent Nobel Peace Prize winners murmured their thanks and moved en masse toward the door. When the last of the press had departed the papal library, the pope turned to his guests.

"Gentlemen, now that the formalities are completed, let us sit so that we may talk." the Pope extended his hand toward three chairs arranged for this meeting. "Please."

The three men sat in upholstered chairs around a low circular table. Atop the table's ornate inlaid surface sat a silver tray with a pitcher of ice water and glasses. The pope served his guests then poured a glass for himself.

"Your Holiness," Egan said, "I wish to thank you again for the courtesy extended to my parents and me yesterday. Attending mass at Saint Peter's was always a dream for my mother, and to be so close to the altar for the Easter celebration and meeting you afterward was an experience of a lifetime. I think she's still walking on air."

"It was a pleasure to meet your parents," the Pope replied, "and I am delighted that they have found their visit to Rome so memorable. President Mensah, how are you enjoying your retirement from office?"

"I am relieved to be an ordinary person once again."

"I envy you. My term of office ends when my employer," the Pope pointed his finger upward, "summons me home. But the burdens of my office are very different from those of a temporal leader. To lead a nation on the verge of war with an aggressive foe—*ach*, the sleepless nights you must have endured."

"As I said, Your Holiness," Mensah replied, "I am relieved. I also take great satisfaction in knowing that my country is a better place than it was when I was first elected."

"You have both done well in that regard," the Pope agreed. "It is our duty as human beings to improve the world around us. In that light, I find your tour of Europe very interesting, especially with regard to you, Mr. Egan."

"How so?" Egan asked.

"Over the past few weeks, you both have enjoyed the hospitality of several heads of state," the Pope explained. "Many, myself included, have welcomed you with the same respect offered visitors with official standing. You have enjoyed tea with the Queen of England and met with my Buddhist counterpart, the Dalai Lama."

"I'm just riding on President Mensah's coattails," Egan demurred.

"I recognize that this treatment is, in part, a swansong for President Mensah, who is departing the political stage. But in you, I sense an ascendancy."

Egan found himself at a complete loss for words while a wide grin broke across Mensah's face.

"Please," the Pope continued, "do not let my words discomfort you. These are simply the musings of an old man who has seen much over many years. I do not know the path that God has chosen for you, but I believe you will continue to improve the world."

35

"...AND I WISH TO THANK THE DORCHESTER COUNTY SHERIFF and the State's Attorney for their thorough and deliberate review of this unfortunate and extremely tragic hunting accident," the Vice President said from the steps of the country courthouse. "Frank Crusca and I were friends for a long time—comrades in the struggle for the working men and women of this great nation. I grieve with Frank's family and will feel his loss for the rest of my life. It is in his memory that I will continue to fight the good fight on behalf of the little guy."

"Mr. Vice President," several reporters called out at the end of the formal statements.

The Vice President glanced at his watch and nodded to the leader of his security detail.

"I guess I have time for a few questions," he said, and then he pointed to one of the reporters.

"Mr. Vice President," Wendy Fry began, "with this incident officially behind you, your attention doubtlessly is returning to the campaign."

"My attention is focused doing my job," the Vice President interjected. "Working with the President to bring about meaningful change and serving the working people of this country are the best ways I know to campaign for my job. But, please, your question."

"A recent poll shows the President in a dead heat with Ross Egan in a head-to-head match-up. Care to comment?"

"On what? Egan isn't running and polls like that are useless. Who cares about a hypothetical contest between the President and a guy who hasn't run for so much as county dogcatcher? Egan ran a power plant, for Chrissake. Don't get me wrong, I have nothing but respect for him and what he did in Africa, but it simply couldn't work here in America. This poll you're citing is about as useful as one that pits the President against Mickey Mouse."

"He'd lose that race!" a bystander shouted back. "At least the mouse knows how to make jobs and money!"

"The only poll that means anything will be taken in November, but enough of this," the Vice President said with a hint of annoyance. "There will be plenty of time over the next few months to talk politics. Today is about Frank Crusca. Anybody got a *relevant* question on that subject?"

"I'VE GOT ONE," HOMER HOPPS REPLIED, WATCHING THE LIVE feed of the press conference. "Patch me through to that cub reporter's smartphone."

McColl tapped a few strokes into her keyboard and a text message window appeared on the upper left wall monitor.

"All yours, Double-H."

FRY FELT HER PHONE VIBRATE WITH AN INCOMING TEXT MESSAGE. It was from her editor. Her eyes widened as she read a tersely worded query, and her hand shot up as the Vice President called for a final question.

"I hope this question is better than your last one," the Vice President said dismissively to a ripple of laughter.

"Where are Frank Crusca's gold coins?" Fry asked.

The Vice President's eyes narrowed, his gaze boring into the young reporter.

"I have no idea what you are talking about, young lady. Who do you work for? Did you even go to journalism school?"

Fry stood her ground. "On the day before he died, Crusca withdrew approximately one hundred thousand dollars from his union's pension fund. He subsequently purchased an equivalent dollar amount of gold coins. This purchase was made from a dealer while en route to his hunting trip with you. The police report makes no mention of any gold coins among Mr. Crusca's personal effects, which leads to two questions: Why would Frank Crusca bring a hundred grand in gold coins on a hunting trip, and where are those coins now?"

36

ON AIR

"LADIES AND GENTLEMEN," DENBY SAID TO OPEN HIS RADIO show, "it is I, Garrus Maximus, the unquestioned conqueror of talk radio, and it is my solemn duty to you to explain the inexplicable and to offer sage and entertaining commentary on a broad range of issues affecting our great nation.

"This morning, like every other morning, I had a thick stack of stuff primed and I was just chomping at the bit for the start of today's program. Well, I know from personal experience that the surest way to get a laugh out of the Almighty is to tell him you got plans.

"So a few hours ago, I was in my home office doing a little show prep. I've got the TV on one of the news channels and that ignoramus who stands next in line the presidency pops up to close the book on his hunting accident. Watching this guy is like watching a car wreck—you know you shouldn't look but you just can't take your eyes off of it. So I watched and, God bless him, the Vice President did not disappoint.

"There's a poll out that pits Ross Egan against the President in this fall's election. Against our great and illustrious leader, this man, who is not even running for office, is in a statistical dead heat. To put it in football terms: it's almost halftime, the score is tied, and the visiting team isn't even in the stadium.

"Since Egan is not running this year, the poll looks four years out and pits him against the President's rock solid insurance policy against assassination, and the career politician and beltway insider gets absolutely crushed by a guy who, in the Vice President's own words, hasn't even run for dogcatcher. Whoever follows this bunch into office might want that job on their resume because there's an awful lot of progressive excrement that'll need to be cleaned up.

"Now, as flattering as this might be to some, Ross Egan shouldn't let this poll go to his head. I frankly would have been disappointed in anything less than a total blowout against the Vice President. In all honesty, I bet my niece's sock monkey would beat that gaffe-prone pinnacle of ignorance, too.

"So this young reporterette from one of the Baltimore papers asks the veep what he thinks of this poll and he just rips right into her. It's a puffball question about a meaningless poll and he takes it like a personal insult.

"The only thing thinner than the Vice President's hair is his skin. But the real reason I bring this little temper tantrum up is that it was very instructive.

"First, the Vice President made light of Ross Egan's accomplishments, stating that what was done in Dutannuru could not work in America. Mr. Vice President, I have news for you—*it already has worked in America*. And, God willing, once you and the President and the rest of their left-wing, ivory-tower elitists are tossed out and your discredited economic, political and social policies are scrapped, what made America great the first time around will do so again.

"The man's colossal ignorance never ceases to amaze me. The agenda of this administration is nothing new. It's been tried time and again and it always, I repeat *always*, fails. Conversely, the simple, elegant, universal truths articulated in our founding documents work every time they're tried.

"Here's the best way to illustrate my point. For roughly a century, the United States has been an economic superpower with the highest per capita GDP in the world. A decade ago, Dutannuru was near the bottom of the GDP list. By some measures, Dutannuru is still a third world country, but their per capita GDP has soared into the top forty percent of nations. If this trend continues, Dutannuru will be on track to overtake US per capita GDP in twenty years—faster if the President's policies of wealth redistribution and economic destruction continue.

"I'll wrap up today's monologue with a comment about gold.

Gold is a big deal these days as people look for an asset that will hold its value while the President abuses the Treasury's printing presses. The Vice President is apparently no longer satisfied with taking his bribes in cash and has moved his graft and corruption onto the gold standard. I say *apparently* because there's no hard evidence that the Vice President took a payment in gold coins from the late union boss, but his stammering, incoherent evasion of the question raised more questions than answers. To paraphrase the immortal bard: The veep 'doth protest too much, methinks.' "

37

"THE VICE PRESIDENT IS HERE, MR. PRESIDENT," THE PRESI-
DENT'S personal secretary announced.

"Show him in," the President answered flatly.

"Mr. President," the Vice President said as he entered the Oval
Office.

"Close the door behind you," the President commanded without
looking up from his briefing book.

The President then closed the book, stepped out from behind the
imposing *Resolute* desk and walked to the seating area in the center of
the room. He motioned for the Vice President to take the seat to his
left.

Both men sat for a moment in stony silence, the most powerful
man in the world glowering at his second-in-command. The Vice
President opened his mouth once, but thought better of it and said
nothing.

"I saw your press conference," the President began, straining to
keep his voice even and calm. "Just what in the devil were you thinking?"

"Mis—"

The syllable barely passed the Vice President's lips when the
President cut him off.

"The question was rhetorical, because I know full well that you
weren't thinking. The press is still largely on our side, but that little
tirade of yours against that reporter will cost us. You will apologize
for your conduct, and you will make this right."

"Of course, Mr. President."

"Good. Now the poll that she asked you about—it's ours."

"What?"

"*Our* campaign is behind the polling on Ross Egan. We are quietly encouraging the movement to draw him into the race."

"If he's polling so strongly, why would we want to run against him?"

The President shook his head, as if the situation couldn't be clearer. "The polls show what we want them to show. A three-way race with Egan splitting the right works to our advantage. The great press he's receiving is designed to fan the flames of interest in him as an alternative to the Republicans, who just haven't been able to agree on a nominee."

"A shame," the Vice President said with a smirk.

"Isn't it," the President agreed. "Egan has the appeal of a populist and there is some big money on the right in search of a new champion. He also sees himself as something of a patriot, so when he's approached with a serious appeal to serve his country in its time of need, I think he'll heed the call."

"If Egan's going to run, he better decide soon or he'll miss the boat."

"I have it on good authority that several of the foreign leaders he's met with recently have quietly probed his interest. He's warming to the idea."

"So how do we play it?"

"Officially, the American people deserve to hear all reasonable voices in the debate on the serious challenges facing our great nation. Until he announces his candidacy, we make no official comment on the hypothetical. Quietly, and with that self-effacing charm you're known for, you can express relief that we're not running against him. And that's how you should spin it when you apologize to that reporter. Telegraph a subtle hint of fear and it will swell the pressure building around Egan to run."

★

THE VICE PRESIDENT GAZED OUT AT THE PROTESTERS AMASSED in Lafayette Park as his motorcade departed from the White House. Among the banners and placards on display, he read the one raised by a man dressed in battle-worn military fatigues:

**YOUR HEALTHCARE
KILLED MY FATHER!**

**YOUR DEATH TAX
KILLED OUR FARM!**

Against the patterned desert camouflage, the Vice President espied a thick blue ribbon worn around the protester's neck. Near the man's heart hung the five-pointed star of the Medal of Honor.

38

NEARLY A THOUSAND YOUNG WOMEN AND MEN FILED INTO THE
SDC Ice Arena, their solemn entry marked by the Keweenaw Sym-
phony Orchestra's skillful rendition of *Pomp and Circumstance*. Flashbulbs twinkled from the stands surrounding the arena floor as proud
families searched for their graduates and basked in the moment.

Once all of those graduating were in place, the dignitaries for the
commencement ceremony processed onto the stage. The academic
robes worn by the faculty and administration displayed the global
depth of their scholarship, doctoral degrees earned from many of the
world's most prestigious universities.

Ross Egan ascended to the stage robed in the colors of Michigan
Technological University, the institution from which he had earned
his undergraduate and graduate degrees in engineering. He recalled in
vivid detail the pride he felt on earning his masters degree, and the joy
that his married life with Maggie would begin just two weeks later.
His was a commencement day in the fullest sense, the day that his
adult life began.

He only half listened to the university president and the other
speakers, his thoughts rushing between past, present and future. He
felt a swell of emotion for the sea of young graduates seated before
him, ready to dive into the wide world. Egan's reverie ended when he
heard the university president begin his introductory remarks for the
commencement speaker.

"...and I am proud and delighted to welcome back to Houghton a
favorite son of Michigan Tech, Ross Egan."

The graduates and the audience rose to their feet, filling the arena with thunderous applause. The President shook Egan's hand near the podium, and then returned to his seat. On cue, the front four rows of engineering graduates raised their mortarboards and tilted them toward the stage. The altered tops spelled out: **EGAN 4 PRES!**

Egan and those on stage applauded the ingenuity and choreography of the statement. As the applause ebbed, Egan adjusted the microphone to his six-foot height and opened the folio containing his prepared remarks. He considered the text for a moment, and then closed the folio and decided instead to speak from the heart.

"My God, it is good to be back home in the U.P.!"

Another surge of applause echoed inside the cavernous arena.

"And if absence makes the heart grow fonder, then my heart is sure to burst with the affection I feel for this amazing place, and for all of you who truly make this beautiful peninsula Heaven.

"My thanks to the university and to all of you for inviting me to share in this celebration of *your* accomplishments. It really does seem like yesterday that I received my last degree and set out on a journey that I could never have imagined. In the immortal words of Doctor Seuss: *Oh, the Places You Will Go!*

"My wish for you is bound in a prayer that I have struggled to live my life by—'May God grant you the serenity to accept the things you cannot change; the courage to change the things you can; and the wisdom to know the difference.' I say *struggled* because a bullheaded Irish engineer like me has trouble imagining anything I can't fix."

The audience rippled with laughter.

"Now, I am of the belief that commencement speakers should talk more about the graduates and less about themselves. This is *your* party and I am just an invited guest."

The graduates loudly cheered and applauded.

"As an occupant of the world that you are about to join as contributing adults, I do feel an obligation to provide, for the lack of better words, full disclosure. Most of you are citizens of the United States by birth. It is your good fortune to be born into a republic that believes at its core that you enjoy certain inalienable rights as a simple consequence of your existence—the two are intimately bound together. The republic exists solely to protect the environment in which each citizen is free to enjoy those liberties derived from their rights.

"The key to understanding how the United States became the greatest nation the world has ever seen, and why we are experiencing the problems that now beset us, lies in a simple truth. The United States is a nation of unique *individuals*, and our form of government functions best when it treats each and every person as a unique *individual*. It is the union of these millions of unique individuals that creates this entity called the United States. *E Pluribus Unum*—Out of Many, One.

"You are stepping into adulthood at a time when the world seems to thrive on affixing labels. You are part of the youth vote, or the male or female vote, or whatever sub-ethnic, racial, socioeconomic category some statistician can devise. Some of this labeling is about as useful as the ERA for left-handed pitchers against ambidextrous batters, on the third Tuesdays of the month, in the second game of a double header.

"There's an old joke about the difference between architects and engineers. Architects, it is said, know a little about a lot, while engineers know a lot about a little. As architects know less and less about more and more, they will eventually know nothing about everything. And as engineers know more and more about less and less, they will eventually know everything about nothing.

"The only reasonable way to categorize the people of the United States is all or nothing. We are one nation made of millions of unique individuals—any other way of looking at it dilutes what unifies us. Politically, it is a tactic known as divide and conquer.

"All of you graduates were born in the digital age and probably had computer chips in your cribs. I'm sure that each and every one of you has a cell phone that can do more than the mainframe computers that put men on the moon. Now, let me ask you a question. How many of you know about WHO IS I?"

All of the graduates raised their hands.

"Great. Grammar aside, this website poses an interesting, if not cryptic, philosophical question. WHO IS I? I guess that depends on what the heck *I* means. For me, I means *individual*. The one. *I*," Egan poked an index finger at his chest.

"We are, each and every one of us, unique and irreplaceable. Each of us is an independent entity, and the only one that has been or will ever be. Individual. Irreplaceable. Independent.

"Who Is I?" Egan thundered. "*I am!* And so is each and every one of you."

Egan beamed a conspiratorial smile at the graduates, who sat transfixed. Egan pointed at those in the front rows.

"Could you all show everyone else here your encouraging message?"

With a sense of anticipation, the graduates quickly filed out into the space between their seats and the stage and turned toward the audience. **EGAN 4 PRES**.

"I do not accept that most of the problems afflicting this country cannot be fixed. I pray for the courage and your help to change what I can. Many will debate the wisdom of this decision, but all I can say is, better late than never!"

The graduates began chanting Egan's name.

"Like many of you," Egan shouted into the din with a broad smile. "Like many of you, I'm looking for a job. Today, I formally submit my application to you, in hope that you and the other citizens of these United States will be my next employer."

Egan waited through another round of applause and chanting.

"The position I seek is my first in public service, but I know that my long career in bringing *power to the people* has prepared me well for the challenges it offers. I belong to no political party. My fellow Huskies, I'm Ross Egan and I'm running for president."

PART THREE

★★★★★★★★★★★★★★★★★★★★

39

WASHINGTON D.C.

MAY 6

"...AND WE'RE BACK TO CONTINUE OUR CONVERSATION WITH THE Vice President."

The Vice President smiled as the host of the Sunday morning issues program, Steve Zane, turned from the main camera toward him. The studio used a three-camera set up, allowing the director to switch between direct shots of the host and guest and an overall shot of them both. The Vice President had done enough interviews to understand when he was on camera, and from where.

"Now yesterday, both you and the President were commencement speakers," Zane said.

"It's that time of year," the Vice President offered. "I was at Annapolis and the President visited his alma mater, Columbia University. Commencement ceremonies are one of the more enjoyable duties of office."

"The newest entrant into a still crowded field of presidential candidates would certainly agree with you."

"I assume you're talking about Ross Egan's announcement yesterday," the Vice President offered. "It certainly helps when you're in front of a friendly audience."

"Any comment on Egan's late entry into the race?"

"The President and I welcome the competition and see a vigorous debate of the issues as healthy for democracy."

As he spoke, the Vice President noticed a crawl running across the bottom of the studio monitor:

TALKING POINT. VERBATIM STATEMENT BY PRESIDENT AND OTHER MEMBERS OF RE-ELECTION STAFF.

STATEMENT DOES NOT MATCH ACTIONS IN PREVI-
OUS CAMPAIGNS BY PRESIDENT AND VICE PRESI-
DENT.

"Historically, there has never been a successful third-party run for the presidency of the United States," Zane continued. "Given Egan's strong polling and the GOP's failure to determine a nominee, should his candidacy be treated on par with those of the traditional major party nominees?"

"Every viable candidate should be taken seriously," the Vice President replied, looking past Zane at the monitor.

LOGICAL RESPONSE.

"If you're asking about the presidential debates, that's really a matter to be decided by the campaigns and the debate sponsors," the Vice President continued. "If Egan continues to poll well nationally, I'd think he would have to be included."

LOGICAL RESPONSE.

"Your tone toward Egan seems to have softened since last month."

"A month ago, he wasn't running and I was being asked to re-spond to a poll based on a hypothetical," the Vice President replied.

"A poll that put Egan in a statistical dead heat with the Presi-dent."

POLL REFERRED TO WAS COMMISSIONED BY THE
COMMITTEE TO RE-ELECT THE PRESIDENT.

"That's a lie!" the Vice President blurted out.

"What's a lie?" Zane asked, stunned by the outburst.

"Why are you running that crawl?" the Vice President demanded, pointing at the monitor.

Zane turned around, but the crawl was no longer on the screen.

"What crawl?"

"I've been watching it on that monitor for the past few minutes—you've been hacked by WHO IS I!"

"Cut to commercial," Zane ordered.

A moment later, the red lights on the cameras dimmed.

"We are off air, Mr. Vice President," Zane said, and then he looked to the control booth. "Did they tap our broadcast feed?"

"If they have, we're not seeing it in here," the director replied.

"It appears that only that monitor was affected," Zane assured the Vice President.

"We're back in five," the director announced.

Both the Vice President and Zane straightened up through the count to air.

"I apologize for that brief interruption," Zane said to his television audience. "We were experiencing some technical difficulties here in the studio. On a related note, Mr. Vice President, the WHO IS I? website's popularity has grown tremendously since its launch at the start of the year. Do you see this development as positive or negative?"

"The site purports to provide only facts, yet if what I just saw on the monitor is any indication, it's not foolproof. I have no problem with the truth and honest reporting, but I do have a problem with the behavior of those behind this site. Laws have been broken and their anonymity does little to inspire confidence."

"So far, everything reported on WHO IS I has proved to be correct."

"That may be, but the *New York Times* and the *Washington Post* do their reporting out in the open. How can you trust the validity of a report without knowing its source? As to WHO IS I's popularity, or Egan's for that matter—both are just the latest new things. And now that Egan is in the race, it will be interesting to see how he fares against the great WHO IS I truth detector."

"What do you mean?" Zane asked.

"What I mean is, let's see how WHO IS I treats him every time he gives a speech. I think it will be kinder."

"On what do you base this suspicion?"

"Egan all but admitted yesterday that he was behind WHO IS I, which makes it a partisan site and not the objective source everyone thinks it is. And if he is behind WHO IS I, then he ought to be jailed."

40

WENDY FRY FOLLOWED THE INSTRUCTIONS OF THE RENTAL CAR'S GPS unit, trusting that the friendly voice was guiding her correctly through what, to a city girl, was *terra incognita*. She had flown into a small airport outside of Traverse City, in what she charitably thought of as a bus with wings. From there, she followed the scenic drive to the top of Michigan's Lower Peninsula, then across the Mackinac Bridge to the state's rural Upper Peninsula. Michigan acquired most of the Upper Peninsula and statehood as a result of President Andrew Jackson's negotiated settlement of the Michigan-Ohio War.

She was thankful to be navigating the stretch of winding, two-lane highway during the day. The sky was cloudless and bright blue and the green of spring was just now arriving at this latitude. As she drove, Fry caught glimpses of a glittering Lake Michigan through stands of birch and pine. Then she saw the wind turbines.

The GPS announced that she had arrived at her destination. Fry turned right off the highway onto a private road, passing a pair of stone pillars that bore the address and a name: EGAN. The road wound through a dense wood before reaching a clearing around a large log home. The round trunks that framed the walls were finished in a clear stain to emphasize the beauty of the wood and the gabled roofs were covered metal panels the color of the sky. A long covered porch wrapped the lower level of the home, its roof supported by columns fashioned from trunks that seemed to grow out of the ground. Rounded stones covered the base of the home and the soaring chimneys.

In addition to the main house, she saw several other buildings on the property, including a large barn. In the center of the circle drive in front of the house stood a flagpole with the US and Michigan flags fluttering in the breeze. Beyond the main house shimmered the placid waters of Brevort Lake.

A man dressed in hiking boots, jeans, a black turtleneck and gray fleece pullover stepped off the porch as she came to a stop in the circle drive.

"Ms. Fry, I presume," Egan said warmly as she exited the car.

"Call me Wendy," Fry replied.

She held out her hand and soon found it wrapped in his warm, calloused paw. Standing a full head taller than Fry, Egan's green eyes and disarming smile immediately struck her.

"Welcome to my home," Egan said. "Or to be precise, my parents' home."

"You live with your parents?" Fry asked, amused at the thought of a presidential candidate and Nobel Prize winner living with his mom and dad.

"When you say it like that, it sounds like I'm still single and living in the basement playing video games and leaching off my folks. I am a widower with no children and my last permanent address was in Dutannuru. And for the past eighteen months I've been on the road living out of a suitcase. For the sake of full disclosure, my father and I are renovating our old lake house for me. It should be ready by mid-summer. Until then, there's plenty of room in the main house."

Fry nodded. "My editor was a little surprised when she received your call. Why me?"

"For the interview? Frankly, it was that run-in you had with the Vice President. I felt badly because you were asking him about me and that seemed to set him off. Now that I'm not a hypothetical candidate, I thought it only fair that you get first crack at me."

"I certainly appreciate the opportunity."

"Make the most of it. And if you don't mind, my campaign pho-tographer will be shooting some pictures as well. We'll be happy to provide images for your article."

"That would be great."

Niki Adashi stepped down from the porch with a travel mug of coffee in hand and a camera and bag slung from her shoulder.

"Wendy, I'd like you to meet my photographer."

Fry's eyes widened with recognition. "You have a Pulitzer Prize winning photographer on your staff?"

"Ross is the reason I have a Pulitzer," Niki offered. "Anyway, I freelance and this opportunity sounded more interesting than the other assignments I was being offered. And with Ross, you never know when lightning might strike again. Oh, your mother has brewed a fresh pot and her amazing cinnamon coffee cake is just out of the oven."

"How 'bout I give you the nickel tour of the place and then we set up on the porch?" Egan suggested.

"Great."

Egan led the way down a gravel path toward the lake.

"So your bio says you were born and raised here," Niki said.

"I grew up in that little house up ahead. That's the original Egan homestead plus a few additions by subsequent generations. My people have been in this area about as long as Michigan has been a state. The Egan family tree is full of loggers, miners, and farmers in the early years. Some eventually set up shop in town and kids started going to college. Each generation doing a little better than the last—the way it's supposed to be."

"If the main house is any indication, your parents have done alright."

"My folks worked hard all their lives and invested well. Did you see those wind turbines on the way in?"

"Yes."

"That's their wind farm. In his retirement, my pa is the largest green power producer in the U.P."

"I guess it doesn't hurt that his son knows something about making electricity efficiently."

"Not a bit," Egan said with a proud smile.

Near the old house, Egan pointed out the homes of his relatives around the large lake—mostly aunts and uncles, and a few cousins. His generation, Egan explained, was the first to spread far and wide beyond the U.P., though most return regularly for vacations and holidays.

"If you can figure out how to earn a living up here, it's easy to have a good life," Egan explained.

Along the shore, he picked up a flat round stone and sent it skipping across the surface of the lake. It hopped several times before disappearing with a splash. Niki captured Egan in profile with the rippled impressions on the glassy water beyond.

On the porch of the main house, Egan's mother set out a tray with steaming mugs and coffee cake.

"Will your parents be joining us?" Fry asked.

"Later, if you like. Both are very private people and politics, like this, is not really their thing. My pa served a few terms as a township trustee and ma was on the school board, but that's about the limits of my family's political ambition. We're not exactly the Kennedys."

"So the big questions is, why do you want to be president?"

"I don't," Egan replied matter-of-factly.

"You don't want to be president?" Fry asked, incredulous.

"What sane person would? I have no burning desire to wield political power, nor does my ego require the attention that comes with the office. I'm not running because this is something I want to do," Egan explained, "but because I possess the knowledge and ability to do the job well, I feel that this is something I *have* to do."

"You say that as if you have no choice in the matter."

"Oh, I have a choice, but the alternative is far worse."

"What's the alternative?" Fry asked.

"Four more years of what is arguably the most destructive presidency in the history of the United States. The damage that's been done is bad, but it can be fixed. Four years from now, the job is going to be exponentially harder. As an engineer, I can see that it's far more cost effective to correct the problems now."

"So you disagree with the changes the President has instituted?"

"I do, and so do a majority of the people in this country, including many who voted for him. I was abroad when the President was elected, but I know leaders like him. Africa's chock full of them—populists who promise everything to get elected; who nationalize foreign investments; who redistribute the nation's wealth. These are thieves who line their own pockets and those of their friends while the people starve. I'm not saying that our President is a murderous SOB like Cudjoe, but their ends are similar, even if they get there by different means. The only difference between a hard tyranny and a soft tyranny is whether or not the iron fist is wrapped in velvet to soften the blow."

"Do you have a plan for America?"

"What I have is better than a plan," Egan replied. "I have the original blueprints for this country."

"You have what?"

"I'm a professional engineer," Egan explained. "The founding documents of the United States—the Declaration of Independence, the Constitution, the Federalist Papers, to name a few—are the blueprints and specifications for our republican democracy. The balance of power defined in these documents is no different than the fuel-air mixture for an engine. There's a sweet spot on the power curve where an engine performs at its peak, and the engine that drives this country is sputtering and running way out of spec."

"Despite your apparent popularity in the polls," Fry said, "you must admit your campaign is a bit quixotic."

"Great word, quixotic. And you may be right that I'm tilting at windmills like old Don Quixote, but what kind of a person stands idly by when they could have prevented a disaster?"

"Presidential campaigns are horrendously expensive and you lack major party backing. Nearly two billion dollars was spent in the last election cycle. How will you fund your presidential run?"

"A mix of self-funding and donations from private individuals."

"So you have some wealthy backers lined up?"

"No, there are no high rollers backing my campaign. I don't need them. This is not to say that I won't take their money, but their contributions will be limited to an amount that I believe every citizen can afford."

"And how much is that?"

"JUST-A-BUCK."

"One dollar?"

"One person. One vote. One buck. JUST-A-BUCK shows anyone

who wants to support me that I'm putting my money, and theirs, where my mouth is."

"Will you be taking matching funds?"

"No. My campaign will be funded solely with my money and the contributions from individual US citizens. No PAC money. No corporate money. No foreign money. No union money. And no redirected tax money."

"Earlier you said you *had* to run. Why?" Fry asked.

"The Founders never envisioned political office as a career choice. In their mind, every individual would pursue their chosen occupation and build their fortune. Only in their later years, when the next generation had taken over the business, would these wizened elders then offer the wealth of their experience in public office as repayment to the nation for the opportunity to prosper. I have enjoyed an incredible career and profited well from my work. It is with profound gratitude that I offer the wisdom of my experience in public service."

"So are you doing this to make some kind of statement?"

"Every action we take makes a statement, but implicit in your question is the belief that I have no prayer of winning the presidency," Egan said with a wry smile. "But I'm in this to win."

"IT'S ALL SET, DOUBLE H," DEB MCCOLL SAID.

Homer Hopps thumbed through the haunting bass chords of Pink Floyd's *Money* with a mischievous grin on his face.

"Then by all means, my dear, open the President's piggy bank."

McColl typed a long string of alphanumeric characters into her computer. The complex password triggered a cluster of programs nested deep within the servers of the President's re-election campaign. These particular servers handled the on-line contributions from the President's supporters. McColl's cluster immediately began monitoring the incoming stream of money and diverting a portion of the funds toward the Egan campaign.

"Thank you, Mr. President, for your most generous support of campaign finance reform," McColl said proudly.

"He has always supported the notion of spreading the wealth around," Hopps agreed. "Only fair it should start with his."

41

"LOYAL LISTENERS, I AM IN A FOUL MOOD TODAY," DENBY ANnounced to open his program. "And my mood has festered since Saturday when two of the candidates who will, in all likelihood, be on the ballot this November delivered the commencement address at their respective alma maters."

"The first was a stump speech by our dear leader to the latest crop of graduates at Columbia University. As he always does with the young skulls full of mush, the President encouraged them to aspire to careers in public service, doubtless working for the regime. Apparently, there can be no higher calling than to be a member of the ruling class. Graduates of the President's alma mater have studied under the right professors and posses the correct pedigree to succeed in telling the unwashed masses how to live their lives.

"I noticed that the President and the rest of the dignitaries were seated in rather ornate chairs, thrones really, on the stage, and it made me wonder. Back in the Thirties, the university enjoyed very cordial relations with the fascist regimes of Germany and Italy. The university president at the time, one Nicholas Murray Butler, said of Mussolini in his 1931 welcoming address to incoming freshmen, 'the assumption of power by a virtual dictator whose authority rests on a powerful and well-organized body of opinion' creates leaders 'of far greater intelligence, far stronger character and far more courage than does the system of election.'

"This was the enlightened, *progressive* opinion at the time, and it perfectly embodies the ruling class's disdain for the rest of us. Butler was also a winner of the prestigious Nobel Peace Prize.

"And seeing the President enthroned at Columbia, I recalled that relations between Columbia and Mussolini were so warm that the dictator personally donated some furniture for the *Casa Italiana* on the university's campus. I just have to wonder if they hauled out one of *Il Duce's* old chairs for the President. That would have sadly been both appropriate and ironic.

"Now, I am used to feeling a sense of vexation when it comes to the leader of the current regime, but it was the second commencement address that really, I mean *really*, set me off. And this came from a place about as far from the hallowed halls of academe, where future government parasites are bred, as one can get—northern Michigan.

"Under most circumstances, I am thrilled when a true conservative runs for elected office. As I have said many times on this program, the Republican Party and conservatism are not synonymous. Being a Republican does not make you a conservative, nor does being a conservative automatically make you a Republican.

"Ross Egan is an example of a conservative who is *not* a Republican. I have met Ross, and I have nothing but respect for the man and what he accomplished for the people of Dutannuru using core conservative principles. On any given day, I would be thrilled with his candidacy for any office, but not today, and not for the presidency of the United States.

"Don't get me wrong. I'm not saying I don't think Egan would make a good president. In fact, I think he is better qualified than anyone else running for the job. The problem is that his timing frankly sucks.

"The election is six months out and the chaos on the Republican side—thanks largely to the minions of the regime—all but assures a floor fight for the nomination and a bloodied and financially wounded candidate going into the fall campaign. Assuming the Republicans fail to unify under whomever they pick, then those dissatisfied with the nominee may look elsewhere. With the current president as the only alternative, these lukewarm Republicans would hold their noses and pull the lever for what they consider a second or third choice nominee. Egan's entry gives those conservative Republicans a tempting alternative.

"Egan now threatens to act as a wedge that splits Republican Party loyalists from conservatives, and that split could provide the opening that allows this president to sneak into a second term with a plurality of the voters behind him.

"This is why I'm against third parties, unless of course they split the left. Third parties do not win American elections. And if we need to have a third party on the right, then let it be a party made of the ruling class, centrist Republicans.

"Ross, I think the world of you, man. But jumping into the race now all but assures the President of a second term, and all but assures the rest of the country four more years of misery and an America gleefully pushed into decline."

42

"WILL YOU BE MARCHING IN THE PARADE?" THE MIDDLE-AGED woman behind the counter at the Devils Lake Dry Cleaners had asked as she handed Mike Unden his uniform.

"Not this year," Unden had replied.

"A shame. Won't be the same without you and your pa."

Not many towns in America could boast of a living Medal of Honor winner among their inhabitants. Devils Lake used to have those bragging rights, but not anymore.

Unden pealed the plastic bag off his dress uniform and laid the garment on the bed of his budget-priced hotel room. The Big-Ag corporation that had bought his acreage unfortunately had no openings for him to work what had been his land. So, for the first time in his life, Unden was idle.

Idle hands are the devil's tool, Unden recalled his mother often saying as he dressed. *That may be, but I'm not idle by choice.*

He was clean-shaven and his hair was trimmed to military regulations. Though years from his honorable discharge, Unden slipped into his dress uniform with practiced ease. Standing before the full-length mirror with his array of campaign ribbons and medals, he felt certain he could still pass inspection. Then he glanced at the box that contained his father's Medal of Honor.

In his protests outside the White House, Unden had worn the medal in honor of his father's service to his country. He never presented himself as a recipient, nor had he sought any benefit or privilege due those honored heroes. The medal simply amplified the gravity of the injustice wrought by the death tax against the estate of a hero.

The medal had assured Unden's entry into the US Naval Academy at Annapolis, allowing the son of an enlisted Marine to earn a commissioned rank. His father had told him that this was the American dream—that each new generation would build upon the previous one and do even better.

He considered for a moment the act of wearing his father's medal today. Wearing the Medal of Honor in protest outside the White House was one thing, but to don the nation's highest military award on hollowed ground troubled him.

In wearing this medal, Unden reasoned, *I mean no disrespect to those who earned it. Rather, I protest the treatment of one of their own by a government those heroes fought and bled and died to protect.*

Unden placed the award around his neck, donned his hat and studied his image in the mirror. Ramrod straight, he was the very picture of a Marine.

He left the hotel and took the metro to Arlington National Cemetery. A number of tourists took note of the stoic Marine, some fathers quietly pointed out the medal around Unden's neck to their sons. No one disturbed him, though a few aged veterans nodded with respect.

Arriving early for the Memorial Day activities, Unden made his way to a remote section of the cemetery. There, in the shade of a Lebanese cedar, he found the graves of his fallen bothers-in-arms. He spent a few moments before the marker of each of the men he knew personally from his time in uniform. Some were friends from his academy days, all frozen in a state of perpetual youth in his mind.

After paying his respects, Unden walked to the mansion at the heart of the great national cemetery. Though used for barely half a century as a private residence, the magnificent home had family links to both President George Washington and Confederate General Robert E. Lee.

Unden found a shaded spot along the colonnade with a clear view of the carved marble block marking the Tomb of the Unknowns. A solemn crowd had gathered for the morning ceremony under a clear blue sky, many there to pay respects to relatives or friends interred at

Arlington.

Just before eleven o'clock, the First Lady took her place on the memorial plaza for the ceremony, accompanied by the Secretary of Defense and his wife. On the hour, the President and the Chairman of the Joint Chiefs of Staff walked past the joint services color guard and processed in silence onto the plaza.

The two men, the civilian and military leaders of the United States, stood respectfully at attention before the simple flat stone slabs set into the plaza—the graves of the unknown soldiers. A military band played the national anthem, after which a soldier brought forth a large wreath stand and set it before the President. With the assistance of the soldier, the President hung the wreath on a stand before the tombs. The President then returned to his spot beside the chairman.

Unden's mind flashed back to his father's funeral as the honor guard fired a twenty-one-gun salute, followed by a solitary bugler playing Taps. Few dry eyes remained as the last of the mournful notes faded from the air.

"Excuse me, sir."

Unden glanced over his shoulder to find the respectful inquiry came from a plainclothes Secret Service agent.

"Yes?" Unden replied.

"I've been asked to bring you up onto the patio."

"Why?"

"The President will be passing that way."

Unden nodded and quickly followed the man behind the cordoned area onto the mansion's patio. On the plaza, the President and the chairman turned from the monument and walked up the stairs toward the mansion.

As both men reached the patio, the chairman, a four-star Marine general, stood at attention and snapped a salute at Unden. Unden returned the salute, and then accepted the President's offered hand.

"It's an honor," the President said respectfully.

"Active duty?" the chairman asked, attempting to reconcile the rank insignia on Unden's uniform with this apparent age.

"Honorably discharged, sir," Unden replied. "I only don the uniform for special occasions."

"Where are you from?" the President asked, trying to place Unden's accent.

"Minnesota, sir."

"What brings you here?"

Unden considered the question and decided that on this day, in this uniform, he would resist offering a brutally honest response.

"Just paying my respects to some old friends."

43

"THE POLLS ARE NOW CLOSED. THE BALLOTS HAVE BEEN TALLIED. And yet, ladies and gentlemen, not only has the fat lady not yet sung, she's still back in her dressing room."

Denby paused as his engineer played a song parody based on *Should I Stay or Should I Go* by The Clash. The musical comedian who created the piece replaced Joe Strummer's wailing vocals with imitations of the GOP candidates.

"Yes, my friends, the *indecision* is indeed bugging me," Denby continued. "We are now just five months from Election Day and what kind of choice are we presented? On the left, we have a progressive reformer—i.e. radical liberal—hell-bent on a second term of social and economic destruction.

"On the right, we have a conservative independent whose first run for elected office is the presidency of the United States. And somewhere in the middle, actually to the center-right, is a six-car pile-up in which no GOP candidate managed to cross the finish line. The President's strategy to inflict chaos on his Republican opposition has worked like a charm.

"Not since men named Truman and Eisenhower sought the presidency has either party headed into its respective convention without a clear frontrunner who could win the party's nomination on the first ballot. Barring some serious deal making, that's exactly what the Republicans are in for this July in Philadelphia.

"The Democrats will stage the typical four-day infomercial to try and resell the American voter on their clearly defective product. I expect the potential ratings black hole for this snoozefest will limit its coverage to the fewest prime-time minutes possible. Some bright network execs are likely trying to figure out how to package it as a half-hour sitcom.

"A truly contested convention is actually the one thing going for the Republicans this year, and for that we can thank the President. Most of today's voters weren't born when Dewey and Stevenson emerged from the smoke-filled rooms of their respective conventions. I expect that veteran newscasters are thrilled with the chance to cover a convention where some actual news might be made. The President's chaos strategy has created something that no Republican in recent memory could—a party convention worth watching.

"And of the iconic outsider on the national political stage, I can report that Ross Egan's name will officially appear on the ballot in all fifty states. Polling of a three-way contest between Egan, the President, and any of the GOP candidates projects a tight race, with the next president winning by a plurality rather than a majority. It is entirely possible we could see our next president win office with less than forty percent of the popular vote, and it is entirely possible that the results of this election will be determined in the House of Representatives.

"My friends, we are indeed living in *interesting* times."

44

EGAN SLIPPED THROUGH A SIDE DOOR AND ASCENDED THE THREE steps onto the stage in the Fox Theater's Egyptian Ballroom. The opulent space was filled to capacity with just over one thousand people cheering his arrival. Clusters of people knotted around the cash bars while servers moved among the attendees with trays of hors d'oeuvres.

"How ya doing?" Egan called out.

The attendees cheered, applauded, and whistled at the grinning candidate, who basked for a moment in the adulation before motioning for a little quiet.

"That was quite a group we had down there in the theater—musta mistook me for Jimmy Buffet or something. This is a great place you got here—a beautiful theater, and a whole lot bigger and fancier than anything up around where I'm from."

A heavyset man dressed in worn denim and work boots held up a homemade sign: BUBBAS FOR EGAN.

"I hear ya, Bubba," Egan said with a laugh. "And while I grew up north of the Mason-Dixon line, I can honestly say the only real difference between a Bubba and a Yooper is snow.

"First off, I want to thank you for coming out to hear what I have to say, and for giving me an earful of what anyone wanting a job in Washington needs to hear. That's what my Fifty-Fifty Tour is all about—visiting fifty state capitals in fifty days, starting with the fiftieth state and working my way back to the first. And if I'm in Atlanta, I'm in the homestretch with only three more of the founding states to go. Your ancestors fought in the War of Independence and that's a heritage that you have every right to be proud.

"I also want to thank you for your bucks. My campaign is only taking contributions from individual citizens, and the maximum allowed is..."

"*Just A Buck!*" the audience thundered back.

"Just A Buck. When I look at our war chest, I know that each and every dollar has a unique name attached to it, and that each was made and given value by the people of this great country. These bucks were born in boardrooms and barns, factories and farms, laboratories and loading docks. These bucks are the result of tireless ingenuity and plain old hard work—the kind of honest labor that makes a person proud and a nation wealthy.

"Our currency is famous for the motto: *In God We Trust.* Our Founders understood the role Divine Providence played in the creation of the Unites States, and inscribed that motto on the instrument that symbolizes the trust we share with each other. Far from being something evil, money symbolizes an agreement freely made between individuals, and it is that trust that gives those coins and slips of printed paper value. No government printing press can make money worth more than the paper it's printed on; it is each and every one of us that performs that bit of alchemy.

"You already heard the rest of my stump speech in the theater, so if you don't mind, I'm going to get myself a drink and something to nibble on and hear what's on your minds."

CAMP DAVID

"PETER," THE PRESIDENT SAID WARMLY, "I AM SO PLEASED YOU could come."

The Secret Service agents escorting Sturla stopped at the doorway to the sitting room, allowing the billionaire to proceed on his own. The President gave Sturla a two-handed shake and locked eyes with his most fervent supporter.

"It is always my pleasure to spend time with you and the First Lady," Sturla replied. "Thank you for inviting me to join you on your respite from campaigning."

"Can I get you a drink?"

"Some ginger ale, perhaps."

The President nodded to one of the house staff and motioned Sturla to a leather club chair as he returned to the couch. Beside him were campaign briefings on his likely opponents.

"This is a lovely retreat," Sturla said.

"D.C. is hot and full of tourists right now, so it's best to be out of town as much as humanly possible. And this week, I'll just lie low and let the Republicans muddle through their convention."

The staffer brought Sturla his drink and set a fresh gin and tonic on the coffee table in front of the President. A television built into the bookcase displayed a reporter standing outside of the convention hall in Philadelphia. The sound was muted, but behind the reporter stood a modest gathering of protesters.

"Those are ours," Sturla offered once they were alone.

"And I appreciate it," the President replied. "It's important to provide the media with the right visuals to accompany the story."

"From now until election day, the Republican candidate will face such protests wherever he or she chooses to appear. It is vitally important that they always appear as the enemy of the people—which is exactly what they are.

"Amen to that. What about Egan?" the President asked.

"That will require some finesse. We must oppose him, to be sure, but not so much that he loses his viability as a candidate. Creating an opposition third party is even more difficult than a shadow party. Egan is the parasite that will drain the strength of your most danger-ous opponent. And if, in the unlikely event that he emerges as a real threat to you, well that's what your opposition research is for."

"I've never seen anything like his campaign before. He says he won't take matching funds, which is a given these days, but we haven't pinned down how he plans to pay for his run. His tax filings show a net worth of a few million, which would barely cover a shot at a minor House seat. And he doesn't appear to be courting any of the usual deep pockets."

"I will have my people look into his finances as well. The money trail could prove useful in October."

As they spoke, the cable news network cut back to the studio feed. A picture of radio talk show host Garr Denby floated behind the anchor.

"Oh God," the President groaned. "Can you believe somebody hired that buffoon as a commentator for the convention?"

"I expect nothing less from *that* network. Their investigations into my political activities are interfering with my business. In your next term, I certainly hope something can be done about regulating both *that* network and Denby off the air."

PHILADELPHIA

"THE FIRST BALLOT IS PRO FORMA EXERCISE," DENBY OPINED from the cable news network's booth inside the convention center. "The delegates are for the most part bound to vote for a specific candidate, and the number of at-large delegates won't tip the balance in anyone's favor.

"The six candidates are holed up in suites around town with their representatives shuttling back and forth between the camps trying to broker the best deal for their guy or gal. What's happening behind the scenes is old-fashioned political horse-trading and we're left waiting for the white smoke to billow from the formerly smoke-filled rooms to signal that we have a nominee. I can only imagine the frantic action swirling around the six hopefuls."

IF ONLY THEY KNEW, MAYA RANDELL THOUGHT AS SHE CHECKED herself in a full-length mirror, listening to Denby's commentary.

"Hon, our guests are arriving," Burton announced. "And for the record, you look stunning."

"Why thank you, my dear." Maya decided she was suitably arrayed and turned to her husband. "Shall we?"

Burton offered his arm and guided his wife through the expansive country home to the entry foyer. The villa and the surrounding vast acreage belonged to friends who were summering in the Hamptons.

Outside, a convoy of nondescript SUVs with dark glass rolled up the long, tree-lined drive toward the home with no sign of any accompanying media.

45

"GOOD EVENING, TRENTON!" EGAN SHOUTED TO THE CAPACITY crowd that filled the Patriots Theater at the War Memorial. "And I thank you for braving that monsoon outside just to see me. You'd think I was Springsteen or Bon Jovi."

The audience roared its approval at the mention of the Garden State's homegrown rock legends.

"Of course, when I think of this historic city, I can't help but recall the motto: *Victory or Death*. Washington's victory here on Christmas Day in 1776 proved a turning point in the war that, until then, was going poorly for those seeking independence.

"Victory or Death—three words that distill the essence of our struggle to live free, to enjoy the fruits of our labors, and to flourish in the liberties bestowed upon us by our Creator. And this struggle didn't end with the founding of this great nation, for it can never end. One of the greatest men to ever serve as president wisely noted that freedom is never more that one generation away from extinction.

"A year and half ago, I stood on the banks of a river, in a place where freedom was just hours from extinction. And those brave men and women who pledged their lives to liberty's defense, chose as their motto those same words first uttered here: *Victory or Death*.

"For us, the struggle isn't so obvious, but it's no less real. Our enemy isn't a tyrant's army standing on the far side of the Delaware, but a gradual, progressive erosion of our freedoms under the false flag of social justice. Instead of cannons and muskets, we face a swarm of legislative and bureaucratic termites gnawing away at our liberties."

★

PHILADELPHIA

"WELL, THAT'S IT, LADIES AND GENTLEMEN," DENBY SAID, TALK-
ING directly to his audience through the camera. "Another round of
balloting has brought us no closer to a Republican nominee. The
mood in the hall is somber as the party, and the nation, are in limbo
over this impasse among the GOP leadership. If there was ever a time
for the national chair to show some *cajones* and broker a deal, it's now."

"Excuse me, Garr," Denby's co-host for the broadcast cut in. "But
there's some kind of disturbance on the convention floor.

The monitors in the broadcast booth, and the image beamed out
to millions of viewers nationwide, showed people fleeing and security
guards wading into a knotted altercation. The guards roughly pulled
combatants from the melee, digging their way to the center of the
disturbance.

"Do we have any footage of what started this fight?" Denby asked
in a voice-over.

The monitors split between the live feed from the floor and a video from a few moments earlier.

"We're looking at either the Michigan or Mississippi delegation,"
the co-host said.

One of the delegates, a middle-aged man with an ample paunch
and thinning pate, angrily scrawled something on the back of a card
stock sign. He then stood upon a chair and held up his message. A
couple of nearby delegates began yelling at the man and grabbing at
his sign. Soon others joined the fracas and the man lost his balance,
toppling into a pile of flailing bodies.

"Did you catch what the sign said?" the co-host asked.

"Not from this view," Denby replied, "but it looks like they're getting to the bottom of the scrum. I haven't seen a pile-up like this
since the closing seconds of the Rose Bowl."

The man at the center of the disturbance emerged with the aid of
some guards and delegates. His forehead was streaked with blood that
ran down his face and shirt. His sign, also splattered with blood, read:
EGAN 4 GOP/USA.

46

HARRISBURG, PENNSYLVANIA
JULY 25

"As I'm sure you're aware," the local morning show host said to open her interview with Ross Egan, "the GOP convention is going on just up the road in Philadelphia."

"I saw something about that on the news last night," Egan joked. "At first, I thought I'd tuned into a wrestling match."

"It appears that you were the cause of the altercation."

"'Cause' is a bit strong," Egan offered. "An expression of support for me..."

"As the GOP nominee."

"...yes, as the GOP nominee, triggered the unfortunate incident. I understand that the gentleman's injuries were less severe than they looked."

"Reports are that he will be back on the convention floor later today for the next vote. Since you're in the neighborhood, would you care to guess who the GOP nominee will be?"

"It really doesn't matter."

"It doesn't?" the host asked, baffled by the response.

"No, not really. My campaign isn't about who I'm running against, but what I'm running for. Mine is a campaign of ideas, not a cult of personality. The reason I'm polling as well as I am is that I am the only candidate with a clue how to fix the mess we're in and the ability to articulate it. What resonates with the people is that there's no magic to what I'm saying, just plain old good sense. Most people know the truth when they hear it, especially since they so rarely hear it in a political context."

"And you're bringing your Fifty-Fifty tour to its penultimate stop here in Harrisburg."

"Yes. I'll be speaking to another sold-out crowd at the historic Forum Auditorium. The tour has been both exhilarating and exhausting, and I've felt a real connection with the people I've met along the way. Amazingly, at some of my stops, I was the first presidential candidate to ever set foot in that state's capital. Seems crazy to me. The way I see it, my best shot of winning this election is to take my ideas to as many people as possible."

"If the polls are any indication, your strategy is working so far."

"Perhaps, but we're still in the summer months and the GOP doesn't have a candidate, so I may be benefitting from the doldrums. There's a lot of campaigning left before November."

CAMP DAVID

"ANYTHING HAPPENING?" THE FIRST LADY ASKED AS SHE ENTERed the study.

She sat beside her husband on the sofa. He was reading. The television in the corner was on with the volume low.

"Some kind of deal in the works," the President replied. "Hook has swung his support behind Vogel, and Widmer is backing Neuske."

"That doesn't get anyone the votes they need to lock up the nomination," the First Lady said, doing the math in her head.

"Quite the opposite. It puts the remaining contenders in a four-way tie. My sources say the two front-runners were playing hardball with the rest of the pack, not offering much in the way of guarantees in exchange for support. The GOP Chair brokered this deal to shift the balance of power. The price of this nomination is going to be very expensive to whoever emerges on top of the ticket."

"You must be very pleased with yourself."

"For this," the President smiled, "I most certainly am."

"Any chance the convention will fail to select a nominee?"

"Given the four left standing, it is entirely possible. But I won't get greedy. Screwing them up this long has been a real blessing to my campaign. It's made them look weak and fractious to the American people."

"While letting you, by comparison, appear presidential and above the fray," the First Lady said coyly.

The television provided a panning view of the packed convention hall. Another vote was in progress and a box with the vote totals filled the bottom of the screen. Amid the professional placards was a scattering of handmade signs that read: DRAFT EGAN!

47

"...AND SO I PROUDLY END MY FIFTY-FIFTY TOUR WHERE IT ALL began," Ross Egan said to his enthusiastic supporters, "in the state that first joined the union and made real the freest, proudest and most prosperous nation the world has ever known. In the history of the world, the United States of America is unique. And when progressives say we are behind the times, that we are not keeping up politically or socially with the nations of Europe or elsewhere, I can't help but shake my head. Since the founding of this nation, people have flocked to our shores to escape the so-called enlightenment politics of every other nation on Earth. What makes us unique among all nations is good, and it must be preserved.

"I thank you for the tremendous outpouring of support I've received since arriving in the First State. It is your passion that will carry this campaign to victory in November. There's not a thing that's wrong with our government that can't be fixed, and not a thing that's right with this country that we can't depend on.

"God bless you all! God bless the great state of Delaware, and may God continue to bless the United States of America!"

Egan paced the stage, waving to the capacity crowd that filled the six-hundred-seat auditorium. Ray Charles' heartfelt rendition of *America the Beautiful* filled the historic opera house along with the roar of a standing ovation. He gave a final wave to the audience and slipped off stage.

"That was quite a speech," Niki said as she handed Egan a cold bottle of water.

"Thanks," Egan replied, his voice slightly hoarse. "What's next?"

"Road trip. VIP lunch in Wilmington. More road trip. Then perhaps a nap before your private dinner with the Randells. We're staying with them at an estate outside Philadelphia, so no hotel tonight."

"Will you please brief me on who's who for Wilmington?"

"Certainly."

"I'm burnt to the point where I can only take information in small bites."

They exited the rear of the theater into the sweltering mid-day heat and humidity. Secret Service agents guarded a line of black SUVs. Egan smiled and nodded to the agents as he climbed into one of the trucks.

"And there is a fresh shirt and jacket in the truck," Niki said.

"Thanks. You've been incredible on this tour. I don't know where I'd be without you."

"In Dover, with a damp shirt and no pictures."

Egan laughed as he settled into his seat and, eyes closed, reclined his head back.

"A quiet dinner with friends," Egan sighed. "I cannot think of a better way to spend the evening."

PHILADELPHIA

"GARR, WHAT'S YOUR TAKE ON THE RUMORS ABOUT A DEAL?" THE network anchor asked.

"A deal has to be cut or this convention will end in utter failure and the GOP will look like a bunch of rank amateurs. After nearly four years of what is arguably the worst presidency in the history of the nation, the Republicans should be riding a wave of popular enthusiasm out of Philadelphia all the way to an Election Day landslide, but they're not. This confusion benefits only the current regime and it has to stop *today*."

"Any thoughts on who the nominee will be?"

"Each of the four camps is convinced that their guy is the top of the ticket, so I'm clearly not talking to anyone who really knows anything. If a deal has been cut, the circle of people in it is very small."

"Well, the delegates are back in the hall for this, the fourth and final day of the convention. We've had another round of speeches on policy issues and the party planks, and the usual railing against the President and his administration. But the lack of a nominee, and the coalescing of the party's hope and enthusiasm around a standard bearer, is noticeably absent."

"In all the years that I've been watching political conventions," Denby offered, "and this goes back to the Fifties with my dad explaining to me what was going on, I have never seen one like this."

"Excuse me, Garr, but the Republican Party Chairman is walking on stage to announce today's vote."

"My fellow Republicans," Brian Frakes called out from the main stage, "my fellow Republicans. After several days of intense negotiations with our six worthy contenders, any of whom I would be proud to see leading our party to victory in November, I am pleased to report that an agreement has been reached that I am certain will unify the party for the difficult campaign ahead. Candidates, if you will please join me."

Frakes turned to face the right side of the stage as the GOP candidates streamed out, waving to their supporters. He applauded the six along with the delegates, who offered a standing ovation.

"First, I am authorized by our candidates to announce that all delegates are now free to vote as they feel best represents the intentions of voters in their home districts. They are all gratified with your support following the first ballot but, standing here with me, they wish to reaffirm that all pledged and bound delegates are released.

"Second," Frakes continued. "Our candidates have united in their support for the person they feel best represents their values, the values of the Republican Party, and the values of the citizens of the United States of America. It is this individual that they as a group wholeheartedly endorse and encourage you to support with our party's nomination."

The image projected out to viewers across the country showed Frakes standing at the podium, center stage, flanked on both sides by three of the Republican candidates. Behind them, a huge LCD video wall glowed with a flowing image of the stars and stripes. The video wall then suddenly turned solid red.

"The name that I am pleased to offer for your consideration as our nominee is..." Frakes said dramatically, "the favorite son of the great state of Michigan, Ross Egan!"

"What the f..." the anchor exclaimed over an open mike before the quick thinking booth operator cut the live feed.

Egan's name filled the LCD display before a stunned arena of delegates. Frakes and the six candidates applauded the announcement. Those delegates supporting the draft Egan movement cheered and chanted his name.

"And with that," Frakes announced over the din. "I call for an immediate vote."

CAMP DAVID

"WHAT THE HELL JUST HAPPENED?" THE PRESIDENT DEMANDED.

He directed his question at Daniel Page, his campaign manager. Peter Sturla sat beside the President with a glass of iced vodka in hand.

"Can they do that?" Sturla asked. "Pick an outsider?"

"Apparently they can," Page replied. "But I'll be damned if I can figure out how Egan swung this. It's unimaginable."

"I pay you to imagine the unimaginable," the President complained.

On the television, Egan's name was officially placed into nomination by the Michigan delegation and quickly seconded. The GOP Chairman then announced a roll call vote. After a quick huddle, the spokeswoman for the Alabama delegation cast all of her state's votes for Egan.

"What does this mean?" Sturla asked.

"It means," the President replied bitterly, "that we're in a *two* horse race."

48

"THIS IS UNBELIEVABLE," THE NETWORK ANCHOR GUSHED. "THE Grand Old Party has just drafted an independent candidate for its presidential nomination. Is this a sign that this party is cracking up?"

"Quite the contrary," Denby said smugly. "Based on everything that Ross Egan stands for, his rock-ribbed conservatism on economic, political and social issues, I'd say it's a sign that party has finally come to its senses about what it truly wants to be. And according to the WHO IS I crawl running across the bottom of our broadcast feed, Egan officially joined the GOP an hour ago. Being from northern Michigan, I guess Ross Egan is the candidate who came in from the cold."

"But where is he?"

"Somewhere nearby," Denby replied. "The Chairman wouldn't make an announcement like that unless it was a done deal."

"What kind of deal would Egan have to cut in order to skip the primaries and still win the nomination?"

"If you are implying that the Republican primaries were a sham and that the fix for Egan's nomination was in from the start, then you have to believe that some vast right-wing conspiracy is at work."

"But how can rank-and-file Republicans go along with this?"

"Republicans are just like Democrats—they like to win," Denby explained. "Egan's ideology fits well with the conservative core of the party and, frankly, a majority of Americans."

"But Egan is behind in the polls."

"The latest polls showed him slightly ahead of any of the Republican candidates—sorry, make that the *former* Republican candidates—

and closing on the President. He was behind because he split the right in a three-way race. If the right moves solidly behind Egan, that split disappears and the President wakes up tomorrow with a double-digit deficit to try to close by November. I don't think rank-and-file Republicans will have *any* problem with that kind of convention bounce."

"The deal Egan must have cut to seize the nomination—is he bought and paid for?"

"Agreements were made, no doubt, but don't think for a second that he sold his soul to be president. That's the secret behind Egan—he *really* doesn't want the job, not like typical politicians who either want it to be loved or are driven to create utopia."

"Then why is he running?"

"Because the country is broke and he can fix it. The guy is an engineer and that's the way he thinks. It's the complete antithesis of what we find in most politicians—certainly in the way he views power. As for the rest of the candidates, look for some to show up in key posts in the administration should Egan win the White House. Those that remain in the House or Senate would rise into leadership positions, depending on the length of Egan's coattails."

"So no one ends up a loser in this deal?"

Denby smiled. "No one but the President."

EGAN SAT IN THE GREEN ROOM BACKSTAGE NURSING A CAN OF Diet Coke as he watched the vote. In addition to his security detail just outside the room, Maya and Burton Randell and Niki Adashi accompanied him. The rest of his senior campaign staff was holed up elsewhere to facilitate his clandestine arrival at the convention center.

Egan's cell phone purred softly.

"Yeah, Dad."

"Is this for real?"

"Is what for real?" Egan replied innocently.

"Don't be a smart aleck."

"Yeah, Dad, I am about to become the Republican nominee for

president."

"No way something like this just happens. How did you and the Randells pull this off?"

"I can't talk about it now, Dad, but I'll fill you and Mom in when I get home this weekend. And this *stays* in the family."

"Damn," Egan's father said proudly. "You got a real good shot now."

"I like my odds. Give my love to Mom."

Egan rang off just as the Chairman called for Nevada to cast its votes.

"Mr. Chairman, the great state of Nevada defers its place in the roll call vote in favor of the great state of Michigan."

"This is it," Maya gushed.

"Mr. Chairman, the great state of Michigan wishes to thank the great state of Nevada for its deference in allowing us to cast the deciding ballots in selecting our party's nominee and the next President of the United States of America. It is the honor and privilege of the Great Lake State to cast all of our votes for our favorite son, Ross Egan!"

The convention hall exploded in cheers as the on-screen tally for Egan showed him officially clinching the nomination. The GOP Chairman allowed the enthusiastic outpouring to continue for several minutes before calling for order and a resumption of the voting. In the end, a smattering of delegates from the home states of the six GOP primary candidates had cast their votes for their local favorites, but the rest went for Egan.

The delegates chanted Egan's name in a rhythmic two-syllable cadence. As Wyoming cast the final votes of the convention, the auditorium again exploded with applause. Then the hall darkened and a brief film on the life of Ross Egan began to play on the video wall. Images of Egan interspersed with anecdotes from family and friends appeared in a documentary style, all seamlessly woven together by the dulcet voice of a renowned actress. Ironically, both the filmmaker and the narrator might have rethought their participation in the project had they known it would be used to promote the Republican nominee instead of an independent candidate.

The beautifully shot film ended with a montage of images of Africa and America accompanied by a recording of Egan's speech on the eve of the war that wasn't. As the final image faded and the slowly flowing flag returned, the stage lights came back up.

"My fellow Republicans!" Frakes shouted into the microphone. "It is my great pleasure to introduce the next President of the United States of America, Ross Egan!"

Egan strode onto the stage to the opening chords of Copland's *Fanfare for the Common Man* and waved to the crowd. He warmly greeted each of the primary candidates and the party chairman before approaching the podium.

"Mr. Chairman, fellow candidates, this convention, and my fellow citizens of this great nation: I apologize for being a bit late to the party..." Egan said, adding a pregnant pause for emphasis. "But how could I decline the gracious invitation of Chairman Frakes to join an organization that my own state claims as its birthplace. I thank you all for such a fine welcome and I humbly accept your nomination for the presidency of the United States."

Egan's acceptance was met with a standing ovation from the delegates.

"Again, I thank you for your affectionate embrace of my candidacy. And to that end, we have one additional piece of business before the conclusion of this convention—the selection of the next Vice President of the United States. On this stage, we are blessed with an outstanding group of individuals. All, as you learned in the primaries, are more than qualified to serve as president, which is the single most important characteristic required in a vice president.

"But it is my sincere honor to recommend to you Florida Governor Lila Oates as the next Vice President of the United States."

Another round of applause erupted from the Florida delegation and spread quickly across the convention floor. Frakes approached the podium and leaned up to the microphone.

"I second the nomination of Governor Oates for Vice President of the United States."

"Chairman Frakes," Egan continued, shouting over the applause, "as we are in the waning hours of this convention, I suggest we suspend the normal voting rules and offer Governor Oates's nomination to the floor for a simple voice vote."

"I approve the suggestion," Frakes replied. "Governor Lila Oates's name has been placed in nomination as our party's candidate for the vice presidency of the United States. All those in favor?"

"Aye!" thundered the convention delegates.

"Opposed?" Frakes called out.

The white noise of conversation could be heard from the floor, but not a single voice rang out in opposition. Oates's primary opponents swarmed her with hugs and offered their congratulations.

"The ayes have it. The nomination of Governor Lila Oates as the GOP candidate for Vice President of the United States is approved. Governor, do you accept?"

Oates smoothed her jacket and approached the podium beaming.

"Mr. Chairman, I gratefully accept my party's nomination for the office of Vice President of the United States."

Frakes shook Oates's hand and then departed the stage with the five remaining former candidates. The spotlight then narrowed on the nominees. Egan offered his hand to his running mate. Oates clasped it with both hands and locked eyes with Egan as the ovation continued. She then leaned close and kissed his cheek.

"I won't disappoint you, Ross," she vowed.

"Ditto, Lila."

Niki Adashi emerged from the wings and walked across the darkened stage carrying a molded aluminum briefcase. She stopped just beyond the circle light and offered the case to Egan with both hands. The video wall switched to display the stage just as Egan opened the case and retrieved a steel machete from the padded interior. The steel glinted in the bright lights and, on the large screen, the dark stains of dried blood were apparent.

Niki retreated from the stage as Egan returned to the podium. The audience grew quiet, realizing the significance of the weapon in Egan's hand.

"I am an engineer," Egan declared. "As a boy, I repaired cars, trucks, and just about anything else that needed fixing. Early on, my pa taught me to always use the right tool for the job."

Egan bent his elbow and slowly brought the machete up from his side.

"The machete is the ultimate outdoor survival tool. It's perfect for dealing with thick brush or any job requiring cutting, hacking, slashing, chopping—can you think of any place else I might put a tool like this to good use?"

"Washington!" the delegates thundered back.

"A year and a half ago, this machete was the right tool for dealing with tyranny. It sent a despot to his grave, liberated millions, and healed the wounds of a terrible civil war. This was the *right* tool at the *right* time.

"In this great country, we are fortunate that our Founders built a system of government based on the rule of law and not men. To change our government, we need not resort to violence. To defeat the soft tyranny eroding our liberties, the *right tools* are the *tools* of the *right*. Conservatism and the Constitution—these are the machetes that we will use to butcher the bloated beast of bureaucracy—"

The delegates roared with approval.

"—to pare back the poisonous profusion of progressivism—"

Another round of cheers and applause as the audience fell into rhythm with Egan's cadences.

"—and to decapitate the dreaded demon of democratic socialism."

CAMP DAVID

"THEY HAVE NOMINATED A MAD MAN," STURLA SAID INCREDU-lously. "How could anyone take this knife-wielding buffoon serious-ly?"

Daniel Page and the President said nothing in response to Sturla, but both men shared a look of horror at the formidable opponent they had created.

49

KEN BUTTREY PARKED THE UTILITY MAINTENANCE TRUCK A-gainst the curb in a neighborhood of expensive homes. It was near dawn and the sputtering remnants of Hurricane Ivy littered the windshield with light sprinkles. The heaviest rains had passed, leaving patches of clear sky visible through breaks in the cloud cover. The stretch of coast between Jacksonville and Hilton Head Island had born the brunt of Ivy's wrath. All that remained of the Category Three hurricane were scattered showers along the Atlantic coast.

Buttrey and his partner, Greg Taylor, put on windbreakers and quickly erected a tent over a sewer manhole. As they set up work lights, a police cruiser pulled up next to their truck and shined a light on them.

"Morning, officer," Buttrey said as the policeman stepped out of the car and headed toward them.

"Can I see some ID?"

Buttrey and Taylor handed the officer the photo IDs that were hung around their necks. The officer nodded and returned to his car.

"If Double-H doesn't vouch for us," Taylor said softly, "we are up shit creek without a paddle."

"We're covered."

The officer returned a moment later and handed back their IDs.

"Your dispatch said there's a blockage?"

"Yeah," Buttrey replied. "Ivy's dumped a ton of water and it's surging through the system. We get problems in the older neighbor-hoods, where the storm sewers cross connect with the sanitary. Roots break free and tangle with other junk to block the lines. Folks get mighty steamed when raw sewage backs up into their basements."

The officer nodded knowingly. "Happened to my in-laws. Hell of a mess."

"That's why we're rodding the line."

"At least the rain has stopped. Today's supposed to be decent."

"Is the Vice President back home?" Buttrey asked.

"Yes," the officer replied. "Why do you ask?"

"We almost never get asked for our ID unless there's a VIP around."

"He's hosting a fundraiser at his place today, so everyone's on duty. Have a good one."

They waited until the cruiser turned down a side street before reopening the rear door of the truck. Taylor stepped up into the truck while Buttrey used a long metal hook to remove the manhole cover. He exposed the subterranean concrete chamber below, its lower half filled with dark, quickly moving water.

"We are all green lights on the eel and ready to launch," Taylor reported.

"Great," the disembodied voice of Homer Hopps replied from half the country away.

The eel was an eighteen-inch long submersible robot. Like its namesake, the sleek machine swam in water by articulating its flexible body, which was an advantage in the narrow confines of a sewer.

With both hands, Taylor carried the eel from the truck to the open manhole. He crouched down and gently dropped the robot into the water. It landed flat on the surface and immediately began swimming in circles, orienting itself to the space. Then it dove under and disappeared.

Buttrey unspooled a thick hose from the back of the truck and snaked it into the sewer line. They weren't going to do anything with the hose, but it maintained their cover. He then joined Taylor in the back of the truck.

Taylor was seated at a console with two small LCD screens. The right screen displayed a map of the sanitary and storm sewers in the area with the relative position of the eel. The left showed the sewer from the eel's point of view.

Swimming upstream against the current, the eel took almost ninety minutes to reach the tap in the sewer main that led to the Vice President's house. While they could have parked closer to the house, doing so would have brought them within the security perimeter established by the Secret Service and drawn unwelcome attention.

"We've reached the back flow preventer, Double-H," Buttrey reported. "The eel has latched on to the side walls of the chamber and is going to work."

The eel had slipped into a chamber about the size of a large shoebox with an inlet pipe at one end, an outlet at the other, and a cleanout pipe in the top. Storm water filled the chamber and pressed a hinged, PVC flapper over the pipe that led to the house. Closed, the flapper protected the house from a sewer overflow.

A simple hack of the county's sewer connection database revealed the make and model of the backflow preventer installed on the line from the Vice President's home. The sixteen-year-old device had passed its annual test inspection this past April.

The eel coiled itself into a flat spiral, wedging its flexible body against the closed flapper. Tiny nozzles along its belly released a pressurized spray of liquid nitrogen directly onto the surface of the flapper. Direct exposure to the extreme cold of the liquid nitrogen turned the PVC brittle.

Water that came into contact with the super-cooled liquid immediately turned to ice, but the exchange of heat went both ways. As the liquid nitrogen absorbed warmth from the surrounding water, its temperature quickly rose explosively past its boiling point. The compromised lid shattered like glass into tiny shards of plastic. The eel shook itself free of the ice and surveyed the damage.

"Would you look at that," Buttrey said. "Blew the flapper door clean off."

"Nice job," Hopps offered as he watched the video feed remotely.

"Told you it'd work, Double-H," Taylor said proudly. "And my eel came through the blast in one piece. I'm sending it downstream to the junction."

50

"Yes, Devon, I watched parts of the Republican conven-tion," the Vice President admitted to the host of the Sunday morning political talk show. "Like many Americans, I watched it with the same morbid curiosity that causes me to stop channel-surfing on some of those reality shows."

"Polling coming out of the convention has Egan up *eighteen points* on the President," Devon Lundford offered in his precise Ivy League diction.

"Eighteen points up in July can easily be eighteen points down at the end of October," the Vice President countered. "Three months is an eternity in politics."

"So you and the President are not concerned about what appears to be a conservative juggernaut heading your way?"

"Conservatism is a political dead end. When the Republicans were in charge of everything, they drove the economy into the ditch. You can't hand the keys back to this bunch. We're still digging out of the hole they left us in, and that hole was a lot deeper than we antici-pated. We're making progress, to be sure, but our efforts to remake the country won't bear fruit overnight. The path we've chosen is long and slow, but it's the way to go. You don't change horses in mid-stream."

"But after four years and several stimulus programs, unemploy-ment is stuck above nine percent."

"And that's proof positive that supply-side, trickle-down eco-nomics doesn't work," the Vice President replied. "We extended the tax cuts for the rich for two more years after the Republicans retook the House and it didn't stimulate the economy one bit. They had it right back in the Eighties when they called it *voodoo economics*. The economy we inherited was the worst since the Great Depression, and it took more than a decade for our parents and grandparents to work their way out of that one. We're seeing some promising signs, but there is no quick fix for this mess."

"Do you have any thoughts on Ross Egan or his selection of Governor Oates as his running mate? If elected, she would be the first African-American woman—or the first woman for that matter—elected to such a high executive office."

"I've known Governor Oates for years, and I personally find her charming and intelligent, but her selection is nothing more than a political stunt. The Republican Party is a white males club and Oates may actually cost Egan some votes among the right wing."

"There's a certain public fascination with Egan," Lundford continued, "which seems only natural considering he is the fresh face in this election cycle."

"What I find fascinating about him is how he's paying for his campaign," the Vice President said. "We don't have a lot of fat cat Wall Street millionaires and billionaires backing our campaign. We operate off of small donations from millions of hard working Americans. Our people have reviewed the public filings of Egan and his campaign. The numbers just don't add up."

"How so?" Lundford asked.

"Egan's running this so-called JUST-A-BUCK fundraising drive. If he got just one dollar from each and every citizen, he'd collect around three hundred million dollars. Not everyone is going to give Egan a buck, so I can't see him breaking a hundred million in donations."

"Egan has stated that he intends to personally finance most of his campaign and he has declined matching funds, as have you and the President."

"But with what?" the Vice President shot back. "His tax filings show he's a millionaire, but he has nowhere near the kind of money needed to self-fund a presidential campaign. Based on his reported donations, what he can now expect from the GOP, and his personal assets—his campaign will be broke by Labor Day."

"Assuming Egan is not so naïve about the actual cost of a national political campaign," Lundford droned, "where do you think he's getting the money for his challenge?"

"Either he lied on his financial disclosures or some of his billionaire buddies are chipping in above the limit. There could even be some foreign money working its way in, but now I'm just speculating. From what we can see, the numbers just don't add up.

"As citizens, we all have to be concerned about to whom our elected officials might be indebted," Lundford opined.

"Nixon took bags of money from Howard Hughes," the Vice President offered smugly, "and who knows if Egan has his own Bebe Rebozo lurking in the shadows. It's in the public's best interest for the press to look into this shady aspect of the Egan campaign."

"As in any good crime novel," Lundford said into the camera, "JUST-A-BUCK."

★

COPPERHEAD, MONTANA

A SMILE CURLED ACROSS HOMER HOPPS'S FACE AS HE WATCHED the Vice President make insinuations against the Egan campaign.

"People who live in glass houses..." Hopps muttered to himself.

51

"LOVED YOUR APPEARANCE ON LUNFORD'S SHOW THIS MORNING," a doyen of the Washington social scene said as she air-kissed the Vice President's cheek.

"Thank you, Larissa," the Vice President replied.

"Good thing that storm finally blew over in time for your party."

"It looked a little touch and go with all the rain, but we dried out enough to get the tent up. And I have it on good authority that the rest of today will be clear and sunny."

"And hot and muggy," Larissa added, dabbing the perspiration from her forehead.

"That's why we have a bar."

The Vice President offered his arm and escorted Larissa to the nearest of three bars set beneath the expansive tent. Eighty guests were expected at the intimate fundraiser, a mix of lobbyists and social climbers there to see and be seen.

The Vice President ordered Larissa a Long Island ice tea and a Belgian beer for himself.

"So, where is your lovely wife?" Larissa asked.

"Touring what's left of our gardens with a few of the other ladies. I'm sure you can find her, but keep an eye out for wet spots. The low areas are still drying out."

"That *damn* global warming is just spinning these storms at us one after another," Larissa said with a honeyed drawl. "Good thing you and the President pushed through that cap and trade program to lower our country's carbon footprint. And not a moment too soon."

"We must do *all* we can to save the planet."

And if some of us make a few bucks off the deal, he thought, *all the better.*

★

THE EEL WRIGGLED INTO PLACE AT A JUNCTION IN THE MAIN sewer line serving the Vice President's neighborhood. It latched into a joint in the pipe just ahead of a manhole and again curled itself into a spiral, partially blocking the flow in the line.

"She's in position," Taylor announced.

"The veep's party is in full swing," Hopps reported over the computer link.

The hackers in Montana had tapped the security system in and around the Vice President's home and had a complete view of the ongoing event.

"He's got quite a nice selection of seafood, if you boys feel like dropping in," Hopps added.

"Think we'll just head into town and find a bar for us regular folk," Buttrey replied. "Maybe get some crab cakes and beer."

"You're making me hungry," Hopps said with a laugh. "It looks like most of the guests have arrived. Now is as good a time as any."

"On it, Double-H," Taylor replied.

Taylor tapped a couple strokes on the keyboard. A moment later, the coiled eel carefully released the remainder of its liquid nitrogen internally. Within the sealed body of the robot, the nitrogen absorbed heat from its surroundings and boiled into gaseous form. As a gas, the nitrogen inflated the eel's flexible skin like a balloon, choking off the flow of water in the sewer main.

Unlike the PVC flapper, the eel's skin did not turn brittle when exposed to the liquid nitrogen. Instead, it absorbed heat from the now-still water in the pipe and created an ice plug.

Deprived of a route to the treatment plant, the mixed flow of storm water and sewage backed up through the network of underground pipes throughout the neighborhood. The sewer lines in the streets quickly filled, reversing the flow back toward the houses. And at only one home did the increasing pressure in the sewer lines find relief.

★

"DEAR," THE VICE PRESIDENT'S WIFE SAID GRAVELY, "THERE IS A problem in the house requiring your immediate attention."

"If you'll excuse me," the Vice President said to his guests. "This should only take a moment."

The Vice President and his wife walked out of earshot.

"What's the problem, dear?"

"I was in the powder room off the foyer when I heard a gurgling in the fixtures. The toilet won't flush and the water in the sink won't go down. And there's a God-awful smell coming up from the basement."

The Vice President shrugged with a sigh. "I'll go take a look."

The odor hit him as soon as he went inside, faint but certainly noticeable. It was like being downwind of an outhouse. He went through the kitchen and took the servant's stair to the basement.

The stench was clearly stronger, so he was closer to the source. He switched on the lights and began looking around. He quickly discovered a stream of pungent, filthy water spilling out through the undercut of the wine cellar door.

The Vice President punched in the access code and opened the heavy wooden door. A surge of dark water flowed across the threshold, soaking his boat shoes and the cuffs of his khaki pants. Instead of the pleasantly familiar aroma of cypress and fermented wine, the Vice President smelled the stench of raw sewage.

A waterline nearly a foot off the floor marked the height of the flooding in the wine cellar before he had opened the door. Fetid water gurgled from a floor drain in the corner of the cellar. The Vice President could think of no way to make it stop.

He was ankle-deep in the floodwater when he realized that the only thing he could do was get out. But first, he went to the tasting table at the center of the room. The base of the table was a rack that held two hundred bottles of wine. He thought about the bottles closest to the floor and decided that even if the corks held, he could never bring himself to drink that wine.

The top of the table was a slab of Red Marinace granite set on a carved wooden frame. The Vice President reached beneath the frame and felt around for the concealed release. The granite top opened like the hood of a car. Inside the frame was a hidden drawer, lined with felt and neatly filled with rows of gold coins. It would take several trips, but he would get his gold out of the flood zone.

He removed an exquisite magnum of red wine from a decorative wooden box and replaced it with coins. Testing the weight, he found the gold considerably heavier than the bottle. He lightened the load slightly to avoid breaking the box and headed upstairs.

As he crossed the threshold of the wine cellar cradling his load, the Vice President slipped on a patch of solids that had collected there when the door was closed. As he fought to regain his balance, both feet slipped out from under him and he toppled forward.

Instinctively, he dropped the box and shot his hands forward to arrest the fall. The heavy-laden box fell straight to the tiled floor and shot a plume of displaced water upward into the Vice President's torso and face. Blinded by sewage, he painfully struck the floor with his forearms. His chest landed squarely on top of the wooden box—it collapsed under his weight while knocking the wind out of him.

It took a moment for the Vice President to catch his breath. He pulled himself up on his knees, grabbed a fistful of coins from the broken box, and carefully arranged them in the crook of his arm. He repeated the operation until he had recovered all of the coins.

COPPERHEAD, MONTANA

HOMER HOPPS AND SEVERAL OF HIS ASSOCIATES WATCHED THE live feed streaming to them from the security camera in the Vice President's basement. They all shared a look of dumbstruck amazement.

"Ladies and gentlemen," Hopps announced, "that man exists one heartbeat away from assuming the duties of the presidency of the United States of America. And yet there he is, in a pool of filth and human waste, grubbing around for the wages of his corrupt political life. It is both tragic and justly poetic."

52

"FAITHFUL LISTENERS ACROSS THE FRUITED PLAINS," DENBY boomed into the microphone, "it is great to be back with you again on this Monday for another excursion into broadcasting brilliance. You already know the program particulars and there is so much to talk about today that I will get straight to it with three simple words: *Shock and awe.*

"I am still shocked and awed by what happened last Thursday on the closing day of the GOP convention. As most of you know, I was there providing color commentary and brilliant insights as only *I* can. The drafting of Ross Egan is perhaps the boldest strategic move I have ever seen a political party make. It is also, by far, the greatest gamble.

"If your aim is to demonstrate to the voting public that your party understands the gravity of the problems that beset our nation and that you are willing to bypass the status quo, then the selection of Ross Egan marks a shift in the Republican Party that we haven't seen since the 1980 nomination of Ronald Reagan.

"As most of you know, I am against third parties because I believe a president should have the support of the majority of voters and not a simple plurality. I was particularly against the independent candidacy of Ross Egan—not on ideological grounds, because I have the utmost respect for him in that regard—but because it promised to split conservatives in a way that would nearly assure the President's re-election.

"Egan's change from independent to Republican and his selection as the GOP nominee heals that fissure and unites party loyalists and independent conservatives into the most potent challenge we've seen to progressivism in a generation. I assure you, the White House has taken notice and many there are still on a twenty-four hour suicide watch.

"Polls this morning show the President down by nineteen points against Ross Egan. Delving deep into the numbers reveals the potential for an electoral landslide the likes of which this country has never experienced. The pounding the Democrats took in the midterms may end up looking like a love tap if the GOP can increase its majority in the House and retake the Senate. The stars and planets are aligning for what promises to be the fulfilment of our conservative ascendency.

"Not to be overlooked is the second big story of national import. I refer you all to the number one video on YouTube, in which our illustrious Vice President pans for gold in the basement of his Chevy Chase mansion. We've linked to it on our website.

"The Vice President is shown in the clip wading through what in elitist circles might be described as *effluvia* to retrieve something from his wine cellar. Nice to know this hero of the workingman has a well-stocked cellar, judging by the quantity of bottles visible through the open door. The highlight of the clip comes when this paragon of political virtue slips on his way out and lands in the muck.

"The quality of the video is quite good, so kudos to the veep for not skimping on his security cameras. Enhanced stills from the video clearly show what Vice President Orpheus descended into the sewage to rescue from his wine cellar, and I can assure you it wasn't a prize bottle of vintage Bordeaux.

"Instead, I ask you to recall that tragic hunting accident involving the Vice President earlier this year. In the aftermath, a question arose about some missing gold coins. The late union boss Frank Crusca reportedly used union pension funds to purchase a hundred grand in gold coins while en route to his ill-fated hunting trip with the Vice President. Those coins, described by some as either a bribe or a payoff, never surfaced among Crusca's personal effects. At least not until now."

53

"AND CHINA'S DECISION TO PARTICIPATE IN THE NEW YORK Climate Exchange has sparked greater interest around the world," the President reported. "India is quietly reconsidering its stance on the matter and may join the exchange in November."

The President was sitting in his private study on a video-conference call with Peter Sturla, who sat in the luxurious interior of his private jet somewhere over the Atlantic.

"With Europe's carbon market in shambles," Sturla said, "this development provides an opportunity to secure an even greater share of the global effort to reduce carbon."

And my investment in the bank that will soon clear all of the transactions on the US carbon exchange will pay out billions in dividends per year, the President mused.

"We will both profit handsomely," Sturla continued, almost reading the President's mind. "An appropriate reward for forcing the United States into acting not just in its own best interest, but in the best interest of the world."

"It's the price of progress."

Daniel Page rapped on the door to the study and the President waved him in.

"Good afternoon, Mr. President," Page said before turning to the video monitor. "And I believe good evening to you, Mr. Sturla."

Sturla gave a polite nod in reply.

"Your special admirer is back in the park," Page said. "I saw him on my way in."

"Special admirer?" Sturla asked, intrigued.

"A protester," the President clarified. "A guy by the name of Un-den. He's shown up at a number of events, usually with a sign blaming me for the loss of his family farm. I even shook his hand after the wreath laying at Arlington—he was in full dress uniform with the Congressional Medal of Honor."

"A war hero?" Sturla asked, as if the two words did not belong together.

"He's a decorated veteran, but the medal belonged to his father. A member of my Secret Service detail recognized this fellow Unden in Lafayette Park afterward and brought him in for questioning. They say he's not a threat, but given his military background they'll keep tabs on him just in case."

"Michael Unden, no middle initial," Page offered as if quoting the Pentagon personnel file. "He doesn't fit the standard presidential assassin profile—he doesn't have three names. Lee Harvey Oswald. John Wilkes Booth."

"Sirhan Sirhan didn't have three names," the President countered.

"He only assassinated a candidate. Mark David Chapman, on the other hand, didn't kill a president, but John Lennon's importance still proves the rule."

The muted television in the study showed the clip of the Vice President searching for gold coins in his flooded basement.

"How many names does a man need to kill a vice president?" the President groused.

"We couldn't be so lucky," Page agreed.

"The Vice President is damaged goods," Sturla said. "He is too great a political liability. You should demand his resignation from office and drop him from the ticket."

"I can't," the President replied. "He has been accused of no wrong-doing. For all I know, he's an avid coin collector."

"I doubt the Vice President's interest in gold coins is purely nu-mismatic," Sturla countered.

"The President's right," Page said. "Keeping the Vice President makes the President look bad, but dumping him makes the President look worse. It's a no-win situation that could cost us the election."

54

MIKE UNDEN FINISHED POURING THE LAST QUART OF OIL INTO his truck's engine when he heard a stern rap at the wood trim surrounding the barn door. He saw two shadowy figures backlit in the bright morning sunlight.

"Can I help you?" Unden called out.

The two men stepped into the barn. Both were dressed in dark business suits and sported earpieces with coiled tubes running down the collars of their starched white dress shirts. Both men held up wallets displaying their badges and official identification.

"Secret Service," the man closest announced. "I'm Vance and this is Young. Are you Michael Unden?"

"I am," Unden replied. "And I've already spoken with the Secret Service and the FBI. My protest is legal and I ain't a threat to anyone."

"Mr. Unden, is it your intent to take your protest to the Democratic National Convention in San Francisco?"

Unden twisted the oil cap back in place and closed the truck's hood.

"I plan to exercise my First Amendment rights in San Francisco," Unden offered as he wiped his hands with a rag. "In fact, that's where I'm heading right now, if that's all right."

"That's *exactly* what we wanted to hear, Mr. Unden."

The response caught Unden off-guard. He barely had a second to consider it when Young drew a weapon and fired.

Instead of a bang, Unden heard only the faintest whoosh of compressed air. A tiny dart bit through his jeans into the meat of his thigh. His knees almost instantly buckled and the world went black.

The two agents donned leather gloves and bound Unden's wrists and ankles with wide Velcro strips. Vance then rolled back Unden's shirt collar, felt the vertebrae along his neck for a specific spot, and affixed a dermal patch fitted with a lithium watch battery. Microthin electrodes imbedded in the patch bit into Unden's skin and completed an electrical circuit with his nervous system. The new circuit disrupted the low-voltage current that normally flowed along Unden's spine.

Unden was just regaining his senses when his body went completely limp. He tried to speak, but could not move his mouth or raise his head. It seemed the only movement of his body that he could control was blinking his eyes. Vance rolled Unden onto his back and looked him in the eye.

"Just take it easy, buddy," Vance said in a friendly tone. "You're about to make history."

Vance and Young fitted Unden with an adult diaper. They then laid him across the rear seat of his pickup. Unden's keys were dangling from the ignition.

"Keep a look out while I take care of the house," Vance said.

Young nodded and took up position in the shadows of the barn where he had a clear view of the house and road.

Vance retrieved a gym bag from his car and entered Unden's house through the unlocked back door. He found the interior was reasonably neat, but definitely a man's home. A small soft-sided suitcase stood on the kitchen floor, ready to be loaded into the truck.

It took just a few moments to locate the spot in the den where Unden and his father once handled the business of their family farm. Beside an old roll-top desk with a laptop stood a four-drawer file cabinet.

He pulled an envelope from his coat pocket and, with his gloved hand, extracted a few pages of paperwork stapled together with a receipt from an out-of-state gun shop. Vance then flipped through a stack of loose filing and randomly inserted the receipt into the pile.

While in the den, he removed his suit and changed into jeans and a work shirt similar to those worn by Unden. He completed the outfit with a pair of distressed boots and a ball cap with the motto *Semper Fi* stitched across the crown. From a distance, Vance could now pass for Unden.

He stuffed his dress clothes and Unden's laptop into the bag, checked that the house was locked, and left through the back door with Unden's suitcase in hand. He glanced at his wristwatch—less than five minutes had elapsed since their arrival.

"Time to move out," Vance announced.

55

"My friends," Denby spoke clearly into the studio micro-phone, "*never* has the distinction between the two major political parties in this country been clearer than what they've shown us in Philadelphia and San Francisco.

"For starters, we have the choice of site for the respective party conventions. The GOP chose Philadelphia—the place where both our Declaration of Independence and Constitution were written, providing the intellectual framework for what made this nation great. The roots of conservatism can be found in Philadelphia because it is there that the ideals laid out in these precious founding documents, the original intent that we strive to conserve, were made manifest.

"The Democrats chose to celebrate the most radical left-wing administration in the history of the United States in one of the most *leftist* communities on the *left* coast. There are a plethora of wonderful things that the city of San Francisco can be proud of, but sane political thought isn't one of them. And in stark contrast to what the Founders accomplished in Philadelphia, we have the Ninth *Circus* Court of Appeals in San Francisco. This is the single most overturned appellate court in the country, and you need look no further than their many constitutionally flawed decisions to see why.

"Take their decision to strike down the Stolen Valor Act, which made it a crime to falsely claim winning a military medal. The case came up because some sleazebag lied about having won our nation's highest military award: the Medal of Honor. This guy argued, and the Ninth Circuit agreed, his right to lie about winning this medal was protected under the First Amendment. Lying, the centerpiece of progressivism as they cannot be truthful about their objectives, is protected speech under the First Amendment. I can't wait for the ruling that strikes down perjury or protects false declarations on a tax return.

"Over the past twenty years, an average of three out of four Ninth Circuit decisions reaching the Supreme Court are overturned! Think about what that atrocious record means to the rule of law when a federal court is struck down on constitutional grounds with such great regularity. Now, this isn't purely a case of activist judges running amok. The Ninth Circuit now covers more people and sees a greater volume of cases than any other circuit court in the country. To deal with their immense caseload, the court utilizes procedures that cannot guarantee a judgment rendered by a majority of the jurists. We've seen the result of these *en banc* rulings in a number of the wackier decisions out of this court. There is an effort underway to split the Ninth Circuit in Congress and I whole-heartedly support the move.

"So, the GOP stages its convention is the city where the Constitution was born, and the DNC parties hardy in a city where a federal appellate court seems hell-bent on rewriting that precious document.

"The greatest difference between the two parties in this election cycle has to be energy. The GOP convention was electrifying and, for the first time in half a century, newsworthy. The Dems, on the other hand, are putting on such a snoozefest that the ratings for the networks carrying this boring infomercial have flatlined. There are community access shows pulling in more viewers than the DNC convention. Nothing is happening. They have nothing positive to promote and under their leadership the country is clearly worse off than it was four years ago.

"I am truly thankful that my deal to provide political color commentary was only for the GOP convention. Watching the Dems' convention is cruel and unusual punishment—far worse than waterboarding or any other coercive technique used on terrorists. And I don't think it will get any better once the President shows up on Thursday to accept the nomination."

56

"RIGHT ON SCHEDULE," VANCE SAID.

From a suite in a downtown hotel, he gazed out a window through a pair of binoculars. Surgical gloves covered Vance's hands.

A motorcade rolled up to the main entrance of the Moscone Center. The Secret Service detail protecting the President and Vice President were augmented by California State troopers and uniformed members of the San Francisco Police Department. Demonstrators, both for and against the current administration, were present in large numbers and kept a safe distance apart.

Both sides grew more animated with the arrival of the motorcade. The rope line between the curb and the main entrance teemed with well-wishers hoping to share a fleeting moment with the most powerful leaders in the free world.

Though unintelligible at this distance, the pulse of the crowd's chanting clearly grew in volume and intensity. Both sides wanted to be heard by the President.

The shades to a second window overlooking the convention center were lowered to just a few inches above the sill, the window beyond opened to the same height. Young sat behind a circular table, staring through a telescopic sight down the barrel of an FN SPR A5M. The buttstock of the sniper rifle was pressed against his right shoulder with the far end of the stock perched atop a bipod.

Through the sight, Young enjoyed a clear view of the curb and the rope line. The motorcade slowed to a stop and the President's security detail were the first out. The friendly crowd cheered the President's arrival, chanting loudly for a second four-year term.

The Vice President emerged from the second armored SUV in the line, waving to supporters as he began walking toward the rope line.

Young scanned the open doors of the motorcade, searching for the President amid the dark-suited men and women. The security detail was on full alert, knowing this moment was among the most difficult in which to protect the President.

The President stepped out of the fourth SUV, his blazer open and ruffling slightly in the breeze. Cool. Calm. Confident. He raised both arms up and flashed his trademark smile to the roaring approval of the crowd. In working an audience, the President rarely disappointed.

Young pulled the trigger and sent a single .308 round spiraling through the narrow opening toward his target. The tinted insulated glass muffled the report of his shot and obscured quick detection of his position from counter-snipers atop adjacent buildings. He expertly chambered a second round and fired.

57

THE PRESIDENT FELT A SHARP TUG ON HIS LEFT ARM, JUST BELOW the shoulder. A moment later came searing pain.

A woman shaking the President's hand screamed as the Secret Service agent standing immediately behind him lurched back and dropped to the pavement. Blood flowed freely from a gaping wound in the man's chest.

For the President, the next few seconds were a blur of dark suited figures swarming around like a tsunami that swept him away. His feet left the ground and he only came to a stop when he landed prone on the rear seat of the armored SUV with Agent Laski sprawled on top of him.

"Templar is secure!" Laski shouted into his throat mike as the SUV door slammed closed behind him.

The cheering outside the SUV gave way to shouting and screaming. More car doors slammed and the leader of the President's detail barked orders for the motorcade to depart. As the motorcade fled the convention center, Agent Laski pushed himself up and onto the rear-facing seat and moved to assist the President up. Then he saw the blood on his hand and the wound to the President's arm.

"Templar is wounded," Laski announced. "I Repeat, Templar *is* wounded."

The President tried to push himself off the rear seat but found his left arm would not respond.

"Easy, sir," Laski cautioned, helping the President into an upright position. "Are you alright?"

"My arm hurts like hell, but that's all."

"We're just a few minutes out from San Francisco General. The ER is standing by."

"Tapper? How's Tapper?" the President asked, his arm throbbing.

"Agent Tapper took a round to the chest. He's in the vehicle behind..."

Laski paused, his eyes narrowing as he listened to an incoming report.

"Understood," Laski replied. "Sir, I regret to inform you that in addition to Agent Tapper, the Vice President was also seriously injured in the attack."

58

"Two for two," Vance said as he closed the window.

Young nodded. He was, after all, a skilled professional.

Unden lay motionless on the bed, helplessly watching the two assassins. They had brought him into the hotel in a wheelchair late on the night of their arrival and left him naked in the Jacuzzi tub until this morning. He had eaten nothing in days, but his captors had fitted him with a nasogastric feeding tube to keep him nourished and hydrated.

Both men quickly moved to place Unden's languid form in the chair behind the rifle. Unden's eyes darted from Young to Vance, keenly aware of what the men had done and that he would be blamed.

Young moved Unden like a rag doll, carefully placing the paralyzed man's hands in the correct position on the weapon to leave clear fingerprints. Beads of sweat rolled off Unden's forehead and onto the gunstock. Prior to loading the weapon, Young placed each cartridge between Unden's thumb and forefinger. The same had been done with the rounds of the nine-millimeter pistol in Vance's gloved hands.

"Done," Young said as he removed Unden's hands from the rifle.

They returned Unden to the bed. Vance reached behind Unden's neck and pealed off the dermal patch. Almost immediately, Unden felt a tingling sensation spread down his spine and over his body. Vance waded up the patch and slipped it into his coat pocket.

Unden grunted softly.

Before he could recover further, Vance placed the pistol in Unden's limp right hand, pressed the barrel under his chin and fired. The shot was loud and the round blew through the top of Unden's skull. The surrounding pillow caught most of the gore and a few stray fibers of eiderdown floated around the dead man's head. Vance quickly checked himself for blood spatter and found none.

"Let's go," Vance said as he stepped away from the body.

Sirens wailed outside as Young slipped through the connecting doors between the adjacent rooms. Both men then dead-bolted the paired doors, securing the separation between rooms. Vance removed and pocketed his gloves, then exited the suite using a handkerchief to operate the door's lever handle.

The hallway was empty except for a housekeeping cart down at the far end. Young stepped out of the adjacent room, laminated convention credentials dangling from his neck, and handed Vance his matching set as they headed toward the elevators.

59

The President winced as the doctor adjusted his sling to support his wounded arm.

"That should do it, Mr. President," the doctor said. "Infection is our biggest concern with wounds like these, but I'm sure you'll be in good hands. You were very lucky."

"Yeah," the President replied. "Thank you, doctor."

The doctor jotted a few notes on the President's chart and left. Daniel Page then entered the room along with Agent Laski.

"What's happening?" the President asked. "How are our people?"

"Agent Tapper is still in surgery," Laski replied. "His condition is critical but they're optimistic he'll pull through."

"And the Vice President?"

"Sir, I regret to inform you that the Vice President was pronounced dead shortly after arrival. He was shot in the head and the damage was too severe. There was nothing the doctors could do to save him."

The President bowed his head slightly and bit his lower lip pensively.

"Thank you, Agent Laski. If you will please wait outside, I'd like to have a word with Mr. Page."

"Of course, sir."

Laski closed the door behind him, taking up position just outside the treatment room.

"Mr. President, in light of this attempt on your life, I agree with the Secret Service and suggest we cancel your appearance at the convention tonight. The nomination is yours and there's little benefit to having you appear..."

"I absolutely *must* address the convention tonight," the President countered. "This attempt on my life is the biggest news story in the world right now, and we have to be on top of it. The Vice President may do more for the campaign as a martyr than a running mate and we cannot let this opportunity go to waste."

60

FOLLOWING A GLOWING VIDEO TRIBUTE INTRODUCED BY THE First Lady, the President walked on stage to the thunderous applause of the convention delegates. He was dressed in a dark suit with an off-white linen shirt and blue tie. His jacket was unbuttoned, the left side draped over his shoulder to accommodate the arm sling. The empty left sleeve was folded and pinned to keep it from flapping as he moved.

The First Lady greeted her husband near center stage with a gentle embrace and then moved out of the light as he completed his journey to the podium. The standing ovation expressed not only support for the man and his agenda, but sincere relief at his survival.

"Thank you!" the President shouted over the din. "Thank you."

The delegates gave their leader a final cheer before settling down.

"Thank you so much for that warm welcome. Today did not turn out quite as I had expected when I got up this morning. I had planned to do many things and to meet with many of you, but sadly that was not to be. Instead, all of us were reminded of how everything can change in an instant.

"The culmination of this convention was to have been my acceptance of our party's nomination for the presidency. And I humbly do accept your kind nomination, and I will strive to be worthy of your faith and trust.

"Following that acceptance, I was to have stood on this stage with my friend, my colleague, my partner in governance for the past three and a half years," the President's voice cracked with emotion. "We were to have soared out of this hall tonight, borne aloft to our second term by your enthusiasm for all that we have changed and your high hopes for the hard work that remains. But sadly, that was not to be.

"Instead, we mourn the loss of a great man, and in his memory we dedicate ourselves to finishing what we started. We will continue to remake America into a fairer and more just nation, to achieve that shining city on a hill, to reach the promised mountaintop of justice and equality for all.

"The Vice President's murder demands justice, not vengeance. Truth, not rhetoric. The rule of law, not mob rule. And in his beloved memory, we shall not waver."

PART FOUR

★★★★★★★★★★★★★★★★★

61

"THERE IS REALLY ONLY ONE THING TO TALK ABOUT TODAY,"
Denby said calmly to open his radio show. "Yesterday, right about the
time we were wrapping up another busy broadcast day, two shots
were fired from a hotel room overlooking the Moscone Center in San
Francisco. The first grazed the President's left arm on its way into the
chest of Secret Service Special Agent Rolland Tapper. A fifteen-year
veteran of the Secret Service, Tapper sustained life-threatening
injuries and underwent eight hours of surgery to repair the damage.
The spokesperson for San Francisco General lists his condition as
critical but stable. The President's injuries were also treated at San
Francisco General and he was released yesterday afternoon. Our
prayers are with Agent Tapper and his family.

"The second shot proved far more devastating. It struck the Vice
President in the right temple and killed him. No further shots were
fired and, aside from some bruises and scrapes among those standing
in the rope line to greet the President and Vice President, there were
no other injuries reported.

"The Secret Service, FBI, and the San Francisco Police quickly
identified the single point from which both shots were fired—the
aforementioned hotel room. Inside this room, they located a weapon
matching the caliber of the rounds fired in the attack and the body of
a man who apparently died from a self-inflicted gunshot wound.

"Authorities have identified the dead man in the hotel room as
Michael Unden of Devils Lake, North Dakota. Unden is a decorated
Marine veteran. He was a trained sniper. Unden registered in the
hotel under his own name, not an alias. The Secret Service was aware

of Unden not as a threat, but as a polite protester. He has been sighted at numerous presidential appearances and has previously been questioned by both the Secret Service and the FBI. Prior to his recent protests, Unden had no history of political activism or affiliation. Unden's protest focused on two issues—the President's healthcare reforms and the death tax.

"To speculate on any of this barely one day after the assassination of the Vice President and the attempted assassination of the President would be both premature and irresponsible. The investigation will continue and the truth, in good time, will be revealed.

"While I disagree with this administration on almost everything they do and continue to hope they fail in executing their radical agenda, we all must stand united with the President in this time of national mourning. There will be ample time during the fall campaign for the ideological and political debate, but for now we are united as Americans in offering our prayers and deepest sympathies to the family of the Vice President."

62

AFTER LYING IN STATE IN THE CAPITOL ROTUNDA, THE FLAG draped casket bearing the body of the Vice President was removed by a military honor guard and carried down the west steps to a 21-gun salute. At the base of the stair, the honor guard placed the casket into a gleaming black hearse for the five-mile journey to the Washington National Cathedral.

People lined the route between the Capitol and the cathedral to pay their respects to the fallen Vice President and his family. The city was somber and quiet.

Beneath the soaring vaults of the cathedral, the Vice President's family and friends found their seats in the pews along with dignitaries and representatives from all over the world.

The funeral service combined a dignified liturgy with uplifting hymns celebrating the Vice President's earthly life and the hopeful promise of life everlasting. Then, for the first time since his brief speech at the convention just hours after the deadly attack, the President rose to speak in public—he would deliver the final eulogy.

The President ascended to the lectern with his chin slightly elevated, his demeanor stoic. His left arm still rested in a sling beneath his jacket, the empty sleeve folded and pinned in place. The President set a leather folio on the lectern and collected himself.

"Arleen, Cynthia, and Victor; members of the Vice President's family, distinguished guests, including our former presidents and first ladies; Reverend Stewart; fellow citizens:

"In his eloquent eulogy to President Kennedy, Chief Justice Earl Warren remarked: 'There are few events in our national life that unite Americans and so touch the hearts of all of us as the passing of a President of the United States. There is nothing that adds shock to our sadness as the assassination of our leader, chosen as he is to embody the ideals of our people, the faith we have in our institutions and our belief in the fatherhood of God and the brotherhood of man.'

"Today, we find ourselves similarly united in our grief over the loss of a great man. To his family, he was a devoted son, a loving husband, and a cherished father. In a long and distinguished career in public service, he was a tireless advocate for the workingman and a powerful voice for those in need.

"The Vice President and I were chosen, in Justice Warren's words, to embody the ideals of the American people and our collective faith in the institutions of our form of government. We cheerfully assumed the heavy burdens of office not out of personal ambition, but out of love for our country and our fellow citizens and a profound sense of duty.

"We can never fully comprehend the mind of the assassin who acted against our nation last week, just as we can never fully grasp the toll of his actions. But for a small distance," the President said, using his right index finger and thumb to measure the space between his heart and the gunshot wound in his arm. "There but for the grace of God.

"What we do know is that such acts of violence are bred from hatred and ignorance. They are the spawn of a fanaticism that threatens our American way of life. And in the face of such bitter evil, we will not shrink. Our struggle for justice and peace, for the dignity and equality of people, will not be deterred. To do so would be a dishonor to this great man, this martyr.

"The world is a poorer place for his loss, but we must rejoice in that we are better for having known him and console ourselves in the hope that he has found his eternal rest."

63

"AFTER A LONG WEEKEND OF GOLF AND EXHIBITION FOOTBALL," Denby said to open the show, "I am fully rested and back behind the microphone for another excursion into the IQ elevating, thought provoking, cultural phenomenon that is *The Garr Denby Show*.

"Like most Americans, I watched the funeral of the Vice President last Thursday and I continue to keep his family in my prayers. While I was never a fan of the Vice President politically, and this goes back into his inglorious days in Congress, his service and interment in Arlington were befitting of the man and his office.

"If there's a nit to pick, it started with the President's eulogy and festered over the weekend as it became the resonant talking point of the state-controlled media. The President eloquently decried the *fanaticism* that threatens our American way of life.

"Over the weekend, fanaticism expanded to 'right-wing fanaticism' and 'conservative fanaticism' as pundits attempted to link the assassin with what the Department of Homeland Security describes as right-wing extremists. You may recall the DHS memo that linked right-wing extremism to frustration with the economic downturn and the general state of the economy.

"If, as the evidence suggests, Michael Unden was the assassin, then one has to ask what drove him to this tragic end. The story starts with Jacob Unden, a war hero and winner of the Congressional Medal of Honor who was the father of the alleged assassin. The apparatchiks on the President's death panel deemed the costly treatment for Jacob's illness a poor investment of healthcare dollars and sentenced this man, who had risked his life for this country, to a nasty death. Jacob committed suicide to spare himself and his son that horror show which triggered Michael's *second* gripe with our beloved leader—the death tax.

"I don't condone murder, and the Vice President's death was clearly murder, but I don't condone robbery either. Unden lost his family farm not through mismanagement, but because his father died and the tax amounted to half the value of the land and equipment. I don't know too many farmers whose net worth isn't largely tied up in land and equipment. Farming is not a high-liquidity business.

"The Vice President's murder is a tragedy. The left's totally expected tack to make political hay from it is also a tragedy. Now that we're through the sympathy phase, the left is working overtime to link Unden to Egan by way of their shared antipathy for our country's abysmal tax code. This is no different than saying that both the President and the Nazis support nationalized healthcare, therefore the President is a Nazi. The logic behind these kinds of arguments is clearly flawed, but logic has never been the strong suit of the left.

"Not to sound crass, but the unexpected vacancy in the vice presidency has proven beneficial to the President's re-election effort. Recent polling puts him within the margin of error against Egan, and no, this is not because of a post-convention bounce.

"Over the weekend, the President moved to fill the vacancy in the order of succession by nominating New Mexico Governor Belinda Delgado for vice president. Both houses of Congress are expected to take up the Delgado confirmation in a special session this week and she could be sworn in shortly thereafter. If confirmed, the President has indicated that Delgado would be his running mate.

"Not to diminish Governor Delgado's qualifications for the job, but the political implications of her selection cannot be ignored. If confirmed, Delgado would become the first female vice president. She would join Gerald Ford as an *unelected* vice president, but she would be the first woman to stand a heartbeat away from the presidency. As a two-fer, she would also be the first Hispanic vice president.

"In nominating a Latina to fill the vice presidential vacancy, the President seeks to diffuse the impact that the election of a woman of

African descent might bring to the race. Democrats hate the idea of Republicans breaking any ethnic or gender barriers, and in fact hate the idea of anyone other than white males being conservative or Republican. The dirty little secret is that the liberals don't want their traditional ethnic base to realize that conservatives really don't care about gender or skin color. You don't have to look a certain way to be a conservative; you have to think a certain way. And to think like a conservative, you first have to *think*."

64

"PEOPLE," DANIEL PAGE ANNOUNCED TO THE GATHERING OF THE President's senior campaign staff, "Labor Day signals the start of the fall campaign and it's a full court press from now until Election Day. That gives us just nine weeks to crush Ross Egan's populist campaign and send his sorry ass back into the sticks of fly-over country where it belongs."

Dressed in gray pants and a white button-down oxford shirt, Page paced in the front of a conference room in the heart of the President's re-election campaign headquarters. Around the table sat the campaign's media strategist, communications chief, point-person for research and policy communications, chief pollster, chief foreign and domestic policy aides, chief operating officer and national finance director. Also present was Zeno Rezi, the DNC research director who managed the party's opposition research at arm's length from the campaign. And near Page sat the President.

"Let's start with money," Page began. "Where are we at, Tina?"

Tina Crenshaw peered over the glasses perched on the end of her tapered nose.

"With a month left to go in the third quarter, the campaign has raised just over six hundred fifty million this year and expended two hundred twenty million to date, leaving four hundred thirty million in cash on hand. Our numbers are a little behind four years ago, but we expect September to be a *big* month."

"Where are we down?" the President asked.

"Our Internet contributions are off as compared to this time in the previous campaign. I expect the economy is taking its toll on this type of discretionary spending. Funds contributed by union PACs representing non-government workers are also down."

"Get me the particulars on both," the President said, "and I'll see what I can do."

Crenshaw nodded and texted the President's request to her assistant. The report would be in the President's hands before he left the building.

"Has the debate schedule been nailed down yet?" the President asked.

"Yes, sir," Page replied. "There will be four presidential debates set on alternating weeks starting on the tenth. The three vice presidential debates will occur in the off-weeks in between."

"Topics and format?"

"Economics, foreign policy, and domestic policy and the environment."

"And the fourth debate?" the President asked.

"Town hall format with direct questioning by the candidates."

"Questions in advance?"

"No. The final debate was their only demand. The rest are by our rules. If need be, we can always kill it at the last minute."

The President nodded. "The public may love this WHO IS I, but I don't want these hackers interfering with the debates. I don't want video monitors anywhere that I can see them—that damn crawl is too distracting. And we have to ban cell phones from the debate venues, otherwise the audience will look like a bunch of bobble heads."

"I'll see to it. Moving on, I know we've all been preoccupied with what happened at the convention," Page continued, careful not to say "assassination," "and August was focused on getting the optics right on the Vice President's funeral, the selection of the new Vice President, and getting the bottom half of our ticket set. But the summer is over and we have a serious challenger to focus everything we have on defeating.

"First, we got blindsided by the Draft Egan move at the GOP convention. I don't know or care how that one got by us, but we cannot afford another screw up like that. The Vice President's untimely death spun in our favor, but it could just have easily finished us off.

"From here on out, it's all about Egan. Our one-time tool for splitting the right is now the enemy. Egan is the face of the right wing, the chief proponent of the kind of twisted ideology that not only destroyed our economy but also led to the brutal attack at our convention. Egan must *be* everything that is wrong with the right. What do we have on him?"

Zeno Rezi consulted the notes on his iPad. At thirty-six, the wiry son of Greek immigrants was one of the youngest people at the table but had proven himself invaluable during the President's previous campaign.

"Egan's bio sums it up pretty well. He is in his late forties, born and raised in the upper part of Michigan, which is like the North Pole with trees. He has undergrad and graduate degrees in engineering from MTU, not MIT. Transcripts are unremarkable and his thesis is unreadable unless you're a gear head. I got some people looking at it, but it's all numbers so I don't expect anything we can hang him on."

The President unconsciously shifted in his seat. His college transcripts and graduate thesis remained safely locked away for precisely this reason.

"Political experience," Rezi continued, "is nil. Egan has never run for office of any kind. He was on the committee that wrote the constitution for Dutannuru and served as an advisor to the president of that country. He was also involved in that nation's public works—utilities and infrastructure. A lot of money was spent getting power, water and such operating after the war, plenty of room for kickbacks and skimming. Rules are different over there, but I might find some graft we can nail to his door. I've got some people looking into it.

"Personally—the guy is boring as hell. Quite shy kid growing up. Dated a little, didn't knock anyone up as far as we can tell. Seems straight, but we're still digging for any *mano-a-mano* indiscretions just in case. Closeted hypocrisy always plays well with the Joe six-pack crowd.

"He's had only one serious girlfriend. He married her, went to Africa because of her, had a kid with her, and lost both in the civil war. Since then, nothing. I got my guys out looking for hookers, titty bars, adult website memberships—anything that puts his personal conduct in contrast with the high moral standards of the right."

Saul Alinsky's fourth rule of power politics, the President silently recalled. *Make the enemy live up to their own book of rules.*

"Egan has spent most of his adult life in Africa," Rezi said, "which makes fleshing out his backstory a little challenging. That and he's a bit of a hero over there so few folks are speaking ill of him."

"Do you have anything we can use?" Page asked pointedly.

"Egan is a global warming skeptic," Rezi replied. "The guy is supposed to be this bright engineer and his thesis was on power generation, yet he doubts the science behind global warming."

Page sighed. "Global warming is out of vogue. The correct term is climate change, and doubting it has spread from conservative Neanderthals to the general public."

"Yeah, but the guy claims to be all for improved efficiency in energy production, storage and use. So how can a guy who is pro-energy efficiency be showing up at his campaign appearances in a full-blown HumVee? And I'm not talking about the softened commercial version, but the original, military grade truck. That pig gets like five miles per gallon, possibly the most fuel-*inefficient* vehicle on the road.

"Second, he's in partnership with his parents on a wind farm on the coast of Lake Michigan. We've gone through their filings and it doesn't seem to add up."

"What doesn't add up?" the President asked.

"Wind farms pump their power back into the grid, selling it to the local utility. We know the rates the utilities pay for green power, we know how much income the wind farm reported on its tax returns, and we know how many turbines this wind farm has operating. I've got some engineers working on it, but at first glance its power output doesn't seem possible. Egan may be defrauding the utility."

"Get me something I can work with," Page said.

The President nodded. "Let's hold this close to the vest until we find the best time to go public."

"Understood," Rezi said. "I'll tell my guys to tread lightly. Egan's got another hinky power plant—that dam where he got famous. Seems the place is off limits. Total lockdown. Other power plants in

Dutannuru have public tours, that kind of thing, but not this one. Just seems odd."

"Have you discovered how Egan is paying for his campaign?" the President asked.

"No," Rezi replied. "I've got every return he's filed from his first job up to last year and there is nothing that indicates the kind of personal wealth needed to fund his run. The wind farm keeps him and his folks comfortable, but not filthy rich. He has some modest investments and an IRA—all penny-ante stuff. The one unusual thing is half-ownership in a new company called Terrafuma Energy. It sprung into existence on the first of the year, so all we got is the filings that created it. Terrafuma's corporate office is a post office box. It has no website, no apparent staff, no other footprint, nothing to indicate what it does or why it even exists."

"Who owns the other half?" the President inquired.

"That's the interesting thing—the rest is owned by Maya Randell and her husband."

The President arched an eyebrow.

"Indeed," Rezi replied. "The relationship between the Randells and the Egans dates back to the Seventies, long before Maya Randell became a billionaire. Egan and his parents are modest millionaires because of stock they bought early on, when Randell took her company public."

"So Randell is the bank behind Egan," Page offered. "Egan didn't announce his candidacy until May, so any flow of cash moving through Terrafuma won't show up until after the election."

"We need to mine this connection further," the President said. "See what other radical groups Randell is funding. Perhaps we can paint her as the puppet master pulling Egan's strings."

"I like it," Page agreed.

"I've saved the best for last," Rezi said, grinning like the Cheshire Cat. "You recall my saying that I hadn't found anything in the morals department to hang Egan with—that's not exactly true. At this point, what I have is only a rumor, but it is too damn juicy to ignore."

"How juicy?" Page asked.

"If we play it right, it'll kill Egan's campaign."

65

"THE MAGIC NUMBER IS SIXTY-SEVEN," EGAN ANNOUNCED TO A gathering of his senior campaign staff. "The voters go to the polls in sixty-seven days. That gives us just over nine weeks to make our case for a change in leadership."

Egan stood at the head of a long oval table. He was dressed in jeans and golf shirt embroidered with his campaign logo. Around the table sat his campaign manager, communications director, IT director, appearance and logistics director, regional campaign directors, foreign and domestic policy directors, head of opposition research, and campaign finance director.

A large video screen on the conference room wall displayed a similar room in Florida populated by Governor Oates and her campaign staff.

"To start, I'd like to commend everyone on both Governor Oates's staff and my team on the excellent job of marrying our two campaigns. I also laud the enthusiasm of your grassroots network in backing our ticket."

"Thank you, Ross," Oates said. "My supporters recognize that we are singing from the same hymnal and that I have not changed a bit to sign on with you."

"Which is what *all* of our supporters are counting on. Since the convention, the integration team has streamlined our joint campaign for the general election and repositioned our assets around the country. Also, we've acquired the full support of the other GOP candidates in a coordinated effort to improve conservative gains in the federal and state legislatures and the statehouses. General Hook has, in the proper military fashion, dubbed the whole enterprise 'Operation Coattails' and has taken charge of that effort.

"We got a big jump in the polls after the convention. It was a great mix of fascinating political drama with a strong resonance to our message. Merging with the GOP transformed us from a third-party curiosity into a viable alternative to the President and his agenda. The President got his post-convention bounce, too, though from a tragedy rather than anything productive."

"Aside from dodging a bullet," the head of GOP opposition research opined. "The assassination attempt gives us a clear example of the type of opponent we're up against. The President is not to be underestimated. When it comes to campaigning, he's about as smart as they come and he will not be easy to defeat. The President and his surrogates are working overtime to tar the political right with the Vice President's murder, linking conservatism as the cause of this lone gunman's effect. The President has authorized a commission to investigate the assassination, which keeps this story alive without reaching any conclusions until after the election. They will hammer us on the fact that Unden was former military, an NRA member, and a frequent protester at presidential appearances in recent months. According to their narrative, Unden opposed the President's healthcare reforms and the death tax, as do we, and his opposition led directly to the Vice President's murder and the attempted murder of the President. Any bad guy who leans to the right is to be used to tar us."

"As bright as the President is regarding politics, he is also incredibly consistent," Egan said. "We know how he and his team think, and how they will react. Most of his inner circle is steeped in the activist strategies of Saul Alinsky and much of what they do comes almost by reflex. But Alinsky's rules work best when employed by an underdog against the establishment. In this fight, the President *is* the establishment.

"So what are we to do? Well, I've read the President's playbook and I think Alinsky's third rule of power tactics suits us well: 'Whenever possible, go outside the experience of your enemy.'

"Where the President seeks to make me the personalized, polarized, demonized focus of his campaign, we will act as if he and his entire administration simply do not exist. We will not engage him or his surrogates. We have the ideas and everything we propose has been proven to work time and again. Our message must always be positive. Better days are ahead for our nation. It's morning in America. Our nation is and must always be that shining city on the hill. A free, prosperous, and strong United States is a benefit to the entire world.

"Our opponents cannot fight us on the numbers—WHO IS I will refute any attempt to distort the record with cold hard facts. That will keep us from getting bogged down in policy wonk minutiae guaranteed to glaze the eyes of most voters. When the campaign speaks, it is with broad stokes. We're communicating a complete vision. The details of our plans are available on our website—nothing hidden, there for all to see—so there's no reason for us to deviate from the big picture.

"A campaign like this moves beyond anything the President and his advisors have ever experienced. And like the rebels who founded this country, we are not fighting against anyone, but rather we are fighting *for* the greater good of everyone."

66

"NIKI ADASHI?" A MAN'S VOICE ASKED.

Niki squeezed off a few final shots from her camera as Egan left the stage. She turned her head and discovered a man approaching that she dimly recognized. He was dressed in a sport coat and tie with press credentials dangling from a cord around his neck.

"Edward Turcott?" Niki offered tentatively.

"Good memory. It's been a while since Dutannuru. Do you have a minute?"

Niki considered the question. She knew Egan had some brief downtime scheduled, then a few private meetings before departing Omaha.

"Yes."

"I'm working on a piece about the night of the Dutannuru miracle."

"Starting with you, that story has been written from nearly every conceivable point of view, has it not?"

"Probably," Turcott said in apologetic agreement, "but it's the assignment I drew. Anyway, the question I have is about the powerhouse. After I left, did you get inside?"

"No. I was only there a few hours after you left and it remained off limits."

"Were they hiding something in there?" Turcott asked.

Niki laughed. "Do you recall what Ross told us when asked what was inside the power plant?"

"Nothing," Turcott replied. "But there's no reason for all that security to protect nothing. Cudjoe wanted the power plant, so I think the place was booby-trapped."

"If it was as you say, then perhaps they did not want us to accidentally detonate the explosives."

"Do you think they would have done it—blown the power plant up?"

"Cudjoe was a monster," Niki replied. "If he wanted the power plant, then I absolutely think Ross would have destroyed it rather than let him take it."

"I see. Are you and Egan close?"

Niki's expression turned guarded.

"My relationship with him is primarily professional," Niki explained with a camera in her hand, "But we are friends—in the strictly platonic sense."

"Hey, I'm stringing for The Gray Lady, not Page Six," Turcott said by way of an apology. "It's just that night at the dam was a life changer for both of you. Who else can relate?"

"For someone who never sought fame, Ross has adapted well and remained remarkably grounded. If you're looking for deep psychological insights into the man, just ask him."

67

"ON BEHALF OF THE COMMISSION ON PRESIDENTIAL DEBATES, I am pleased to welcome you this evening to the first of four presidential debates. I am Dale Redmond of NBC News.

"Tonight's subject is the economy. The rules of this debate are simple. Over the next ninety minutes, I will ask a series of questions. Each of the candidates will then have two minutes to respond, followed by a period of discussion. I will encourage the candidates to ask follow-up questions of each other. If they do not, I will.

"And now, let us welcome our candidates for the presidency of the United States."

The audience seated in the Don Powell Theater at San Diego State University applauded enthusiastically as the President and his challenger appeared from opposite sides of the stage. Both were impeccably dressed, every element of their attire—from the suit to the cufflinks—selected to craft the most positive image. Egan referred to the process as "packaging."

"Good luck, Ross," the President said warmly as they met at center stage.

"And to you as well, Mr. President," Egan replied as he shook the President's offered hand.

They retreated to podiums on their respective sides of the stage, adjusted their microphones, and mentally girded themselves for battle. The audience quieted down as Redmond removed a binder clip from a stack of index cards.

"Prior to the start of tonight's debate," Redmond said, "there was a coin toss backstage and the President won, so he will receive the opening question."

The President nodded that he was ready.

"In the summer of 1992, the nation emerged from a recession that was both brief and mild in comparison to our current economic climate. The successful aspirant for the presidency that year ran his campaign with the simple slogan: 'It's the economy, stupid!' I think it's fair to say that the topic of tonight's debate is first and foremost in the minds of a majority of the American voting public," Redmond said. "Mr. President, our country remains mired in what many observers liken to the malaise of the 1970s. While the market down-turn that ushered in this period of lingering economic difficulty preceded your election to the presidency, as we approach the end of your first term, strong signs of recovery remain elusive. What do you propose to put the economy back on a solid footing?"

The President began, "To understand where we are now, you have to remember the tremendous economic mess I inherited when I took office. The near total collapse of the nation's financial sector brought about by greed and speculation on Wall Street, financial deregulation, and lax oversight wasn't something that could be fixed overnight. The US economy is not a sports car that can turn on a dime, but a lumbering leviathan. The actions we've taking are turning the economy in the right direction, but there's no quick fix to get us out of the hole we're in."

As the President spoke, Egan noted that the attention of some audience members repeatedly shifted between the stage and their laps. More than a few had defied the President's ban on cell phones and were checking WHO IS I for its on-the-fly critiques.

"The steps we've taken to stimulate economic growth are bearing fruit. In most regions of the country, housing prices have stabilized and the market for new and existing homes shows positive signs of improvement. During my first term, we've added millions of jobs, and the economy has shown positive GDP growth over the past seven quarters."

Murmurs rippled through the auditorium as the attention of many audience members shifted from the stage to their smartphones. WHO IS I confirmed the President's limited assertions, but clarified that those added jobs were more than offset by the millions more lost during the prolonged downturn. The modest improvement in the nation's unemployment number resulted primarily from the elimination of millions of long-term idled workers from the unemployment calculation reducing the overall official size of the labor force and not from job creation. It also noted that only the public sector experienced significant job growth, a trend that had an overall negative net impact on the national economy.

WHO IS I further noted that the U-6 measure of national unemployment averaged 15.2 percent during the President's first term, never dropping below 14.6 percent. The demand for labor in the US remains weak. And while GDP had been positive over the period specified by the President, the rate of growth never rose above two-tenths of a percent.

"The economy isn't roaring yet," the President stammered, distracted by the sudden loss of audience attention, "but most economists agree that the worst of the recession I inherited has passed and our economy is poised for a substantial recovery.

"Lastly, my program seeks not to simply restore our economy, but to correct significant flaws in our economic system that are the root cause of the recurring boom-bust cycle and, of course, the terrible disparity between the rich and poor in this country. The sweeping healthcare reforms passed by Congress and that I proudly signed into law addresses a sector of the economy where costs for individuals, businesses, and the government were skyrocketing, yet millions had little or no access to affordable healthcare.

"The Republican-controlled House has squandered the people's time and money attempting to repeal these vital healthcare reforms, which are essential in bending the cost curve down and, in the long run, reducing the federal deficit. The healthcare status quo was a bullet train to economic disaster and the reforms veered the nation away from certain financial suicide.

"The economy and jobs are my top priority, and will continue to be my top priority in my second term. But fixing the economy takes more than just money—you cannot have economic justice without social justice."

"And how do you plan to address the nation's economy, Mr. Egan?" Redmond asked.

" 'Those who cannot remember the past are condemned to repeat it'," Egan offered. "While specific details differ, the current economic downturn is similar to others in our nation's history and those experienced elsewhere in the world.

"And many of the supposed solutions adopted by the President and his economic team were tried before with similarly dismal results. For example, Japan's booming economy of the late Eighties suffered a spectacular crash in the early Nineties. Subsequent economic intervention, classic Keynesian stimulus with massive public sector spending by the Japanese government, led to a lost decade of economic growth from which they never really recovered.

"Hoover's progressive agenda of domestic spending after the crash of Twenty-nine, and Roosevelt's massive expansion of this policy in the Thirties, had little positive economic effect. In fact, most economists now agree that stimulative spending by Hoover and Roosevelt actually prolonged the Great Depression.

"The thing is, we know what works. The United States slipped into a depression in January of 1920 after the relatively new Federal Reserve began raising the rates on money it lends to banks. In response, instead of priming the pump through increased spending as we're doing now, the government cut taxes and spending. A year and a half later, the economy healed and the Roaring Twenties began. A similar policy in the Eighties created an economic expansion that ran for much of the next twenty years.

"A century of government intervention based on the theories of John Maynard Keynes has failed to produce one success story, and in fact proved that the interventionists do more harm than good. I'm an engineer, and when I look at a flow chart of how this beloved theory allegedly works, I see something I know for a fact *cannot* work. The idea that the state can take money out of the economy—through increased taxes, increased debt, or inflating the money supply—skim a little off the top, then pour what's left back into the economy and expect the whole thing to hum along indefinitely is the economic equivalent of a perpetual motion machine.

"My economic plan is simple. Cease stimulative actions by the government because they don't work. Cut government spending— and yes, everything is on the table. No sacred entitlement cows. Cut taxes in the immediate short term, and completely restructure how the government receives revenue over the next few years.

"I am a believer in dynamic, Darwinian capitalism. Businesses blink into existence and go extinct. They adapt to changing conditions or die. They defeat competitors or are overtaken. The invisible hand of the marketplace, and not the whims of the ruling class, determines the winners and losers.

"While not all government regulations are bad, those that effectively raise barriers to entrepreneurs distort the organic marketplace. These barriers are often the spawn of lobbyists seeking to protect their corporate masters from the threat of a more efficient competitor. I propose that all government regulations be reviewed for intent. Job growth in this country does not come from large established concerns, and should not come from the already bloated and wasteful public sector. In a vibrant economy, entrepreneurs fuel job growth and they must be encouraged."

"So you want to cut Social Security and Medicare?" the President charged.

"As part of a long-term restructuring," Egan replied calmly, "both should be phased out and replaced with programs based on sound investment principles and not a pyramid scheme."

"Pyramid scheme?" the President bristled. "The integrity of Social Security has never been in question."

"That's the problem," retorted Egan. "It should have been questioned from day one and exposed for the fraud that it is. The Roosevelt administration sold Social Security to the American public as government insurance and not a tax, but defended its constitutionality before the Supreme Court as a tax and not insurance because the government does not have the power to compel an individual to purchase anything. In truth, the government lied to both the Supreme Court and the people as to the program's true purpose— providing the government with another way to tap the incomes of productive American wage earners.

"Social Security only works if more people pay money in than take money out. As soon as the numbers get close to equal, the pyramid collapses. The same is true for public sector and large group pensions, which is why so many states, cities, and entities with large unionized workforces are going bankrupt. Geometric growth in public or private payrolls is impossible to sustain in the long run and will *always* lead to the collapse of these pension funds.

"Current obligations must be met, but to achieve sustainability in the long term, we must transition to a program that generates individual wealth independent of corporate, union, and especially government control."

"Which leads us to tax policy," Redmond said. "Mr. President, the tax rates put into effect during your predecessor's tenure in office were set to expire almost two years ago. At the time, you signed into law an extension of those rates for an additional two years. With a significant tax increase looming at the start of the New Year, what is your agenda for your second term?"

"My opponent says he plans to cut taxes," the President replied. Well, I cut taxes two year ago and our current economy is proof positive that his supply-side, voodoo economics simply doesn't work. If anything, it hampered our deficit reduction efforts and cost the government money. I wasn't thrilled about cutting taxes at such a difficult time, and I've been proven correct.

"This time around, I will let the tax rates for our country's wealthiest individuals return to their appropriate level. Those who have benefitted most should and must pay their fair share. I promise that working Americans will not see a dime of new taxes taken from their paychecks. I will also continue to work with Congress to overhaul our tax code. Economic justice and social justice go hand in hand."

"Brief and to the point, Mr. President," Redmond said, receiving a ripple of chuckles from the audience. "Mr. Egan, your thoughts on tax policy?"

"First, a point of clarification," Egan said. "The tax rates for all Americans are the same today as they were when the President took office. The bill the President signed into law maintained the status quo and did not cut taxes. The stimulative effect of these tax cuts took place several years ago, when the taxes were actually cut. The positive economic effect of these tax cuts was pronounced. Tax cuts, economically speaking, continue to bat a thousand.

"I am sure the President will sigh with relief when I say that this does not mean you can cut taxes indefinitely."

Egan paused for the laugh.

"A zero percent tax rate might sound like a blessing, but it starves the government and prevents it from undertaking those essential duties assigned to it by the Constitution, like defending the nation from foreign aggression. At this extreme, a zero percent tax rate equals zero revenue for the government.

"Going to the other extreme—and please don't get any ideas, Mr. President—is a confiscatory tax rate of one hundred percent. The government takes *everything*—lock, stock, and barrel. The economy shrivels to nothing and, in very short order, government revenue evaporates. Like the zero rate, a one hundred percent tax rate quickly equals zero revenue for the government.

"Like any business," Egan explained, "the government should be run in a way that maximizes its income. I like pie, so I'm going to equate our economy to a juicy apple pie."

Egan paused as the audience laughed.

"Unlike the pies my mom bakes, the government's pie grows or shrinks depending on how much of it the government leaves for the rest of us. It can have a big old slice of a tiny pie, like something that popped out of an Easy Bake oven. Or, it can have a thin slice of a pie that would win a spot in the *Guinness Book of Records*. The thin slice is a whole lot more pie.

"My father taught me that fifty percent of a hundred dollars is less than ten percent of a thousand dollars. There's a sweet spot for taxation that maximizes the amount of revenue the government can take in. Raising the rates from that spot cuts revenue because it shrinks the economic pie. Lowering the rates again cuts revenue, but the impact here comes as increased deficits or cuts in essential government services."

"This is nonsense," the President countered. "Our nation enjoyed times of prosperity with tax rates significantly higher than they are now. And the Reagan tax cuts conservatives so proudly boast about exploded the deficit and greatly increased the federal debt."

"Anyone who passed introductory economics, or ever tried to make money, knows that income and expense are two separate items on the balance sheet. In the example you cite, the Reagan tax cuts more than doubled government revenue as the economy grew. Had government spending remained steady, those tax cuts would have generated surpluses that could have been used to pay down the debt. Instead, government spending in all areas exploded to absorb the tax cut windfall. Like the rest of us, the government should make as much money as it can, spend within its means, and sock a little away for a rainy day.

"Now, Mr. President," Egan continued, "in addition to allowing the so-called tax cuts for the rich expire, I understand that you and your committee of tax advisors are looking at additional ideas for raising revenue. Is it true that ideas like a value added tax and a tax on net worth are on the table?"

"We are considering a number of reasonable ideas for enhancing revenues to the federal government," the President replied. "The two you cited have been used successfully elsewhere."

"I'd be interested in hearing what your definition of *successful* is," Egan countered. "To the best of my knowledge, those taxes in combination with a progressive income tax have always resulted in economic stagnation, the devastation of individual wealth, and revenue shortfalls. Sounds like a lose-lose to me.

"Taxing income and wealth effectively punishes people for being productive. It's both anti-capitalist and, to use the President's turn of phase, *socially unjust*. I propose to completely scrap the current tax system in favor of one that taxes consumption rather than production."

"I'm confused, Mr. Egan," the President said snidely. "You seem to be speaking out of both sides of your mouth. Are you for or against a national VAT tax?"

"That's probably just my Yooper accent throwing you off—doublespeak being your native tongue," Egan quipped back. "I favor a national tax on the sale of all goods and services *in lieu of* our current tax code, not in addition to it. Taxation simply becomes part of every consumer's decision to buy a good or service."

"But such a tax would hurt the poor," the President argued.

"Hardly," Egan replied. "The burden of this tax applies to everyone equally—and isn't equal treatment under the law what we all want? And built into my tax proposal is a poverty line refund for every citizen of the United States. The government sets the poverty line—the income level below which a person is deemed to be poor. The refund equals the tax that would be paid by someone earning right at the poverty line who spends every dollar they make. The net result of this refund is that nobody pays one red cent of tax until their earnings rise above the poverty line. The real benefit of this form of taxation is that it rewards saving, which puts more money to work in the form of loans and investment."

"Mr. Egan," Redmond interjected, "such a sweeping tax reform would be difficult, if not impossible to enact."

"Indeed it would," Egan agreed. "The first major hurdle is Congress, which uses the tax code to favor friends, punish enemies and solicit contributions from lobbyists. The consumption tax would strip them of this power. Crucial to my proposal is the passage of a constitutional amendment to deny Congress the ability to levy any form of income tax. Once we drive a stake through the heart of our bloodsucking tax code, we don't want it coming back from the dead.

"Another power that I will fight to strip from the government is the ability to print money. Every time the Federal Reserve increases the money supply, the government steals a sliver of value out of every dollar already in circulation. *Steal* may be too strong a word—the right term for government appropriation of private wealth is *taxation*. Since no good was created or service provided to give these new dollars value, then the government must have taxed them into existence. The only way to stem this subtle, underhanded form of taxation without representation is to return to the gold standard. That way, the marketplace can function as it should and the money we make can maintain its value.

"These fights won't be easy, but what I'm proposing is sound economics, not crackpot Keynesianism. Dutannuru employs the exact system I propose and it works *perfectly* for both the people and their government."

"Thank you, Mr. Egan," Redmond said. "Mr. President, the sweeping healthcare legislation you championed and signed into law continues to be a source of much debate, and it serves to highlight the issue of government entitlements. Your opponent recommends that all government expenditures be put on the table in the conversation on cutting the budget deficit and the growing national debt. You follow the more traditional path of respecting the distinction between discretionary and non-discretionary spending and approaching the nation's budgetary shortfall through revenue enhancement. Given the growth we've seen in non-discretionary spending and debt service, and the lack of growth in the national economy, is it now time to address those untouchable items on the national budget?"

"Contrary to what my opponent believes, there is no quick fix to our nation's economic problems. Deficits incurred during my first term in office reflect both falling revenue due to the terrible recession I inherited and increased spending by the government to stimulate economic activity and to steady the financial markets with quantitative easing. We've sought advice from the finest economic minds in the country and crafted policies grounded in sound economic theory. My economic council is a who's who of men and women with Nobel Prizes in Economics—these people know what they're talking about when it comes to reviving and restructuring our nation's financial house.

"The signs of improvement we're seeing prove that we are making progress toward full recovery, complete with gains in both jobs and housing. I caution patience as our policy initiatives slowly work their way through down to the roots of our economy.

"With regard to entitlements, these are the social safety net that keeps those most vulnerable of our citizens from financial ruin. Social Security, Medicare and Medicaid are fundamentally sound programs of proven benefit to millions.

"The same is true of federal unemployment insurance, which has a proven stimulative effect on the economy. Unemployment insurance injects demand directly into the communities hardest hit by unemployment, demand that translates directly into jobs.

"The healthcare reforms that I signed into law are just now slowly taking effect. Change is difficult, but with so many millions of Americans unable to obtain affordable healthcare, these reforms were absolutely necessary. The system we had was broken. Costs were out of control. Those that could afford medical care got it, and those who couldn't were out of luck. Those with pre-existing conditions were out of luck. Those whose job offered no medical benefits were out of luck. The elderly, the poor, and the folks most in need of medical care were all too often out of luck.

"Entitlements are part of the social contract our government has with the people of the United States. It's there in the Constitution, the requirement for the government to promote the general welfare.

"As the economy recovers, the government can scale back on stimulus investment and eliminate wasteful tax cuts for the rich, shrinking and eventually eliminating the budget deficit. The course proposed by Ross Egan is both reckless and irresponsible."

"Your question, Mr. Egan," Redmond said.

"Reckless and irresponsible," Egan repeated to start his rebuttal. "If that's not the pot calling the kettle black.

"In his farewell address, President Eisenhower offered this warning: 'We cannot mortgage the material assets of our grandchildren without risking the loss of their political and spiritual heritage. We want democracy to survive for all generations to come, not to become the insolvent phantom of tomorrow.' The reckless and irresponsible spending of the past few years has brought that insolvent phantom much closer to today.

"The debt amassed under this administration exceeds the most extravagant, reckless, and irresponsible spending by any government in history. The President famously complains about the deficits run up by his predecessor, yet his deficits dwarf them by comparison. And any return on the President's so-called investments are decidedly negative. Thomas Jefferson had it right when he declared: 'It is incumbent on every generation to pay its own debts as it goes.'

"Nobel Prizes or not, the President's economic dream team is profoundly wrong. The theories they espouse fail every time they're tried and they should be tossed onto the trash heap of bad ideas. In fact, the only time these theories should ever be discussed is so that future generations can learn and hopefully avoid repeating these mistakes.

"To be clear: There are *no* signs of a recovery on the near or distant horizon, and nothing that this administration has done or is now doing will create the conditions in which a recovery can occur. This economy is, at best, barely treading water.

"The claim that unemployment insurance stimulates the economy and creates jobs is *insane*. Only fifty-five cents out of every dollar in unemployment insurance gets spent by the unemployed, so the vaunted multiplier effect of this investment is actually division. And for all the billions spent in extended unemployment insurance, not a single private sector job has been created. If the government really wanted to reduce our appallingly high unemployment rate, it would leave the money consumed by these bloated federal programs in the economy where it would create jobs.

"The very term 'entitlements' offends me. Among the inalienable rights granted to all people, the three explicitly identified in our founding documents are life, liberty, and the pursuit of happiness. This is not a *guarantee* of happiness, but the right to *pursue* those goals and activities that satisfy us. It is the right to work toward something—the right to create, build, and achieve. No one is entitled to the fruits of another's work, rather they are entitled to go out and work for their own. Democracy ceases to exist when you take away from those who are willing to work and give to those who are not.

"The great difference between conservatives and progressives lies in how we view the rest of humanity. Conservatives believe that what we achieve over the course of our lives is a matter of the talent we possess and the choices we make. There will be winners and losers in the end, but each of us has an equal opportunity to play.

"Progressives believe in equality of outcome—regardless of what paths we take, all roads lead to the same end. There are to be no winners, because winning is unfair. That makes losers of us all in the end—all except the people rigging the game to achieve this unrealistic, utopian fantasy. These folks make out quite well on the deal. Tyrants always take care of their own.

"I fully support having an economic safety net, but not as a permanent lifestyle choice. Perpetually extending unemployment benefits only dampens the incentive of many idled workers to accept any form of employment. It locks able-bodied people into a form of economic slavery and, judging by the current crop of alarmist campaign ads with apocalyptic warnings about conservatives cutting these programs, it smacks of the worst kind of vote buying.

"My main objection to federal safety nets is that they violate the principle of subsidiarity that requires matters be handled by the smallest, lowest, or least centralized competent authority. The solution to any human problem starts with the individual, then the family, the community, the state, and as a last resort, the nation. Instead, we manage the entitlement welfare state with the largest, highest, and most centralized bureaucracy possible. In truth, there are very few problems in everyday life that require federal intervention.

"I do believe that every federal program should be reviewed and the vast majority either cut or eliminated. And the laws that make the budgets of the so-called entitlement programs untouchable must be repealed. Federal entitlement programs offer few benefits that couldn't be provided better and more efficiently by sources closer to the individuals in need."

"Thank you, gentlemen," Redmond interjected. "I have the final question of the evening, which is on healthcare. Mr. President, healthcare reform is the signature legislative accomplishment of your first term, and arguably the most controversial. The reform package was singled out as the key issue in the midterm elections. The current Congress has made several attempts to repeal or defund the reforms and polling shows it remains both divisive and unpopular among voters. Given the rapidly rising cost of healthcare and the millions of uninsured in this country, few would argue that some kind of reform isn't needed, but how do you address the concerns of the American people over these particular reforms?"

"I did not write the historic healthcare legislation that became law", the President opened. "The reform package that passed both houses of Congress and that I signed into law may not be perfect, but it is a monumental step in the right direction. It addresses the problem of the staggering number of people without health insurance, people just one illness or accident away from complete financial ruin. It addresses corporate greed in the healthcare and pharmaceutical industry, attacking the exorbitant profits raked in by these corporations at the expense of the American people.

"All Americans have a right to affordable healthcare. Greedy corporations, on the other hand, exist solely for profit and are not motivated by their social responsibility. It is the duty of government to step in and reorient the priorities of our nation's healthcare system.

"Where my administration has not been as successful as I would have liked is in our effort to educate the American people about the benefits these reforms will have on their day-to-day lives. We have to do a better job of getting the message out. I remain confidant that as more elements of the healthcare reforms come on line, the fears raised against the reforms will be proved ignorant rhetoric and not reality."

"Mr. Egan, your question," Redmond said.

"Messaging, Mr. President?" Egan asked wryly. "The problem your administration has in winning the support of the American people for the healthcare reforms isn't P.R. It's B.S."

The audience and even Redmond couldn't suppress a chuckle at the remark.

"The healthcare reforms that Congress created and the President signed into law promise a bureaucratic behemoth the likes of which our nation has never seen, coupled with a decrease in both the quality and quantity of healthcare services. There is nothing wrong with the system we enjoyed before these crippling reforms that could not have been fixed at the doctor-patient level.

"The public's skepticism over this monumental piece of legislation is twofold. First, it puts a government bureaucrat in the position to decide the quality and even the duration of our lives. The British system, on which these reforms were modeled, rations healthcare and denies life-extending treatment to people that an actuarial table deems a poor investment of healthcare dollars. This is *wrong*. This is *immoral.*

"Second, when has the government ever provided a good or service better than what can be found in the free market? The profit motive creates the drive to find the most efficient balance of the three things that every consumer wants—quality, efficiency, and cost. The government simply lacks the motivation to provide us with the best healthcare at the best price because they tax the money out of our wallets before we're even sick. Government is not a solution to our healthcare problem, government *is* our healthcare problem.

"The employer-based healthcare system we have today is an unintended consequence of government intervention in the free market—specifically the wage and price controls enacted by the government under FDR. In order to compete for workers, businesses began offering healthcare benefits in lieu of wages. This was the first step in disrupting the efficient balance of the healthcare free market because it made consumers indifferent to costs. The root cause of skyrocketing healthcare costs is the lack of a free and open market for these services, and the President's healthcare reforms only worsen the situation.

"Fixing this problem is fairly simple. We start by scrapping both the healthcare reform law and the employer-based system, and restore a marketplace where the person receiving the service is involved in the payment for that service. The government does not coerce, but rather encourages each individual citizen to establish a health savings account. The encouragement is in the form of a financial incentive that guarantees a minimum return on investment for money placed in these accounts. From these accounts, individuals can then choose to purchase catastrophic health insurance and pay directly for routine medical services—all from the free market.

"These accounts start the day you're born and stay with you for the rest of your life. Any money left in your account after you die goes to your heirs, like any other asset. And since it's not tied to a job, it's totally portable. In a free market, healthcare costs will drop with the more efficient flow of money and services between healthcare consumers and providers. It's a fix that puts the matter squarely in the hands of the least centralized competent authority—the *individual*."

"Your reforms put the entire system in the control of the greedy corporations that are causing the problem," the President railed. "It's this kind of lockstep, right-wing ideology that got us into this economic mess."

"Is there a question in there, Mr. President?" Egan asked.

"You plan to scrap everything and start over with individuals buying their own insurance. Doesn't that put the insurance companies in the driver's seat, picking and choosing only the healthiest customers and denying coverage to people with preexisting conditions? Isn't your free-market solution fundamentally unfair to the vast majority of Americans?"

"Quite the contrary," Egan replied, "and I refer you and anyone else who wants the details of this proposal to my website. As to your specific question, Mr. President, there would be an initial period in which the private healthcare companies would have to take on all applicants regardless of any preexisting medical conditions. The government would assist the healthcare insurers in maintaining a minimum level of profitability during the early years of this reform— we won't cap how much they can make, just guarantee they won't take a loss due to customers with expensive medical conditions.

"The idea is to encourage universal participation in the savings accounts and in acquiring catastrophic insurance. And we expect the tax rebate every citizen will receive each year should cover most, if not all, of that expense. This will help make the decision to acquire adequate coverage a no-brainer.

"The United States will enjoy a robust, free market for healthcare and the budgets of federal and state governments will enjoy significant financial relief once freed of this onerous entitlement."

"It is time for your closing remarks, gentlemen," Redmond announced. "I thank you both for a substantive debate of the issues before the American voters this year. Mr. President, the floor is yours."

"Thank you, Dale," the President said. "The value of these debates in educating and informing the voting public cannot be underestimated. They are an essential part of our election process.

"The journey we as a nation began on my first day in office has been a difficult one, but we knew that rebuilding the shattered dreams of America on a foundation more sound and fair, a foundation more inclusive and diverse, a foundation set atop the granite bedrock of our universal belief in a nation where we are judged solely by the content of our character.

"With all the progress we've made over this difficult road, we cannot afford to turn back, to return to the failed policies of yesterday. I have cleared the wreckage of the previous administration, plowed the still-fertile soil of America, and planted a new crop that only now is bursting up with new green shoots. I delivered on my promise for bold changes in the ways our country worked, but most have barely begun to take effect.

"The choice could not be more clear. My opponent offers us reruns of a disaster we have no desire to relive. I offer the promise of new ideas and the vision we deserve for a better tomorrow."

"And your closing remarks, Mr. Egan," Redmond said.

"The people of this nation have been statistically sliced and diced in about as many ways as one can imagine—by race, age, gender, ethnicity, faith, income, geography. We are all hyphenated Americans of one kind or another, and this hyper-sorting of the voting public aids the efforts of political strategists in the electoral equivalent of divide and conquer.

"In truth, the only relevant distinction that needs to be drawn between Americans at election time is by class. Country Class," Egan said, holding up the palm of his right hand. Then he drew up his left, "and Ruling Class.

"Ruling class elites dominate national politics and populate elective offices and bureaucracies around the country. The ruling class operates like a machine whose sole purpose is to increase its power. The rest of us are the country class. The ruling class—which includes the President—are all OPM addicts."

Egan pronounced the acronym as "opium."

"I object to such a slanderous statement," the President interjected. "I demand an immediate apology for your unfounded remark."

"If you would let me continue, Mr. President, the substance I'm referring to is far more seductive and potent that any narcotic, and it's perfectly legal. The OPM I'm talking about is *Other People's Money.*

"The members of the ruling class have, as their sole defining characteristic, a disdain for anyone who actually produces anything of value, because they do not. Using the power of government, they lay claim to money they had no hand in earning and spend it to increase their hold on political power. The crony capitalist friends of the ruling class benefit and the rest of us are punished.

"The game works something like this—the ruling class divides the country class into two basic camps: makers and takers. The makers are the people who perform productive work and create the wealth of our economy. The takers either work in government or subsist on government handouts—their primary source of income is the redistributed tax dollars of the makers.

"The goal of the ruling class is to have just enough makers to keep the economy going, but not enough that the makers could vote the ruling class out of power. Our progressive tax system and the federal entitlement structure are designed to create a permanent majority of takers who will vote for the ruling class in perpetuity.

"This addiction to other people's money isn't satisfied with spending the tax dollars of today's producers, it now devours those of generations yet unborn. And with every dollar of debt and every dollar printed out of thin air, the ruling class pushes this country ever faster toward the abyss of financial collapse. Over the past century, the ruling class has proven itself a poor steward of the economy and those powers that it has usurped should now be returned to the people. Replacing the tax code and restoring the gold standard are two vital steps in curing this disastrous addiction."

68

"SEE YOU IN TWO WEEKS, MR. PRESIDENT," EGAN SAID CONFI-
dently as the two candidates shook hands at the conclusion of the
debate.

Both men chatted for a moment with the moderator before retreating to their respective sides of the stage. In New York, studio
anchors took control of the broadcast and immediately began dis-
secting the debate with their panels of political experts.

The impeccably dressed First Lady strode on stage and dutifully
kissed her husband's cheek.

"You did well," she whispered in his ear.

"You're being charitable," the President replied through clenched
teeth. "Let's get out of here."

The President and his wife politely endured an abbreviated meet
and greet with university dignitaries before making their exit. They
found Daniel Page waiting for them in the armored SUV.

"Talk to me," the President commanded once the doors were
closed.

"You held your ground," Page replied, "but lacked bite."

"I expected the SOB to come out swinging, but it was almost like
I didn't matter. Couldn't fluster the guy."

"You played it like a pro," Page offered. "You are the President
and you have to remain above the fray. This is the public's first
opportunity to see you side-by-side and you came off confident and
presidential. This debate didn't cost you anything."

"Egan was boring," the First Lady sighed. "I bet the focus groups
lost interest as he droned on and on—especially women. You were far

more eloquent and handsome."

The President gazed out as his motorcade pulled away from the auditorium. He absently rubbed his left forearm, feeling the fresh scar beneath his jacket and shirt. Nearby, he noticed his opponent's security detail. Amid the dark SUVs stood Egan's menacing HumVee.

"To win this election," the President said, "we have to get dirty."

69

"DID YOU SEE THE DEBATE, LAST NIGHT?" DENBY ASKED TO OPEN his final show of the workweek. "Man-o-man, what a whooping our dear leader took from a man the sycophant media derides as a back-woods engineer.

"What we got last night in San Diego was a perfect display of the contrasts between conservatives and whatever the left calls itself these days. Have you noticed that conservatives in this country have never felt the need to rebrand themselves, to attempt to reinvent themselves with a shiny new sobriquet? The word *conservative* has never become a pejorative like *socialist*, or *liberal*, or *progressive*.

"And what about this ridiculous crowd of milquetoast ninnies trying to fool voters by pretending they have no label at all. Talk about spineless—it's like a football team that's afraid to wear their uniforms. It's bad enough that you're all liberals, but you should at least be confident enough in your beliefs to admit that you're liberals.

"There's no doubt what Ross Egan is. And last night, he laid out the case for conservatism that would have made the Founders and Honest Abe beam with pride. I haven't felt this way about a presidential candidate since Ronaldus Magnus went up against that clue-less peanut farmer. And not in a generation have the voters been offered so clear a choice.

"What's funny is that our friends on the left opine that a vote for a conservative is a vote to go backwards. Let's see now. A vote for the progressive gets us higher unemployment, higher debt, higher taxes, lower GDP, higher crime rates, lower graduation rates, a weaker military, rising unrest in the world, and a waning superpower status.

If going backwards means the opposite of all that rot, then put that transmission into reverse and punch the gas, baby. Pedal to the metal.

"For those of you looking to score the debate, you need go no further than the WHO IS I-ometer that we've placed up on the website. While I, your humble host, can provide you with a dazzling qualitative assessment of each candidate's performance, the WHO IS I-ometer objectively determines just how far a candidate strays from objective reality. Ross Egan batted a thousand last night, triggering no objections from WHO IS I. The President—not so much.

"We'll be back in a few."

70

DANIEL PAGE LOITERED OUTSIDE THE PRESIDENT'S OFFICE A-board Air Force One while the nation's chief executive conferenced with the Senate majority leader. The President had just completed a grueling swing through the Midwest that mixed official business with campaign stops and fundraising before heading to Barcelona for the G20 Summit.

"Come in," the President said as he cradled the phone.

Page closed the door behind him. The President mentally switched gears into candidate mode.

"How did we do?" the President asked.

"Press did a decent job covering your speeches, great optics from the factory and solar sites. Your PAC pulled in a few million from the fundraisers. All in all, a productive run into the heartland."

"Didn't feel like it," the President groused. "Crowds look thinner and less enthusiastic than four years ago."

"You were the hot new thing then. The danger of your job is overexposure, and the voters are easily bored. Familiarity breeds contempt."

"Any good news?"

"The Chinese have quietly put a lot of money into an American energy company."

"How much?"

"North of a billion, and there's no apparent reason why. The company has no advertised product line, no proven field of consulting expertise, and no patent filings on record. It simply sprang into existence at the start of the year and cut a monster deal with Beijing."

"Any idea why?" the President asked.

Page smiled. "The company is Terrafuma Energy, a privately held concern owned by Maya Randell and Ross Egan."

"The Chinese have poured a billion dollars into Egan's pocket?"

"Looks that way. The bigger question is what are they buying with their money? That flap back in the Nineties over campaign contributions by the Chinese nuns pales in comparison to this."

The President smiled. "We always suspected Randell was bankrolling Egan's campaign, but this is better. The right has called me a socialist for years, yet their guy is bought and paid for by the People's Republic of China."

"We don't have any real proof to back that claim," Page said.

"There's an old saw about LBJ spreading a rumor that his opponent for a congressional seat had sex with pigs," the President said. "When his campaign manger complained there wasn't a shred of truth of the charge, LBJ remarked that he just wanted to make the man to deny it. It's the seriousness of the charge that matters, not the facts."

"Understood, but with Beijing directly involved, this is a bit stickier than a normal scandal. I know we have to play this card, but we need to be careful how we play it."

The President nodded. "Connect the dots as best you can. I have a private meeting with President Xaio in a few days. I think I'll press him on it. There are consequences to backing my opponent."

71

THE PRESIDENT SMILED POLITELY AS HE AND HIS CHINESE COUN-
terpart shook hands. The scene was a typical one dutifully played out
by various world leaders before the media covering the G20 Summit.
The two men sat in identical upholstered chairs, a small table set
between them with glasses and carafe of ice water.

With the greeting fully documented, summit security escorted the
press from the room, leaving the two leaders and their translators
alone for this private session.

"President Xaio," the President began, "I wish to start by offering
not just my thanks, but the thanks of future generations around the
world who will benefit from your far-sighted decision to make China
a founding partner in the carbon exchange. This makes our two
nations allies in addressing the root causes of man-made climate
change and signals the joint leadership of our two nations in averting
the disastrous consequences of unchecked greenhouse gas emissions."

"Thank you for your kind words," Xaio replied through his trans-
lator. "Our decision to partner with the United States in the carbon
exchange was made in the best interests of not only the Chinese
people, but all the world's people. Our rising position among nations
is accompanied by rising responsibilities. The exchange is a well-
designed mechanism for effecting the change we desire."

"I am pleased to hear that China takes its position in the world
seriously. I certainly hope that enlightened outlook will extend to
monetary policy."

Xaio's eyes narrowed slightly.

"Unlike gas emissions, which affect the shared atmosphere of our planet, currency policy is a sovereign matter. I believe in careful management of our currency's value. To allow the value of the yuan to rise and fall freely on the open market invites the danger of speculation by unscrupulous opportunists, as was the case in England and Southeast Asia."

The President caught the veiled reference to his political patron, but his outward expression remained impassive.

"Of greater concern to China is the falling value of the dollar," Xaio continued. "It affects both the value of our currency and the value of that portion of our foreign reserves held in your currency. China remains opposed to your country's policy of manipulating long-term interest rates through large purchases of your own treasury bonds. This policy exports your inflation to emerging economies like China. A continuation of such a financially dangerous policy may force us to reconsider our benchmark for the yuan."

"I will certainly take your concerns under advisement as I and my economists craft policies to guide our nation toward sustainable prosperity," the President replied, acknowledging that this line of discussion was fruitless. "I do have a specific topic of exchange between our two nations that I wish to discuss—your nation's recent agreement with the private US firm Terrafuma Energy."

"I am unfamiliar with this agreement," Xaio lied.

"China's National Energy Commission has transferred several billion US dollars to Terrafuma Energy this year. My government has only recently become aware of these transfers and we are understandably curious about the specifics of this energy consultation agreement. Such a lucrative deal between our two nations is typically celebrated, not concealed."

"As I said," Xaio countered, "I am unfamiliar with this agreement. If you like, I will make some inquiries."

Gotcha, the President thought.

"I would appreciate that," the President replied.

72

"PETER, THANK YOU FOR TAKING MY CALL," THE PRESIDENT SAID.

"It is always my pleasure to speak with you, Mr. President," Sturla replied. "To what do I owe the pleasure?"

"China," the President replied. "They're upset with our policy of buying our own debt."

"As they should be. Their extraordinary holding of dollars loses value with each purchase. They've already exchanged some of their dollar reserves for other currencies to reduce the impact of your buy-backs, but their holdings are too large to dump the dollar entirely. Such a move would be disastrous for the yuan."

"Xaio hinted that if we continued our policy, China might reconsider their benchmark for the yuan."

"Interesting. I thought it would take longer for them to play that card. This could be the opening we've been waiting for."

"Should I apply more pressure with another debt purchase?" the President asked.

"Yes, but not until after the carbon exchange opens. As planned, we'll leverage the sale of those emissions credits to finance our move on the global currency markets. Things are moving faster than I anticipated," Sturla admitted, "but we are ready for this coming opportunity to truly change the world."

MORAN TOWNSHIP, MICHIGAN

NIKI FOUND ROSS IN THE BARN, BENT OVER THE HOOD OF HIS HumVee. Cables ran from a laptop computer on the workbench to several points on the engine. Music poured from wall-mounted speakers, filling the garage with the recording of a Seventies rock concert. Thunderous guitars raced through a frenetic song and Egan rose up, socket wrench held like a microphone, joining the band in a screaming chorus.

"Gonzo! Gonzo! *Gonzo-oh-oh!*"

"May I interrupt your performance for some campaign business?" Niki asked loudly, announcing her presence.

Red-faced, Ross retrieved a tiny remote control from the workbench and paused the music. The garage instantly fell silent.

"Sorry about that," Ross offered.

"You are a man of hidden talents."

"Singing not being one of them. What's up?"

"I spoke with Maya—Terrafuma's deal with Beijing has been noticed. The President brought it up with Premier Xaio in Barcelona. Chairman Chen informed Maya of the conversation."

"It wasn't going to stay under wraps forever," Ross said with a shrug, "not with that much money changing hands. Is that my sweater?"

Niki wore an Irish fisherman's sweater over a peach turtleneck. Black jeans flattered her lithe figure and leather boots defined her slender calves.

"Your mother found it for me. She said there was a nip in the air."

"You look *much* better in it than I ever did," Ross said, moving closer to Niki. "Of course, there are other ways to stave off the cold."

"Are there now?"

Niki gazed into Ross's green eyes and then reached up and pulled his face close. She kissed him fully, passionately. She then felt his arms encircle her, drawing her torso tightly against him. Through the woolen bulk of the sweater, she felt his heart racing in time with hers.

Neither could pinpoint the moment when their relationship, which had always been friendly and professional, began to develop a romantic facet. Neither was an adolescent subject to hormonally fueled infatuation, and the strongest emotional bond they shared was grief over the tragic loss of Ross's wife and son.

Gradually, the kiss slowed, lingering until both came up for air.

"That's one of them," Ross said softly.

"Still, we have to be careful. You are a public figure, even here."

"I know."

Niki reluctantly withdrew from Ross, denying her physical desire for him out of love and duty.

"Maya is prepared for the inquiries that will likely be made regarding Terrafuma," Niki said, resuming her professional demeanor as Maya Randell's unofficial representative to the campaign.

"Good, because the President's team will go after us hard on this."

73

ON AIR
SEPTEMBER 26

"AND WE'RE BACK," DENBY ANNOUNCED TO HIS MILLIONS OF RA-
dio listeners. "As I opined in the opening monologue, I think Ross
Egan clearly outmatched the President in the debate that took place
last night at the Air Force Academy's Arnold Hall in Colorado. It
was a thoughtful discourse on foreign policy and the challenger had
little trouble in an intellectual battle of wits with the unarmed
incumbent.

"The idea of American exceptionalism came up as the focal point
of Egan's thinking, and this theme resonated in his responses. The
consistency of this central premise was clear with regard to America
as the world's dominant superpower and the emergence of China as a
potential superpower; on foreign aid and how we deal with our
friends, our foes, and the UN; and the ongoing threat of terrorism
and militant religious extremism.

"Foreign policy has always been a weak point with the current
administration and our standing in the world has suffered for a lack
of coherence that emanates from the Oval Office. After last night's
side-by-side, I'm convinced coherence won't be an issue for a potential Egan administration.

"I think the high point of last night's debate came during a spir-
ited exchange on illegal immigration. This is treated in most circles as
a domestic policy issue, but Egan correctly recognized its foreign
policy implications.

"The President favors a do-nothing approach to securing our nation's borders, coupled with a quick path to legal status and citizenship so these undocumented aliens can be assimilated as quickly as

possible into the ranks of dependent Democrat voters.

"Egan, in brilliant contrast, recognizes that the exodus of people from their Central and South American homelands into the United States as not just a border security-slash-illegal immigration issue, but a foreign policy *opportunity* as well. And to clarify this point, we have as our guest today, GOP candidate Ross Egan. Ross, thanks for taking the time to speak with me today."

"Given that more folks are probably listening to your program than last night's debate," Egan offered, "I'd be a fool not to. Thanks for inviting me back."

"During last night's debate, you turned the conversation to a topic framed normally as a domestic issue: illegal immigration. In fact, I dare say you turned the topic completely on its head. For the sake of some audience members who did not see you put the President on the ropes with this, please lay out your plan for handling our growing problem with illegal immigration."

"My pleasure. Both parties recognize that the vast majority of people who enter this country illegally do so out of desperation. They are leaving behind their homes and family in search of opportunity, no different than the ancestors of most US citizens.

"Another way to look at it—these people are voting with their feet. As I've said on many occasions, American exceptionalism is not rooted in geography or natural resources, but in a system of laws that guarantee the rights and liberties of the people by restricting the power of the federal government. Our Constitution is what allows each and every citizen of this country to employ their talents and ingenuity to their fullest. That's what most of these illegal immigrants are after, the opportunity for a better life.

"Now, I'm a Yooper, which means I'm used to long winters with tons of snow. To my way of thinking, something must be mighty wrong with the governments of our neighbors to the south if their people are fleeing those tropical paradises in droves to look for work in my neck of the woods. And you can bet, they wouldn't be leaving if jobs were plentiful back home. So, here's my plan.

"First, we beef up our border security because some bad folks are sneaking into the country with drugs and guns and we must put a stop to that. And while the United States welcomes immigrants, we prefer they come in the right way and follow our laws.

"Second, for those who slip by or are already here—it's our fault if we didn't catch them. If they plan to stay, they have to register immediately as undocumented aliens with status as economic refugees. Refugee status will bring most of these people out of the shadows and make them less susceptible to abuse and intimidation."

"What about deportation?" Denby asked. "Didn't these folks break our laws by entering the country illegally?"

"Illegal entry into the country is a violation of our laws, but I propose fines over deportation for this specific offense. Under my proposed tax system, every *citizen* receives a poverty line tax refund from the government."

"This is so no citizen earning at or below the poverty line pays any taxes, correct?"

"Yes," Egan replied. "These economic refugees would not receive this refund as the fine for their illegal entry into the country. They would also never be eligible for citizenship until they leave the country and return legally. I would also close the *jus soli* form of natural born citizenship to eliminate the anchor baby route to citizenship for illegal aliens."

"There will be those who decry your proposal as unfair, that the door to citizenship shouldn't be closed to these people."

"The door isn't closed, only this underhanded route to citizenship, but that's not the real issue. If the United States is taking in refugees, we have to ask ourselves why. There must be a fundamental problem with the places these people come from that is driving them to come here. And the best way for us to fix our illegal immigration problem is not to build a better wall, but to fix what's wrong on the other side of our borders. We want these people to remain citizens of their homelands so they can vote against the regimes that drove them out and vote for the kinds of reforms that can bring them home. Citizenship isn't what draws these people here, and based on where I live, it certainly isn't the weather. These people come here for opportunity and security.

"This exodus from Latin America is a tragedy," Egan continued.

"Ignoring its root cause makes us collaborators with these corrupt regimes. The policy I propose is designed to encourage reform in the nations that have forced millions of their desperate citizens across our borders."

"And these fleeing millions, as economic refugees, come out of the shadows and participate fully in our economy," Denby offered. "They can take jobs, establish credit, buy homes and put their kids in school—just like any legal resident alien. The only difference is that they don't get the tax refund and they have to vote in their home country's elections."

"Right," Egan agreed.

"That's what I like about this policy," Denby said. "It treats the disease, not just the symptoms."

74

EDWARD TURCOTT SWATTED AT A FLY BUZZING AROUND HIS head. It was hot and humid in that tropical way that had soaked his clothing through to his skin within minutes of leaving the air-conditioned comfort of his rented Land Rover.

Despite the rapid pace of reconstruction throughout much of what had once been Safo, this small village by the riverside could have emerged intact from Conrad's *Heart of Darkness*.

Turcott ambled to an open-air bar with a mixed collection of tables and chairs under a thatched roof. The place was half filled in the late afternoon.

"Nimako?" Turcott asked the bartender.

The bartender looked up from his tabloid and gestured toward a man seated at a table with a view of the slowly moving river. The man had deep black skin and sunglasses to match. He tilted his head back and drained the remnants of a bottle of cold beer. Turcott set a few bills on the bar and ordered two more bottles of the brand the man was drinking.

"May I join you?" Turcott asked as he approached Nimako's table.

Nimako turned his head toward Turcott and studied him from behind his dark glasses. He nodded. Turcott slid down into a battered chair and set one of the beers in front of the African. Nimako drained two inches out of the bottle and nodded his gratitude.

"So," Nimako said, "how may I help you?"

"You know who Ross Egan is?" Turcott asked.

"Of course. He is a very famous man in Dutannuru."

"He is a very famous man in my country as well. I am looking into his life here, *before* he became so famous. I understand that you are a man who can help me in my research."

Nimako took another swig.

"You are looking for things that Egan might wish you not to find, eh?"

"Things that I can prove are true," Turcott replied.

"My business is not as good as it was in the old days. Some of my activities are frowned upon by the Dutannuru government."

"You would be well compensated should your assistance prove useful."

"What is it that you seek?"

"Egan has something hidden inside the powerhouse at the Umoja Dam. I need to get inside that powerhouse."

"Difficult, but not impossible. Security there is still very tight."

"I'm also chasing down a rumor, to see if it's true."

"Do rumors need to be true in the politics of your country?"

"Not always," Turcott admitted, "but in this case, I must have proof."

"What is this rumor?"

"Ross Egan bought a woman."

"A woman?" Nimako laughed incredulously. "You mean a prostitute?"

"No," Turcott replied icily. "A slave."

75

DANIEL PAGE ENTERED THE ROOM WHERE THE PRESIDENT AND his debate team were preparing for his third televised encounter with Ross Egan. The furnishings that populated the large space had been pushed against the outer walls to create room for two podiums and a central desk for the moderator.

"To understand my opponent's position on the environment, just look at what he chooses to drive," the President said. "Your truck is one of the least fuel efficient vehicles ever offered to the American people. It barely gets half the gas mileage of a Ford Model T. I have no problem with a soldier in harm's way driving a vehicle like that, but soccer moms and commuters shouldn't be clogging our roads and wasting fuel with them.

"As an engineer, Ross Egan claims to be all for energy efficiency. He claims, in fact, to be some kind of an expert on the subject. If his personal choices are a sign of that expertise, then he is the wrong man for the job of leading the United States to a sustainable energy future."

"I think that's it, Mr. President," the debate coach offered, "a knife to his ribs."

Page motioned to the President that he needed a moment of his time.

"Great work, everybody. Let's take a break and be back in twenty."

The President grabbed a water bottle and sat down in a rocking chair. Page sat opposite the President on one of the displaced sofas.

After the first two meetings, charitably declared draws by the mainstream media, the President felt it was time to go after his opponent with direct and personal attacks.

"How is the prep going?" Page asked.

"Well. There's a lot of emotion tied up in energy and the environment, but not a lot of facts for this WHO IS I site to parse. I can open it up a little without worrying about some crawl disputing my point. Energy and the environment are two areas where Egan is vulnerable, and we're going to take the fight to him."

"In that case, I brought you some more ammo. We got the goods on Egan's wind farm." Page rapped his knuckles against the cover of a thick three-ring binder. "I won't bore you with the engineering analysis, but the turbines on the Egan farm cannot generate the quantity of electricity they claim to be selling."

"So they're defrauding the utility?" the President asked with a smile.

"That's the only plausible explanation. I have some of the speechwriters distilling this report into sound bites—it's damning as hell."

"Hell is exactly where we need to damn Ross Egan."

76

"DOUBLE-H, CAN I HAVE A WORD WITH YOU?" DEB MCCOLL asked.

She stood at the door to a horse stall in the resort's large barn, a messenger bag slung over her shoulders. Hopps was brushing down the golden buckskin coat of his prized Akhal-Teke after their daily ride. The horse whinnied softly, clearly enjoying the attention. He set the brush into a bucket and fed the horse a handful of apple slices.

"Sure. Let's step into my office."

Hopps closed up the stall and accompanied McColl to the stable office next to the tack room. The barn was largely empty, save for the half dozen horses Hopps and his wife transported with them. Spring had brought with it a foal that had become the mascot of the WHO IS I team and had been named Liberty.

McColl pulled up a stool as Hopps dropped into a wooden office chair behind the desk. The office radio was tuned to Garr Denby's show and the host was discoursing about a fatuous federal court decision allowing the government to regulate an individual's mental activity under the Commerce Clause.

"Whatcha got?" Hopps asked as he turned down the radio.

"The Vice President's assassination—something about it just doesn't add up."

"Seemed pretty straightforward to me. What's troubling you about it?"

McColl set an iPad on the desktop and roused the device out of sleep mode. The screen displayed a web of lines connecting nodes—a digital mind map. She tapped one of the nodes and a photograph filled the screen. It showed Unden and his father dressed in hunters camouflage, armed with rifles, posing with the body of a large buck.

"Look at their rifles," McColl said.

Hopps studied the image closely but failed to discern what McColl was trying to show him.

"I pride myself on possessing a wide breadth of knowledge," Hopps admitted, "but sadly firearms is not among my fields of expertise."

"I'm an army brat, so I do know something about firearms. Look at the bolts on their rifles. Unden's father is holding a right-handed weapon. Unden has a left-handed model."

"So, Unden was a southpaw."

"Most likely. Left-handed rifles are the exception rather than the norm. The choice is based primarily on your dominant eye."

"Dominant eye?"

"Everybody has one eye that's stronger than the other. This is the master eye, or dominant eye. Doesn't matter if you're shooting pistols, rifles, or arrows, you *always* use one eye to site a target. If Unden is shooting lefty, he has a dominant left eye."

"It makes that much difference?"

"It's the difference between a hit or a miss. Unden was a Marine sniper, and a good one according to the news reports, so they would have dialed him in with his dominant eye."

McColl returned to the mind map and located a second photo. It showed the rifle mounted on a bipod, resting atop the desk in the hotel room.

"This is the weapon used in the assassination. It's a right-handed rifle," McColl explained. "Now, I checked and the company that makes this rifle doesn't produce a left-handed version."

"Can a southpaw fire a right-handed rifle, like Hendrix playing right-handed guitars upside down?"

"Sure, the problem is chambering the next round."

McColl braced her elbows on the desktop and held her arms as if aiming an imaginary rifle.

"I shoot lefty, so I'm familiar with this problem. With a bolt-action rifle, you work the bolt to load a round, fire, and then work the bolt again to load the next round. If I'm a lefty using a right-handed rifle, I have to reach over the barrel work the bolt. Doable, but awkward and a bit slower, even for someone really familiar with the weapon."

"Okay, lay it out for me."

"Unden's out of the military for a few years and he hunts with a left-handed rifle. He decides to off the President and Vice President and sets out to purchase the firepower necessary to do the job. He buys a right-handed rifle and mount and, with just a few days to practice with the weapon, uses it to near perfection."

"You don't buy it?" Hopps pressed.

"It's possible Unden could have fired, reloaded, and fire again, but unlikely. And here's the clincher."

McColl brought up a copy of the FBI report on the assassin's rifle.

"You hacked the FBI?"

"I pulled his Marine service records, too, just to be thorough. I'm sure they didn't even notice I was there."

Hopps smiled, certain McColl had left no trace from her illegal trespass.

"The ballistics report confirms this is the rifle that fired the two shots," McColl continued. "Fingerprints show that Unden held this weapon and the gun shot residue test of his hands indicates he recently fired a weapon. The problem is the fingerprints. The FBI pulled Unden's prints, both fingertips and palm, from the rifle. The location of these prints shows that he could have only held the rifle like this—"

McColl crouched back into firing position, this time shooting right-handed.

"The clincher is in his service jacket. During an overseas tour, he was injured in an off-duty altercation."

"Bar fight?" Hopps guessed.

McColl nodded. "A bottle was broken and a tiny sliver of glass struck Unden's right eye. The damage wasn't severe, but it degraded his vision in that eye."

"So there is no way Unden could've made these shots firing right-handed?"

"None."

"So somebody else pulled the trigger and left poor Unden to take the blame," Hopps surmised.

"Which leads us to logistics. A political convention is a big-ticket event that fills hotels for miles around the hall. How does a guy like Unden land a primo hotel within walking distance of the convention center just days before the event?"

"More important, a room with the perfect view of the convention center," Hopps offered. "And if Unden isn't the shooter, how did he get there?"

"His truck was valet parked at the hotel," McColl replied. "He drove, or to be precise, I believe he was *driven*. The FBI tracked his credit card use from North Dakota to San Francisco and even pulled security camera images of him pumping gas. Grainy shots, and he always has a ball cap on that obscures his face, but the license plate is clear."

"So the FBI has a definite trail of Unden driving across the country and checking into the hotel, where he kills the Vice President and wings the President before taking his own life. Open and shut case?"

McColl nodded. "The evidence against Unden is so overwhelming that there is no reason for the FBI to look deeper."

"But *you* did, I take it."

"Yes, and I found something very interesting. Every time Unden's truck stopped for gas, another vehicle stopped for gas, too. Not always at the same gas station, but always the same rental car, at the same exit, at the same time."

McColl ran through a series of still photos taken from gas station security cameras. Each showed the same vehicle and the same driver pumping gas. There did not appear to be any other passengers in the car.

"This car and Unden's truck get different gas mileage," McColl explained, "so it's highly unlikely both would pull off the highway at the same time unless they were travelling together."

"And if Unden is an unwilling patsy, then we have at least two other people involved," Hopps said. "How'd you piece this together?"

"I spotted the chase car in two of the FBI's photos," McColl replied. "Once I knew Unden couldn't have made the shot, I followed the other car. It led me to look at credit card numbers, and the rest fell into place. The same card was used to rent the car, to pay for fuel, food, and motels on the trip, and to rent the connecting room *next* to Unden's in San Francisco. That connecting room also happens to be wheelchair accessible."

"Which is how you might bring an incapacitated man into a hotel without drawing much attention. Very clever."

"Still not the best part, Double-H. The credit card the assassins used is part of the same block of numbers we found swirling around the President's on-line piggy bank."

One of Hopps's bushy eyebrows arched up like an angry cat as he quietly considered the implications of McColl's findings.

"You make a convincing case," Hopps said. "But the trick is how to point the authorities to this line of inquiry without exposing our other activities. I think I'll run this past our patrons."

77

"GOOD EVENING, MR. PRESIDENT," EGAN SAID WARMLY AS THE two candidates met center stage at the Jesse Auditorium.

"Ross," the President replied flatly as he shook Egan's offered hand.

Both men smiled as they met, cameras recording the moment, though the President's expression seemed less genuine, as if he would rather be anyplace else but here. They then greeted news anchor Hannah Douglass, who stood beside the moderator's desk, before all three took their places for the third debate.

"Mr. President," Douglass began, "in January, either you or your opponent will be sworn in as president. The oath of office includes a solemn vow to preserve, protect, and defend the Constitution of the United States. When the current Congress was sworn in almost two years ago, the Republican leadership felt it necessary to open its session with a recitation of the Constitution to remind lawmakers just what it was they had sworn to protect and defend. The debate over the constitutionality of government actions and constitutional interpretation is nearly as old as the document itself. How do you view the Constitution?"

"Thank you, Hannah," the President began. "The Constitution is a remarkable expression of a political vision. It describes the framework of a government that is of, by, and for the people. It also establishes the rule of law as the operating ethic of our nation. As you noted, debate over the meaning and intent of the Constitution began while the ink was still wet on the page, and this debate is a good and healthy thing. There are those who view the Constitution within the rigid confines of originalism, and others who see it as an artifact of its day whose meaning has ebbed with the forward progress of our nation and the world around us.

"I believe the Constitution is as relevant now as the day it was written. It's a living document that's relevance must be interpreted anew with each step in the evolution of our ongoing experiment in democracy.

"I do not agree with those primarily on the right who revere the Constitution as some sort of sacred text, as if the Framers descended from a mountain with it chiseled in stone tablets by the finger of God. Our nation is a work in progress, and the Constitution simply provides the guidelines within which our national government must operate.

"The Constitution was by no means perfect when it was first ratified, and the Framers themselves knew there was much work left undone. The failure to abolish slavery and establish equality for all men and women was clearly the most significant missed opportunity for this country to live up to its professed belief in the self-evident truth that all people are created equal. To the Framers, that meant all white men were created equal among themselves and more equal than everyone else. It's only through an enlightened, progressive view of the Constitution as a living document that it ultimately addressed our nation's original sin and expanded liberty to the slaves and suffrage to women.

"As a constitutional scholar and elected official, I find that the Constitution's bias toward the individual renders it a charter of negative liberties with regard to government's role in promoting social justice and the common good. It is in addressing these weaknesses in the Constitution that my administration has been most effective in serving the American people."

"Thank you, Mr. President," Douglass said. "The question now goes to you, Mr. Egan."

"This is an ideal question to start this debate because our respective understanding of the duties and limits of government are rooted in how we view the Constitution," Egan said. "While I respect the President's constitutional scholarship, I approach the Constitution and the supporting documents left to us by the Framers with a humbled respect and gratitude after my experience on the council that wrote the constitution for the nation of Dutannuru. It's one thing to argue political theory from the comfortable confines of an academic ivory tower, and quite another to debate natural law and the rights of man knowing that the results of those heated discussions will have an immediate and lifelong impact on the citizenry of a nation. In crafting Dutannuru's constitution, we drew heavily upon the founding documents of this country. We did so because the principles our Constitution so clearly articulates are directly responsible for the success of these United States.

"Consider that the nations in this hemisphere are the offspring of the European colonization of the New World. None has a monopoly of natural resources or favorable geography, yet only one rose from the wilderness to become a global super power. Only one.

"And less than two hundred years after the rebels shook off the chains of tyranny and reclaimed the God-given right of liberty for themselves and their descendants, that *one* nation of free people set foot on the moon.

"The accomplishments of the United States are unequalled in the history of human civilization, both in the pace of our nation's intellectual and creative output and its sheer magnitude. And there is a simple reason for this—the Constitution.

"In fashioning a form of limited government whose authority lies only within the bounds of a few enumerated powers, the Founders unleashed the potential energy of the entire populace. Unfettered by the tyranny of an oppressive state, the people did what came naturally—they created and they prospered.

"I do not share the belief that the Constitution is a living document, that its intent is malleable and can be refashioned to suit particular political ends. Such a belief is akin to football referees replacing the chains used to measure a team's progress toward the goal line with rubber bands. Like a yardstick, the restrictions placed on the government by the Constitution are not meant to be elastic.

"While I greatly admire the Constitution, I readily concede it is an imperfect work. It was, after all, created by imperfect beings. That is why only the people, and not any of the three branches of government, have the power to alter and amend the Constitution.

"The Constitution is the political DNA of our nation and the source of our exceptionalism. It is far and away the finest expression of faith in the individual."

"So, in nominating judges to the Supreme Court, you favor strict constructionists, Mr. Egan?" Douglass asked.

"I do," Egan replied, "and the Constitution is clear on this point. Congress writes the laws, and the courts judge whether those laws are constitutional. It does the people no good if the court's basis for measuring the constitutionality of a law flexes from one decision to the next, or if the result of a decision is, in effect, the creation of a new law.

"Each of the three branches is limited in what it can do by design, which is a good thing. Judicial activism oversteps the constitutional bounds of the judicial branch, in effect usurping the constitutional authority of the legislative branch. Judicial activism is a means of creating laws that legislators could not or would not pass, and that in most cases the people do not want. Where the Constitution is silent on an important issue, it is up to the people to provide the courts with guidance through the amendment process. Judicial activism is to be avoided."

"Any rebuttal, Mr. President?"

"Judges who share my belief in the Constitution as a living document are essential to the continued progress of our democracy. I will continue to appoint judges whose thinking is not limited by archaic notions of originalism."

"Since you raise the topic of Constitutional amendments," Douglass said as a segue, "I offer my next question to you, Mr. Egan. In your campaign literature, you propose not just one but four amendments to the Constitution. Not since the drafting of the Bill of Rights have so many amendments been offered for discussion. Is our nation in such dire straits that only an overhaul of the Constitution will remedy the situation?"

"If by overhaul, you are asking if I favor a constitutional convention to rewrite the Constitution, then my answer is an emphatic no.

The amendment process is more than adequate for addressing the fundamental issues that affect this nation.

"A century of progressive attack on the liberties enjoyed by our citizens—liberties that make this country the envy of the world—have exploited a fundamental flaw in the design of the Constitution. John Adams identified this flaw early on when he commented that our Constitution was made only for a *moral* and *religious* people. It is wholly inadequate to the government of any other kind of people.

"Enlightened progressive socialists in high office and on the courts, who are often both amoral and irreligious, pervert the explicit meaning and common sense woven into the Constitution to their own ends. In the case of abortion, they have created an unresolvable wedge issue that festers in our national psyche and provides cover for their other dangerous but less emotionally charged actions.

"Justice Blackmun identified the crux of the abortion problem in his majority opinion in the landmark *Roe vs. Wade* case. He wrote that the Constitution does not define *person* in so many words. Blackmun's comment begs the question: Where in the Constitution does an inferred right to privacy trump and explicitly enumerated right to life?

"The life amendment I propose seeks to rectify the deficiency Blackmun identified by defining the life of each individual person as existent from the moment of conception until natural death. Given the unresolved conflicts over life and death, and the marvels medical science has produced in just the past twenty years, this is a matter that should and must be decided by the people.

"The rest of my proposed amendments are more pragmatic. The tax amendment eliminates Congress's power to levy an income tax by repealing the Sixteenth Amendment. This is essential to shifting our country to consumption-based taxation. The citizenship amendment would revise the Fourteenth Amendment's Citizenship Clause to eliminate the granting of *jus soli* citizenship. Lastly is an amendment to regulate congressional conduct regarding pay, job perks, and self-exemption from laws applying to all other citizens. This amendment wasn't necessary when public service was something you did toward the end of a productive life, but in this age of career politicians and bureaucrats who regard the public purse as a personal piggy bank, this amendment's time has come."

"Mr. President," Douglass said politely.

"There is so much wrong with these proposed amendments that I hardly know where to begin. The right to abortion is a matter of settled law and this so-called life amendment usurps a woman's right to choose. And *natural death*? This would prevent physicians from compassionately assisting those suffering with painful, debilitating medical conditions from ending their lives with dignity. Forcing a person to continue a life of agony is morally hypocritical and simply cruel.

"Progressive taxation of income is a necessary tool at the government's disposal for serving and promoting the general welfare. Its elimination—a classic Republican pander to the rich—undermines our efforts toward creating a more just and equitable economic system.

"To deny birth right citizenship to the children of people who, in many instances, have risked their lives to reach these shores is again cruel and flies in the face of everything this great country stands for.

"And as to your amendment to rein in Congress, good luck with that."

"Why thank you, Mr. President," Egan said. "And since your rebuttal illustrates to the voters the vivid differences we offer, I have no further comment."

"Returning to the proposed life amendment," Douglass said to Egan, "in addition to ending abortion and physician-assisted suicide, wouldn't it by necessity end the death penalty as well?"

"If we are to be consistent, yes," Egan replied. "A while this stance might be troubling to some death penalty proponents, it is far less morally hypocritical, to borrow the President's term, than defending the right to life for convicted murders while simultaneously championing the right to end innocent life in the womb."

"Moving to the environment," Douglass continued, "Mr. President, your administration has sought to strike a balance between energy production and environmental protection, especially with regard to man-made climate change. Your efforts to curb our nation's greenhouse gas emissions have resulted in legislative and executive actions both lauded and decried. How do you view where we are as a nation now, and where we need to be in the future?"

"Change is never easy," the President replied. "But the effects of man's activities on the environment are undeniable. The scientific facts speak for themselves and the finest minds are of one voice in raising this alarm.

"The most significant foreign policy accomplishment of my presidency is one we chose to undertake unilaterally for the benefit of all mankind. The New York Climate Exchange will open for business next week in a display of free market capitalism with a social conscience. It's an exchange driven not by profit for profit's sake, but profit for the planet's sake. Our carbon emissions must be reduced, and we don't really care how it happens as long as it does happen.

"The hard work of creating a private exchange for the public good is done, and over the next four years my administration will work to bring other nations on board to globalize the marketplace for carbon credits. China has joined us as a charter member and we are currently in serious discussions with India and much of Europe. By the end of my second term, I fully expect scientists around the world to report that the amount of carbon in our atmosphere is leveling off or even showing the first signs of declining.

"As important as curbing greenhouse gas emissions is, I fully recognize our nation's need for reliable sources of energy. We have made great strides with clean, renewable sources of power, and transitioning from fossil fuel vehicles to hybrid and electric vehicles. I got the ball rolling in the right direction and we must keep it moving."

"Mr. Egan," Douglass said.

"The President and I are on the opposite sides of many issues, and this is certainly one of them. The President accepts the alarmist position on face value because it serves his purpose of increasing government control over the individual. As an engineer, I have trouble with any hypothesis that boasts such a poor experimental track record and is so deeply mired in politics. All I'm willing to say about the earth's climate is that we don't know nearly enough about it and any decisions we made now, especially economy altering national transformations, would be done in ignorance.

"As president, I would fund basic research in climatology and put a constellation of satellites in orbit to collect as much data as possible. These are important scientific questions and they need answers based on facts, not politics.

"That said, I am all for energy efficiency in our buildings and vehicles and will certainly support improvements in existing technologies and the development of new technologies."

"If you encourage efficiency, then why do you drive a HumVee?" the President sneered. "Its fuel consumption might as well be measured in gallons per mile."

"As with far too many things, Mr. President," Egan replied, "you clearly don't know what you're talking about."

"I take it you are a climate change skeptic?" the President countered.

"The appropriate term is *realist*," Egan replied calmly. "The facts don't support your rhetoric, and often contradict it."

"I have a few facts of my own," the President said smugly, "starting with your hypocritical wind farm scam."

78

UMOJA HYDROELECTRIC POWER PLANT, DUTANNURU
OCTOBER 13

"...AND THIS IS WHERE TANU BAAFI SURRENDERED TO ROSS EGAN," the soldier said proudly.

Wearing camouflage fatigues and a black beret, the young soldier escorting Edward Turcott pointed to a circular marker of white stone that had been set flush to the earth near the edge of the helipad.

"Incredible," Turcott said with a feigned touch of awe in his voice.

"I was here when it happened. Tanu Baafi surrendered Safo on this very spot."

Turcott snapped a few pictures, and then scribbled some short-hand notes onto a small pad.

"There is something else I would like to see," Turcott hinted.

"The power house," the soldier said knowingly. "Visitors are not permitted."

"So I've heard. Still, control of this power plant was recognized by both sides as vital." Turcott lowered his voice. "I understand that arrangements have been made."

Turcott tapped an envelope concealed in his multi-pocketed vest. The soldier checked his watch and gave a curt nod of the head. Both men began walking toward the dam.

"Few are authorized to enter the power plant," the soldier explained. "Before reunification, very high clearance was required. Very tight security."

"And now?"

"The danger has passed. This plant requires few workers to function, mostly for maintenance. Security has been reduced to appropriate levels. A two-man patrol will soon finish their sweep of the area round the dam and move on to the perimeter. They will return in twenty minutes. You must be out of the powerhouse before then."

As they neared the powerhouse, Turcott saw a pair of armed men walking away along the fence line. His escort then guided him around the side of the powerhouse and held out his hand.

"As I told your associate," the soldier said distastefully, "I require payment before I let you inside."

Turcott pulled the envelope from his vest pocket and placed it in the man's palm. The soldier quickly thumbed the stack of bills inside and nodded satisfactorily. He pocketed the envelope and unlocked a side door to the powerhouse.

"You have ten minutes. Knock when you are ready to exit. It will be *bad* for both of us if the patrol returns and you are still inside."

"I understand," Turcott said.

Turcott stepped through the doorway into a windowless vestibule. The soldier closed the outer door behind him. A single bulb illuminated the entry space. He opened the heavy inner door and discovered an eerie darkness. The air that greeted him smelled stale and musty. The space beyond was deadly quiet.

Careful to remain in the shallow aura of light from the vestibule, Turcott stepped onto a metal platform. His hand fumbled along the wall until it found a bank of light switches. The first caused the lights immediately overhead to flicker to life. He found the platform was the upper landing of stair that led down several flights to the powerhouse floor.

He flipped each switch to illuminate successive bays of the powerhouse. The cavernous space expanded with each bank of lights until it spanned the entire length of the building. The concrete structure showed its scars, clear evidence of past damage and repair. Cudjoe had ceded Dutannuru a ruin and Egan had vowed the despot would find the same if he ever took it back.

And instead of massive generators harnessing the kinetic energy of the river to power a nation, Turcott saw six gaping holes in the thick concrete floor.

79

"COME ON IN, DANIEL," THE PRESIDENT SAID AS HE FINISHED UP his morning security briefing.

Page waited until an aide retreated from the on-board office with the briefing books before entering and closing the door behind him.

"Mr. President," Page began, "I have some interesting news regarding Egan in Dutannuru."

"Our October surprise?"

Page shook his head. "Still working on that, but our man is making progress. What I do have ties back to Egan's background as an engineer. In the last debate, we went after him for cheating his power company."

"The numbers don't lie, and he didn't refute it," the President said smugly. "I scored some points there."

"Yes, Mr. President, but there may be a problem. Do you recall the Umoja Hydroelectric Dam?"

"Where Egan gave the speech that made him famous?"

"Yes," Page replied. "It's not operational."

"Was there an accident? I didn't hear about anything in my briefing."

"No. The facility was apparently never repaired after Safo ceded it to Dutannuru a decade ago."

"Wasn't that power plant Cudjoe's main objective?" the President asked.

"It was. And in Egan's own words, if Cudjoe took it back, he would have found it in the same condition as he left it. Everyone assumed the plant was booby-trapped and, if forced to retreat, the

Dutannuru army would destroy it. Nobody thought to take Egan literally, but it makes sense. Why repair a vital power plant that's within a stone's throw of a hostile enemy?"

"If the Umoja plant doesn't work, where is Dutannuru getting their power?"

"That's the million dollar question," Page replied. "Dutannuru made it look like the plant was operational as a feint, believing Cudjoe would one day try to take it back. Egan not only rebuilt Dutannuru's electrical infrastructure, he managed to hide an entire power plant. Tracking back the network of high voltage transmission wires, we believe it's located on a military base just outside of the capital—about as far from the Safolese border as they could get it."

Page laid several photographs on the President's desk.

"I've had some experts look over these. Aside from some emergency generators, they can find no sign of a conventional power plant large enough to meet the needs of Dutannuru. Given the presence of an industrial scale desalinization plant providing a ready source of fresh water, they speculate that if there's a power plant here, it's nuclear."

"How could Dutannuru have built a nuclear power plant without our knowing about it?" the President asked, pondering the implications.

"The Japanese and the Russians both have reactor designs that are basically plug-and-play, and if they paid a premium for discretion..."

"So it's possible."

"No one really pays much attention to that part of the world," Page explained. "And Egan's engineering background includes nuclear energy. What makes this all the more suspicious is his wind farm. It really is generating electricity, but those big windmills can't be doing the whole job. Like the Umoja Dam, Egan has concealed his real source of power."

"You need permits to build or operate a power plant," the President mused.

"He has the required permits for his wind turbines, but not for any other type of power generator. Oddly enough, when they installed the turbines, Egan and his father pulled permits to drill monitoring wells scattered all over their property. We don't have any of the reports, but they test the ground water regularly."

"If he's taken such elaborate measure to hide his power source, odds are it's either illegal or environmentally dangerous."

"Or both," Page agreed.

"I have to consult with the Attorney General," the President said, "but I believe this pattern of suspicious behavior constitutes probable cause."

"Egan has scheduled a press conference at his family farm to address the issues you raised in the debate," Page said as he flipped through his notes. "This is so perfect it's almost poetic. His press conference is set for the same time as the inaugural opening bell of the carbon exchange."

The President smiled at the thought of celebrating the fulfilment of his boldest environmental accomplishment while simultaneously exposing his rival as an environmental fraud.

80

"THANK YOU FOR COMING OUT ON SUCH A BEAUTIFUL DAY," ROSS Egan began.

He stood beside his HumVee on a clearing along the northern shore of Lake Michigan, speaking to a gathering of reporters. The sun shone bright in a clear sky, the forest surrounding them ablaze with autumn color. Egan was dressed in blue jeans, a dark blue turtleneck and a wool sweater.

Egan's SUV was parked next to a fenced enclosure surrounding a metal clad pole barn. Thick electrical wires ran from the gable end of the barn to a row of freestanding utility poles going out to the main road. In the distance, towering wind turbines spun slowly in the breeze off the lake.

"The President said a lot of things during the last debate—things that were at best empty rhetoric, at worst flat wrong. I've asked you all here today to address two of the latter.

"Most of you already know that I don't pay much attention to what the President says, especially when he's talking about me. Politics can be an ugly business and I knew what I was in for when I decided to run. The President is fighting hard to keep his job. I respect that. But in the last debate, he crossed the line. He insulted both my parents and my truck. In most parts of this country, those are fighting words.

Several reporters chuckled at the remark that would likely emerge as that evening's sound bite from the campaign trail. Niki stood nearby with members of a Secret Service detail recording the scene with her camera. Egan opened the driver's door of the HumVee and stepped up into the vehicle.

"The President claimed I wasn't walking the walk on energy efficiency by driving a gas guzzling SUV," Egan continued. "He actually claimed that Henry Ford's original Model T got better gas mileage than this beast of mine. Now, I can haul a lot with this truck, but what the President's shoveling is a mighty big load."

Egan pressed the start button and the throaty sounds of 6.5-liter V-8 turbo diesel roared from the vehicle's engine compartment. He punched the accelerator a few times, revving up the volume and intensity of the sound.

"According to the President," Egan shouted over the revving engine, "I just burned about a gallon of fuel and haven't moved an inch. I assure you that not one drop of diesel died for this demonstration."

Egan tapped another button on the dashboard and the vehicle fell silent.

"Did any of you near the back of my truck see or smell anything?" Egan asked. "Any exhaust coming from my tailpipes?"

"Just a clear liquid dripping out," a reporter replied.

"No need to call the EPA," Egan said with a grin. "It's water. I won't bore you with the details about what's under my hood—especially since I can't because of a non-disclosure agreement—but I can assure you it's not available from the factory. Not yet, anyway. What I am authorized to say is that the prototype engine in my old HumVee was created without a single dime of DOE funding, and it *will* change the world. And to prove the point..."

Egan shifted the truck into drive and silently moved the vehicle forward a few feet.

"What you heard when I started my truck was computer generated engine noise," Egan explained. "Folks get a little too curious when a big truck like this rolls past without making a sound. And around here, it's a good idea to give the wildlife a heads up that you're coming down the road. There's enough deer hit around here without driving in stealth mode.

"Which gets us to the bigger issue—the kind of vehicle I drive is *none* of the President's damn business. The government should play no part in telling private companies what to make and private citizens what to buy.

"As to the matter of my family's wind farm, if the President has any evidence that my parents and I are cheating the electric company he ought to bring it forward and have charges filed against us. Now if you'll follow me."

Egan led the reporters to a bank of utility meters that stood just outside of the fenced enclosure.

"The electric company uses these meters to measure how much power we're delivering so they can calculate how much money to pay us. These are the electric company's meters and they verify every month that the readings are accurate.

"The President's accusation against my family and me is based on the assertion that there is no way that our windmills could generate the amount of power that we're selling to the electric company. Given the President's support of green power sources and all the subsidies the government provides for wind farms—of which my family has taken none—I find it ironic that his charge against me is rooted in the inherent inability of wind generators to provide a steady flow of power. If the wind doesn't blow, the electricity doesn't flow."

One by one, the blades of the wind turbines in the distance slowed to a stop.

"I have to admit that the President is absolutely correct—our wind turbines are *not* providing the power that we are selling."

Egan smiled as he let his admission sink in.

"Are you admitting to charging the utility for more power than you delivered?" a reporter asked pointedly.

"No, I simply agree with the President that wind turbines are an unreliable power source. There is no way our turbines could provide the steady, reliable flow of power that we're delivering. In fact, if you look closely at these meters, you'll see that only one has stopped. That's the one connected to our wind farm. The rest are still spinning away and clean, reliable power is still flowing out into the grid."

"If not wind, then how are you generating this power?" another reporter demanded.

Egan smiled. "The *how* is my life's work, the product of exercising my individual right to pursue happiness."

81

SANDRA GIFFORD SAT IN THE PASSENGER SEAT OF A BLACK SUV bearing government license plates. The vehicle sat idling on the shoulder of the main road that led to the Egan family farm, one of several in the strike team deployed for this operation. The in-dash display carried a live feed of Egan's press conference.

The cell phone in Gifford's hand purred with an incoming message: RAID IS A GO! She clipped the phone to her belt and switched on her throat mike.

"All right people, we're going in. Watch yourselves—these folks own firearms and may react badly."

A panel track containing a detachment of agents from the FBI's elite Hostage Rescue Team (HRT) pulled out first to lead the assault. A trio of matching SUVs filled with FBI and EPA field agents immediately followed suit. A second panel truck brought up the rear—this one containing EPA hazardous materials gear and equipment.

Gifford's cell phone vibrated and she quickly answered.

"Egan's security detail has been notified that you're in play," the FBI Director said. "Tread lightly. Everything you do in the next few minutes will be on national TV."

"Got it. We're heading onto the property."

The convoy raced along the two-lane road and turned up the gravel drive onto the Egan property. Police lights flashing, the five vehicles roared down the wooded drive toward the clearing.

Egan looked past the reporters gathered around him and the utility meters at the rapidly approaching vehicles.

"Ross," Niki said with concern.

"I see 'em. Don't know what this is about, but just keep shooting pictures."

Niki nodded and trained her camera on the unexpected intrusion. Secret Service agents moved into protective position around the candidate. Robin Boyd, the lead agent, drew close to Egan.

"Sir," the woman said softly. "There's no need for concern over your safety. This is a joint FBI/EPA operation regarding your power source. Their authorization checks and it's been cleared with my superiors."

"No advance warning?" Egan asked.

"None, sir. We just got word now."

As the vehicles closed in, they fanned out to form a perimeter. The lead truck remained on the driveway, gravel crunching under its tires as it came to a stop. The rear doors on the truck flew open and eight figures clad in black riot gear and armed with combat assault rifles leapt out.

Boyd motioned for her team to remain with the candidate while she conferred with the FBI lead agent. Weapons drawn but pointed down, the detail moved Egan to the far side of the HumVee.

News cameras recorded the unfolding scene. Live feeds of the raid on the Egan farm streamed out to the twenty-four hour news channels and the Internet. Encountering no resistance, the strike team quickly assumed a defensive posture, securing the area around the fenced building.

"Special Agent Boyd," Gifford said as she assumed command of the scene. "I'm Special Agent Gifford. I understand that you were just notified of our arrival."

Boyd curtly shook Gifford's offered hand. "Washington was a little light on the details. Why is the FBI coming down on a presidential candidate like a Mexican drug lord?"

"Standard procedure when securing a location where the occupants are known to be armed."

"A couple of hunting rifles hardly makes this Ruby Ridge. And these folks are about as supportive of law and order as any you'll find."

"That may be, but I have a warrant to search these premises."

"We both know this stinks," Boyd said.

Gifford shrugged. Boyd motioned for her team to escort Egan over. She then introduced the candidate to the FBI special agent.

"To what do I owe the pleasure?" Egan asked politely.

"Sir, I have a warrant to search this property and all structures located on it for an illegal power generator."

Gifford handed Egan the search warrant, which he quickly reviewed.

"What you're looking for does not exist," Egan said flatly.

"With all due respect, sir, you admitted to possessing an unknown power generator during your press conference."

"True," Egan said, "but my generator is not illegal."

"That is for the experts to decide. Will you now show us your generator?"

"No."

"You refuse to comply with a lawful search?" Gifford asked sharply.

"You miss my point. Your search does not cover *legal* power generators. I am under no obligation to show you technology that I am within my legal rights to own."

"The Attorney General and a federal judge aren't so sure. The installation of test wells on your property indicates a concern over groundwater contamination. We are seizing the annual reports for those wells from the testing lab. Illegal discharges into the groundwater fall under the purview of the federal and state environmental regulators."

"Again, my energy-related activities on this property are not governed by any state or federal regulations and are therefore legal," Egan replied. "But let's cut to the chase, Special Agent. You are welcome to the test reports, which show no contamination of any kind. I will not cooperate with your illegal search. If you want to see my generator, you'll have to break the door down in front of all these cameras."

Egan nodded his head toward the pole barn.

"Clear a perimeter around that building," Gifford ordered as she turned away from Egan. "Cut the lock on that gate and get that building opened. EPA, suit up to go inside."

Gifford had Egan and his security detail moved behind the EPA's panel truck. Bolt cutters made short work of the padlock on the fence. The HRT agents found the inconspicuous door to the pole barn a bit more daunting. After several blows with a battering ram, the locked steel panel sprang free of its hinges. Several of the reporters gasped as a roiling gray cloud billowed out from the barn's interior.

"Pull back!" the leader of the breaching unit ordered.

"What the hell?" Gifford spat.

"Don't worry," Egan said nonplussed. "It's mostly steam."

The door fell through the haze and clanged loudly against a concrete slab. Through the opening, the pole barn's interior appeared dark and shrouded in fog. EPA agents dressed in tightly sealed, orange chemical suits cautiously approached the building. An LCD monitor in the back of the EPA truck displayed a live feed from the camera mounted to the lead agent's helmet.

In the distance, an engine loudly coughed to life.

"Another surprise?" Gifford asked suspiciously.

"Emergency generator," Egan replied matter-of-factly. "My folks don't like it when we lose power—messes up their DVR. First time we've had to run it for real in years."

"Why's that?"

"Your men will have the answer to that question shortly."

In single file, the four men stepped toward the open doorway. The lead man entered the barn with a Geiger counter. He slowly swept the air in front of him with the external probe for any sign of radiation.

"Only normal background radiation," the man reported.

The rest of the EPA team filed into the barn. Each carried sensors for a variety of toxic or volatile chemicals. A dull hum filled the interior of the barn, the deepening sound of rapidly spinning equipment slowly winding down. As the vapor dissipated, the team saw a pair of steam turbines bolted to the floor. Piping ran from the generators to the rear of the building. There, they found a red-hot puddle of molten metal and a perfectly circular hole cored through the floor. The leader crouched over the twelve-inch diameter opening and aimed a flashlight and helmet camera down the shaft.

"Are you seeing this?" the agent asked.

"Roger that," Gifford replied.

The powerful beam cast by the EPA agent's flashlight was simply swallowed by the deep void. For as far as he could see, the interior lining of the shaft was as smooth as glass.

The agent noticed the remnant of a stainless steel bolt on the floor. He picked up the fragment with his gloved hand and dropped it into the hole. It quickly disappeared from view and, if it reached bottom, it made no sound.

Egan's iPhone vibrated against his hip and he checked the screen. It was his father.

"Can I take this?" Egan asked Gifford.

Gifford nodded. Egan accepted the call and set the phone on speaker mode.

"Yeah, pa?" Egan answered.

"I'm watching your press conference—very exciting."

"I know."

"Just thought you should let those FBI folks know that the head of the electric co-op called and a good bit of the eastern UP just lost power."

82

THE PRESIDENT SMILED AS HE WATCHED THE VIDEO MONITORS in Peter Sturla's well-appointed suite overlooking the trading floor of the New York Climate Exchange. All of the cable news channels carried the unfolding story of the raid on the Egan family farm. A spokesman for the Justice Department had delivered a brief statement regarding the search, followed by a terse "no comment" from the White House Press Secretary.

"An interesting development don't you think, Mr. President?" Sturla asked.

"I love the optics, especially Egan in handcuffs as the FBI hauled him away for questioning."

"That clip will be in the next round of ads from my political action committees, starting tonight. They will juxtapose you as the stalwart environmentalist versus Egan the polluting eco-terrorist."

"I look forward to seeing them," the President said.

"We first need some footage of you opening the climate exchange."

"I really do like the acronym—NYCE," the President offered, pronouncing the four letters as a word.

"It will be very *nice* indeed to those invested in the exchange," Sturla quipped.

The President smiled warmly at the thought of his part-ownership in the privately held bank that would process all of the exchange's transactions. That single asset in his blind trust would make him a billionaire many times over before the end of his second term.

"Mr. President, the Chinese Ambassador has arrived," the aide cheerfully reported. "And everything is ready for your opening remarks."

"Thank you, Lindsey. We'll join him shortly."

AMBASSADOR LONG STOOD WITH THE CHAIRMAN OF THE EX-change and a small entourage in the anteroom to the balcony over-looking the trading floor. The President arrived with his security detail and a group of aides. Both men moved to the center of the room and shook hands.

"Ambassador, it is a pleasure to see you again," the President said warmly. "Thank you for being here today."

"I am pleased to meet with you as well," Long replied. "And it is indeed my honor to represent the People's Republic of China on this most important occasion—important both for the relations between our two countries and for the future of the world."

"I couldn't agree more. China's commitment to partnering with the Unites States in curbing greenhouse gas emissions bespeaks your nation's leadership role on the global stage. I believe China's partici-pation in the NYCE will allow this exchange to flourish where pre-vious efforts have failed."

"It is truly fortunate when national and international interests coincide."

"Gentlemen, it's time," the chairman of the exchange announced.

The chairman opened a sliding glass door and led his distin-guished guests out onto the balcony. They were met by applause accompanied by a recording of the Marine Corps Band playing *Hail to the Chief.* LCD screens mounted to the railing glowed with images of the US and Chinese flags.

The NYCE trading floor was a cavernous two-story space popu-lated with islands of workstations and flat screen displays. Laid out with an efficiency of purpose, the room employed LED lighting and various recycled and renewable materials in keeping with the envi-ronmental mission of the exchange.

"Ladies and gentlemen," the chairman announced into a microphone, "it is my great honor to present the President of the United States."

Traders cheered from the floor, thrilled to share the moment with the man whose political will made the NYCE a reality.

"As many of you know, I am a firm believer in capitalism," the President said. "Capitalism, when employed correctly, can be a tool for good. I believe this exchange will be a shining example of capitalism as a tool for social and environmental justice.

"I wish to thank Ambassador Long and the People's Republic of China for their partnership with the United States in the founding of this exchange. Both our great nations recognize the dangers of climate change and our responsibilities as citizens of the world to address a problem largely of our own making. With that, I am proud to declare this exchange open."

The President motioned for Ambassador Long to join him in pressing a large ceremonial button. Automated bells built into the balcony railing peeled loudly, provoking another cheer from the brokers and environmentalists on the trading floor. The President shook the ambassador's hand for the cameras recording the historic event, both men smiling broadly.

In an exclusive agreement, NYCE acquired the entire annual allotment of emissions permits from the governments participating in the climate exchange at a fixed price. The exchange opened with the permits offered to emitters at a higher, initial public offer price of $25 per metric ton of carbon dioxide emitted.

As the sole, legal market in which this peculiar pollution commodity could be acquired, the owners of NYCE hoped to recoup much of their initial investment during the day's trading and turn a profit on every trading day that followed.

The President glanced at the big board as he left the balcony and saw that bidding had already driven the price-per-ton up forty-five cents. NYCE was his proudest accomplishment, and not because he had any delusions about its potential impact on the global climate.

"Gentlemen," the chairman said enthusiastically as they returned to Sturla's suite, "it may still be morning but I believe a toast is in order."

A cart draped in white linen had been rolled into the suite during the opening bell ceremony and a uniformed steward was filling slender glass flutes with champagne. Starting with the President and the Chinese ambassador, servers distributed glasses around the room.

"To the New York Climate Exchange," the President offered with his glass held high, "may it prove to the world that capitalism can be an instrument of good."

"Hear, hear!" the gathering responded.

Daniel Page waited as the President mingled with guests and donors in the suite, taking in the scene and imagining how he would describe it in the book he would eventually write. The video monitors switched from coverage of the opening bell back to the unfolding story of Egan's apparent arrest by the FBI.

"What's happening?" the President asked softly as he moved next to Page.

"Egan's on his way to the FBI office in Traverse City for questioning. Whatever he was doing in that barn was more powerful than anyone considered."

"How so?"

"The good news is that, fortunately, that part of Michigan is lightly populated. Bad news is most of those folks are without electricity. Something happened when the FBI kicked down the door to Egan's barn that cut the power to thousands of homes. The sudden loss of power triggered a cascade failure that's spread to adjacent sections of the grid, including Canada. Since this wasn't weather related damage, power should be fully restored in a few hours."

"Any big cities lose power?" the President asked.

Page shook his head. "It didn't make it as far as Madison or Detroit. We'll spin it to make it look like the power failure was Egan's fault, but there's a catch."

"Which is?"

"With the loss of power from Egan's farm, the local utility has been forced to increase output from one of its older coal-fired plants."

"I trust you'll find a way to spin that to our advantage, too," the President said as he tapped his glass against Page's. "The silver lining here is that the old plant will have to buy plenty of emissions permits. In fact, I'll bet news of the blackout is already having a positive effect on the permit price."

A crawl running across one of the screens beneath a business news anchor listed the permit price up to $32.13 per ton.

83

ON AIR

"YOU KNOW WHO I AM," DENBY DECLARED TO OPEN HIS BROAD-cast. "You know *what* this is, and you know *why* we are here. So let's dispense with the pleasantries and get straight to work. We have a lot to cover and only three short hours in which to do it.

"Just a few hours ago, GOP nominee Ross Egan was taken into custody by the FBI for questioning. He has not, as yet, been charged with any crime. These are the known facts and anything else you may be hearing from the mainstream media apparatchiks is either idle chatter or malicious campaigning for the President.

"As to the raid and arrest—am I the only one who finds the tim-ing suspiciously convenient for the President? The term that comes to mind is *October Surprise*. The President, arguably one of the world's biggest cheerleaders for climate change regulation and the greening of our nation's economy, launched a baseless allegation during the last debate, in effect accusing Ross Egan of fraud and conspiracy. And his complaint, get this, is that windmills—which all tree-hugging liberals just love as long as they don't have to see them from their tony enclaves—are so inefficient that they could not possibly generate the amount of electricity Egan claims he and his parents are selling to the local utility.

"The utility never complained that they weren't getting the power and, just before the start of this program, released a statement that its audits of the meters on the Egan property accurately reflect the amount of power it received from the Egan wind farm.

"So instead of asking Egan to voluntarily come in and answer some questions about how he is generating electricity, the regime roars in locked and loaded like they've cornered public enemy number one—though in the eyes of the regime desperate to stay in power, Ross Egan *is* public enemy number one.

"In the process of arresting Egan in the most publicly damaging way possible, the regime inadvertently triggered a regional blackout that they're now trying to pin on him as well. Remember friends—it's not the facts that matter to the left, it's the seriousness of the allegation.

"All we can say for certain is that Ross Egan knows a hell of a lot more about energy than our President, and he has done far more as a private citizen to empower people than our President has in his long and distinguished career of political agitation and community organizing.

"In a related and similarly breaking story, the regime unleashed its latest horror on us this morning to the fawning adulation of the liberal media. Like most of the laws and policies proffered by this administration, the New York Climate Exchange—which we all know is anything but *nice*—was cobbled together out of dead ideas like the regulatory equivalent of Doctor Frankenstein's monster. That monster was jolted to life this morning by edict and has been unleashed on the world. *Or so we thought.*

"As we have discussed at length on this program, free markets exist in the absence of government, not because of it. The Wall Street we all know started with a group of twenty-four traders under a buttonwood tree in Manhattan, not because the President at the time willed the exchange into existence. So the NYCE is not a true exchange but a political wolf dressed in free market finery.

"Now, there are a few dirty little secrets about the President's climate exchange. First, the government has no desire for American industry to reduce its carbon emissions. To do so would eliminate the government's income stream from the sale of the permits. It's like the tax on gasoline—if we stopped using internal combustion engines completely, the government would lose billions of dollars in revenue. The government makes more money off the sale of each gallon of gasoline than all of the oil companies combined, and they do nothing to bring that product to market. By way of the tax code, and now this exchange, the government has a vested interest in things staying just as they are and taxing the status quo.

"The second dirty little secret is that the *real* green objective of the NYCE is the money that will line the pockets of investors backing it. Make no mistake—the climate exchange is not a charitable institution or feel-good non-profit. There is some very big money behind the exchange and they expect a solid return on their investment."

"*But Garr, but Garr,*" Denby said in a mock simpering falsetto of a leftist, "*aren't these well-intentioned investors entitled to a return for the good the exchange will do? I thought you were a cheerleader for the free market.*"

"Yes I am, but this is anything but free market entrepreneurship. This exchange is crony capitalism at its worst. The President used the power of the government to create a market that otherwise has no earthly reason to exist. By design, his well-heeled political backers got an exclusive franchise to market the government permits and the President, through his not-so-blind trust, gets a cut of the action that could make him a multi-billionaire.

"I say *could* because there is a tragic, or from my point of view karmic, flaw in the design of this parasitic exchange. The NYCE is based, as I said earlier, on the hope that the engine that drives the private sector will continue for the foreseeable future to be carbon-based.

"Imagine, if you will, a technological innovation in the realm of energy production that completely alters how we create the power that drives our economy. Such an innovation would torpedo this artificial market for carbon permits and take those who hoped to profit from it down as well.

"My friends," Denby said with an undercurrent of delight in his voice, "just such an innovation does indeed exist."

84

IN A SUITE ON THE OPPOSITE SIDE OF THE TRADING FLOOR, MAYA Randell and her husband sat in a pair of leather club chairs observing the opening day of trading. She was sipping a cup of green tea while her husband enjoyed an espresso.

The monitors in the Randell's suite silently displayed feeds from the exchange floor and several of the cable news and business channels. The room was filled with the sound of a Garr Denby webcast that filled one of the monitors. Shortly after noon, the news channels all abruptly switched to a live feed from China. Their respective reporters were staged along the security fence outside of a large industrial facility near Beijing.

"This looks interesting," Burton said as he used a remote to mute Denby's audio and increase the volume on one of the newscasts.

"...and I am standing just outside Beijing Power Plant Number One," the reporter announced. "We have unconfirmed reports of unusual activity at this, the oldest of the coal fired power plants serving China's capital city. What this unusual activity might be, we can only speculate, but the presence of the Chinese military indicates the seriousness of the situation."

Army trucks and soldiers on foot raced into position. Several of the trucks towed field equipment that the soldiers quickly trained on the power plant.

"And from this vantage point," the reporter continued, "we cannot tell just what the Chinese army is aiming at the plant."

One by one, powerful floodlights cut through the dark to illuminate the power plant's towering smokestacks. Most of China's ever-growing demand for electricity was sated with coal, and the thick smog that blanketed Beijing was the price its citizens paid for that power.

The first of the smokestacks shuddered as a cloud of dust burst out from around its base. It rose up ever so slightly and hovered for just a second before collapsing straight down as if a trap door had sprung open beneath it. Its siblings disappeared in similar fashion, replaced by the growing cloud of dust.

"...the soldiers are cheering," the reporter said, confused at the unfolding scene. "The collapse of the smokestacks here at Beijing Power Plant Number One was not an accident, but rather a precisely controlled demolition. The remainder of the power plant is still intact and, from what I can see, the lights are still on in China's capital city."

One of the monitors chimed and the screen switched into videoconference mode. Computers at both ends of the call connected. The Chinese Chairman Chen Yung-Chin appeared on screen, seated in his Beijing office.

"*Wan shang hao*, Chairman Chen," Maya said in greeting.

"And a good day to you and your husband," Chen replied.

"I trust that you are monitoring the opening of the climate exchange."

"I am indeed, with great interest. The price has quickly risen past forty US dollars per metric ton. Demand for carbon permits appears quite strong."

"Demand is largely a matter of perception," Maya posited. "Artificial scarcity alone causes the price of these permits to rise irrationally. The awakening of a new reality will bring it down as quickly as your smokestacks."

"And with it, the houses of our mutual enemies."

Burton tapped the Bluetooth headset on his right ear and uttered a one-word command: "Sell."

85

"MR. EGAN!" A GAGGLE OF REPORTERS SHOUTED IN UNISON, clamoring for attention as Egan emerged with a pair of his Secret Service bodyguards.

Egan signaled he would be with them in a moment. It was a brisk fall evening with a hint of snow in the air. Aware of the national news value of the situation, the local police had established traffic controls on this section of the city's downtown and cordoned off an area for the press.

Camera trucks filled the two-lane street and the adjacent parking spaces in front of the four-story building that housed the FBI Resident Office. Egan waved to his father, who stood with the rest of his security detail and their vehicles on the opposite side of Front Street.

"You want me to handle this?" Egan's attorney asked.

"Naw," Egan replied. "They need to hear it from me. I would appreciate it if you'd fill my dad in on the highlights."

"Sure."

As his lawyer departed, Egan approached the awaiting press.

"It's been a long day and I don't have anything prepared, so let's get right to your questions."

Egan pointed to a reporter from the local paper.

"Have any charges been filed against you?"

"If they had, I don't think I'd be standing here talking to you," Egan replied with a laugh. "The FBI and the EPA simply had some questions and I was forthcoming in all of my answers. I wish to be very clear on this point: my energy research has not violated any laws or regulations imposed by the local, state, or federal authorities."

"What about the claim that you defrauded the electric company, that your wind mills could not generate the quantity of power you were selling?"

"Two separate questions. The claim that I defrauded my local utility is baseless. I have provided documentation and affidavits confirming that my parents and I delivered every watt of power for which we were paid. Regarding my wind mills—I never claimed they were the *sole* source of the electricity we were selling."

"But you claimed you were selling green power," a reporter countered skeptically.

"And I stand by that claim. My power source is as green as wind and solar, but far more efficient. And unlike wind and solar, my power source can work anywhere in the world, day or night, and it poses no environmental threat in the event of a natural or man-made disaster. It also powered the collapse of the climate exchange earlier today."

"So you admit your campaign is funded by the Chinese government?" a reporter asked pointedly.

"My campaign is funded solely by Just-A-Buck contributions from individuals and my personal financial resources. I have taken no foreign money whatsoever."

"But how could the Chinese have done what they did if you didn't sell them the technology? Is it even legal for you to have sold it to them?"

"I didn't sell China a thing. I licensed my innovation to Terrafuma Energy, and I received fair-market value from them for my years of work. Terrafuma Energy, in turn, negotiated a deal with the Chinese government to upgrade their fossil-fuel power plants with the technology I created. Terrafuma Energy has and will continue to receive fair value for these upgrades. And Terrafuma's shareholders, of whom I am one, will benefit from this transaction.

"What Terrafuma did is no different than a pollution controls company installing scrubbers on China's smokestacks—except that my technology eliminated the noxious emissions completely. Regarding your second question—Terrafuma's attorneys fully reviewed the deal and there are no laws in China or the United States that prohibit the sale of purely commercial power generating or emissions control technology. Terrafuma's deal with China is perfectly legal and has already made a noticeable cut Beijing's infamous smog."

"But in collapsing the climate exchange, haven't you and your Chinese partners damaged a vital force in combating man-made global warming?"

"Assuming I accept the premise of your question, which I don't, then emitting carbon into the atmosphere is bad because it's altering our planet's natural pattern of warming and cooling. The climate exchange sought to control the emission of human-generated carbon and make a few individuals very rich. By definition, it needed to restrain human activity by robbing individuals of their resources, namely money. This kind of exchange is not free market capitalism— it's taxation.

"My innovation eliminates the emission of human-generated carbon and provides every nation on earth with real energy independence."

"And it's going to make you very rich," a reporter offered with a derisive snort.

"It already has," Egan replied with a laugh. "But that is my due as the creator of something from which you and every other person in the world will derive a benefit. What I've done fundamentally shifts the global economy away from fossil fuel-based energy to a clean, green power source that will provide as much power as we need for as long as there is a planet. I ask you this: Which candidate has done more to achieve the stated goals of the environmental movement— the President or me? And don't I deserve to reap the rewards of my labor, or is the wealth my invention will create somehow unfairly stolen from those who couldn't conceive what I've done?

"Yes, I expect to become extraordinarily rich because of my invention, and every dollar of that wealth represents newly created value. Every dollar *fabricated* by the President and his ilk was taken from someone else. The left does not create wealth, *they confiscate it.*"

Egan noticed his father standing across the street pointing at his watch.

"I've got time for one more question," Egan announced, and then pointed at a young reporter.

"Could you comment on the blackout resulting from the raid on your family farm? When will your power plant be back on-line?"

"Like any parent to their child, I am very protective of my creation. The raid by federal agents triggered a self-destruct mechanism I installed to defend my right to intellectual privacy. The blackout was caused by this politically motivated raid ordered by my opponent's administration. Since the President and his supporters are so troubled by my ability to create clean power, I leave it to them to pick up the slack. In the meantime, I understand that an idled coal-fired generator has been brought back on-line and a plume of carbon-rich smoke is now billowing into the atmosphere. Thank you."

Egan ambled across the street with his security detail and slipped into the back of the HumVee. His father was in the passenger seat with a Secret Service agent behind the wheel. In the back seat, Niki switched off an LCD screen mounted in the back of the driver's seat.

"They carried your impromptu press conference live," Niki said as he sat down beside her. "You handled it quite well."

"Thanks," Ross said as he slumped into the seat and buckled in.

Niki took his hand and gave it a supportive squeeze.

"The combined disasters of the raid and the NYCE collapse have driven the President into hiding," Niki reported. "He has cancelled all of his scheduled appearances."

"We've bloodied him badly," Ross said, "but the President is a political animal. This isn't over until one of us concedes on Election Day."

"During your detainment, Maya sent over some research materials that require your immediate consideration."

Niki set an iPad on his lap and handed him a pair of ear buds. Ross drooped his head and sighed.

"How important?"

"Vitally important," Niki replied. "*Do it now*, important."

86

THE PRESIDENT CRADLED THE PHONE, HIS EAR ACHING FROM THE marathon conversation with Peter Sturla. He slumped back in the sofa, his collar button undone and his tie lose and slightly askew.

"How bad is it?" the First Lady asked sympathetically from the doorway.

The President simply rolled his eyes. "The kids finally asleep?"

The First Lady nodded. She padded softly across the floor and sat beside her husband, offering comfort.

"Today was a catastrophe. For a few short hours, we were billionaires. Then as quickly as we made all that money, it was gone. And not just gone—it took a big chunk of our blind trust as well."

"What's left?"

"Not much. We still have our pensions, the house, and the college fund, but the rest went down with the exchange."

Much of the first couple's personal wealth stemmed from sweetheart deals and inside information found within an expansive circle of political friends and supporters. Not bribery or graft per se, but quiet nudges at certain investments that always paid spectacular returns.

But the New York Climate Exchange was different. Here, the President had forced the creation of an economic entity that would not just serve his progressive agenda, but would allow him to amass the kind of wealth associated with the greatest dynastic families in American history. It was the kind of fortune that would place his name alongside the Astors, Rockefellers, and Gettys—making him not just a friend of Peter Sturla, but an equal.

"Sturla's calling in every favor," the President explained. "There will be a blue ribbon investigation and we'll be pressing for federal intervention in the market to protect the national economy. Problem is, the stock market had a record day following the collapse of the exchange. Denby had a field day with this on his radio show, even running an extra two hours until the market closed."

"I heard he claimed the only thing that could have a more positive effect on the economy, short of your defeat, would be the repeal of your healthcare reforms. Nothing makes sense anymore."

"Worse still, the exchange is on the hook for the full purchase price of the carbon permits."

"Oh my God!" the First Lady exclaimed.

The President nodded solemnly. "And with the collapse of the exchange, both China and the Republicans in Congress are pressing for immediate payment of their accounts. Peter put the lion's share of his personal fortune in escrow to cover the opening day and all his money is now frozen. This could wipe him out."

The crawl on a mute television reported Egan surging in the polls with a twenty-point lead over the President.

87

MORAN TOWNSHIP, MICHIGAN

"YOU WISHED TO SEE ME, SIR?" SPECIAL AGENT BOYD ASKED AS Egan greeted her at the door to his house.

"Thanks for coming, Robin," Egan replied. "I know this has been a long day for both of us, but I just came into possession of some information that I couldn't sit on until morning. And since you're the lead on my protective detail, I decided it best to start with you."

Egan led Boyd into the great room that overlooked the lake. As a fire blazed in the fieldstone fireplace, she saw a wine glass on the coffee table beside a tablet computer.

"I know you're on duty, but can I get you anything?"

"I'm fine, thank you. Exactly what kind of information have you acquired, and from what source?" Boyd asked warily.

"I cannot speak to the source, but if what I have is accurate, the attack on the President and Vice President wasn't the work of a lone gunman."

"Show me."

Egan offered Boyd a seat and handed his iPad to her.

"Just press play."

Egan sat in a leather club chair with his wine glass and waited as Boyd watched the presentation. Though digitally altered, the voice narrating the program methodically laid out the case for Michael Unden being another victim of the assassination and not the perpetrator. Twenty minutes later, Boyd found herself staring at the obscured faces of the two men likely responsible for the attack.

"My God," Boyd said softly.

"That's why I got myself a drink."

"If this analysis pans out, the investigation moves from lone gun-man to a much broader conspiracy—something well beyond these two men. How did you get this?"

"I'm not quite sure how it got on just my tablet, but whoever sent it targeted that specific device. It's not anywhere else I receive email or surf the net. Niki discovered it while the FBI was questioning me—she triggered it by using my password to log on. I didn't see it until I was on the way back home. Attached to that presentation is a file that contains all the photos, documents, and interconnected links."

"I'll need to take this tablet into evidence."

"It's yours."

"If this proves Michael Unden's innocence," Boyd said, "then the whole course of the government's investigation has just taken a very dangerous turn.

88

THE OASIS APPEARED AS A DISTANT SMUDGE, LIKE A MIRAGE ON the horizon. As the helicopter closed the distance, it grew into a tiny island of green fixed in a vast sea of Saharan sand. Turcott found himself staring at his destination and wondered if his fascination was simply due to his purpose or something hardwired into his DNA, a biological instinct to move toward a source of life.

The pilot set the aircraft down near the southern edge of the oasis, kicking up an angry cloud of sand in the process. Turcott waited for the dust to settle before exiting. As the light brown haze grew more transparent, he recognized Nimako waiting for him.

"Edward, it is very good to see you again."

Turcott smiled at Nimako. Such an effusive greeting from Nimako meant his agent was looking forward to being paid well for his services.

"Is he here?" Turcott asked.

Nimako nodded. "The man's name is Mustapha. His *khaima* is this way. He awaits us."

Nimako guided Turcott through the oasis—a lush explosion of grasses, date palms and other flora that Turcott could not readily identify. Passing by a small herd of goats, they arrived at a sprawling complex of tents. Men stationed around the *khaima* were all armed.

"Our host is a man of importance here," Nimako said softly. "He is *bidhan*—a white Moor—and we are infidels. I caution you to treat him with respect. These people are easily offended."

A guard stationed at the main entry to the tent offered a slight bow and motioned for them to enter. Turcott removed his sunglasses, but it still took several seconds for his eyes to adjust to the dimly lit interior.

The man Turcott assumed was Mustapha reclined upon a layer of embroidered cushions. He was dressed in the simple robes of a nomad, his gaunt face and leathery skin bearing witness to a lifetime in the harsh desert. Younger men stood by watching warily, sons and members of the extended family.

Nimako approached Mustapha cautiously in a low bow, speaking carefully in a Hassaniya dialect of Arabic. Mustapha nodded to Nimako and motioned for Turcott to approach and be seated. Mustapha spoke with a gravelly voice, his steely eyes on Turcott. He then paused for Nimako to translate.

"Our host humbly extends his hospitality to you and thanks you for the honor of your visit."

"Please tell our host that I am honored by his hospitality and may the many blessings of Allah be upon him and all who dwell here."

Mustapha smiled with stained and crooked teeth, nodding his thanks for the polite gesture. The young men served tea and set a bowl of dates between their patriarch and Turcott.

"How may I be of assistance to you?" Mustapha asked through Nimako.

"I am looking for information about a man, a foreigner like myself. I understand this man may have come to an arrangement with you regarding a woman who served you and your family."

Turcott diplomatically avoided referring to the woman as a slave, knowing the practice was officially illegal despite the fact that nearly twenty percent of Mauritania's populace was enslaved. He offered a photograph to his host, a candid shot of Ross Egan standing with a group of people backstage before the first presidential debate. Mustapha studied the image intently for several minutes.

"I remember this man well," Mustapha declared, pointing at Egan. "The others I do not know."

"Please, tell me about the man."

"Very tall, with red hair—looked like the devil," Mustapha said, musing through his memory. "He came by truck with a group of men, all black except for this man. The men were armed, but gave us little cause for concern. If there was to be trouble..."

Mustapha let the thought trail off with a smile. The sons grinned as well, doubtless the bones of those who did cause trouble lay beneath the sand.

"These men brought machines with them, and they used them to test the water and the plants. They even took blood from some of our animals, with our permission, of course."

"Of course. Please continue."

"I permitted some of my servants to help these men in their work. They freely explained their purpose and showed kindness to the children. After several days, this man *desired* one of my servants. He wisely did not attempt to take the woman and we began to discuss the matter."

"Do you recall your negotiations with this man?"

"He was a stubborn haggler," Mustapha said with admiration. "But in the end I knew that the ache of his flesh would win me a fair price."

"And what did you receive in exchange for your servant?"

Mustapha shook the sleeve from his right forearm to reveal a golden wristwatch. The precision timepiece seemed utterly absurd in this place.

"He prized this watch and did not wish to part with it," Mustapha explained, "but this was my price."

"May I see it?" Turcott asked.

Mustapha considered the request, then unfastened the band and carefully offered the watch to his guest. Turcott accepted the watch respectfully with both hands and was careful to keep it in Mustapha's view at all times.

The black dial read: OMEGA SPEEDMASTER PROFESSIONAL. The case and band were fashioned in yellow gold and the chronograph showed little wear for its time in the desert. Turcott flipped the watch over and discovered an inscription etched into the back along with a date a quarter century in the past. The inscription simply read: ROSS LOVE MAGGIE.

89

"THIS COULD BE THE ELECTION," DANIEL PAGE UTTERED ABSENT-ly as he finished the final page of Turcott's report.

"Thought you'd like it," Turcott said, stifling a yawn.

They were seated in Page's office at the President's campaign headquarters. Turcott arrived straight from the airport, jetlagged from the long flight nearly halfway around the world.

"If only you could have found the woman," Page said.

"Trail is cold on her after Egan left the oasis. The Mauritanian government has record of Egan and his associates entering the country, but nothing about a woman accompanying them on the way out. A bribe at the border would have handled that. Same with Dutannuru's border records. Really, there's no way to know if she's even still alive. But you have the video statement of the man who sold his slave to Egan. And you have this..."

Turcott pulled a small white box from his soft-sided briefcase and handed it to Page. The top of the box was embossed with a single word: OMEGA. Page removed the box top to reveal a gold watch with a black dial.

"This is Egan's watch?" Page asked.

Turcott nodded. "Mustapha is a cagy haggler, and he drove a hard bargain. But I figured it was worth the price, which is itemized in my expense report. On the way back, I stopped by the Omega factory in Switzerland and had them do a full rundown on the watch. Egan's late wife purchased it as an anniversary present. Kind of ironic that a high tech guy like Egan would have a manual watch, but maybe it was just the practical thing to do seeing as they were living in Africa."

"Your report indicates you found photos of Egan wearing the watch?"

"He was part of Mensah's inner circle, so he shows up in photos at various official functions. He always has the watch on, right up to the time when he made his research trip into the Sahara. Since then, he only wears cheap digital watches."

"Any chance this Mustapha is lying? Maybe he just stole the watch."

"Why make up such a story, all but admitting he sold a human being?" Turcott asked. "Slavery may be tolerated over there, but it's still illegal. And Egan went into the desert with armed men, soldiers. I don't think Mustapha and his tribe of goat herders have the balls to rob a group that could wipe them out."

"Playing devil's advocate, it's one thing for a Westerner to have a fling or hire a hooker, and another to buy a sex slave."

"Character is how you act when you think nobody is looking. For all we know, Egan bought the woman, did what he wanted with her and dumped her in the desert before he returned to Dutannuru. When he made that trip, it had been a few years since his wife's death. Lust and opportunity are powerful motivators."

"Who else knows about this?" Page asked.

"You, me, and my man in Dutannuru, but he's been paid well so he'll keep his mouth shut. Speaking of payment..."

"I'll authorize the transfer to your account immediately. You've done a magnificent job, really fantastic. This might just win us the election. The President and I won't forget that."

★

AFTER TURCOTT LEFT, PAGE CLEARED HIS AFTERNOON SCHEDULE to plan how to detonate the slavery bombshell on the Egan campaign for maximum impact. He was furiously scribbling on one of the white boards that lined his office when a rap on his door interrupted his brainstorming.

"Daniel?" Tina Crenshaw said cautiously through the cracked opening.

"My door was closed for a reason," Page growled without turning from the white board.

"I know, but this simply can't wait. We've been robbed and a *lot* of money is missing."

"Okay, you've got my attention," Page said.

Crenshaw closed the door behind her and took a seat opposite Page at the small conference table.

"As you know, online donations are down as compared to our previous campaign. This has largely been written off as a combination of the flat economy and voter fatigue," Crenshaw explained, "but then we noticed irregularities in the traffic at our website. Statistically, a fairly high and steady percentage of visitors who opt to view a donation page actually give money. This is not just true for us, but for every entity that solicits donations in this manner."

"I'm familiar with the research. The decision to donate is made before most of these folks access the site."

"It's not typically an act of impulse," Crenshaw agreed. "Our ratio of visits to donations has deviated significantly from the norm, meaning that either a number of these folks are having second thoughts after clicking on the page or something else is at work. The odd thing about this deviation is that it has held steady since May, week in and week out."

"So our deviation is an artificial distortion?" Page asked.

"Yes," Crenshaw replied. "Once we recognized the pattern, I put our best programmer-analysts on the problem and they uncovered a Trojan Horse embedded in our web server. They tracked our redirected funds back to the persons responsible for the theft."

"I hope they ripped it out." Page fumed.

"I instructed them to leave it in place for the moment."

"What the hell for? If you know who did it, cut 'em off and turn the evidence over to the police."

"Our website was hacked by the Egan Campaign," Crenshaw said.

"Are you absolutely certain of that?"

Crenshaw smiled at Page's incredulity.

"My programmers infiltrated the site receiving our funds, and only then discovered it belonged to the Egan campaign. Our donation page is mirrored within their site—they simply collect our donations just as we would. I tested the mirror page and my modest donation appeared on my credit card statement as if it went to us."

"You can prove *all* of this?" Page asked.

Crenshaw handed him a bound report of her investigation. "Right down to the campaign bank account receiving our money. Correcting for the deviation, they've stolen roughly a hundred million dollars. Egan is using our supporters' money against us."

Page considered the quantity of politically explosive material in his office as a devious smile curled the corners of his mouth.

"Tina, Halloween may be a few days away, but today is Thanksgiving and Christmas all rolled into one."

90

THE PRESIDENT DID NOT GREET EGAN ON STAGE AS THEY HAD AT the start of the three prior debates. As they emerged from the wings before the audience in Georgetown University's Gaston Hall, the President offered only a curt nod of the head before turning toward the moderator and his applauding supporters in the audience. Egan took the hint and did the same, making a point to acknowledge the pool photographers that, tonight, included Niki Adashi.

"The rules of this debate are a little different," moderator Mary Dewan announced as the audience settled down. "The candidates have chosen a town hall format for their fourth and final meeting, and the questions will be drawn from those provided by our audience members."

The candidates each moved to their respective spots on the stage. The podiums that had anchored them in place during the three previous encounters were replaced with upholstered high-back bar stools and circular café tables that held a wireless microphone, a legal pad and pen, and a glass of water.

"...our first question of the evening comes from Corrine Snyder, a graduate student here at Georgetown," Dewan said, "and it's for Mr. Egan."

"Good evening, Corrine," Egan said as Snyder approached one of the fixed microphones set in the main aisles.

"Good evening," Snyder replied nervously before reading from her question card. "Mr. Egan, your campaign for the presidency has been largely free of negative campaigning and personal attacks on your opponent. You have sought to elevate the level of discourse beyond knee-jerk response to offering detailed plans based on a well-defined political philosophy. What do you see as the fundamental choice that needs to be made by America's voters on November 6?"

"Corrine, I'm glad you liked how Lila and I kept our campaign out of the mud. I'll admit I've had some heated conversations with a few of my advisors, who all have a lot more experience at this than I, but the strength of our campaign lies in good conservative ideas and not hollow rhetoric.

"As to the fundamental choice, it's thankfully not about which of us you'd rather have a beer with. Political campaigns are, at their best, a battle of ideas, a war of words. And words have meaning."

Egan slowly roamed the stage as he spoke, using his tone and body language to engage the audience. The President, half-seated and half-standing, patiently watched and listened.

"The terms 'socialism', 'communism', and 'fascism' have come to mean different things to different people, but they all share a common intellectual root in the idea of political power achieved through the fusion of many individuals into a single bloc. The word *fascist* is derived from the Italian word *fascio*—to bundle—and it was used there a century ago as a synonym for union organizing. Generically, these are all forms of statism.

"Our national motto, *E Pluribus Unum*, reflects the idea of strength from the union of many into one. There is sound logic in the concept of strength in numbers.

"Where our motto and the founding documents of this nation differ from the ideology behind statist movements lies with the individual. Republican democracy defends the rights of the individual. Statism suppresses them.

"The President has been called many things during his quest for office and in his first term, some fairly and some not. The label he seems most comfortable with is *progressive*. It has a nice ring to it, sounds positive and forward thinking. After all, who could be against progress?

"Progress implies movement. Not aimless wandering, but directed movement toward a specific goal. Making progress means getting closer to that goal. If the President and his policies are progressive, then toward what goal are they moving us? If the ends justify the means, toward what ends?

"The progressive outwardly has nothing but the best intentions, but we all know with what the road to hell is paved. Politics is not played on a level field with a left side and a right. Instead, the field steeply slopes either down toward the hell of tyranny or up into the golden light of liberty.

"I speak often of American exceptionalism, and the greatest mark of this exceptionalism is how far we as a nation have scaled that steep, difficult slope. No other people in history have set foot as high on that glorious mountain and breathed the rarified air of liberty. As a conservative, I want to set solid anchors to prevent a slide back down the mountain and to enable our continued ascent.

"Abraham Lincoln put it best when he said, 'We all declare for liberty; but in using the same word we do not all mean the same thing. With some the word liberty may mean for each man to do as he pleases with himself, and the product of his labor; while with others, the same word may mean for some men to do as they please with other men, and the product of other men's labor. Here are two, not only different, but incompatible things, called by the same name— liberty. And it follows that each of the things is, by the respective parties, called by two different and incompatible names—liberty and tyranny.'

"The fundamental choice before each and every American voter is not between right and left, but between *right* and *wrong*."

Egan paused after this final word before calmly retreating to his place on the stage. The President was on his feet, watching Egan cross in front of him.

"If I may," the President said as Egan raised the water glass to his lips, "I wish to ask a follow up question of my opponent."

Dewan looked to Egan, who shrugged and nodded his assent.

"I must agree whole-heartedly that the fundamental question before the voters is one of right and wrong," the President said directly to Egan. "Last week, you admitted to an arrangement with China that is largely funding your campaign and was responsible for the collapse of the New York Climate Exchange. The financial and environmental damage of that failure to this country is incalculable..."

"It's zero," Egan interjected.

"What?" the President asked, flustered by the interruption.

"If your question is how much the collapse of the climate ex-change will cost the people of the United States, the answer is zero, unless, of course, your friends who backed that monumentally bad idea fail to pay what they owe the governments of China and the United States for the carbon permits they bought. What's incalcula-ble is how much I have saved the American people in lost wealth and productivity that would have resulted if the exchange hadn't failed.

"And regarding my personal finances," Egan continued, "my wealth is the reward for decades of hard work in creating an energy technology that will be an inestimable benefit to all mankind. *I earned it.* I created something that previously did not exist. I licensed what I created to a privately held American company. This company stands to make a lot of money from my technology for its owners. China paid a fair price to upgrade their power plants, and I am certain that the people of Beijing who are enjoying cleaner air and bluer skies would tell you the price they paid was well worth it."

"So you say," the President countered, "but the facts of your sweetheart deal with China and your collusion to ruin a financial exchange should and must be fully investigated."

"I welcome it."

"And not just the unsavory Chinese financing of your campaign, but the outright theft of millions of dollars in contributions from my campaign by the Egan Campaign."

The bemused expression that came over Egan's face was not what the President expected as he leveled that charge.

"Agents of the FBI are at this very moment raiding the offices of your campaign, questioning key members of your staff and securing evidence of this crime."

"I assume you are talking about the redirect of online contribu-tions from your campaign to mine."

"So you admit it," the President charged.

"I have been aware of the situation for some time," Egan replied matter-of-factly. "It was first brought to my attention in early June, and we have been cooperating fully with the Michigan State Police in their effort to determine the person or persons responsible for this crime. And I can state with absolute certainty that not one cent of the redirected money has been used by my campaign—it's all in a State Police escrow account."

"Why hasn't this money been returned to my campaign?" the President demanded.

"There are complications with the redirected money," Egan explained. "Even though there is no physical money, no stack of bills, the electronic transactions are evidence of an ongoing crime that's still under investigation. Returning the diverted funds might tip off the people who hacked both our campaign websites, making an arrest more difficult. Your public airing of this crime tonight has rendered that point moot. The more significant complication lies with identifying the victims of this crime."

"*I* am the victim," the President declared.

"No, you are not," Egan countered. "While I agree that the redirected money was intended for your campaign, none of it actually got there. The money was, in fact, *not* stolen from you."

"If not from my campaign, then from who?" the President demanded.

"As a lawyer, Mr. President, I am certain you will agree that your loyal contributors are the injured parties. The money was fraudulently taken from them along with their credit card information. Is it not *they* who must be made whole?"

"Of course," the President stammered, "but shouldn't my supporters' intentions be considered as well?"

"Without contacting them, the police cannot be sure just what their intentions were. Perhaps they only wanted to donate ten dollars to your re-election effort, but the redirect turned it into a hundred. The stolen money must be transferred back to its original source and each victim notified of the theft. It's the right thing to do."

The President glowered at Egan. "If the police have been investigating this crime for the past two months, why wasn't my campaign notified?"

"The police couldn't be sure your campaign wasn't behind it. You have to admit, something like this would be a hell of an October surprise, especially with Election Day less than two weeks away."

"That's an outrageous lie!" the President shouted.

"I'm not accusing you or your campaign of anything, Mr. President. There was, however, another irregularity that forced the police to keep you out of the loop—it seems there is a problem identifying the victims."

"I thought you said the police had all of the transaction details."

"I did, but the details apparently weren't much help. Each of the contributions was for an amount less than two hundred dollars. This, you may recall, is the legal threshold for mandatory reporting of the contribution. And aside from the credit card numbers—which were, amazingly, all from pre-paid, untraceable cards—the rest of the online forms were a jumble of random words and numbers. To the police, this seemed as curious as the redirected funds."

"We're dealing with computer hackers," the President said derisively. "They simply altered the data to cover their tracks."

"The police considered that possibility, but some very bright folks who work for a friend of mine dissected the redirect programs and found no sign of any tampering with the data as it flowed from your campaign to mine."

Egan rose from his stool and slowly approached the President.

"These savvy programmers then began tracing the incoming contributions and discovered that each and every one originated from the *same* computer. And I think we both know which of your many supporters has, or at least had, pockets deep enough to afford illegally funneling more than a hundred million dollars into your campaign."

"I don't know what you're talking about," the President exclaimed, standing his ground.

"That, Mr. President, remains to be seen."

"The next question," Dewan announced, trying to reassert control over the debate, "is from junior Evan Richmond and is for the President."

Both candidates withdrew from center stage as Richmond made his way to the microphone. The President took a drink and shot a glance off-stage at his campaign manager. Page gave a slow nod of his head. The President set his glass back on the table and turned toward the audience.

"Mr. President," Richmond began, "One of the main themes of your opponent's campaign has been to liken progressive entitlement programs to the monstrous evil of slavery. Mr. Egan has gone so far as to call for the slaves of government dependency to be freed under a new Emancipation Proclamation. I am the product of a single-parent home and a number of federal programs have helped keep a roof over my family's head, put food on our table, and provided the grants I needed to pursue my education here at Georgetown."

"Hoya Saxa," the President offered with a fist pump, inciting an appreciative response from the audience.

"Hoya Saxa, Mr. President," Richmond replied with a broad smile, forgiving the interruption. "As someone who is making something of myself with the investment of federal aid, I do not feel trapped in dependency, nor do I consider myself a slave. Under your leadership, more has been done to level the playing field for all Americans than at any point since the New Deal and the Great Society. How do you counter your opponent's arguments that entitlement spending does more harm than good?"

"I must first commend you on your accomplishments. The fact that you are here, at one of the most prestigious universities in the world, speaks volumes about your drive and determination. If federal entitlement programs gave you the boost you needed, then I say it was money well spent. And I'm sure we're going to get it all back, with interest, in the taxes you'll be paying after you graduate. You are the norm and not the exception."

The President strode toward center stage, closing the distance between himself and Egan. His suit coat was unbuttoned, one hand holding the microphone, the other casually placed in his pants pocket.

"Regarding Ross's analogy—I don't see it. Then again, I have little first-hand experience with slavery."

The President stopped at the café table next to Egan's chair, standing opposite and slightly taller than his partially seated opponent in what he hoped would become the 'above the fold' photo in every newspaper in the country tomorrow morning.

The two candidates studied each other for just a second, and Egan felt the fury concealed behind his opponent's congenial façade. The President pulled his hand from his pocket and held it palm up barely an inch above the table, fingers gently closed around a concealed object.

"In fact, all I know about slavery I discovered *second hand.*"

As he pronounced the last words, the President uncurled his fingers and tilted his hand to allow a gold watch to slip from his open palm onto the tabletop. In the bright stage lights, he saw the reaction he had hoped for—the barest hint of recognition and a subtle drain of color from Ross Egan's face.

The President lowered his microphone, turned his back to the audience and the cameras, and leaned across the table close to Egan.

"Checkmate, you son of a bitch," the President hissed softly.

Egan ignored the taunt and picked up the watch to look at the back. Maggie's inscription was just as he remembered it.

"Oh, it *is* your watch, Ross," the President nearly whispered. "We checked it out thoroughly, even had it cleaned and tuned, just for you. All those years in the desert can take a toll on a precision timepiece. Fortunately, you left it in very good hands."

The President moved away from Egan, raising the microphone back to his mouth as he turned to the audience.

"Getting back to the question, I must defer to my opponent regarding slavery—he is, after all, the expert in this area. Several years before sudden fame plucked him from obscurity and thrust him onto the world stage, Ross toiled in a tiny African country. He was a widower who, for years, had buried himself in his work. It was during a trip deep into the Sahara Desert that an opportunity, or I daresay a temptation, presented itself—one that sadly gave him something in common with more than a few of this nation's Founding Fathers—*Ross Egan bought a slave.*"

Egan withdrew in thought, ignoring the President's continued attack.

"Ironic how the same conservatives who rail against entitlement programs as a form of slavery put forth a candidate who secretly practices the real thing. What is known of this heinous transaction came to light from the nomadic chieftain who sold what he describes as a beautiful young female to my esteemed opponent. The woman in question had been this man's slave for only a few years at the time of her sale to Ross Egan. She served primarily as a domestic, but satisfied *other* of her master's needs."

"Though officially illegal, the slave trade still exists in Africa today. The going rate for a slave in that part of the world is so low that they are considered a disposable commodity. The chieftain recognized my opponent's *prurient* interest in his slave and set a price many times what he paid for her. *And he got it.*

"Ross Egan bought another human being as his personal property, for God knows what purpose. And the price he paid in trade for the young woman who became his slave," the President said, pointing at the dumbstruck Egan, "was the gold watch given him by his late wife as a token of her love."

Egan found his feet and the audience saw on his face pained bewilderment. He clasped the watch tightly in his hand and walked off the stage.

Tears streamed down Niki's face as she stoically recorded Ross Egan's embarrassed retreat and the moment his campaign to win the presidency died.

91

Robin Boyd oversaw Egan's abrupt retreat from George-town, coordinating with D.C. law enforcement to clear the path to Reagan National Airport, where a chartered jet sat prepped for the next campaign stop.

"...Cherry Capital Airport," Boyd informed the pilot. "Repeat, the destination is Traverse City. The candidate is heading home."

"Roger that," the pilot replied. "Updated flight plan will be filed by the time you get here."

Boyd switched off her mike and sat back against the seat of the SUV. She was in the first of three black SUVs racing through the streets of the nation's capital with a police escort.

"Helluva thing," the driver offered.

"What?" Boyd said absently, her mind elsewhere.

"Buying a slave—I mean this is the twenty-first century, not the old South."

"I don't know what to make of that," Boyd admitted.

As the convoy sped through traffic lights and intersections closed in a rolling fashion along their route, Boyd felt her cell phone vibrate with an incoming call. The caller ID was blocked. She answered and identified herself.

"Agent Boyd," an electronically altered voice began, "you received a package of information pertaining to the attack in San Francisco, correct?"

"Yes."

"The pre-purchased credit card used by the unknown suspects— check the numbers against those used for online contributions into the President's campaign. They match. Money from the base account was also transferred to two offshore accounts. Follow the money and you will find the shooter and his accomplice."

"Are you saying Peter Sturla is behind the attack?"

"Follow the money, Agent Boyd, and you will find the truth."

HOPPS DISCONNECTED THE CALL, CERTAIN ITS BREVITY PREVENTed a trace back to him.

"Think she'll bite?" McColl asked.

"Egan trusts her, as do the Randells," Hopps replied. "She'll pass it on to the FBI. And if they are as good as you, then a pair of killers will soon find themselves stateside facing a federal murder charge that carries the death penalty."

92

MORAN TOWNSHIP, MICHIGAN
OCTOBER 31

EGAN'S SECRET SERVICE DETAIL DROPPED HIM OFF AT HIS PAR-
ents' front porch. It was mid-afternoon and an early snow was
blowing in lightly off Lake Michigan. Egan ran the soles of his boots
over a stiff bristled brush to clean the treads before stepping inside.

"Glad to see you made it home in one piece," his father Leon said,
not rising from his seat on the leather couch in front of a roaring fire.
"The way the press is going after you, I wasn't sure there'd be much
left."

"You and me both," Ross replied as he hung up his coat.

"There's a bottle of red on the bar if you're drinking, unless you
need something stronger."

Ross pulled a round-bowled glass from the rack and poured in
several fingers of the merlot. His mother appeared from the kitchen
with a tray of hors d'oeuvres.

"You didn't have to go to the trouble..."

She cut him off with a look. "It was no trouble at all, dear, but
don't spoil your appetite. I have a venison stew for dinner and an
apple pie for dessert."

Rhetta curled up on the couch beside her husband and studied
their son with an expression that barely concealed her pained concern. Ross took a sip of wine and stared into the fire as he collected
his thoughts.

Since his abrupt departure from the fourth debate, Egan had been
holed up with his running mate and senior campaign staff in Traverse
City, struggling to counter the damage caused by Egan's non-re-
sponse to the President's shocking allegation. The press had likened

his abrupt disappearance under the onslaught of the President's damaging offensive to Hitler's retreat into the bunker.

"I wanted you to hear it from me," Ross said flatly. "It's over. My campaign is finished."

"How can it over?" Leon asked. "This ludicrous story can't be true, can it? Tell me it's not true."

"I won't lie to you, and I won't discuss it. The bottom line is that I cannot offer an honest defense to the President's charges, and I will not try to lie and weasel my way out of it. Even if I could somehow win the election, I would be damaged from my first day in office— four years of a hated, lame duck president. The country deserves better."

"The President is not a better man, nor is he a better leader," Rhetta countered.

"Thanks, Mom. And while I agree with you, it doesn't change the facts. As president, any legislation I backed would die in Congress, probably without a sponsor. I would actually be worse than a lame duck; I'd be a leper president. The only thing that I could do that the country would agree with is resign during my inauguration speech. Loyal Lila would be guilty by association and her presidency would be only slightly more effective. It's over."

"What will you do?" Leon asked.

"Not much I can do. On Friday, I'll issue a statement that I've suspended my campaign. Then we'll close up shop."

"You were so close," Leon said bitterly. "After four years of this looter regime, we had a chance to set things right. You were the country's best hope."

"We waged a campaign of ideas and the people responded. Hopefully they won't toss the message with the messenger."

"I'll drink to that," Leon offered, raising his wine glass up in a toast before taking another drink.

"Have you heard *anything* from Niki?" Rhetta asked.

Ross shook his head. "I don't expect to, either. This is too much. I've lost her."

93

"Mr. President, the Director of the FBI is here to see you," the President's secretary announced over the intercom.

The President initialed a few documents and closed the folder.

"Please show him in."

The President greeted the FBI Director at the door and handed the folder to his secretary. He returned to his seat behind the *Resolute* desk and motioned for the Director to take a seat in a guest chair.

"Sir," the Director began, "there's been a significant development in the investigation of the assassination."

"Oh, I thought the case against Unden was open and shut."

"So did we. But on further review we now believe Michael Unden was another victim of the attack, a fall guy. At eight this morning, local time, a joint US-Mexican assault team raided a compound and arrested the two men we believe executed the attack. They are currently being questioned."

"They committed a capital crime—will the Mexicans allow them to be extradited?" the President asked in astonishment.

"In this case, yes," the FBI Director replied. "The political repercussions would be too great. We are also dangling the possibility of a lesser sentence for these men in exchange for their help in exposing the full extent of the conspiracy."

"And are these men cooperating?"

"They are. Mr. President, you were not the target of the assassination attempt. The Vice President was."

"But I was shot."

"You were superficially wounded, which was the intent."

"But why?"

"The election. Your poll numbers were down and the Vice President's gold scandal apparently made him an even greater drag on the ticket. The assassination was staged to elicit voter sympathy and eliminate what was seen as an obstacle to your re-election. "

"But I was shot! Who the hell thought shooting me was a good campaign strategy?"

"According to the men in custody, Peter Sturla thought exactly that. And his strategy worked—you pulled even in the polls afterward and your selection of Governor Delgado as Vice President has proven quite popular."

"The son of a bitch had me shot."

Simmering, the President buzzed his secretary on the intercom.

"Yes, Mr. President."

"Get Peter Sturla on the phone, now."

The FBI Director interjected, "Mr. President, I'm not sure that's a good—"

The President held up a finger a cut him off. A moment later, the call to Sturla was patched through. The President put the call on the speaker. They heard the drone of jet engines in the background.

"Good morning, Mr. President. I have been meaning to call you regarding this nonsense over campaign contributions. In light of the pending indictment—"

"You thought perhaps a pardon might be the quickest way to resolve the matter."

"Yes."

"And would you like that pardon to cover murder as well?"

"I-I don't know what you are talking about," Sturla stammered.

"What are the names of the men you have in custody?" the President asked the FBI Director.

"Vance and Young. Both ex-military, part-time mercenaries, and on Sturla's payroll."

"The FBI has Vance and Young and they are cooperating, so the pending indictment is the least of your worries. "

"But, Mr. President, we have a long history."

"Yes, and we have both profited from our relationship, but two men are dead and I could have been killed. Of all the boneheaded ideas."

"Mr. President, I swear I had no knowledge—" Sturla lied.

"Save it for someone who cares, Peter. I swear that I will not rest until you pay for this."

The President pressed a button on the speaker and ended the call.

"Coordinate with the CIA and NSA to locate Sturla and bring him in."

"Yes, Mr. President," the FBI Director replied.

"If Peter Sturla ordered the assassination of the Vice President, then he is public enemy number one."

94

"JUST SIX DAYS REMAIN UNTIL ELECTION DAY," DENBY AN-
nounced to open his radio show. "And what a difference a week has
made. Just one week ago, Ross Egan had such a clear and commanding lead over the President that a complete sweep of the Electoral
College map was a distinct possibility. The tectonic, visceral shift in
the country that was within sight just seven days ago promised to be
unlike anything that any living person had ever witnessed, and I
daresay the only event comparable in our nation's history was our
transition from colony to country.

"The renewed sense of optimism surrounding the all but assured
outcome of this election was already being felt in the stock markets. It
was as if a long and particularly harsh winter was finally releasing us
from its icy grip, and the first green shoots had burst up into the
sunlight. Our hope was tangible, but it apparently was not to be.

"To the left, evidence is secondary to the seriousness of the
charge. You don't have to prove your opponent did X, you just have
to get them to deny it, and deny it often enough that they are sub-
consciously linked with the charge.

"We do not know the facts of this matter. We do not know if this
woman was a slave or a servant or something else entirely. We do not
know what Ross Egan's intentions were in entering into this transaction. All we do know is that the President delivered the charge with
devastating effect and Egan has responded with silence. At this point,
I would much prefer if Ross Egan had denied the charge because
whatever this is, it's worse.

"So where does that leave us? With less than a week until a majority of voters cast their ballots we have the two badly damaged frontrunners and a slew of third-party eccentrics looking to avoid the wreck in the final lap and pull off an upset victory. Next Tuesday night is going to be a long one.

"And lost in the media frenzy over the slavery allegation is an actual scandal concerning millions of dollars in illegal contributions flowing into the President's re-election campaign. His staunchest backer, former-billionaire speculator Peter Sturla, was indicted this morning by a federal grand jury. A representative of the Justice Department, which has taken over the case, issued a statement clearing the Egan campaign of any wrongdoing with regard to the theft of Sturla's illegal campaign contributions. The statement further commended the Egan campaign for their cooperation with the investigation. I suspect this story will not see the light of day among the mainstream media until after the election.

"Sturla has apparently fled the country ahead of the indictment and there is some concern that the President may issue a pardon to his long-time mentor and confidant. I find this doubtful now that the FBI is reporting that the disposable credit card used by the persons responsible for assassinating the Vice President and murdering Michael Unden is part of the same sequence of numbers used by Sturla to illegally fund the President's campaign. Two persons of interest in the murders have been detained abroad and questioned and are currently en route to the United States."

95

"THAT WAS THE BOYS GUARDING THE FRONT DRIVE," RHETTA Egan called out to her husband as she cradled the phone. "Maya and Burton are here, and they've brought Niki with them."

"Here?" Leon asked, surprised.

"Coming up the drive."

The Egans stood at their front door waiting as a dark gray SUV with tinted glass pulled up the gravel drive. Niki emerged from the vehicle, accompanied by the Randells.

"We apologize for dropping in unannounced," Maya said as they stepped onto the porch. "There was really no choice."

"Oh shush!" Rhetta demanded. "You are as good as family and always welcome."

"As are you, child," Leon said as he engulfed Niki in a tender embrace. "As are you."

Niki buried her face in Leon's shoulder as a flood of emotions welled up. She sobbed briefly before regaining her composure.

"I was not sure how I would be received," Niki admitted hesitantly as she dabbed a tear from the corner of her eye.

Rhetta threw her arms around Niki protectively, the action erasing all doubt about their affection toward her.

"Dear," Rhetta said, her voice a tear-choked whisper, "you are the best thing to happen to our son since we lost Maggie and baby Quinn. You made him whole again, and for that I will always be grateful."

"Whatever Ross did or didn't do has nothing whatever to do with you," Leon added. "If it's possible, I hope you can find it in your heart to forgive him."

"Has he spoken with you about this situation?" Maya asked.

"No," Leon replied. "All we know is that he won't defend himself or offer any kind of explanation. He's gonna scuttle his campaign."

"Ross believes he's lost you," Rhetta said to Niki.

"Where is he?" Niki asked as she withdrew from Rhetta's embrace.

"Holed up in his house," Leon answered. "Please, talk to him."

Niki nodded, stepped off the porch and began walking down the path toward the lake. The two couples watched her disappear around the side of their house.

"No sense standing here in the cold," Leon declared. "Can't have you southerners catching frostbite or something just because the temperature is below fifty."

The Egans welcomed their guests inside and, after a brief flurry of activity in the kitchen; all were soon seated by the fireplace with a mug of tea or coffee. It was early afternoon and sunlight streamed through the barren birch trees casting a warm glow on the polished woodwork of the log home.

"How has he been?" Maya asked.

"Closed," Rhetta replied. "Distant. Not himself at all."

"As hard as it is for me to believe something like *that* of my own son," Leon offered, "there must be a kernel of truth for it to have hit him so hard. My son has always owned up to his failings—this retreat is completely out of character."

"Maya and I have known Ross for a long time," Burton mused, "and we got to know Maggie and him as a couple quite well. Had Ross been with her when she was attacked, do you think he would have given his life to save her and their child?"

"What a question to ask," Leon replied. "Without a doubt he would have done all he could to protect his family, or died trying."

"We believe that same instinct is driving his actions now," Maya said. "There is more than a kernel of truth to the President's allegations, but it's a past that is best left in the past. As you can already see, no good has come from this revelation."

"You think Ross is taking this terrible beating from the President and his ilk to spare us some embarrassment?" Leon asked with a snort. "A bit late for that. Most of the press thinks we're illiterate Eskimo hillbillies with our snow mobiles and hunting rifles. Our son knows that no matter what foolish thing he might do, the worst we'll feel is disappointment. Our love for him is unconditional."

"He's not doing this for us," Rhetta realized.

"Niki?" Leon offered, and then he shook his head at the obvious. "My God, he must *really* love her."

"He does," Maya said, "and she loves him. But their relationship is—complicated. Niki is a *very* private person. Had their relationship come to light with the media circus of the campaign—it would have been very difficult for her. Add this to the mix, and it would have been more than she or their relationship could bear."

They heard the sound of footsteps outside, and then Niki and Ross walked across the back porch and entered through the French doors. All eyes were on them.

"Niki and I have talked," Ross announced. "I want to thank you all for your love and support. Tomorrow, I will issue a statement suspending my campaign, and hopefully this will all be over."

96

DENBY OPENED THE FINAL SEGMENT OF HIS PROGRAM'S FIRST hour with an instrumental bumper cut from The Doors classic song *The End*.

" 'This is the end, beautiful friend'," Denby recited the song's familiar lyrics somberly as the music faded. " 'This is the end.'

"Shortly after the top of the hour news break, Ross Egan will make an announcement at the Jefferson Memorial in Washington D.C., likely ending what, until last week, was the best hope for driving a stake through the undead heart of vampire liberal progressivism and returning this country to the founding principles that made it great in the first place.

"Now the best we can hope for is Egan still managing to pull out a win, followed by four years of bureaucratic gridlock that leaves in place all of the current regime's destructive, rotgut legislative victories. The alternative is worse—four more years of the worst presidency in our nation's history and the bankrupting of the republic.

"I'm not saying it's time to call it quits, head to a tropical island with strong banking privacy laws and live out the rest of my life as an expatriate, but that day may be closer than I ever thought possible.

"We will carry Ross Egan's announcement live, and then see where we go from there. Back after the break."

97

BUSLOADS OF DEMONSTRATORS FILLED THE PLAZA, FROM THE TI-
dal basin sea wall to the steps of the Jefferson Memorial. The day was
cool and overcast. Left-wing groups from around the country came to
protest the first public appearance of Ross Egan since the final
presidential debate. Only a few of the signs they carried were of the
homemade variety—the rest were the glossy product of professional
graphic designers produced just for the occasion. The crowd bore all
the markings of a rent-a-mob.

Uniformed D.C. Metro police officers manned security check-
points and lined temporary barricades, maintaining access and order
in and around the memorial. Police helicopters orbited overhead,
complementing sniper teams deployed on the ground. The steps
leading up to the memorial portico were kept clear save for an
outdoor projection screen that organizers of the demonstration had
brought so the crowd could witness the historic collapse of Ross
Egan's bid for the presidency.

Members of the press awaited Ross Egan's arrival inside the memorial. A simple podium with microphones stood near the base of the
towering bronze statue of Thomas Jefferson. Egan would face due
north as he spoke, with a view through the portico of the Washington
Monument, and beyond, the White House. Three manned video
cameras were strategically placed in the rotunda, their raw feeds to be
shared by the televised media.

A rope line kept the journalists and photographers several feet
back from the podium. Niki Adashi stood at the rope carefully
adjusting the settings on her camera.

"I guess it's only fitting that we're both here at the end," a man's voice said.

Niki turned and saw Edward Turcott walking toward her. He was clad against the weather in a leather jacket, his press credentials dangling from a lanyard around his neck.

"What do you mean?" Niki asked.

"You and I were there when Ross Egan became *Ross Egan*. But like a meteor, he streaked brightly across the sky before eventually crashing down to earth."

"You seem to be enjoying this," Niki said distastefully. "Building someone up only to tear them down again."

"Journalistic Darwinism," Turcott said with a shrug. "Look, I know you're part of Egan's publicity team and what he did in Africa was great, but at the end of the day should he really be running *this* country? I don't think so."

"I think he would have made a fine president, perhaps as good as that man," Niki said with a tilt of her head toward Jefferson.

"News flash: Jefferson bought slaves, too."

The incensed crowd outside roared to life, chanting *Hell No! Egan Must Go!*

Turcott glanced at his watch. "Like him or not, Ross Egan is always punctual. I'll miss that when he's gone."

"Sir, you have to get behind the line," a police officer informed Turcott sternly.

Turcott lifted the rope cord and slipped in beside Niki. She trained her camera toward the portico and captured Ross Egan's arrival. He strode into the rotunda confidently. His long wool cashmere topcoat was unbuttoned down the front, fluttering as he moved. Egan chose a dark blue suit for this occasion; the creases on his pants were razor sharp, the tailoring impeccable. He was clean-shaven, alert and calm—not at all the image of a man mired in the political scandal of the century.

"Get a good picture of him quitting," Turcott whispered into Niki's ear. "I'll need it for the book I'm writing about how I brought him down."

Niki turned from her camera. "*You* did this to him?"

"Uncovering his dirty little secret is going to put me front row in the White House briefing room, on top of the *Times* bestseller list, and it might even win me a Pulitzer. Then you and I will have a matched set—one for making him, and the other for breaking him."

Camera flashes marked each step of Egan's long, slow walk to the podium. He moved purposefully through the gauntlet, each footstep tapping softly on the marble floor.

"I have a brief statement to make," Egan said in a business-like tone. "I will take no questions afterward. I am here today to discuss the serious charge leveled against me by the President. While I might take issue with the speculation and inferences, the factual substance of the President's claim is correct. I did, in fact, purchase a slave. There is nothing that I can offer in my own defense."

"I just hope I can find the woman he bought," Turcott whispered. "The victim's side of a story like this would add some serious seven-figure sizzle to my advance."

Niki felt her hands tighten on the camera body, knuckles bulging white under the taut skin. She pivoted about and struck Turcott's face with the lens. Turcott staggered back, dazed by the blow. Niki then furiously smashed her camera on the floor.

"You seek to profit from a woman's pain?" Niki shouted at Turcott. "You are *evil*."

Niki ducked under the rope line and stormed straight toward Egan, her eyes on fire with rage. Egan's Secret Service detail quickly closed in around him and a pair of burly police officers moved to intercept her.

"It's alright!" Egan called out. "It's alright. She's with me."

The officers each grabbed one of Niki's arms and looked to Egan for confirmation.

"She's okay," Egan said reassuringly. "Let her go."

The officers released Niki. She took a deep breath, trying to re-gain her composure before proceeding at a more measured pace. Egan waited at the podium in silence as Niki approached. He turned as she stepped onto the platform and they stood for a moment, face to face. Then she touched his cheek.

"To be truly free," Niki said softly, "I *have to* do this."

Egan saw the plea in her eyes and nodded that he understood. He stepped back, ceding the podium to Niki.

"Ross Egan has said he will offer no defense against the President's claim that he bought a slave," Niki began. "I am here now to refute that false claim.

"I am Niki Adashi. Though I was not born here, I am an American citizen. The country of my birth no longer exists, and the people who live in peace in the new nation of Dutannuru are most thankful for all that Ross Egan accomplished on their behalf."

The crowd outside jeered and booed loudly as Niki spoke. She ignored them and continued on.

"As a young woman, I worked for Ross Egan and his wife as a nanny for their child. The Egans helped many people during the Safolese civil war, and made many enemies in the Cudjoe regime.

"One day, my mistress and I were taking food and medical supplies to a village. The fighting was far away, so we thought the journey safe. A Safolese raiding party attacked us. Our military escorts were killed and we were captured. They smashed," Niki choked back a sob, "the baby on the ground and killed him. Maggie Egan and I were both raped many times. We were beaten terribly. Because Maggie Egan was white and an American, they killed her."

The sounds of the protesters outside quieted as Niki continued her story.

"I was taken across the border, far into the Sahara Desert, and sold to a vile man named Mustapha. The work was hard, and I was raped often. I became pregnant three times, and I was often beaten. Now, my body can no longer bear children.

"I was held in bondage in the desert for several years. My family believed me dead, and those who survived the civil war had fled our old village. My prayers for deliverance from Mustapha were answered when Ross Egan found me in the desert.

"I swear that I have never had sexual relations with Ross Egan. I have not had sexual relations with any man since my liberation. I cannot.

"Ross Egan is not Mustapha!" Niki declared, fighting back the tears. "Ross refused to defend himself against the President in order to protect me. He was willing to suffer public humiliation and defeat because of lies rather than reveal my plight and break his promise to me.

"Ross Egan could have easily defeated the President's lie by telling the truth, but he would not harm me to win this election. He came here today to end his campaign, to withdraw from the public stage in false infamy, to spare me the trauma of a public revelation of all I had suffered. Ross Egan is not a politician like the President—Ross Egan is a man of great honor.

"For me to be free of the demons of my past, I must let them go and make my peace with all that I cannot change. My victory comes in my survival. What was done to me does not define me." Niki turned to Ross. "I am so much more."

Ross smiled. He had told her that as he transported her out of the desert.

"Not one of us is perfect. This president standing behind me owned slaves, but the good of his life, and what he and the other Founding Fathers gave to all Americans, far outweighs the bad. President Lincoln, who freed the slaves, was not perfect, but his good deeds far outweighed his sins. Ross Egan is not a perfect man, but in his actions you can clearly see, he is the *better* man.

"Mr. President, you are wrong! Ross Egan never bought a slave. He never *owned* me. Ross Egan *saved* me."

98

"ROSS, I AM ALMOST NEVER AT A LOSS FOR WORDS," GARR DENBY said to open the interview, "But I have to admit that Niki Adashi left me speechless."

"That makes two of us," Egan agreed.

"I mean, if you listen to the tape after we cut back from your press conference last Friday, there's what seems like a minute of dead air before I could make words come out of my mouth. I am a highly skilled broadcast professional and this kind of thing never happens on this show. Well, almost never happens.

"So, for anyone living under a rock, let's recap. The President's opposition research team uncovers a nugget of information about you that they think is your kryptonite, your Achilles' heel. The President drops this bombshell during the final debate, hoping you won't have enough time for effective damage control. The President's October surprise: Ross Egan bought a slave.

"The media lapped it up because it fit the template. Conservatives are mean-spirited bigots—so it only makes sense that a white conservative would own a black slave. Conservatives are the oppressors, and they have nominated an evil Simon Legree as their candidate. The op-eds practically write themselves.

"Now, when the left lies, they try to insert a sliver of truth to make what they're saying appear reasonable. In this case, you did in fact pay to acquire a woman who was being held as a slave, correct?"

"Yes, that is correct."

"But that little fact was all they knew, and from it they spun a narrative that transformed you from an enlightened man who toppled a dictator and saved the planet into the most evil man on the planet. In less than a week, you went from being the likely winner of the presidency in a landslide victory to something lower than dog excrement. And you did nothing to counter this flow of unadulterated sewage being dumped on you by the left."

"I couldn't fight the lies without revealing the whole truth," Egan explained. "And revealing the whole truth meant sacrificing a woman who suffered unimaginable horrors. I couldn't do that just to win a political office."

"In the modern vernacular, you couldn't toss Niki under the bus to achieve your political ambitions."

"Sacrificing Niki for the presidency would be like selling my soul."

"So Friday, just days before the polls open, you emerge from your self-imposed exile to..."

"Quit," Egan said, filling in the blank. "Every conservative on the ticket was being hurt by the charge against me. To give these bright and energetic men and women a fighting chance, I had to provide a face-saving way for them to distance themselves from me. It was the best outcome that I could salvage from a bad situation. This election has always been about more than me."

"So what happened on Friday was not staged?"

"That deer-in-the-headlights look you saw on my face when Niki charged the podium was absolutely genuine," Egan admitted with a laugh.

"Then she delivered a speech about truth, integrity and freedom that would have made Doctor King proud."

"As I said, she left me speechless, just like you."

"But you quickly recovered and got back in the game none too soon. Weekend polling shows you once again pulling away from the President by double digits. The only fly in the ointment, as it were, is the absentee ballots cast during the fog of the slavery allegations."

"That's why we need to get the word out to all those folks who, after everything hit the fan, may have decided to sit this election out, that their votes still matter."

"That is absolutely right," Denby concurred. "At this moment, the hope for an American renaissance has never been brighter, but it is up to *We the People* to live up to our heritage and reclaim our birthright."

"I'm very optimistic that we can remind the people of this great nation about the truth of American exceptionalism," Egan said.

"I won't keep you because I know you have a few more campaign stops on the West Coast before you head back to Michigan to cast your ballot. May I just wish you good luck and Godspeed."

"To us all, Garr, to us all."

99

MORAN TOWNSHIP, MICHIGAN
NOVEMBER 6

OUTSIDE THE TOWNSHIP HALL, MEMBERS OF THE PRESS FAR OUT-numbered the voters of the sparsely populated district waiting to cast their ballots. If the bumper stickers on the backs of trucks and even a few snow mobiles were any indication, Egan's advantage among the hometown voters was insurmountable.

Egan arrived at the polling place at nine in the morning with his parents, Niki, and his security detail. He was dressed casually in jeans and a heavy wool sweater, looking vigorous and outdoorsy. With her ever-present camera, Niki set to work documenting the historic day.

"I have something I need to take care of inside," Egan shouted to the media waiting the required distance away from the polling place. "But I'll pop over when I'm done."

One television cameraman accompanied Egan into the hall. He and Niki followed Egan as he presented his credentials and queued up for a booth. The process moved quickly and he ceremonially fed his ballot into the scanning machine.

"So, who'd you vote for?" a reporter from Detroit asked with a laugh as Egan emerged from the hall.

"The American people," Egan replied.

TRAVERSE CITY, MICHIGAN

"BOYS, THE WEST COAST POLLS ARE CLOSING," RHETTA EGAN EX-citedly sang.

She shared a long couch with Niki and Maya in the sitting room of the Grand Traverse Resort's presidential suite. All three were still clad in plush white robes, their natural beauty enhanced by a day at the resort's spa that pampered them from head to toe.

Ross Egan stood on the patio with his father, Burton Randell and Garr Denby. All were dressed casually, enjoying the view on this clear, starry night with a glass of port and a fine cigar. They had spent the afternoon challenging their modest golfing skills on Gary Player's Wolverine course, followed by a gourmet dinner with the ladies served in the suite.

"Shame we can't smoke these inside," Denby opined.

"We're probably breaking the rules doing it out here," Leon offered, "but I'm sure the management will let it slide just this once."

"Did you send my thanks to your crew in Montana?" Ross asked Burton.

"I did, and I expect they are watching the returns with the relief that comes from a job well done."

"It's not over, though. They'll have to lay low until the inauguration. Then I'll pardon the lot of them for any rules they might have bent a little in exchange for their expertise."

"They're all patriots and I'm sure they would be proud to serve their country."

They finished their cigars and reentered the suite in time to see the first tallies posted for the eastern states. From New England to Florida, the east coast was awash in Republican red. The President managed to pick up a few electrical votes in states that divided their electors proportionately, but Egan was off to a commanding lead with the opening returns.

"The big question now is coattails," Denby opined. "Just how many rock-ribbed conservatives are going to ride your wave into Washington?"

Ross shrugged with a smile, happy to enjoy the evening with family and friends. Burton tapped away on the glass screen of his tablet computer, skimming through raw data returns and crunching the numbers almost as quickly in his head.

"I don't think you'll be lacking for politically sympathetic company in D.C.," Burton offered. "You may even have a larger majority in both houses than the President enjoyed during his first two years in office—enough to possibly run your amendment proposals out to the people."

Denby raised his glass high. "Power back to the people, where it belongs."

"Hear, hear!" everyone else replied.

"*JUST AN HOUR AFTER THE WEST COAST POLLS HAVE CLOSED,*" THE NEWS anchor reported, "*and we are confident in calling the election for the presidency of the United States for Ross Egan...*"

"Congratulations, son," Leon said, with a bear hug.

"*...huge voter turnout has turned even the bluest of states red and we are looking at an electoral sweep that could rival that of the Eighty-Four election.*"

"We are so proud of you," Rhetta said before leaving a bright red lip print on her son's cheek.

Using the sleeve of her robe, Rhetta carefully tried to remove the smudge.

"*...Ross Egan will be the first unmarried president in well over a century,*" a political analyst offered. "*He's a self-made billionaire and now, the next leader of the free world. That has got to make him perhaps the most eligible bachelor in history. The D.C. social scene will be abuzz with who will be on his arm for important state functions.*"

Amid their private celebration, the suite phone rang. Niki pressed the mute button to silence the television. The phone rang again.

"I know you are *dying* to do this," Ross said to Denby with a mischievous smile.

Denby set his glass down on a side table and dramatically picked up the phone.

"Ross Egan's suite. This is Garr Denby. To whom do I have the pleasure of speaking?"

Denby put a hand over the receiver as he stifled a belly laugh.

"Yes, Mr. President, he is here and I will be so very pleased to get him on the line."

Egan accepted the handset from Denby, who mouthed the words

Thank you.

"Good evening, Mr. President," Ross said respectfully. "Thank you, sir. And, yes, good help is *very* hard to find."

Leon elbowed Denby who was near tears with laughter.

"I appreciate that, and I look forward to working with you and your staff on the transition over the coming months," Ross continued. "Again, thank you for the call, Mr. President, and good night."

"So he's conceded?" Maya asked.

Ross nodded.

"*Ding dong,* this presidency is dead!" Denby said with a laugh.

"Yeah," Ross replied. "And now the real work begins."

100

ALL BUT NIKI LEFT THE PRESIDENTIAL SUITE FOR THEIR OWN rooms to dress for the victory party in the resort ballroom. She remained at his mother's request to capture a few final candid shots of Ross before his first public appearance as president-elect.

They dressed separately, and when Niki returned Ross had to pause to appreciate her transformation.

"My dad would say that you clean up real good," Egan offered.

"And what do *you* say?" Niki asked as she set her camera case on the bed.

"Since you are my date tonight, thank you."

I do require some assistance, if you don't mind."

Niki turned on her heel to reveal a zipper opened down to the small of her back. Egan considered making a witty, intimate remark, but immediately thought better of it. That Niki would expose herself to him in this way was a significant expression of trust and he would not make light of it.

Her back bore the faded reminders of distant abuse, scars the plastic surgeons had softened but could never fully erase. As he slowly eased the zipper up, Ross paused and kissed a scar at the base of her neck. Niki did not flinch and murmured a soft sound of pleasure.

"All set," Ross reported. "Mom wanted the tie shot?"

"That is what she requested."

Ross turned up his collar and set a patterned silk tie around his neck. He tried to suppress a smile as Niki shot away with her camera, fumbled the knot, and had to start over.

"This is the one part of the job I will least enjoy," Ross said, failing on the second attempt.

"You're just nervous," Niki said as she set her camera on the bed. "Allow me."

Ross clasped his arms behind his back, standing tall. She adjusted the tie's length against his torso and then expertly wound the cloth into a classic four-in-hand knot. Niki surveyed her handiwork, and then finished the job with a gold tie tack.

"You'd make a fine valet," Ross mused as he looked in the mirror.

Niki returned her camera to its case and came back to Ross with the gold watch that he had exchanged for her freedom. He had not worn it since that day in the desert when he had given it to the slave owner Mustapha.

"Twice this watch was given for a noble purpose," Niki said solemnly, "and now it has returned to you. Please wear it tonight for Maggie and for me."

Ross held out his left arm and allowed her to slip the gold linked band around his wrist. He felt the weight of the timepiece and recalled the day he received it and the day he gave it away. He glanced at the watch face and noted the moment.

"Thank you. Now it's time we got going. There's a room full of people downstairs and a nation beyond waiting for me."

Niki kissed his cheek, and then moved toward the bed to retrieve her camera.

"Leave it," Ross said. "There will be plenty of people taking pictures. And as of now, you are no longer my official photographer."

"I'm not?"

"No," Ross replied as he opened the suite door for her, "but there is another job opening I would like you to consider."

101

"...AND WE MUST FIGHT TO HOLD THE GAINS WE HAVE MADE FOR WORKING men and women, for the poor and the disadvantaged. This fight is over, but the struggle remains and we must move with progress and commitment toward an ever-brighter future.

"I wish to express my deepest gratitude to all of my supporters—you were the bedrock beneath my feet during these most challenging, most exhilarating years of my life. Thank you, God bless you, and may God continue to bless the United States of America."

The capacity crowd in the resort ballroom cheered and applauded as the President concluded the second-most anticipated speech of the evening. The image of the defeated President then faded from the projection screens that flanked the stage. Denby stepped back into the light, microphone in hand, beaming his broad, infectious smile.

"Like most of you, I have been longing to hear our President make that speech since the day he was elected," Denby told the crowd. "Today, the people of this great nation told the politicians in Washington the direction that defines positive progress, and it's one-hundred-and-eighty degrees from where we're currently headed. And without any further ad-libbing from me, it is my honor and distinct pleasure to introduce the next President of the United States, Ross Egan!"

Egan stepped into the spotlight smiling and waving to the crowd as the band launched into a swing version of *Hail to the Chief.* He shook hands with several people along the edge of the platform and then embraced Denby at center stage. Denby handed Egan the micro-phone and stepped back into the shadows, leaving the new president-elect alone to bask in the adulation.

"Thank you!" Egan said over the din of applause and cheering, which only made the friendly audience increase their volume.

"Egan! Egan! Egan!" the crowd cheered.

"Thank you!" Egan shouted again, smiling and motioning with his free hand for quiet. The crown joyfully disobeyed the request and gave the man of the hour a five-minute standing ovation.

"Thank you so much for the enthusiastic welcome!" Egan said. "Governor Oates, or should I say Vice President-Elect Oates, and I are simply overwhelmed with the results of this election. The American people have, in record numbers, put their confidence in Lila and me, and we promise that we will do everything we can to deserve it.

"Just a short time ago, I received a phone call from the President congratulating me on my victory and offering his full support and that of his administration during the transition. It was a hard-fought, passionate campaign and I thanked the President for his service to the country.

"In the coming weeks, the vice president-elect and I will set to work on getting our administration up and running by Inauguration Day. We will be meeting with the leadership of the next Congress to establish our legislative priorities. We will also be finalizing a number of Executive Orders that I intend to sign shortly after I am sworn in. There's a big job ahead of us, but we have all proved that America is more than up to the challenge.

"I am pleased to report that tonight I offered what I consider the most important post in my administration to a highly qualified individual, and that my offer was accepted without hesitation. And there will be no confirmation problems with this appointment either—which is great because I intend to put this talented individual to work on Inauguration Day. The post I'm referring to is that of First Lady."

Many of the women in the ballroom cheered loudly, recognizing quickly what Egan had just revealed—America was in store for a presidential wedding.

"My reign as an unmarried president and supposedly the world's most eligible man will be thankfully brief," Egan said, and then he turned and extended his arm to the right. "I am pleased to introduce to you and the country the future First Lady of the United States, Niki Adashi."

As Niki stepped into the light and joined her fiancé on stage, the band launched into a soulful rendition of *America the Beautiful.*

ACKNOWLEDGEMENTS

As an author, I get by with a little help from my friends. I am deeply grateful to the many generous people who lent a hand in the effort to tell this story.

To Edwin Feulner and his brilliant team at the Heritage Foundation for an insider's look at Washington and a laser-like view of the issues that challenge our nation; the always Honorable Daniel Ryan for his constitutional insight and all things legal; Jim Brandstatter for putting me on the O-line for the big play; BJ Keepers for helping me shoot straight; Bob Johnston for drinks and cigars at the Winston Churchill Bar; David Limbaugh for his timely editorial help and the gift of his excellent book *Crimes Against Liberty*; Don Povia and HHR Media Group—publicists extraordinaire in media new and old; Brian Farkas for his unflagging support and insatiable enthusiasm for this book; Mike Cox and Stu Sandler for their political insights; Marcie Gates and Joyce Brewster, my early readers; Tina Bibbs and my sharp-eyed Kathleens for their careful read of the page proofs; and to Zingerman's Roadhouse and Connor O'Neill's—a pair of fantastic Ann Arbor eateries that kept my writing fueled with pimento cheese burgers and salmon boxties.

A special thanks goes also to: my agent Esther Margolis and her outstanding group at Newmarket, my superb editor Jack Langer, and the folks at Dunlap Goddard for taking on this challenging project.

I follow the advice Mark Twain gave to Rudyard Kipling: "Get your facts straight first, and then you can distort 'em as much as you like." Any errors resulting from my 'distortions' are my own.

And always, I thank my family for their love and encouragement.

BIBLIOGRAPHY

I drew on a number of fascinating resources in the writing of this book that I recommend for anyone interested in further reading on the history and issues presented.

The Declaration of Independence
The Constitution of the United States of America
The Federalist Papers, Alexander Hamilton, James Madison, & John Jay
The Art of War, Sun Tzu
We Hold These Truths, John Courtney Murray, S.J.
The Road to Serfdom, F.A. Hayek
The Fatal Conceit, F.A. Hayek
Rules for Radicals, Saul D. Alinsky
Getting America Right, Edwin J. Feulner & Doug Wilson
How Capitalism Will Save Us, Steve Forbes & Elizabeth Ames
Economics in One Lesson, Henry Hazlitt
Liberal Fascism, Jonah Goldberg
Meltdown, Thomas E. Woods
Liberty and Tyranny, Mark R. Levin
Crimes Against Liberty, David Limbaugh
Atlas Shrugged, Ayn Rand
Mr. Smith Goes to Washington, Columbia Pictures (1939)
The Sting, Universal Pictures (1973)

I must also note that Joan Saccary's anecdote in Chapter 20 is taken almost verbatim from Hillsdale College President George C. Roche's remarks introducing keynote speaker Governor Ronald Reagan at the 1977 Ludwig Von Mises Memorial Lecture.

ABOUT THE AUTHOR

TOM GRACE is the internationally bestselling author of *The Secret Cardinal*, *Bird of Prey*, *Twisted Web*, *Quantum*, and *Spyder Web*. His books have been translated into several languages, pirated, and placed in the library at the South Pole. He is an architect in private practice with projects ranging from private residences to genetic therapy labs. He lives in Michigan with his wife and children and is at work on his next novel. To learn more about Tom Grace, visit www.tomgrace.net.

AUTHOR'S NOTE

An interesting thing happened during the production of this book. Two very talented and experienced freelance editors turned down the opportunity to work with me on *The Liberty Intrigue*. Both thought my novel was engaging, well-written, and timely, but both declined due to the same pre-existing condition: liberalism. The idea of a likable conservative protagonist was too great a leap of imagination, even in a work of fiction. One apologetically offered that he would like to refer me to a conservative editor, *but he didn't know any*. When it comes to cultural bias in the media, I think that says it all.

WILLCUTT

Made in the USA
Lexington, KY
20 March 2012